THE MAGDALENE MANDALA

Michael Bradley

Manor House Publishing Inc.
www.manor-house.biz
905-648-2193

Library and Archives Canada Cataloguing in Publication

Bradley, Michael, 1944-
    The Magdalene Mandala / Michael Bradley.

ISBN 978-0-9736477-9-2

    I. Title.

PS8553.R226M34 2006   C813'.54   C2006-903035-9

Copyright 2006-10-30 by Michael Bradley.
Published October 15, 2006
Manor House Publishing Inc.
(905) 648-2193
First Edition. 336 pages. 147,686 words. All rights reserved.

Book cover artwork: *Marie Sorrowful* from an original engraving by
the artist DAVID SILVERBERG B.A., R.C.A., F.R.S.A.,
17 Hillside Ave., Wolfville, Nova Scotia B4P 2A9
Website: www.davidsilverberg.com
david.silverberg@n.s.sympatico.ca   Special thanks to the artist for
his kind permission to reproduce his etching, *Marie Sorrowful*.

We gratefully acknowledge the financial support of the Government
of Canada through the Book Publishing Industry Development
Program (BPIDP), Dept. of Canadian Heritage, for our publishing
activities.

The Magdalene Mandala is a work of fiction. All content is owed in
its entirety to the imagination of the author. Any and all characters
and situations are solely the creation of the author. Any perceived
resemblance to real people/events in the pages of this novel is purely
unintentional.

For my wife, friend and companion, Joëlle Lauriol.

Foreword

Bradley is back! Michael Bradley, a familiar name to many readers, is the author of literally dozens of critically acclaimed non-fiction books, including several on the Holy Grail (he recently wrote *Swords at Sunset* tracing the Holy Grail to Niagara and Vermont and served as a researcher for *The Da Vinci Code* movie)

But fans of Bradley's fictional work have been waiting since the 1970s for his next novel, following the success of *Imprint* and *The Mantouche Factor*, which together sold more than half-a-million copies after being re-released in mass-market paperback format.

Now the long fiction drought is over with the release of a new novel. And what a novel: *The Magdalene Mandala* draws on Bradley's enviable reputation as a Holy Grail expert to lend authenticity and reality to a plot that twists and turns at a rapid pace, bringing together everything from murder and intrigue, to organized religion, political cover-ups, Jesus Christ, Mary Magdalene and the Holy Grail.

Set in the near future, *The Magdalene Mandala* introduces a new heroic figure – Canadian-American adventurer Marc Rennsalaer – who teams up with an exotic, leggy linguist Mariko O'Shaugnessey.

Together they make a desperate journey through France and England to protect a priceless parchment and its shocking secrets. In hot pursuit are sadistic forces determined to destroy all evidence of the West's genuine Christian legacy. At risk: The survival of the truth behind the Western world's oldest religious heritage – and the lives of Rennsalaer and the two women he loves. Intriguing, pulse-pounding adventure at its best.

Added to this intoxicating literary mix are detailed descriptions of ingenious low-tech survivalist devices from an intriguing boat design to lethal air cannons. *The Magdalene Mandala* is an original in every sense of the word.

- **Michael B. Davie,** author, *Poetry for the Insane: The Full Mental.*

About the Author:

Michael Bradley is the nom de plume for Michael Anderson de Sackville, American by birth; Canadian citizen since the mid 1960s.

The famed researcher, author, amateur historian and anthropologist was born in Talladega, Alabama in 1944. He was educated at Agincourt Collegiate in 1963 and Dalhousie University in Nova Scotia from 1964-1967; He became a Canadian citizen on Dec. 1, 1965.

Nominated for the Nobel Prize (Biology) by Nobel Laureate, Konrad Lorenz in 1979; Bradley refused special Doctoral degree program offered by Dalhousie University. Throughout the 1980s, he served as a lecturer at various institutions of higher learning, including: the Princeton Institute for Advanced Study, Vanderbilt University, York University, Yale School of Divinity, and Kennedy-King College. (Chicago).

Bradley is a winner of the DeMille Writing Award (poetry) and Dennis Writing Award (prose) (both Dalhousie University). He was elevated to the rank of Knight of Malta in 1989 for activities in carrying medical supplies to remote villages in Central America in 1983 while conscripted to the Canadian International Development Agency (CIDA) in the design and manufacturing of five and ten metre boats for impoverished Caribbean fishermen.

Michael Bradley is the author of literally dozens of critically acclaimed books, including prior bestselling novels ***Imprint*** and ***The Mantouche Factor***. A recognized expert on the Holy Grail, Bradley served as researcher for ***The Da Vinci Code*** movie and wrote the non-fiction trilogy on the Grail that concluded with the recently released ***Swords at Sunset*** (Manor House Publishing).

Prior non-fiction works include: ***The Cronos Complex, The Iceman Inheritance, Chosen People from the Caucasus, The Black African Discovery of America, Holy Grail Across the Atlantic,*** and ***Grail Knights of North America.***

Michael Bradley resides in Toronto with his wife, writer Joëlle Lauriol. ***The Magdalene Mandala*** is his third novel and 24th book.

Part One

What a personage says or does reveals a certain moral purpose; and a good element of character, if the purpose so revealed is good. Such goodness is possible in every type of personage, even in a woman.

Aristotle: *The Art of Poetry*

1

Lining up *Jester* to thread the high central archway was a little worrying because I was uncertain of the current's strength.

I could see no roils or ripples curling from the abutments, but the lighting wasn't very good and I feared crashing the boat. Just then, however, the low sun flared behind me. It had found a rent in the brooding cloud cover before it sank into the waiting teeth of the Massif Central. The ancient sandstone of the bridge in front of me turned suddenly from dark grey to vibrant dusty rose, and its shadowed archways flicked from sooty to royal purple. Incongruously, distant thunder rumbled with the splash of claret sunset. And so the floodlit girl fell off the bridge with a drum roll.

My mind registered that it must be a girl because of the moth-like flutter of cloth from the balustrade. Her skirt billowed up briefly when she hit the water. It was as if some lumpy creature had come suddenly up from the depths to snatch an exhausted insect that had fallen on the surface. Just before she went under completely, I saw a pale blob for an instant. It might have been her face, and then it was gone in the centre of a widening ripple that lived for some seconds in the lazy current. The limpid water of the summertime Garonne River was hard to stir, and her splash made no sound that I could hear. There did not even seem to be any foam from the splash, but maybe the shadows absorbed it. In any case, it all happened unexpectedly and my view was obscured.

I shoved *Jester* into reverse and I did see, or thought I did, a long pale object spearing upward from the middle of the ripple for an instant before it, too, slid beneath the surface and the loom of the boat's oncoming bow. My mind told me that this must be an upward reaching arm, and it seemed to wave a thing that was just a blacker shadow with glints of gold. I remember thinking, stupidly, "The Lady of the Lake," before *Jester's* prow blotted out the scene and then itself disappeared in the darkness beneath the span. It was purple darkness only for an instant because the sun was suddenly switched off by low overcast skies or sullen mountains to the west.

While the stone archway was sliding over the stern, some hint of movement caused me to glance up. Silhouetted against indigo clouds and shy stars peeking through small rents in them, two shapes were leaning over the bridge's balustrade. One shape seemed to extend itself, like some lengthy and stealthy thing flowing down a wall – and fired a gun; I saw a reddish yellow flash with a few sparks. I ducked, which did no good whatsoever since I only increased the size of the target. I heard a metallic whine off the taffrail, along with a soft "phutt" sound that was aggrandized into a magnificent fart by the bridge tunnel. Then the stone closed overhead and the two shadows were gone.

Under the bridge, in the archway tunnel of solid stone, the sound of churning, reversing water was like being right beside Niagara Falls on the promenade. But I knew it was hopeless. You can't stop a boat like you can stop a car. *Jester* had passed over the woman, and might have pinned her under the water. I spun the wheel hard over to port with the idea of giving the victim some room in which to surface between the main hull and the starboard outrigger, but there was not much clearance in the tunnel.

Jester's speed had been much reduced in that fierce burst of full reverse, but not halted. The roar of water ceased as we glided out from under the other side of the bridge. I de-clutched the engine just before I scrambled behind the windowed wheelhouse.

How were the gunmen to know that the wheelhouse was steel, and that the glass was really polycarbonate?

I glanced quickly back under the arch, but saw no one struggling amid the black serpent coils of disturbed water. Next, I peered intently toward the top of the span, and saw two dark shapes watching from this side, now, as the boat drifted away from the bridge with hardly a ripple. Two more "phutts" sounded almost simultaneously, and along with them came two sprays of sparks. A clang like a bell sounded from somewhere forward, and water splashed close astern. Then, the two dark forms turned away and diminished until they were covered by the balustrade.

They disappeared. I heard doors slam and then a car accelerating from idle to urgent with a squeal of tires along the invisible pavement atop the dimly lighted bridge.

The victim could not have known, nor the gunmen, that *Folderol Jester* was a decidedly odd craft. The boat did not have a conventional propeller, but a kind of low-speed, high-volume jet drive. The impeller was enclosed, so there were no exposed sharp whirling propeller blades to cut anyone into small and bloody pieces. My mind was remembering this even as I fumbled my way back to the wheel.

The Old City's medieval market quay should have been almost dead ahead when *Jester* emerged from the tunnel, and I half expected that its lights would be shimmering on the water. I'd done no nighttime navigation for a while, and as I spun the spokes of the wheel I noticed only a few pinpoints of light amid the distant jumbled and angular shapes curving past the bow. The old market wharves, my planned destination, showed no lights at all. The market cobblestones glistened in only the barest glow coming through *Le Port Romain's* wide windows under the city wall. It was easy to forget how the world was changing. It continually came as a surprise, in small ways. Only the palest light from the Old City flickered enough to give me some aid in turning the boat.

Further ahead upstream, as the bend in the river wheeled into view, I could glimpse in the distance an uneven straggle of multi-coloured lights sparkling from the New City like a broken necklace in a deep vault. The New City of Moissac had been built in more modern times just where the mighty Tarn River flowing from the far northern hinterland of eastern France joined the east-west flowing and equally mighty Garonne. But the glitter of the more modern New City did not reach down the river to the old bridge. Dark Age night was again asserting its rule over medieval Moissac. The fuel shortages starting almost a decade ago back in September of 2000 had dictated ongoing electric frugality and, in the Old City at least, narrow twisting streets prevented these surviving dungeon lights from escaping beyond the ancient crennelated battlements.

Turning took time, some backing and filling in the dark, because the channel of the upper Garonne is not so very wide for a boat fifty feet long, especially with the onset of summertime low water. But at last it was done and I aimed the bow back toward the centre span. The bridge was neither golden nor picturesque since the sun had gone, and especially from this shadowed upstream side. It was a heavy dark medieval thing that hunched over the water. A dragon gloating over prey. The archways were flat black against a scaly black of indistinct stonework.

I pierced the dragon with a stab of the searchlight. But I could see or hear no swimmer in the light. Although there was no propeller to do fatal damage, could the boat's hull have struck hard enough to knock a girl unconscious? Or – my mind was racing – could one of their shots have hit her? But no, the sound effects had accounted for all three bullets. Could the long length of the hull have pinned her under long enough for a shocked victim to fill with water? Or... had the reversed jet not only slowed *Jester*, but also pushed the girl ahead of the boat toward the Old City side of the bridge?

Visibility had not been good with the Old City shuttered and that had also been while I was cringing from the "phutts" before the car squealed away, and naturally before I had turned on the searchlight.

But with the shock and surprise transforming into a kind of dull foreboding, I did things methodically. First of all, I lifted a life ring from the wheelhouse coaming and then unsnapped the searchlight from its mounting. I could hold the light in one hand and direct its beam as I wished, while the other hand could toss the life ring if necessary. I throttled back to dead slow, once I got the boat turned about, and again aimed her bow toward the inky hemisphere beneath the middle of the bridge. I swept the searchlight methodically over the water. There was now hardly a ripple left from the earlier disturbance of full reversing in the tunnel. I would have seen anything floating, would have heard anyone swimming. *Jester's* steam engine never did more than breathe in soft sighs even when it was working very strenuously; and the deeply immersed jet produced only a chuckle of turbulence on the surface – except in the frenzy of emergency reverse on full throttle.

As for the sounds of traffic on the bridge, rush hour was over and Old Moissac isn't exactly a metropolis. In any case, with the petroleum shortage, there were noticeably fewer cars on French roads after work. So, there were few auditory or visual distractions, but I didn't see anything.

It then came to me, belatedly, that the two men in the car might well have hit her on the head, or tied her arms and legs, before tossing her over... if, as it clearly seemed, these two men, as I supposed they were, had been trying to kill her. What about that black object that the pale arm had held aloft? What about the golden glints of metal in the shadows? A weight and chains?

While this was churning through my mind, I brought *Jester* to a dead stop with compensating bursts of forward and reverse. After dropping the life ring to the deck and re-mounting the searchlight in its fixture so that its beam stared once more into the archway, I jumped and scrabbled over the main hull's cargo and out onto the outrigger platform.

Levering off my size 12 Nikes against the edge of the plywood decking, I remembered not to dive head-first into the river. No telling what sharp objects might be sticking upwards from the bottom. Folks in these parts had used the river as a dump for centuries. So I lowered my rather lanky six-foot two-inch frame gingerly into water that was not all that warm. It was only June. Cold winds still chilled the water, especially on overcast nights like this one.

I hoped that the weak current would carry *Jester* safely down to the bridge where the hull would fetch up gently against one of the stone pylons.

I Australian-crawled my way from *Jester* and, swimming now, went under the stone span of the Moissac bridge again. Within the half-lit tunnel, my arms made echoed surf. It wasn't hard to imagine rhythmic surges of some giant thing almost upon me. When I reached the other side, where she had tumbled in, I treaded water, took some deep breaths, exhaled half of the last one and dived. I have fair breath, having grown up scuba and snorkel diving on the Florida coast – with military training since. My first dives that evening probably lasted more than a minute.

It was, of course, pitch black down there. It was not very deep, though, only nine or ten feet. The canal route is supposed to have a dredged channel of three metres. I fought my way down to the muck and mud at the bottom, and began feeling around with my arms and hands. I had a very good idea of where she had gone in – more or less the middle of the centre span, the widest span. If she was still there, I would eventually find her. Probably it would be too late, of course.

I encountered no soft and clammy object that might be a drowned female body. But on the fourth dive, my hand encountered a smooth and squarish thing already half-settled into the bottom ooze. I felt around this, discovered that it had a handle, and knew it for a briefcase. Surfacing with it, I saw golden hinges, tabs and locks. I had the vague idea that it might contain some identification. It was black vinyl-covered aluminum. It wasn't heavy. Treading water, I drained it out, although I couldn't snap it open. It had combination dials on the locks. After it dribbled more or less empty, and this did not take long because the halves did not fit together snugly, I placed it carefully on its side on the surface.

It floated well enough on the quiet water in the eddying lee of a massive stone abutment. The wavelets were not so importuning as to splash up to where the two sides of the case closed together. It was not waterproof, by no means a top quality case. Then, I noted that its brass fittings suddenly winked out. *Jester's* light had swung away.

These observations may have flitted around my brain, but they cost no time. As soon as the case was bobbing on its own, and thankful for the short rest, I dived once more. This time, I could only stay down there for perhaps a minute or less. I searched the area carefully again, and stretched my time down there to the end. Coming urgently toward the surface I saw a bright oval blob swirling around crazily on the water above me. Searching? Had the men in the car been plagued with second thoughts? Had they come back with a flashlight to make certain? This notion caused my heart to kick, and it was already pounding in my ears. And this jolt caused me to lose control and snort water in.

No matter what awaited above, I kicked upward in desperation, the water searing my nose, throat and lungs in agony. I surfaced gasping, my vision dark and heart pounding heavily. I kept seeing a thousand points of light, as the elder George Bush had once put it, but the bright oval of incandescence had flitted off elsewhere. A blurred glance upward seemed to rule out shadows hanging over the bridge, and no one shot at me while I clung to the abutment fighting for breath and vomiting Garonne out of me. It had been a bit closer than I wanted to admit, and I had left no margin for that scare with the crazy light, but I was also morally sure there was no body on the bottom.

2

I splashed over to the briefcase and, using it gingerly as an aid of marginal flotation, kicked slowly back toward Jester in the relative security of the bridge tunnel. There was no loom of the boat's hull framed in the archway as I half expected, but the beam of the searchlight was slicing up the night outside like Darth Vader in a tight spot.

I splashed my way slowly out of the archway mouth and saw that *Jester* had drifted over toward the north bank. She was also performing a ponderous pirouette in mid-channel, rebounding from the back-eddies upstream of the arch pylons. Her bow no longer faced the bridge archway, as I had left her, but was turning with slow resolution toward the remaining gems of Moissac New City. *Jester* would, however, be inevitably pushed toward the smaller arches on the northern side of the larger central tunnel. I figured *Jester* was too wide to fit through them, so there was nothing desperate about the situation.

The beam of the light quickly homed in on my position, but somewhat shakily.

It was quite obvious that someone had gone aboard during the ten minutes or so that I'd been doing the Jacques Cousteau thing; and that person was most probably the victim who had fallen from the bridge.

The men, who had been up on the bridge, if they'd returned, would obviously not have hesitated to shoot. They had not hesitated before. The searchlight, after questing crazily, had now pinned me in a circle of water that was painfully bright. Did I discern a sleek and drooping shadow at the wheelhouse behind the light?

Or... had *something* come aboard? But even in my chest-burning and befuddled state, I doubted that it could be what it resembled – a smooth and glistening giant bat, wings all folded, the size of a small man. I ruled out a Transylvanian vampire. Romania had not yet been admitted to the European Economic Community; its nationals could not work along French canals and as for a terrifying Transylvanian tourist, the season for them had not really started. At the same time, an errant medieval Moissac gargoyle with nautical yearnings seemed equally unlikely.

Whatever it was, the creature was managing the searchlight with inexperience while trying to light my way back toward Jester. The light was effectively blinding me, so I closed my eyes when I could as I splashed. Things seemed to be under control, after a fashion. I relaxed a bit and, since I didn't know the answer to who or what was aboard, I let my mind play with those things that I did know. This is a habit of mine.

There is no current to speak of in the summertime Garonne, at least not in stretches of the river that interlock with the Canal du Midi. A total of 53 locks within a distance of three hundred kilometres tend to subdue water's natural frivolity. *Jester* had drifted sideways in the channel because of a sudden cold, southerly mountain breeze off the snow-capped Pyrenees.

The south of France heats up very quickly on spring days, but nights can be cool on the Garonne-Aude waterway. What happens is that when the sun gets low, updrafts from the day's heat cease abruptly. And, as the last layer of heated air rises from the surface land and water, low pressure results. This low pressure attracts the cold evening breath of the Pyrenees during this time of the year.

Later, of course, during late June, July and August, the sun's heat lingers in land and water, creating updrafts all night. But the chill of the Pyrenees does not then invade the lowlands during high summer because, by then, the Pyrenees themselves have warmed up.

Splashing slowly toward *Jester*, trying to keep that light out of my eyes, I noticed that the few southern stars visible between the low clouds were not rocking on rounded wavelets as before, but were sizzling on sharp-crested little puckers of cats' paws from the south. There was both excitement and urgency in this frantic dance of starlight reflections.

The face that was reflected up at me in the dark waters and shimmering starlight just astern of the briefcase could not really be called handsome anymore. The Indonesian landmine that had propelled me into the trunk of a palm tree had crushed the right cheekbone and had fractured the right side of my jaw in several places. The right cheek was, not, therefore exactly symmetrical with the undamaged left one, and the right jaw line was lumpy, and both were also adorned with a tracery of only now-fading white scar tissue.

But, I suppose, the face could not actually be called disfigured. The American and German surgeons in the U.S. military hospital in Germany had really done a remarkable job of reconstruction, all things considered. I suppose that it was worth the agony of the operations and the months of drinking vitamin-enhanced meals through straws.

I noticed that my hairline wasn't receding – yet – in spite of my 38 years, but the hair wasn't much to write home about anyway. It was neither blond nor black, but a light mousy brown that was also too fine to control. It fell in an unruly shock over my forehead and right eye more often than not. The eyes went with the hair – not that slightly disturbing leonine yellow that I've seen sometimes, and not dark brown either, but a sort of very light brown in which some women had claimed to see grey or green highlights. But these were usually the same women who were impressed by my cheekbone and jaw line scars. If they'd seen the rest of me, which some had from time to time, they would have fallen madly in love with me... or the scars... which some had from time to time.

The nose reflected back at me in the jittery Midi starlight just went along with my general build. It, too, was long and a bit lanky, but regular enough and not lumpy as it hadn't encountered the Indonesian palm tree.

I suppose that we now come to my mouth, which I had sometimes considered from time to time. Was it weak or strong? It was certainly rather wide and, when I smiled, curved up sharply at the edges. But my lips were a shade too full to go with my tall, thinnish build. My lips should have been thin, too, I suppose. There had been some criticism, among women in whom I wasn't particularly interested, that my mouth betrayed a weak sensuality... which is why their own perfection could not satisfy my latent disreputable appetites. And, to be fair, I suppose that this must have been true after a fashion. Their self-proclaimed perfection, usually fairly dull, had not come close satisfying me.

The reflection fragmented, as perhaps befitted the existential angst of modern Western man, when the breeze intensified just as I kicked lazily close aboard *Jester's* port outrigger. I grabbed at the edge of aluminum float as it slowly pivoted away, and swung the briefcase up the two feet up onto the outrigger's plywood deck. It clunked and scraped as I pushed it safely inboard. These sounds were impressed on my memory because my ears happened to pop at that same instant. My perceptions suddenly became much sharper. I just hung onto the outrigger, treading water, feeling the slight cooling current as *Jester* drifted and pulled me gently.

After a minute or so, I porpoised and levered myself up onto the deck. The light was almost point blank at me, so I closed my eyes.

"Éteignez la lumière, s'il vous plait," I called out in my atrocious French. "Turn off the light," I added for good measure.

"How?" came back the surprising query. I didn't want to believe my French was that bad. But I generally go with the flow. "The trigger thing on the... er... handle."

After a few seconds of fumbling, ended by an audible click, the eye of the searchlight subsided into amber, and then into a tiny ruby glow that faded out reluctantly: An angry Cyclops chilling out. There was now no light on the water to attract curious eyes. There was only shy starlight between clouds, the small jewelled necklace of the New City's riverfront upstream, and that southern rosy snow-glow of the distant Pyrenees catching the last light of a sun already beneath the horizon.

I looked up toward the poop deck. She wasn't obscured by the glare of that searchlight any longer, but illuminated by the buttery glow seeping through the wheelhouse windows. What I had taken for drooping bats' wings was, in fact, a very sodden darkly hued raincoat of some shiny material. It wasn't buttoned or belted. Drab looking attire was plastered beneath it.

I heaved myself to all fours when goose bumps started to crinkle my skin. Heaved was the operative word, for I had ingested a fair quantity of river on that last dive. Looking around, I saw that *Jester* was pivoting in the little breeze and it now seemed strong enough to carry her across the sluggish current. To gain courage to undertake that stumbling struggle over the clumsy cargo up to the wheelhouse, I fumbled the fenders off the outrigger deck with one hand and pushed them overboard. In the tradition of barges, and for sheer practicality, my fenders were small auto tires. They were not only better than yachty pneumatic bumpers, but much less likely to get stolen.

The Pyrenees breeze was drifting *Jester* inexorably toward shore on the New City side of the Garonne. The boat would fetch up against the bank, eventually, or up against the concrete retaining wall that protected some short and apparently random stretches of the canal side. But I rather thought that *Jester* would ground beneath the truly gigantic weeping willows that not only adorned this Moissac portion of the Canal du Midi route, but also provided a picnic area for local French families. These willows already had the feathery look of summer. Just half a month earlier when *Jester* had passed them, their bare branches had barely been turning green.

I stumbled my way off the outrigger deck and up to the wheelhouse. By now I'd more or less regained that proud Homo Sapiens stance that supposedly distinguishes us from the lower anthropoids. My reflections on this achievement constituted a disadvantage in computing her first statement.

"I'm very happy you decided to throw it in," she said.

Her "very," was "veddy," the accent cool, crisp and English with a lilt from Hibernia. But it was all somewhat disconcerting coming from a partly Oriental face with apricot coloured skin, delicately slanted eyes with baby-thickened lids and the usual centre-part treatment of what looked like lustrous black hair in a page boy cut. This latter was currently rather too lustrous, being sopping wet and somewhat clinging. The real problem was her eyes, not that I mind epicanthic ones at all, but I was not used to blue irises sparking ingenuously in the starlight from that sort of face. She certainly had arresting or even disturbing features, but I couldn't decide then if she was attractive or not.

It must have been the shock of this, plus lingering hyperventilation, that atrophied my brain for a few moments. *I'm veddy happy you decided to throw it in...?* The pathetic too-brief vignette of that upraised arm sinking down under the water came back to me.

"The Lady of the Lake..." All things considered, I must have said this in a puzzled kind of choking way. For an instant I had imagined a hedging Sir Bedivere lying to dying King Arthur about the legal, proper and wilful disposition of certain valuable personal property, to wit, Excalibur. My helplessly blurted statement turned the tables. It was her turn to be surprised. Her eyes widened and I saw that they were, indeed, blue. It had not been a trick of starlight or some unpleasant chemical pollutant dripping from my own lashes.

"How… how... how did you know?" she asked, stunned in wide-eyed wonder. Then she added in a puzzled, musing way: "I only *fell* onto this boat... "

Even my befuddled brain suspected that this last statement was only figuratively true and figuratively accurate. It was also becoming rapidly apparent that we were both a bit confused, not just me. For instance, I should have done something seamanlike. With greater windage aft, *Jester* was turning lazily on the water, her bow coming around to point back toward Bordeaux. But I just couldn't think of anything to do and, besides, I knew that the canal banks here were mostly soft. And the fenders were over the side. So, I just knuckled water out of my eyes, and then looked at the gracefully curtseying willows that seemed to be gliding toward us, and around us, like giant women dancing a stately gavotte that nonetheless had deceptive speed. In a few moments *Jester* slid beneath the bowing bell of a withy skirt, its fringes brushing me and my stowaway as the boat crept into secret darkness beneath the tree.

"Hold on," I said, grasping the young woman's arm and gripping the top of the wheelhouse at the same time. But we grounded gently, after all, probably because the lee outrigger pushed against some bottom ooze as the riverbed shelved up. That Pyrenees evening zephyr wasn't a hurricane and the river was fairly narrow so that *Jester* wasn't blown far and didn't attain much speed. Still, inertia is a surprising force. I had expected a bump that could cause the uninitiated to stumble. I felt *Jester* working her outrigger into the muddy bank and quiver to a stop.

She would have to be tied up, of course, but for now the breeze pinned her to the shore securely enough. I glanced back toward the stone bridge, gratified to see that its span and arches were obscured by swaying willow tassels. We would be even more obscured for anyone on the bridge. And, as I looked with great care, I didn't see much movement on it. As I scanned the shallow rise of the span, distant thunder growled like a pack of dogs in pursuit of a fugitive.

This old bridge is the first of several that one encounters when coming upstream into Moissac, a wide stone span that lopes across the Garonne in nine bounds. The Garonne is still fairly wide at Moissac – a few hundred yards depending on the season – if not very deep, and this gave creative scope for bridge construction. Medieval builders, with exquisite care for symmetry, had made their arches with increasingly wider leaps from each shore to exult in the high central archway that permitted boat traffic in mid-channel.

Eight sturdy pylons tried to comb the flow that was curving around an invisible and nearly circular bend just upstream from the bridge. This loop of the Garonne formed a moat embracing most of Moissac Old City before the river abruptly curved the other way toward the New City further upstream. The pilot book for the Canal du Midi said that currents could be tricky both upstream and downstream from the bridge, especially at springtime high water. Just two weeks earlier, when I had made a nervous trip under this same – but then much lower – bridge, unruly tendrils of current had indeed curled and creamed obliquely from the water-worn buttresses. But now that it was almost summer, the black water flowing through the even blacker archways barely pulsed in rhythm with drowsy just-awakened cicadas.

I had wanted to be tied up at the quay in Moissac's old market before the storms came on, if possible, because even on a river thunderstorm gusts could be dangerous. Storms seemed both more sudden and more intense in the highlands, if also shorter-lived. I had wanted to pass this bridge before any vanguard wind hit the water. A gust could swing a boat against a stone bridge buttress, and at low water the inevitable tumble of submerged medieval masonry around an old abutment could damage a hull. Now, of course, I would not be tying *Jester* to Moissac's wharves tonight, but the shelter of the willow should be safe enough.

Now that *Jester* was motionless, snuggled cozily against the riverbank, I climbed up and stood on top of the wheelhouse to get a better view. Because the bridge was a long gentle up and down ramp, I could even see thin wedges of glistening pavement below the balustrade at each end of the span.

There was very little traffic over this bridge, anyway, because it was the old medieval bridge that had been renovated in the 1950s to accommodate two very narrow lanes. A wider steel bridge that had been built in the 1930s had been destroyed during the war and so the medieval one had been pressed into temporary postwar service. Two newer bridges had been constructed since, in the '70s, and these had carried the modern traffic for the most part. Now, of course, there was much less traffic than before over any of the bridges. The mist-fuzzed lights placed at rather long intervals along this 15th century span were, naturally, a postwar addition. As an energy-saving measure, however, only one light of every four was turned on.

This light was sufficient, barely, to show me that only a few pedestrians and vehicles at lengthy and irregular intervals were crossing over the arches. I saw pedestrian heads as dark blobs moving along the top of the balustrade, and vehicles as moving glows that illuminated old stone and cracked asphalt. There was no noise. The stone sidewalls must have reflected it back to the pavement and the air had become more humid, muting sound.

From June 24, the feast day of St. Jean Baptiste, and the day when the summer season officially begins, the latest edition of the *Canal Pilot Book* said that this old bridge would be draped with multi-coloured lights at night and provide a remarkable sight. I had never seen this bridge decorated for the summer because I had planned my travels differently. And now, even now, or perhaps especially now, there were more exciting places to be in summertime than Moissac.

Unless the endless negotiations with OPEC improved, or unless the West solved the immediate oil problem by simply invading all of the Middle East and 'liberating' the oil fields from 'rogue' countries while we still could, I might never see these strings of coloured lights at all. However, I could at least imagine that if the lights were chosen with care and some artistic sensitivity, they could enhance the ancient glow of the golden sandstone. But knowing the ruthlessly commercial instincts of small town France as I did, I had the suspicion that the Moissac bridge had been bejewelled with neon, and might be again.

But there were no colourful lights now to confuse my long and thorough scrutiny of the span, and the lamp standards provided just enough illumination to know for certain that nothing suspicious was on it. A slow dripping of small vehicles and bicycles crossed the misted bridge, skittering their own small wan pools of yellow headlights and dim sparks of taillights across the broken pavement of the span. No car hovered at the far end, toward which the accelerating automobile had gone. A thin and broken trickle of hunched pedestrians hurried along the walkways, hastened by the distant rumbles of thunder, and no one seemed to be loitering. But the near end of the bridge was blanketed by the line of willows, of which our own was one, leaning well out over the water, and so I couldn't tell what might be there.

This perspective of the bridge from a landlubber's point of view, so to speak, told me a great deal. Sure, times had changed, and there was less motorized traffic over the bridge, but – as I thought about it – maybe even more bicycles than before. But there was still some traffic on it. This fact argued that the girl had jumped over the balustrade the instant she had seen the two men, otherwise someone would probably have noticed a struggle. There was no knot of curious pedestrians looking over the central arch, no vehicles stopped beside the walkway there and no sound of an approaching police car. Police forces all over Europe had been enlarged, and were more responsive these days than previously.

They had to be if a semblance of modern society was to be maintained.

All this argued that she had recognized the men, which meant that she had seen them before. Her behaviour and theirs suggested that they were after something and she knew very well what it was. But their silencers and indiscreet shooting also told me that they would just as soon kill her outright, so long as whatever she was carrying was lost along with her. This fact seemed to rule out drugs, money or sexual molestation.

I began to feel the young woman's eyes intently on me as I finished scanning the bridge. When I bent and dropped to the deck, she looked steadily up into my face. "Do you see them?" she asked anxiously.

I shook my head curtly. "No. Nothing."

"That dive of yours…" she began "I… I waited for you to come up. With the light. I waited for you to come up… and… I searched…" She paused and swallowed the frog in her throat. I mean this almost literally because it sounded like a tiny croak, or choke.

I managed a grin of sorts. "So, instead of waiting around on this damned boat for me to come up, you felt like going into town and having a couple of glasses of vin ordinaire."

"What…?" she questioned. She tried to comb the stringy hair out of her face with a jittery hand. She didn't understand masking fear with humour. Studying that earnest, blank and wholly exotic face for a long moment, I decided that she had never known enough fear and uncertainty to acquire the defence of bravado.

But she was quick. Even in her present state, she flickered a smile. "Oh. Yes. I see," she almost whispered. "The beau geste."

"I wasn't all that anxious to come up," I said. "They had guns." I didn't add that her antics with the searchlight had very nearly killed me more effectively than the gunmen.

An intake of breath. "Oh," she said. Then, a tentative query or contradiction: "I didn't hear any explosions…"

Her eyes were still wide with shock, and guileless so far as I could tell. Her rather pointed chin jerked sharply in the start of a shiver, but she bit her lip to stop it. She had started to tremble. I slid the companionway hatch back across the wheelhouse, and the golden glow from the muted interior light flowed up to bathe her skin from mild Cheddar cheesy into apricot life.

"I'll show you the evidence in the morning," I replied. "But for now you have to get warm, dry and out of this breeze. Step down carefully. Hold those handrails there. Be careful on the… er, stairs… the ladder's steep." I guided her down as far as I could crouch, and stretch an arm. Only a four-foot descent, but best not skittered down in slippery nylons. She had lost her shoes. She looked up when she reached the bottom. I went down after her.

I pulled at the massive handle of the uninviting stainless steel door that led into the cabin. There was so little room in the wheelhouse that I had to nudge her very gently out of the way, and then I reached around and into the cabin to flick the light switch. She now clearly looked most forlorn and bedraggled in the sodden coat. I noticed that it had the current stylishly wide and impractical sleeves. "Here," I said, "drop that coat on that grate thing" – I pointed to the floor of the wheel-house – "and you'll have a hot shower soon." She looked at me while she shrugged out of the coat with some difficulty. It splattered onto the drain grating like a wet sheet.

"I don't want to seem inhospitable," I said and smiled, "but you're dripping wet. I have to tie the boat up, and I'll be right back in a few minutes. In the meantime… take off your clothes and just drop them on the grate."

She was really shaking now with chills, and hugging herself. She nodded. "Oh, and I'm Marc," I added as an afterthought. "Mariko," she replied, her voice quivering.

"It's warm in there," I said, gesturing toward the cabin. "Straight back there's a … bathroom… where you'll find towels. There are shirts in one of the closets."

I was about to turn to climb the steps when I remembered. "Oh, and watch your step, Mariko. There's a high… lip… around the door."

When I reached the deck, I turned to look back down at her. Obviously, her eyes had been following me. "It's okay… all right… You're safe." In spite of the wheelhouse and cabin light now spilling softly from the open hatchway, I didn't close her in. "Don't worry."

She barely nodded while she hugged herself.

Me, when thunder rumbled deeply and nearer, I scrambled off the poop deck, and onto the outrigger platform again, climbing, stumbling and cursing en route over rounded shapes under the tarp. These were casks I planned to deliver to my business partner Marcel Bouchard. No one on *Jester h*ad to walk into town for a couple of glasses of wine.

The boat had found a comfy berth for herself, snuggling her outrigger right against the soft turf bank. So far as I could tell by looking and feeling down in the darkness, the tire-fenders were squeezed cozily between the aluminum float and soft earth. The height of the bank was convenient, too, because I could make one long step from the outrigger deck onto the trembling sod. Clearly, this ground was saturated, and was just avoiding being mud. The rains of the spring had probably raised the river level high enough to put some of this water meadow under water just weeks before, and the water table had since subsided only a couple of feet.

The ground would get a lot harder and drier very quickly. It would soon suddenly become much hotter in the Midi, and also the thirsty roots of each willow tree along the bank drew up a couple of hundred gallons of water each day – I remember reading this once and being amazed.

Willow roots aplenty looped out of the turf around our tree, and there's nothing much tougher than an old gnarled willow root. I tied *Jester's* nylon bow and stern warps to these with much confidence. The only proper bollards were cemented into a concrete retaining wall that began beyond the little willow-park about a kilometre further upstream from the bridge. But it would be an exposed mooring. I much preferred being under the tree, even though we were closer to the bridge. This proximity even had advantages, so long as withy tassels provided a virtually one-way view.

After securing the warps, I stood up slowly, enjoying the new grass beneath my bare feet, the softness of the night air under the tree and the soothing evening's cricket song. At least, at first I thought they were crickets... or cicadas. I admit to limited knowledge of small creatures. I cocked my head to listen, and then it came to me that the rasping and plinking was orchestrated, not a cacophony. Not crickets or cicadas. Frogs along the canal bank. Probably small, green peepers, from the sound of them. Perhaps they were similar to those of Florida or Indonesia that could make a disproportionate racket for their size, because these French ones were giving quite a performance too. Their stately, almost melancholy cadence resembled the heartbeat plucking of a fretted violin.

A motor scooter, popping and buzzing, turned onto the willowed end of the bridge and started across toward the Old City. I brushed the withy curtain aside and peered, an action that suddenly reminded me unpleasantly of Timor. A single pool of light was jiggling along on top of the balustrade followed by a round head seemingly rolling along with it. The light contracted into the distance and the mosquito whine of the motor faded.

Now, what had that old fisherman told me so long ago? When frogs sing slowly and all together, it is a sure sign of rain. The slower they croaked, he had insisted, the more it would rain.

Even back then, and that would be almost thirty years ago, I had been sceptical. But I duly looked westward toward distant Agen and even further Bordeaux. The weather in France, as all over the world, generally comes out of the west toward the east because of the earth's rotation.

After a few moments of squinting though a thick fringe of willow withies, the western sky flared with lightning. I began to count. Twenty seconds before the distant sound of thunder reached me. Only about twenty miles away now, over Agen, give or take a few miles, the sky rumbled more deeply and distinctly than the more distant growling earlier. The frogs chanted sadly on, although I thought they were supposed to welcome moisture.

I turned back to the boat and made that long step aboard. Light from the Moissac bridge was pulsing through the willow swaying gracefully back and forth in the Pyrenees breeze, and so briefcase hardware kept winking coyly up at me. I picked the case up and wrestled my way over the slippery, rounded casks to the wheelhouse. In the instant before I slid the hatch open to go down, another and stronger flare in the western sky reminded me that my Nikes were still on the outrigger platform where I had shucked them before going for my swim.

Weary as I was, I considered just leaving them there. Knowing that willow bark was the source of acetylsalicylic acid, aspirin, I wondered if, when it rained, a weak solution of it might do something good for my athlete's foot. But they were my only decent pair of running shoes and I preferred them dry, so I scrabbled over Bouchard's casks yet again.

Returning to the wheelhouse after still another mild adventure surmounting the lumps piled under the slippery plastic neo-tarp, I descended the companionway. But something warned me not to take the briefcase into the cabin. Not just yet. At least, not until I learned what was going on. Every day, even in France, men mug, molest and rape young women. The victims are often beaten, sometimes knifed, but not shot very frequently. There is seldom premeditation in these crimes.

But both gunmen had used silencers, which indicated a certain forethought, not to mention money. And they had had a car. These days, that also indicated financial resources. A sordid local mugging would seem to be ruled out.

I noticed that only her coat was on the drain. I picked it up, wrung it, and hung it on the oilskin hook above the grate. Then, I wiped my feet as best I could against the rungs of the drain grate and upended the briefcase on it. The coat was long enough to cover most of the briefcase, and they both were black. Good enough for the moment.

I switched off the wheelhouse light. Darkness foundered Jester and, until the wave of it passed with the return of some night vision, I just stood there and listened to the frogs.

A light truck was coming over the bridge, an Innocenti three-wheeler or a small Citroen from the sewing machine sound of it. Not smooth enough for an Evolution or a Smart. And it was heavily laden because the driver shifted down just to come up the modest grade to the central archway. Then it chattered down toward me and the willows in a crescendo of seamstress virtuosity.

After a moment, I could see enough to reach for the refrigerator-type handle of the cabin door. It had once secured an old-fashioned cold room in a beef processing plant. I pulled the heavy steel door open, feeling the rubber seals parting reluctantly from steel lips around the sill. No need to look. I knew three inches of coaming rimmed the bottom of the door. The lady or the tiger? I suspected it would be a bit of both.

3

By the time I was looking at Mariko over the rim of a cup of hot chocolate, rain had come streaming in from Agen and Bordeaux along the usual Atlantic weather corridor.

The old Florida fisherman had been right, the slower the cadence of the frogs, the more rain there would be. So, the rain proved to be heavy and it would have drummed on *Jester's* deck but for the shelter of the willow. As it was, it hissed down the withies with surprising vehemence, and only the stronger gusts spattered the deck. We could hear this because all four portholes of the cabin were open for ventilation. But I had lowered the external steel storm covers so that the only light – and I kept it very low – slanted down onto the water on one side and onto the new grass beneath the tree on the other.

Given the night, the rain, the willow and the bare minimum of light, I figured that *Jester* was invisible for all practical purposes. My determination to remain concealed and our dim lighting within *Jester's* long and rather narrow accommodation reminded me somewhat of a movie about submarines.

This metaphor became dramatic when our pallid illumination paled altogether in a strobe of lightning reflecting off the water. At times, explosions crashed directly over us, and made us seem like actors in *The Hunt for Red October*. Once we heard the crack of a branch and the crackle of a tree limb falling, and I almost felt like speaking into a tube to give Sean Connery a damage report. It was a late spring highland thunderstorm, but more violent than usual.

I had returned to the cabin to find her hunched on the port settee with her face in her hands. She was wearing my blue flannel shirt and had a flannel sheet bundled clumsily around her legs. She looked up when the cabin door opened, and said nothing when I pulled it shut and swung the inside handle to close it on its seals.

"I still couldn't see them on the bridge," I reported briskly. I'd been gone for a few minutes and hoped she understood I'd looked carefully.

She had tried to comb her hair with her fingers, at least, and her eyes followed my every movement as I rummaged in the closet for dry clothes. I had noticed then that her hair was indeed a lustrous black. Her nose was ridged and straight, although only gently raised between her eyes, and these were not quite as almond-shaped as I had first thought. They were, however, still blue... but lighter now, in better light, with touch of green. These oceanic eyes had followed me out of the cabin as I headed aft with dry jeans and a shirt draped over my arm. My wet jeans and shirt had had some time to dry a little. At least they hadn't dripped too much down the narrow corridor.

Once in the head... bathroom... set across the aft-most few feet of *Jester*, I had noticed her grey skirt and white blouse hanging neatly from the showerhead where they could drip into the plastic sitting-tub. Purely utilitarian bra and briefs hung the opposite way on a hanger hooked over the steering shaft.

Dodging these items as well as I could, I had dowsed myself with hot water using the flexible attachment. I had then also draped my own clothes carelessly over the showerhead and steering shaft, but had left some space between her things to encourage air-drying.

After a few minutes, I had returned to the cabin, discovered dry socks in a drawer and had sat on the starboard settee opposite her to put on the Nikes. I then had stood up to rummage in the closet beside her settee, with her eyes following everything I did. Feminine attire was not well represented on *Jester*, but I had gradually acquired a small collection that could be stretched to serve emergencies. I found a pair of Jordache jeans and a bulky cotton knit pink-and-blue horizontal striped crew necked pull-over that had been inadvertently left aboard by a woman who had looked about the same size as she did. I found a pair of thick cotton socks and a pair of Adidas in the bottom of the closet. I had turned, smiled and had handed these things to her. "I hope they fit, more or less," I'd said.

She had stood up and combed her hair back with a quick gesture. She had seemed hesitant, but then she quickly unwrapped the flannel sheet and had bundled it onto the settee beside her. She needn't have worried. My plaid shirt fell off her shoulders and reached almost to her knees. She had taken the clothes with a sort of downcast nod and had almost scuttled aft. The bathroom door had closed definitively, and I'd heard the click of the bolt lock. Presently, I had heard the sound of the shower running. But by then I had turned to the stove, microwave and coffee maker.

Within an hour, all of our more immediate needs had been met. Mariko had had a hot shower. I had had a hot shower. Mariko filled the pair of small-sized Jordache jeans like they had been made for her. The rather bulky cotton knit crew-necked jersey with pink and blue horizontal stripes had definitely not been made for her. She looked teenish in white socks and the pair of Adidas running shoes that were only one size too large. She looked somewhat exotic with the towel wrapped around her head turban-style. This, she had explained when she had emerged from the steamy bathroom, was to blot her hair dry since I had no blow-dryer.

We were outside of a large vegetable omelette with a side order of leftover *saucisses à la Catalane* that I had made yesterday, not all that successfully, and which frying had sadly improved. It was difficult to scale down Rousillon and Languedocienne recipes for one person, sometimes, though I was winning more battles nowadays than I lost in the taste department. Mariko had, however, apparently been impressed with my haute-upscale collection of copper-plated stainless steel cookware. At least, she had cocked an eyebrow. I had taken this for appreciation. Just as I had taken the suddenly wry mouth for less than an accolade for the garlicky Spanish sausages.

All this had come with coffee, not afterwards in the French manner, but with, in the American way. I had waited a decent interval, and had come on with hot chocolate. My intention had been entirely honourable, to soothe tense and, perhaps, over-garlicked stomachs. I had been listening to Mariko's story.

But suddenly, and mostly because of Mariko's lying, I wanted a beer. So I took my half-emptied hot chocolate cup to the galley, and washed and rinsed it. And all the while I was wondering whether it was unfortunate that I was, perhaps, just a few years too old. I was becoming miffed that a young woman – and an oddly attractive young woman, I had decided – was being dishonest with her rescuer. Just a few years earlier I wouldn't have cared whether she had been lying or not. Opening *Jester's* small refrigerator and grasping a beaded can, I decided that my present annoyance with Mariko wasn't a tragedy. It made life simpler.

I came back into the cabin with a pop-top of Silver Bullet. You can still find Coors in France, sometimes, but it costs. I fizzed it open and slurped. The cost was worth it. You can have your Amstel, Heineken and Union Spazier. To me, European beers have a soapy taste. If I can't get Corona which, when and if available at all is exorbitant, I usually manage to get Coors, Bud or Canadian. I keep it cold, like a barbarian.

Without seeming overly curious or interrogative I had learned that her full name was Mariko O'Shaugnessey. She was half-Japanese and half-Irish. Her father had been a technician, whom the RAF had sent to Japan to help install some fancy new Doppler radar system for weather fore-casting. Sean had met and married Yoko, Mariko's mother, a horticultural expert. Mariko had been born in Osaka, Japan. I believed all this without question. It was much too unlikely not to be true. It explained her disturbing blend of Celt and Oriental.

In return for this, I had told Mariko that my full name was Marc Rennsalaer, spelled like that but pronounced Rensler to make things easy, that I was American by birth, Canadian by adoption and education, and a quasi-engineer and boat bum by inclination. I was a science and technical writer, when possible, by profession. I hadn't told her about Somalia, the Gulf War and Timor.

As for herself, in due course, Mariko had told me that she had attended the University of Armagh where she had double-majored in Classics and in Linguistics. Her mother had counselled botany and cellular biology, but in this matter the Celtic influence had triumphed. Mariko had won a scholarship to Oxford for some original work on North African linguistic elements in the *Book of Ballymote,* but this had not blossomed into a secure and respectable, if obscure, academic niche. I gathered that her perspective had proved too intuitive for her thesis advisor, although she had done brilliant and surprising work as a graduate student. I had believed all this, too.

The mutual dissatisfaction between Oxford and herself had coincided, she had told me, with an unfortunate relationship that had left her disenchanted with more than Oxford. So, she had simply left Britain to do some low-cost travelling on the Continent. Her vague intention had been to study Gaulish and Breton literature en route, but not much had come of it so far. This was at least plausible.

Mariko's increasingly easy conversation had suddenly become contrived at this point, and I sensed that she dropped words like "Tectosages," of which she could safely assume I would be ignorant, just to convince me of her story. It had seemed to me that during this part of the conversation Mariko's eyes kept avoiding mine. She said she'd come south to look into traditions that one Celtic tribe of pre-Roman times, the Tectosages, had preserved Greek mathematical and literary material.

So, I just sat facing Mariko, nodding and smiling and sipping the Coors. And I also kept remembering that the eyes of my confidant and girlfriend Joëlle had never yet avoided me, nor anything else I could think of. I'd be meeting up with with Joëlle soon enough.

Strangely enough, I happened to know a fair amount about Tectosages. This ancient Celtic tribe had greatly assisted my adaptation to France, had helped me to find a good friend and had even played a part in my finding a place in the canal life of the Midi.

I had seen some barrows along the shore of the étang leading to Narbonne when I had first sailed *Jester* into French waters, and I had been intrigued by them. Like everyone else, and perhaps more than most, I knew a little about the megalithic works of Brittany and Britain – under the minor and soothing information category labelled "Stonehenge." This knowledge had come from researching newspaper feature stories. There were also megalithic constructions on Malta. But I had never heard that the Mediterranean coast of France had some too.

After almost two days of bureaucratic red tape just getting *Jester* safely and legally moored along Narbonne's Canal de la Robine – a spur line of the Canal du Midi – I was ready for a break from the hot and stuffy offices of French officialdom. A few hours in Narbonne's air-conditioned library had satisfied my curiosity about the barrows. Well, almost.

Tectosages is a Latin name from Roman times. It had been applied to a Celtic tribe that had inhabited the region around Narbonne when Rome had annexed this part of Gaul in 127 BC. There were many impressive geometric earthworks, simple non-geometric mounds and megalithic dolmens, south of Narbonne when the Romans had occupied Languedoc. Most of these works have been destroyed or obscured by later construction, but a few still exist in the more remote and sparsely inhabited places, including those barrows I had seen on the shores of the étang. The Romans had naturally assumed that the Celts then living in the area had also built the earthworks and megalithic monuments, and because of that had called them Tectosages or "wise builders."

Knowing that Greek mathematicians had fled to southern Gaul about four hundred and fifty years earlier in 580 BC, the Romans had also assumed that the Greeks had taught the Celts geometry. Today, however, archaeologists know that the Celts migrated into southern France along the Danube about 1500 BC, while the first megaliths and earthworks around Narbonne were constructed at least 2500 years before that. No one knows who actually raised them, or how this unknown early culture had developed such impressive geometry and measuring methods. No one who writes textbooks, that is. Joëlle and a few other people I later met in Narbonne claimed to know all about the ancient megalith builders.

Facing Mariko O'Shaugnessey as I was, however, I thought it politic not to mention a cultured megalithic civilisation that had existed long before the invasion by savage Celts.

Twisting half around from Mariko to adjust the angle of a steel porthole cover behind me, I idly commented that her reference to Greek mathematics must mean Thales of Miletus, later Pythagoras himself and then his disciples. They had reputedly found refuge in southern Gaul, somewhere south of Narbonne, after they had been expelled from Magna Greciae because of their curious blend of mystical and mathematical religious beliefs.

When I turned back, I found her looking at me with narrowed almond eyes that had very little to do with Oriental genes. I could almost hear her computer rebooting. She smiled, however, and nodded her agreement. But I could even believe this Tectosages part of her story, too... up to a point.

The unfortunate incident on the nearby Moissac bridge was, she had supposed, just one of those random acts of senseless violence perpetrated against women. She had been at the New City's modern library on the north bank of the Garonne, where Moissac's ancient archives were now housed under climate-controlled conditions, trying to find some reference to the Tectosages tribe this far to the west. No one had ever been able to discover the precise extent of their historical domain.

After a day in the library, she had been walking back toward her bed-and-breakfast place in an old quarter of Moissac on the south side of the river. She'd been looking forward to scouting around for a working class restaurant in the medieval Old City once she crossed the bridge. A car had cruised up beside her. It had stopped. Two men had got out and had tried to force her into the car. The objective had been rape, she supposed. At any rate, she'd struggled. She had her briefcase with her in which were the notes covering the afternoon's research on Tectosages-related matters, and she had used the briefcase to good effect. But it hadn't been enough. She supposed that she had been pushed over the balustrade in the struggle. Naturally, I didn't believe a word of all this.

First of all, no one had ever heard of Tectosages west of Carcassonne, according to the conventional literature. Mariko had been a bit too intuitive for Oxford, perhaps, but even lack of conventionality is a relative term. Her blouse was conservative, her skirt was conservative and her lingerie, if it could be called that, was unexciting. Now that she was in the Jordache jeans and the jersey top, I could see that her figure was extraordinary and yet her own clothing had not even been chosen to complement her curves, much less advertise them. I felt certain that someone like Mariko would stick to approved academic sources while even supporting an unconventional interpretation of them.

Second, the central arch of the old bridge wasn't all that high and if she'd been pushed over that almost shoulder-high – for her – balustrade, she'd have fallen head first into the water unless she had somersaulted completely. But there was no height for a complete somersault, and I had seen her go in feet first.

And third, she had tried to hold that briefcase aloft even as she was going under. "I splashed down in front of your boat," she said. "It moved so that I could go between two parts of it. There were pipes under there, and it was covered over, so I could just hang on." Both her innocence and her nautical ignorance were charming. I nodded.

She continued: "And then you drove the boat back and forth looking for me, and I could only stay under it holding on. The first chance I had to get out from underneath was when you finally stopped the boat and swam away. I tried to help you with the light," she said, "but the boat kept drifting and turning." She bit her lip delicately again, probably not knowing how attractive the habit was, when she added: "And that last dive. You were down so long..." Her long lashes quivered and fluttered onto cheeks that had gradually become rather golden again because of the shower, nutrition and warmth. "I... I... thought you'd drowned."

Then she shook her head, and looked up, smiling. It was convincing, shaking off the past gesture, but I thought her concern was also genuine. She had played much the same scene with palpable shock previously up beside the wheelhouse. Take Two was just a bit over-acted, that's all.

Of course, we'd rehashed the story a couple of times, as people will after a harrowing experience. We had chatted while the *saucisses à la Catalane* had been frying, and while the American-style coffee had been dribbling into its basket filter. I couldn't blame her for starting to get tired of the script. But this last time, with the cold beer can in my hand; I remembered something I had forgotten to ask in earlier renditions.

But, just as I was about to open my mouth to ask it, scents of distant orange, apple, cherry and apricot blossoms wafted subtle perfume through the porthole. Although there were scattered fruit trees in Tarn-et-Garonne, as all over the Midi, the scent was so definite and distinct that it could only have come from a very large concentration of trees. It must have come from the orchards south and west of Bordeaux in the Landes. Almost a hundred miles away. I was humbled by reverence that such delicacy had been carried so far by the violence of the storm's wind. I breathed it in, and it sweetened me. So, thankfully, I began more patiently and gently than I had intended.

"When I first came up beside you, after my swim, you said – and I remember being puzzled by it – *'I'm very happy you decided to throw it in...'* What did you mean? Throw what in?"

She looked at me with mild surprise, and then squinched her eyes shut. She was obviously trying to think back to something that was quite trivial to her. Then she brightened with lively eyes, it was genuine, and she even laughed for the first time since we'd met. "The towel, of course." She restated it for my benefit. "What I meant was... *I'm very happy you decided to throw in the towel...* decided to stop looking for me. At first, because you kept going back and forth under the bridge and I had no chance to get out of the water so long as the boat was moving. And later, because I was truly afraid you had drowned diving for me..." She trailed off as if it should be clear by now, but then my rejoinder popped into her memory by association. She stared at me. "Then you said *'The Lady of the Lake'*... "

"And you were stunned by it. Remember what you said?" I asked.

She looked down, concentrating. Finally, "No," she shook her head, "I can't remember."

"You blurted out... 'How did *you* know?'"

"I did?"

"Indeed." I paused, sipped. "And that has been intriguing me. Want a beer?" She shook her head, so I got up and walked to the galley, took another Coors from the small supply in the small refrigerator, and popped the top.

I ambled back. "For me, it is all clear now, given my confused mental and physical state just after that last dive. When you hit the water, the last thing I saw of you, while I was reversing and turning to give you some room, was your arm raised up. You were holding something – your briefcase, we know now – and it was the last thing to go under. Your waving arm reminded me of the Lady of the Lake. Just popped to mind," I shrugged. I slurped. "Then later, when I came up to you at the wheelhouse, you said 'I'm *very happy you decided to throw it in*' and, well, I guess my last sight of you was still lingering in my oxygen-starved brain because I thought of reluctant Sir Bedivere. You know, the chap who dithered over throwing Arthur's sword into the murky mere."

She looked up, impatience thinly masked by courtesy. Her eyes flickered to my beer can. *Is he getting drunk? Did I jump from a frying pan into a fire?* I could almost hear her thoughts. I smiled and sat down, across from her. "What's the salient point about Excalibur?" I asked.

"Excalibur...?" She frowned, shook her head, focussed on me.

"Value, Mariko." I considered the Coors can, and sipped thoughtfully. "You might say it was a sword of destiny... a fell and fateful symbol of hope and power. Arthur will return when he's needed, so the legend goes, and the Lady of the Lake has Excalibur in a security deposit awaiting withdrawal."

She was smiling at me in an impatient and somewhat patronising way, waiting for me to continue with my irrelevant ramble.

"That briefcase was as valuable to you as Excalibur was to Arthur. You tried to save it even as you were sinking in the Garonne. It was also just as valuable to those two men."

Mariko smiled in a friendly way, and stretched. She fumbled the turban loose and folded the towel neatly. Then she looked up, smiling brightly, while she finger-combed her damp hair back into a semblance of a page boy. "Well," she said, looking at a watch we both knew had succumbed to shock and drowning, "thanks to your kindness, I feel much better. I really shouldn't trouble you further. You've been *so* gracious." She looked down at herself. "If I can borrow these... "

"Of course", I said casually.

"I'll return them tomorrow. I shall."

"Fine."

She turned then to go aft and retrieve her clothing. She was back in just a few moments with folded garments over her arm and her under-things discreetly hidden beneath the bland grey skirt. She paused on her way to the cabin door, turned and extended her right hand. She looked at me too brightly and I met her eyes steadily.

"Mariko O'Shaugnessey," I said, ignoring the hand and not getting up, "they had silencers on their guns. They were trying to kill you, not rape you. You know it. I know it. But I do wonder why."

4

Mariko shook her head slowly. At first I thought she was hard and strong enough to be pretending she was sorry for me. You know – poor, drunk over-imaginative man – and all that. But then I knew, as her head kept gesturing negative, that it was a last long denial from a desperately weary young woman, as I now realised. Her skin was grainy beneath the quickly fading flush of recent nutrition and temporary relief from stress. She couldn't have been more than about twenty-five, and yet there were shadows beneath her eyes not caused by *Jester's* dim lighting. Tiny wrinkles crowded into the corners of her eyelids and mouth.

And she was a frightened young woman, too. Her mouth twitched once or twice before she relinquished control and her lips began to quiver. She bit her lip again, but it didn't help. Then she closed her eyes tightly to try to hold herself together, but that didn't work either. She lost some control, but she never lost any dignity. As the first tears skittered down her cheeks, long fingers came up to cover her face so that I would not witness her defeat.

I closed my own eyes for a second, worried and tired, and heard her rounded bottom plunk back down onto her seat. I opened my eyes just as she shifted her clothes onto the settee beside her and folded them over absently. She covered her face in her hands again, and choked back a sob. I slurped and I waited, but not too long. We didn't have too long, maybe. "Mariko, how long have they been after you?"

The answer came, at last. "Ten days."

"Since where?"

"Glastonbury."

My head jerked to full attention. Then I sighed. And slurped again. "Oh, dear," I said.

Her head had stopped its continual, gentle shaking negation, but now the finger-covered face nodded softly in resigned affirmation, showing that she fully understood that I now understood. Well, *some* of it... Glastonbury was the home of the Lady of the Lake. It explained her shocked reaction up at the wheelhouse. But I was no nearer to knowing the cause of it.

"So... What makes that briefcase such a fell and fateful thing?" I said in the best mock-legendary intonation that I could manage.

She sniffled a little laugh. Then she got up and threaded her way back to the head where I heard toilet paper being bumpily unrolled, a nose blown. I heard the fridge door suck open, a tinkling of cans. Mariko appeared in the cabin doorway with a silver Coors in each hand. "Do you mind?" she asked.

"Not at all."

She extended one toward me in a kind of preoccupied way, and I nestled it beside the cushion for future use. Mariko remained standing a moment, as if undecided about things, but she flicked her hair back with the now-freed hand, and plunked herself down again. Her bottom was even rounder with a supply of contingency tissues in her hip pockets.

Mariko hesitated. She tugged at her lower lip with small teeth, as if working out what to do. She considered for a long time, looking down, and I sensed genuine apprehension. "I would tell you about what I have…had... in the briefcase... except that it doesn't matter now," she said finally as she regarded me earnestly. "It... it might put you in danger, you see, if someone got the idea that you knew about... you had seen it... and you've already done a great deal for me." She shrugged, and smiled warmly at me. "I mean it. Truly. And it can't matter now. It's lost."

So, her earlier dishonesty had been from trying to figure out a story that wouldn't involve any further or future risk for me. I was pleased with that. "Ah… not necessarily," I said.

Her head jerked up and she stared at me. Then she seemed to relax, or relapse, and ran her fingers through her hair again. "Oh, I know. I suppose you're saying that you're willing to dive for it."

I nodded, but vaguely.

She smiled, genuine gratitude and great regret. "Thank you. But it wouldn't do any good, you see. What's inside couldn't withstand a long soaking in water. I didn't think of that when I wrapped it," she added bitterly.

"I see," I said. It wasn't difficult to put two and two together... up to a point. "A book. Or a manuscript, then." She had studied literature and linguistics, after all.

She smiled and snuffled a laugh. She nodded. But then any amusement at my persistence drained from her face. "But it would do you no good to know, and possible harm."

"I've already been shot at," I pointed out.

She looked at me doubtfully.

"Oh, I know you don't believe it," I said. "Or about the silencers. I said that I would show you in the light. But, in any case, I think you know it's true." I paused. "Or... you're afraid it's true."

Mariko sighed, and finally nodded. "I did hear a funny sound...

under the boat... and something clanged not far from me."

I remembered this sound when she admitted it. Other events had made me forget it. "I hope to hell they didn't put a hole in the outrigger. Oh, well. We'll see." I knew that *Jester*, loaded as she was amidships with Bouchard's wine, and with the afflicted outrigger virtually ashore, would not list much even with a hole in this float. I'd have to check carefully when there was light. I looked up at Mariko, holding her eyes. "Yes. Well, something clanged – as you put it. I know a bullet when I hear one... I've heard them before," I added.

Mariko nodded slowly. She hesitated for some moments. "It's just one page of vellum – calf-skin. Parchment is actually lamb skin", she added almost as an after-thought. "I rather think it must be copy, probably medieval. Seventh or Eighth Century? It is... was... in fairly good condition. I'm not certain what it was."

"What do you think it is?"

She pursed her lips, and shook her head as if to clear it. "I don't truly know," she mused, "but I think it was important."

"But you must have some idea. You're a linguist, after all."

"True... " Mariko smiled wryly. "Unfortunately, that didn't help much. It took me two weeks to find out that the script is genuine Tiffinagh, with, I think, an Ogham rebus – I could recognise *that*," she looked up brightly. Then she subsided back into puzzlement. "At first I thought it was some sort of monkish code..." she mused. "They were rather obsessed with cryptic parchments during the medieval period," and she glanced up again, obviously adding this as a gloss for me, "until I discovered that it was mostly Tiffinagh."

"A North African script, still used by Berbers in places, but anciently and somewhat curiously also used in pre-Christian Scandinavia." I said this mostly to myself while reaching for the cached Coors, and when I turned back to her found her regarding me with a slightly cocked head and a questioning eyebrow.

"You are full of surprises, Marc Rennsalaer." She said it somewhat wryly. "A boat bum who is familiar with Thales of Miletus and with Tiffinagh?"

"Newspaper articles," I said matter-of-factly. "I told you I was a writer of sorts. I once did a piece on the controversy surrounding the Peterborough Petroglyphs. Peterborough, Canada. When I was at the University of Toronto, I got interested in the glyphs and proposed an article to the *Toronto Star*. They didn't take it, but I did a lot of research. Some of the glyphs seem to be Tiffinagh."

"Tiffinagh? In Canada? Who says so?"

"Well, Barraclough Fell said so," I noted innocently. I was not surprised to see her grimace and indulge in a slight snort. "And then David H. Kelley also said so," I added. Her mouth opened. I nodded. "I interviewed him," I said, and paused. "As for Thales of Miletus, well, general education *does* exist outside of Europe, Mariko. Why, I even know the Pythagorean Theorem. Engineers have to learn it," I said, "…you know, that right triangle and hypotenuse thing. And it's only a step from there to Pythagoras himself and then back to Thales." I popped into the new Coors.

Mariko finally pulled her pop tab without breaking a nail. She tried a tentative gulp. Then she looked at me and smiled. "I do apologize," she said. "I'm veddy sorry."

"The language…?"

"That's the curious part. I don't know from my brief study of it. Not Greek. Not Latin. Not Aramaic or Hebrew. Not in clear, that is, which is why I must now suspect a cipher."

"But Tiffinagh symbols still represent phonemes," I said. "Even a cipher would reflect a language's general sound. It must sound like *something*."

"It took me so long to identify the script for certain that I had only just started trying to figure out the language when… when… "

"When you were attacked."

She nodded. "Yes." She looked up. "I really was at the library in Moissac today, Marc. It's not the biggest library in the world, but I've been using whatever I could wherever I found myself. But I wasn't interested in Tectosages." She flickered the briefest of rueful smiles. "For ten days I've been working on the parchment. And travelling." She bit her lip again, and delved behind for another tissue. "And now it's gone."

"Where did you find this thing?"

"In a tiny church. The church of Saint Mary Magdalene in Glastonbury." She paused so long that I thought she had finished. But then she continued as if puzzled herself. "I don't know why," she said helplessly. "I just decided to go to Glastonbury to see the Abbey. I was working out a personal problem. Of course, I've been there many times before. One of the premier sites of early Celtic learning in England… But this time I noticed a tiny church not far from the great Abbey. I never saw it before, never even heard of it. It's truly very small… " She trailed off, remembering.

Then she looked up again and smiled. "Not so small for me, but you'd have to stoop to pass through the door." She paused, gathering the memories. "Well, no one was there. It seemed like no one ever came there, but it was open. Somebody had opened it."

"Probably a National Heritage caretaker from the Abbey."

She nodded. "That's what I think… Anyway, the place was quite decrepit. I looked around and I leaned against the little altar. It was falling apart, just loose stones, really… But of course I didn't know that when I leaned against it." She spread her fingers, shrugged. "It started to lean and slide. It didn't actually collapse or anything, it just... *shifted*." She glanced at me as if expecting to be doubted. She clearly felt guilty.

I nodded sympathetically.

"There's not so much to tell," Mariko added, quickening the pace of her story, as if to get it over with. "At the bottom of the pile, I could see a deep space between some stones. I saw a glint like dull metal. I then looked more closely. It was a small box, and it had been pried apart by the shifting of the stones. It looked like metal had been torn all around the edge, if you know what I mean. I wasn't paying attention to the box because I could see a roll of vellum – *parchment* – inside." She stopped, and shrugged again.

"Go on, Mariko."

She grimaced. "I don't know what came over me," she said. "The long and short of it is that I just reached into the crevice and pulled at a piece of parchment. It came out neatly. Nothing ripped or was turned to dust or anything like that. There was writing on it. I took it." She almost glared at me in defiance. "I know I shouldn't have done, but I just took it and stuffed it in my briefcase."

"All right," I said mildly.

Mariko bit her lip again, suddenly but briefly. "But I was worried about the altar. I shoved the stones back into place one-by-one. It was easy to see how they had slid, you know. After it was done, and I certainly did a neat job on the altar, you may be sure; I simply hared away from that place."

Even I knew, or thought I knew, that "to hare" is British for "to run". But I wanted to make absolutely certain of Mariko's meaning. "Hared? You mean that you actually ran?"

She nodded. "For a hundred yards, at the least. Then I slowed. I remember that someone called to me that the bus had already passed a minute before. They must have thought that I was running for the bus."

"I see," I said. "Mariko... Why did you run? Did you hear anyone approaching the church?"

She regarded me with a puzzled expression. "Because I'd stolen something, of course. No, I heard nothing. And I didn't pass anyone on his way to the church. I told you that no one seems to go there."

"Yes. You did." I paused. "Mariko, what colour was that small box? It may be important."

"A sort of dull silver. Like pewter. Or lead... Why is it important?"

I shrugged. "Maybe it's not so important, after all. At least not right now." I cleared my throat. "When... ah... when did you first know that someone was after you?"

"Today," she replied, "when the car came up to me on the bridge."

"But you said..." I must have looked startled.

"You asked when I first *knew*, Marc." She got up in the narrow corridor that boasted standing headroom. She hugged herself. "That's when I first *knew,* but I had this feeling that I was being followed from the start. Even in Glastonbury when I finally did visit the Abbey later."

"Maybe it was just guilt," I suggested.

She nodded readily enough. "That's what I thought, myself... at first... But then I began to notice the same men wherever I went, the same two men... No matter what city I was in. They followed me everywhere. Glastonbury. London. Oxford."

"How did you travel? Car?"

She shook her head. "Trains and some buses in Britain. I've no car."

I regarded her with new respect. Ten days of travel by train, especially these days, called for quite a bit of endurance. And buses were very infrequent, at least in continental Europe. She must have done a lot of waiting in stations, but not much sleeping. She probably had not done much good eating, either. I didn't bother to ask her the usual *'are you sure you were followed?',* or *'how can you be sure you were followed?'* – because she had very nearly been killed in my presence. I tried to save our time and energy. "So, that's why you left England and came over here... to try to get away from them."

"Not entirely. There was also the relationship of which I spoke."

"Yes. That."

She nodded, and paced the length of floor between the bunk-settees. I noticed that the rain had stopped hissing. Random drops spattered *Jester's* deck when the porthole curtains billowed. I followed Mariko with my eyes, like a spectator at Wimbledon. Quite obviously she was more than upset. She was angry. But not, I thought, about the possible loss of her life so much as angered at the loss of a scrap of parchment. "Mariko O'Shaugnessey," I said quietly, "what did you find?"

After the ground we had covered, she must know that it was patently clear, to both of us now, that she'd discovered something of great value to someone. Or great threat.

She turned to face me. "I *think* I may have found another Gospel," she said. "It was a copy of the original, of course. Perhaps even a copy of a copy. But if my hunch is right, it may well be the oldest Gospel. It might also have been the most important one."

"And the author...?"

"I found the first clue only today, in fact. In Tiffinagh phonems... *Mir-yam Mag-da-la...* Mary Magdalene." She paused. "You don't have to know the language to recognise that."

"The woman with seven devils...?" My knowledge of the Bible was sketchy, except for inaccurate quotations.

Mariko smiled wryly. "Perhaps... so the Church would have it – but I prefer to think of her in another context."

"Yes...?"

"Yes. There's evidence that she was the most devoted apostle of them all. One of the Nag Hamadi texts – not the text actually entitled the so-called *Gospel of Mary Magdalene*, which seems likely to be a forgery – hints that she may have been more than that."

"Like what?"

"The *Gospel of Philip* in the Nag Hamadi library says that Jesus and Mary Magdalene often walked alone together. And that they kissed on the mouth. Philip also said that she was the beloved disciple of Jesus. All this may mean that Mary Magdalene had been married to Jesus."

"Couldn't she just have been his mistress?"

"Not likely, Marc," she smiled wryly. "Back then, under Jewish law the penalty for promiscuous behaviour was stoning to death... for the woman, of course. Also, if there had been rumours that Jesus and Mary Magdalene were living like that, then he would not have attracted any following at all."

"I see." I hesitated. "Mariko, how reliable are these texts, the Nag Whatever-It-Is?"

"Nag Hamadi." She paused. "Since they were buried in the Egyptian sand for almost two thousand years, they are more reliable than the canonical gospels, in my opinion."

"Why?"

"Because they weren't subjected to any editing by the early Church. All biblical scholars know that the New Testament wasn't standardized in its present form until more than three centuries after the time of Jesus, and by then the Roman Church was claiming leadership of all Christianity. Much was rejected as not conforming to Roman doctrine, and what was accepted was heavily edited to make it conform that much better. So, a genuine account by Mary Magdalene would certainly illuminate the New Testament story of Jesus' life," she concluded.

"And now, Mariko O'Shaugnessey, I must ask the obvious question."

She stopped pacing, faced me and nodded as if agreeing. Then, she sat on the opposite settee again, blew her nose and slowly looked up.

"After you had had a chance to think it over," I began, "why didn't you just take your piece of vellum to the Heritage people and admit the whole incident?"

Mariko stood up and began to pace again. I waited.

"There are not many opportunities, even at the best of times, for linguists. Especially for female linguists. These aren't the best of times."

"No."

"I was fortunate. I was approached to be a... protégé... of a respected Oxford professor."

"I see."

"The same one who, so I learned quite recently, has just published a journal article based on North African linguistic elements in the *Book of Ballymote*."

"Your small claim to linguistic fame."

She nodded, brushed her hair back and crossed her arms.

"Hence the trip to Glastonbury," I surmised. "Soul searching."

She nodded again, smiled grimly and brushed her hair back impatiently. "If I had admitted the discovery, Marc Rennsalaer, do you know who one of the experts would have been to whom the parchment would doubtless have been given for study?"

"I think I can guess."

"Yes. Well, I found that I was tired of being a… convenience."

"So you would prefer the risk of physical rape, to use your euphemistic account of the incident on the bridge, to intellectual rape?"

She stopped pacing once more and looked at me with what seemed to be mild surprise. "Now, that is an exceedingly insightful observation, Marc Rennsalaer. I will have to think carefully on it. But yes, on first reflection, I might well agree." She began pacing again, but more slowly. "As a woman, I've learned that our bodies were obviously designed to be taken by men and to be inseminated so that reproduction can result. I don't argue with the biology. But the mind is another thing, the thing that makes us fully human in a way that transcends gender. I will not have that violated."

"We boorish North Americans have a term for it, Miz O'Shaugnessey, which I won't repeat here."

"I've heard it, of course. Mind-fucking. Very apt." She paused and gazed at me thoughtfully. "By the way, Marc Rennsalaer, was your observation also in the nature of… an offer?"

I had not considered this and it took me by surprise. I managed a faint smile, but quickly felt it fading. "I would have to think about that very carefully," I replied cautiously. I couldn't think of anything else to say, so I waited until Mariko had paced beyond me toward the galley, and then I stood up in the central aisle between the bunks and pushed through the cabin door.

Then, I checked the coat. It was almost dry. I picked up the briefcase and it didn't drip. When I turned back into the cabin, Mariko was sitting slumped on her settee with her hands between her knees. She looked up, and I held the case out to her.

5

Mariko had wrapped the page of vellum – "parchment" to me, although she had explained the technical difference – in folded-over plastic sealed with cello tape. She had been right, it would not have survived any long submersion, but then it had not suffered one. There had been only a few beads of water within the plastic sheath. However, there had also been some unprotected paper photocopies within the file compartment and they were truly soaked.

"Tiffinagh alphabets," she explained as she arranged them flat on the rest of her settee and attempted to blot them. There were obviously too many for her bunk alone, and so I transferred some sheets to the top of my mattress and stood leaning against the cabin door.

"Thank you, Marc. That was considerate." She threw up a short and weary smile. "We...I...can dry them that much faster."

Once she'd slowly and carefully blotted everything dry with tissues from her hip pockets, she put the parchment and wrinkled papers back into her towelled-out case. She closed it finally, taking a last reluctant peep inside before it clicked shut. Mariko regarded the numbered dials for a split second. She politely didn't lock it, though I could feel her wanting to, and she bent to place it carefully on the cabin sole beside her settee. She looked at the floor width doubtfully, and she sat back up.

"Believe me," I grinned, "I'm not about to steal it. My life in France has been generally placid and uneventful... up to now." *Too placid? Too uneventful?*

"I'm veddy sorry," she said again. "Habit." She smiled ruefully and fingered her hair. I think that she would have blushed, and maybe she even did blush, except that her face suddenly became so drained with fatigue that there wasn't much blood to work with.

"That long shuttered section between the galley... ah... kitchen... and the head ... bathroom ...has some storage underneath." She couldn't just leave the case beside the settee. The central passageway was so narrow that even the briefcase's modest thickness partly obstructed it. That was one of the few drawbacks of *Jester's* design. All the amenities from settee-bunks to stove and refrigerator to computers had to be on one side or the other of the long sunken corridor that gave standing headroom for everything and yet kept the hull low. But the design had so many other advantages that this was a minor inconvenience. I'd got used to it.

She stood up with visible effort, smiled to cover it, and made her way aft. A few moments after she disappeared through the galley, I heard a metal door roll up. She exclaimed: "Holy Mother of God. I say." I noted that instinctive Irish had been quickly smothered by educated English. There was a long minute of silence while she couldn't resist examining the space-saving Toshiba laptops with Pentium IV processors, and the external CD ROM and diskette drives. I heard a scuffle and shuffle among the lower shelves as she finally settled the briefcase between books, files and plastic diskette holders.

But I could almost feel her eyes following the cables leading across the low ceiling to whatever modules might be behind the other metal barrier. Certainly, a printer, at the least, she would conclude. There was also a high-resolution scanner and two digital cameras. She was a good guest, however, and resisted any temptation to pry. Anyway, I didn't hear the second door roll up.

However, space considerations had dictated that some materials had to be divided between both sides of the boat. So, when I heard a faint brush of denim, I figured she'd knelt to scan the portside CD library under the work shelf. Finally, the door rolled down and chunked solidly into its plastic seal.

I sipped Coors, but she didn't reappear quickly even though there were only a few short steps to cover. I glanced up to see her leaning against the… er… doorway, looking down at me thoughtfully. She shook her head slowly. "Just a typical boat bum," she said.

Mariko fingered her hair distractedly, and took a couple of preoccupied steps into the cabin, her fatigue momentarily eclipsed by interest. "Marc Rennsalaer…" she said softly to herself, "… where have I heard…" Then she sat down on her settee, modified that almost immediately into stretching out on it and finally propped her cheek on her elbow. She gazed at me steadily before her eyes began to droop.

"A prophet is not without honour, except in his own country," I quoted incorrectly. And, "sufficient unto the day is the evil thereof," I intoned. Not that these statements meant anything in particular, but they generally fitted my context. And, besides, I was getting a bit tired myself.

"How do you get connected?" she finally asked.

"Satellite dish." I sipped. There was an optimistic half can remaining, as Karl Marx had once observed. "I'll show you tomorrow."

Mariko closed her eyes and nodded, accepting the fact of staying aboard *Jester* for the night. She was obviously not anxious to walk across the bridge to her bed and breakfast place. If it existed, that is. But perhaps she had just not been in France long enough to call such an establishment a pension. I had not seen her blot a passport or any money from the briefcase, but perhaps she carried these necessities elsewhere. The grey skirt had big zippered pockets.

She yawned, but daintily, patting her lips with long fingers. She sat up again. "Tell me more about Marc Rennsalaer," she said. For something to do to keep herself awake, she did the wrong thing. She fumbled for the can on the shelf and drained her Coors in a few long gulps, like a veteran. She subsided once more onto her elbow and blinked.

I figured from past experience that the best way for a man to put any woman to sleep is to tell her a long, rousing war story. I began by explaining how my military experience had moulded my subsequent life orientation, as a television interviewer had once put it. But before I even got out of boot camp at Paris Island, she had gathered her rolled-up clothes under her cheek as an extra pillow.

My descriptions of exotic Somalia – a candidate for Solomon's Ophir, to judge from the products as described in the Bible, although Ophir could have also possibly been Saba in ancient Yemen – had elicited a response of deep, regular breathing. I kept on describing Somalia's myhrr and frankincense trees, bushes really, emphasising that you had to be cautious of the ones that moved. They were almost always attached to an armoured car.

I waited a while before I raised her bunk's wooden safety rail. She didn't budge when its safety tabs snicked into place. At least she wouldn't fall off her bunk into the corridor if she rolled over in a troubled sleep. I floated the flannel sheet down over her because nights on the water could be cool and her bunk's portholes were partly open. Then I turned off the single dim cabin light.

Lying in the darkness opposite her settee, I listened to the slow rhythm of Mariko O'Shaugnessey's deep, regular breathing. Well, snores, really. But gentle ones. They did not put me to sleep, but made me restless instead. I also continued listening to diminishing celestial grumbles as the retreating thunder contributed occasional comments on my thoughts.

Rape is one of those words that can be surprisingly elastic. Applied pedantically to women in a purely physical sense, it is the traditional female fate worse than death... and yet Mariko O'Shaugnessey, as a human being, had feared intellectual rape much more deeply than mere physical usage. In this sense of mental and emotional violation of propriety, rape could also apply equally well to a man.

For example, once I had been so patriotic that I had interrupted an engineering education, and an impending career and marriage, to serve my country. For some reason, at the age of nineteen I had suddenly felt it was time to fulfil my military obligations to the American Republic.

As a proudly newly-minted U.S. Marine, I had survived Paris Island and was shipped out to Somalia. Although some of my friends at university had always been more than a little critical of U.S. foreign policy, which had always exhibited a high degree of overt or covert military intervention, service in Somalia could not be frowned upon. We were there *only* to see that UN-sponsored food got distributed fairly to a starving population.

And that seemed to be true… in the beginning. But the "CIA", that catch-all term meaning Washington's hidden agenda under any number of alphabet agencies, rapidly undermined this purely humanistic policy. Not only did it quickly become obvious that pro-Western elements got more food, but soon UN food convoys had started to be used for smuggling arms to supposedly pro-Western and pro-American paramilitary forces. These mini-armies were usually controlled by local warlords, disguised as Colonels, who were otherwise making fortunes in the slave trade.

The American goal in supporting these thugs was to build democratic states around them. Not unlike the same strategy with Diem in South Vietnam a generation earlier. It therefore didn't take long for sincerely progressive Arab leaders to turn toward their only other source of support, Communist and Socialist movements. As these movements gathered momentum among those committed to social and agrarian reform, they could be labelled as terrorist and revolutionary. Opposition to them did not have to remain covert by subverting the UN; it could hopefully become overt using the American military. Although I had a few encounters with mobile myhrr and frankincense bushes, I was transferred to the bigger show that was televised by CNN and all other major networks as the exciting spectacle of Desert Storm.

On the scene in Kuwait, the real character of Desert Storm's assault quickly became apparent. True, Sadam Hussein was rabidly anti-American and anti-Western… but that wasn't the point. Iraq's army, *on paper* the fourth largest in the world, could not be considered any danger to the United States. This army was, however, in spite of its inefficiency, a potentially lethal threat to a country as small as Israel.

The entire rationale for Desert Storm was simply to fight a proxy war on behalf of Israel, while Israel itself remained officially uninvolved. Aside from that, Desert Storm was useful for testing new U.S. weaponry in a hot war against a paltry adversary, an opportunity that had been scarce for a while.

Iraq had been set up for this war. Kuwait had been drilling obliquely beneath their borders to tap into Iraqi oil pools far beneath the sands. This meant that while the visible part of the drilling operation was in Kuwait, the drill beneath the surface was slanted on an angle so as to tap into Iraqi oil fields. Iraq was naturally incensed and had asked the

American ambassador if the United States would be upset if Iraq put a stop to this robbery. Iraq was assured of complete U.S. disinterest in the matter. So, Iraq had invaded border areas of Kuwait and had put a swift end to the oblique drilling technique. The U.S. then tried to use this action as a pretext for intervening against Iraq.

However, the American public didn't want to go to war over this kind of local dispute. Since Vietnam, Americans had long since stopped trusting anything their own government ever said, including the danger posed by Iraq to 'human freedom'. And the American government had not dared to admit that the danger was only to Israel because too many American voters might have been both pleased and relieved about that. Best not to bring *that* out into the open. So, the inspiration had to appear to come from Kuwait.

The U.S. then had spent $6-million on a public opinion study to determine what *would* incite comfortable Americans to go to war, a war that was urgently necessary for Israel and therefore must happen. It also had to happen because Israel's nuclear capability was applying not-so-subtle blackmail on the U.S. government. If the United States did not take care of Iraq, Israel would. Instant, if brief, nuclear World War III. Being the chosen people, the children of Israel did not fear a nuclear... er... *holocaust*... as much as other people. Indeed, so long as the children of Israel were around on Judgement Day, they might even welcome the coming of their Lord. So, the United States and whatever allies it could arm-twist into a semblance representing world opinion, simply had to fight a conventional war against Iraq... whether the benighted and naïve American public wanted to or not.

But what could provoke American outrage? That was the rationale behind the $6-million public opinion poll. The answer? Atrocities committed against babies, that's what.

And so this was duly scripted as the great Iraqi maternity hospital atrocity. Iraqi soldiers had supposedly burst into a Kuwaiti hospital and, besides murdering and raping both nurses and new mothers, had killed scores of helpless infants in incubators. President George Bush referred to this 'incubator atrocity' in many speeches and the American public had duly endorsed Desert Storm in an outburst of moral outrage headed and orchestrated, of course, by *The New York Times*.

However, this particular atrocity never happened. This was well known to all the military in Kuwait, of whatever nationality or political stripe. I had even visited the Kuwait hospital in question and had interviewed Kuwaiti doctors and nurses who had supposedly been on duty at the time. The atrocity was news to them.

Consider. Fifty incubator atrocities required fifty incubators. Were we to believe that Kuwait, with presumably clean desert air, required ten times as many infant incubators per maternity bed as smog-bound Los

Angeles hospitals? Naturally, no one had counted. North Americans had simply reacted to President Bush's assertions.

Now, I've always had a certain amount of automatically ingrained sympathy for Israel resulting from incessant media propaganda. I might therefore have even been willing to fight directly for Israel if only anyone had asked me. However, I drew the line at being a military pawn for Israel, paid by the United States, fighting in a trumped-up war based on too-obviously concocted media and presidential propaganda. It seemed like a Somalia re-play. I vowed never to trust any authority again, although I might have to appear to obey it.

However, it had been an Indonesian landmine that had destroyed my engineering career. After Desert Storm and while stationed at Riyadh, Arabia, I had received the letter from my fiancée in Boston about her imminent marriage to a Business Administration grad. He had not been as patriotic as I, but he had been considerably more intelligent. I discovered that I wasn't devastated by the news, after all, and I got an inkling of why I had joined up in the first place. This letter had coincided with the approaching end of my hitch and so, like many other soldiers before me, I had signed up for another three years. Not that I was patriotic any longer.

One reason was that, after the Dear John letter, I simply had no other clear direction in life. The other was some suppressed excitement, not appreciated at the time, about the wide world. The Marines had taken me to Somalia, Kuwait and Arabia. I would probably never have seen such places otherwise.

The Corps, as every Marine calls it, next sent me to the Philippines. The U.S. was discreetly helping the Quezon City government to fight Islamic rebels who had gained some support in the southern islands of the republic. These were fanatical Islamic extremists and, of course, were capable of any cruelty... but that wasn't the point. Their movement happened to be strongest in those remote areas where the president's family grew poppies and refined heroine.

After a time, I was approached while on leave in Manila by a man who was obviously "CIA." I could easily obtain a secondment to join, on contract, another alphabet agency which was supporting East Timor's rebellion against Indonesia. This would entail a raise in pay and rank, but officially I would remain on the USMC payroll. After some advanced training in small arms, sabotage and unarmed combat, I and a few others were trickled into East Timor from the Philippines by way of Sarawak, Brunei and Borneo. We had not thought of ourselves as nasty Western mercenaries.

Why Timor? Or, East Timor? There was the fairly obvious fact that it produced inexpensive high-quality heroin, which the "CIA" needed to finance its operations with untraceable money. There were also rumours of extensive petroleum and mineral deposits on the eastern end of the island. These were reasons enough for an independence movement against Indonesia. But there was also the less obvious fact that the Western allies wanted some potential military base between China and the Anzacs now that China was expanding economically. Military expansion might follow. Timor was seen as the last fallback position if the Philippines were invaded by China as they had been invaded by Japan two generations earlier.

Except for ourselves, I never saw many East Timor freedom fighters. But, nonetheless, I had learned about the island's history and culture by various means. There was Mei Ling and, of course, Mariko had reminded me of her.

In point of fact, I was not injured directly by the Indonesian landmine in the road outside the supposed rebel stronghold of Dili. An Aussie sailor walking beside me had bought it and his flying body parts had propelled me into a coconut palm's trunk. I had suffered a fractured spine, broken leg, broken arm, broken shoulder, broken ribs and a concussion in the blast. Even in the small Dili hospital, when I woke up, it became apparent that I had also suffered some sort of brain damage. I had lost almost all of my math skills.

I could manage only the most rudimentary arithmetic, and even that had tired me out. Algebra and calculus were gibberish, and they have always remained so. The numbers kept moving and getting jumbled. By compensation, though, my reading improved because the letters, which had always been a bit mixed-up before, had become clear and they remained stationary.

The psychiatrists were of the opinion that my partial amnesia was due to 'shell shock' or 'battle trauma', and perhaps it was. Engineers need fairly sophisticated mathematics and I had studied it at MIT. They had been among my best subjects. But now that I wasn't going to be an engineer, and I had accepted this long before the psychiatrists did, I had to find another way of making a living.

I began to look into things that I had mostly ignored before. Engineers have seldom been noted for their cultural, social and humanistic orientation. Only Frank Lloyd Wright and Buckminster Fuller have been, in our own time, engineers who achieved prominence as public spokesmen on wider issues. It had not taken long after I started reading about history for me to realise that if I had studied the humanities previously, I might have gone to war anyway, but never proudly, innocently and ignorantly.

One thing about the American military is that they do take very good care of their soldiers. The hospital library in Germany would get any book that a patient might want. If it was not on their own shelves, they would borrow it through the German library system. If that wasn't enough, all the libraries of Europe were available. And, of course, there were superb computer facilities. While waiting for my spine to heal, and during the long months of physiotherapy, I had had plenty of time to read… now that I could.

By the time I received my honourable discharge, I not only had the glimmerings of a new direction in life, but some help to pursue it. I didn't want to return to Boston and I couldn't return to MIT. The Veterans' Administration made it possible for me to attend the University of Toronto, and I also had a small disability pension. There was also a surprisingly large Special Operations pension – hush money from the "CIA." This is still regularly paid to me in France. I had always lived frugally in the orphanage, and had never had much social life, so it came naturally to divide my time between studies and voracious reading in the new fields I was studying: history, archaeology, anthropology, German, comparative religions, English literature and art history. Eventually, after I'd got used to reading, perhaps it was inevitable that I would begin to write. I had submitted articles to newspapers and magazines. A few pieces were accepted and published. The money was laughable.

One thing I was particularly studying in my spare time, because it had affected me in profound ways, was recent history. I felt that I owed something to the Islamic world, and that the Jewish one owed something to me. I was both surprised and appalled at what I learned. And I had vowed, among many other things, that I would never believe media again, although I might write for it. It had gradually also dawned on me during student discussions that what had been common knowledge among soldiers, topics of ribald conversation from Kuwait to Timor, was not well known to the general public in the Western World.

I began scribbling *War Crimes*, the real story behind the headlines about Somalia, Desert Storm, the Philippines and East Timor. *War Crimes* was told plainly, from a soldier's point of view, and I can say that it was honest. I researched the media coverage and propaganda, history, politics and culture as thoroughly as I could as background, but I stuck to places that I had been and to events that I had experienced. I was able to provide illustrations from photos that I had taken myself and had smuggled out.

Now, I don't want to imply, and I made it clear in *War Crimes*, that we modern Westerners were any worse than modern non-Western tyrants and the traditional ones of antiquity. But we were no better, either. Mao-tse-tung, for example, had supposedly executed twenty million Chinese over the course of five years, while we consign that many people to death each year by perpetuating profitable exploitation and misery in the Third World. The difference was only that we modern Westerners refused to admit it and our media did not give coverage to it. *War Crimes* was intended to cause thought and talk.

The book had concluded with the observation that our Western crimes of cultural and religious prejudice, always disguised and presented as humanism and responsible globalisation, would inevitably provoke retribution. I had targeted our dependence upon Middle Eastern oil as the most obvious means of punishment.

To my astonishment, *War Crimes* was almost immediately accepted by a respected British publisher and I was offered a fairly good advance, but it took almost a year and a half to be released. I had already dropped out of the University of Toronto, deciding that whatever I could learn there I could also discover in books, and maybe even better. I didn't aspire to teach anything, so I required no degree or 'union card' as all students called it, and I had already decided to try being a writer. Not a serious book author, mind you, but just a freelance newspaper and periodical writer.

The ready acceptance of *War Crimes* by a publisher had therefore caught me by surprise, but it had not changed my mind about my own evaluation of myself and it had not changed my plans, such as they were, for the future. In fact, I had already found a job as a junior promotional writer to augment my pension and I intended to keep the job. Aside from income, it provided constant opportunities to develop my writing style and it provided contact with newspaper and magazine editors.

However, the fact that someone had taken my ideas seriously enough to want to publish my book made me think that perhaps I should take it more seriously myself. I had re-read the manuscript, an obligation connected with some significant editing and minor modifications into British spelling anyway. The book had ended on a somewhat pessimistic note, forecasting a not-too-distant energy crisis in the West. And there were already daily and increasingly ominous signs of it. Perhaps I should take heed of my own predictions in *War Crimes*. What did this mean for my own future?

Since the end of my engagement and through all of my experiences since, I'd had, of course, occasional casual liaisons. Perhaps I was just not highly sexed, but I had never met a woman other than Mei Ling who had tempted me enough to consider marriage. And she was at the bottom of the Sulu Sea in the twisted wreckage of a fishing boat. Anyway, I was not sure what marriage might mean at the close of the 20th century. I had no strong desire to have any children and marriage was basically only a social structure for making reproduction more secure for women and children. Therefore, what use was I to a woman?

I had been thinking for some time, and the feeling was even stronger after having to re-read *War Crimes*, that living alone on a boat would suit me. Living on water would insulate me from most people. And even a hundred yards of water was a fairly effective moat in the event of social disruption. I had been preparing myself by reading about sailing and I had taken every opportunity to go sailing on Lake Ontario and at cottages. Some students had boats or, more correctly, their families had boats and cottages.

I had always lived frugally, as I've said, and I been proceeding slowly with my plans to get by as a freelancer while eventually living on a boat along the Intercoastal Waterway between New York and Key West. It would be a small boat, mainly just for me, but with room to accommodate friends occasionally, even including, perhaps, girlfriends.

The acceptance of *War Crimes* had accelerated these nautical plans and had changed them from vague to specific. I had seen a curious vessel in Brunei, Borneo on the way from the Philippines to Timor. It had been called an *orembai*, a large central hull with outriggers – a much larger central hull, in proportion, than any conventional trimaran. The *orembai* in Brunei had been built of teak and bamboo with Chinese junk sails on its strange hull. Since I had had three days to spend in Brunei, three days that had stretched into 10 due to transportation snafus, I had examined the craft and had gone out fishing in the Sulu Sea with the crew.

More as something else to do besides read books in the German hospital, I had once doodled with this type of boat in order to work out a way of making a better one with modern materials. An *orembai* strong enough to have saved Mei Ling in the storm. It was also as close as I could get to the nostalgia of forever-lost engineering. The calculations were simple enough for my curtailed abilities, but sufficiently complex to provide a challenge. The exercise had turned into a fantasy. I had imagined a folding *orembai* and, between reading books, I had sketched it out. The notion was that I could trailer it to the Gulf of Mexico, the Caribbean or the West Coast without having to experience any heroic sea sagas. I was weary of heroic sagas. I could then keep on seeing the world without undue risk. But in the end, I had done a rough costing and had discovered that it was so expensive that, in spite of its theoretical advantages, I could probably never afford it.

One evening shortly after the book contract had been signed, I had taken out the yellowed plans for the folding *orembai* and had begun assessing them with a view toward having proper plans drawn from my sketches. A faded Polaroid snapshot of Mei Ling had fallen out of the crumpled and folded sheaf of plans. With my upcoming book as well as the design in mind, I decided to call the boat *Folderol Jester*, and to add new features to make an unpredictable future more secure.

The *War Crimes* advance had permitted me to start having the crazy folding *orembai* constructed in a local metal fabrication shop. My own income and savings could keep construction going, whether or not the book was a success, once the basic hull was completed. I could save on rent. My *orembai* could fold into a travel trailer. I could park it and live in the trailer, in some Toronto driveway, and the money saved would be used for gradually finishing it. As I had thought in the German hospital, I could trailer it to keep on seeing the world, when I had saved enough for a truck to pull it. And I could also add travel articles to my repertoire.

Then, one spring day while walking to work near Bloor Street and University Avenue in Toronto, I happened to notice a sign denoting the French Consulate. I suddenly remembered that my mother had been French when she had met and married my father, a U.S. Marine stationed at NATO headquarters in Belgium. Both my father and mother had died in a Virginia car accident shortly after his return to the States with his young wife. I retained only the vaguest memories of them.

There on Bloor Street, quite unexpectedly, it had come to me that I might have some claim to French citizenship. This had never occurred to me before. I was American and had once had been so proud of it that all other nations had seemed pallid and insubstantial.

But, of course, my perspective had changed. I hadn't become exactly anti-American, as many of my student friends had always been and some of my Canadian colleagues were, carefully, beneath their breath. But American policies, attitudes and lifestyles had become increasingly distant to me. I now regarded the United States much as a nostalgic rustic republican might have viewed Imperial Rome. I could see why France had pulled out of NATO when I had never understood before, and could also see why France now led the opposition to globalization.

My commitment to America had become a wistful ideal betrayed by those who ran the country. The power of democracy had long ago – I had personally pegged it at the long-ago assassination of John Kennedy – been nullified by the simple expedient of ensuring that all candidates had to be acceptable to the power elite. Differences between candidates were kept carefully minor... except for issues of concern to vociferous special interest groups, and the political power of such groups was also carefully balanced and divided up between major candidates. This gave elections the semblance of contention, the trappings of choice. But the basic character of the United States had long ago become a non-issue. America's vaunted democracy had become a farce of meaningless voting.

But also, on a less philosophical note, if *War Crimes* proved to be correct about an imminent energy catastrophe for the West, I could think of better places to be than in the U.S. along the Intercoastal Waterway. The Waterway ran through highly populated states with acute economic disparities, whose racial problems were not wholly unrelated to these same inequities and therefore through areas of intense racial polarisation.

One could reasonably expect a lot of social chaos and violence in the many cities along the U.S. Inland Waterway, especially with a country and a mixed people lacking a long tradition of cultural cohesion and which had never before been subjected to material hardship. Also, after *War Crimes* did get released, I might not be all that popular among mainstream Americans, anyway. And these were the very people who would, most probably, represent the authority and any justice that might still be operable in a changed world. Since East Timor, I had vowed, if at all possible, to avoid any personal involvement in political and so-called philosophical controversies or violent conflicts.

Later that day, during the lunch hour, I had discovered that I had, indeed, a claim to French citizenship after a period of residency. I already knew about the Canal du Midi, of course. Almost everybody has at least heard about it, particularly anyone interested in boats. After I had read a few library books about it and the countryside through which it ran, the *orembai* under construction seemed just as suited to the Canal du Midi as to the Inland Waterway. And I didn't have to sail it there. Because of the unexpected success of *War Crimes*, I had been able to ship my boat to the Mediterranean.

However, one thing had always bothered me a little and had begun to trouble me much more in recent months. Was it enough merely to live and to survive? Even in southern France? If one was cynical about humanity's ability to practice compassion and intelligence, lacked the desperate urge to reproduce, and also doubted the existence of the God of Churches so that serving "Him" was a base hypocrisy, then what justified one's life except the fear of death? I may have failed at many things, but I knew that I wasn't a coward.

And then Mariko O'Shaugnessey had fallen off the old Moissac bridge in front of *Jester* with a page of what she thought might be a lost Gospel of Mary Magdalene.

6

M ost things are relative. For instance, last evening, the upstream side of the Moissac bridge had reminded me of a dark dragon that was hunching and coiling its way over the Garonne from the medieval depths of Moissac Old City. Its intent was to cross the river and devour the New City up ahead, a symbolic return of the Dark Ages caused by the petroleum crisis.

But now, as I looked up from my examination of *Jester's* hull, sunrise was changing everything. This side of the stone bridge was now soft rosy pink, and the old stonework appeared as dimples and not as slimy scales. It reminded me of the texture and colour of how I imagined the skin of a new baby's bottom might look, although I had never seen one. A New World was being born, you see. Timeless swans were gliding over timeless water down near the archways. Basking in a rare flush of warm political correctness, I conceded that this world would not necessarily have inferior human potentials, but merely *different* ones.

From upstream around the bend of the Garonne where the New City's glass and concrete would be glowing like rubies, the river arced toward me like sparkling wine pouring from an emerald decanter of grass and trees. Even up in these highlands, the valley of the Haute Garonne was now in full summer foliage and the Massif Central pushed up near heaven. Wisps of purple cloud over toward the sunrise horizon were all that remained of the storm. Grey puffs with pearly edges floated overhead. The Old City's walls, battlements and turrets were no longer shadowed, but streamed sunrise pennants.

I was reasonably happy with my inspection of the hull. The good news was that Mariko's clang had not been a bullet piercing an aluminum outrigger. The bad news was that it had been a bullet deflecting off the steel central hull. I had a dent to pound out, and a streak of painting to do to prevent rust. But this could wait a while.

Getting *Folderol Jester* under way took only about fifteen minutes. It wasn't necessary to fire the boiler from cold because I always kept it on simmer during the nights of my canal trips. The steam engine ticked over to supply hot water and to keep the generator going and thus supply electricity for the refrigerator and the computers. One thing about a steam engine is it can use almost anything that will burn. Previously, I had used heating oil because of its convenience. Last winter, though, I had collected trash and dead wood as I had no wish to use heating oil I didn't need, even though I could certainly have got a purchaser's permit. After all, *Jester* was also a home and her merchandise supplied people.

Now, however, instead of heating oil cracked from petroleum, the boiler was being fed old-fashioned coal oil. This had almost disappeared from the market during the 1970s because automotive fuel could not be made from it, at least not fuel of sufficiently high octane for modern high efficiency car engines. You could sometimes find small bottles of coal oil in the occasional hardware store. Usually it was pine scented and exorbitant, fuel for mock-antique old-fashioned wick lamps. These days, however, the coal mines of Belgium, northern France and the Ruhr were again being worked with pre-World War II frenzy. Only severely rationed coal had saved Britain during the last harsh winter.

And wick lamps had suddenly become quite modern once more. Workaday coal oil in barrel quantities had even begun to be available early this spring as formerly obsolete distilling factories had been rudely awakened into new service. It was, of course, still fairly expensive. But there would be no shortage of it until automobiles and home furnaces had been converted to burn it. It was much more convenient than gathering trash and dead wood, even if it wasn't nearly as volatile as petroleum oil. Convenience meant saving time, and time was still money.

So, I valved coal oil into the boiler and watched the east grow brighter while waiting for a head of steam to build up. There was no noise to awaken Mariko, and I suspected that unless she was disturbed she would be sleeping for a long time. The past ten days of travel and apprehension had taken their toll, not to mention the sudden fear that had impelled her to jump off the bridge, but the final climax of recovering her parchment had done her in.

When I awakened just before dawn, a long habit, Mariko was in the same position on her bunk. There had not been one new wrinkle in the flannel sheet. Although it seemed obvious she wouldn't be moving for a while, I'd left a prominent note on the toilet seat top, held down by a plastic bottle of after-shave. I wrote that I had to risk going to Moissac market. She was not to appear on deck until I came for her. She was not to open the porthole covers any higher than they already were. She was to be careful about making noise. She could play with computers to her heart's content, but there would be no Internet connection for a while. I had recommended the CD-ROM on *Folderol Jester*, suggesting that it might prove useful. Me? I thought she would probably gloat over her parchment, so I had also mentioned the CD-ROMs on various languages and of various dictionaries. I had suggested that she might scan her damp and wrinkled Tiffinagh alphabets and put them on diskette.

The needle climbed to sufficient pressure, and I eased *Jester* away from the grassy bank. I was careful, though, as I headed upstream, to keep beneath the line of huge old willows as long as I could. Their trunks leaned out over the river. Some of their tassels floated on the water and streamed lazily down toward the bridge with the current. I was primarily concerned with surveillance from either the bridge itself or from the nearly adjacent old Moissac market. From their point of view, that was their last contact with Mariko and the vessel that had passed when she went into the water. If they had any training in surveillance and stalking, they would try to pick up the trail where they had lost it. The old bridge.

The only question of consequence, the one that would eventually answer all the others, was who they were. Who had been watching that little church near Glastonbury Abbey? And, since Mariko had emphasised several times that she had seen no one near the little church, they must have used long distance surveillance. A telescope. Or a high resolution video camera with a telescopic lens. And the church must not only have been under long distance surveillance, but also under long term surveillance. Mariko had gone to Glastonbury on a whim and yet they had noted her visit to the church. How long is long-term surveillance? Weeks or centuries? Who was so interested in whatever Mariko had accidentally discovered there? For, remember, they had never got inside the briefcase and she had carefully repaired the altar.

However, since I could not answer the all-important question of who *they* were, and I since was certain that Mariko was puzzled too, I retreated to those trivial considerations that seemed within my grasp. I liked to think of this habit as the quirk of an exacting intellect that overlooked no detail that might possibly prove useful, and sometimes this actually turned out to be true. But, I knew, much more often it was just a way of avoiding imponderable, threatening reality.

Therefore, I had been giving a great deal of thought to the general situation and to specific events as they must have appeared to the eyes of the gunmen. Preoccupied with Mariko, and possibly startled by her choice to leap blindly off a bridge instead of being chivvied into their car, they could not have seen much of *Jester* when they peered into the river where Mariko had fallen in. By the time that extended arm had fired down in reflex, *Jester* was mostly into the archway. The shot had hit the brass taffrail, had ricocheted off the round tube, leaving a bright, oblong dent that awaited Mariko's inspection. So, they had seen only the extreme stern on the sunset side of Moissac's old bridge.

Then, they'd run across the bridge to see *Jester* emerging on the upstream side. But that side was under overcast skies that had made all of the day dreary, and it was sunset and therefore in the shadow cast by what after-light the sun gave in its dying moments. And again, they could have seen only the stern. True, "*Folderol Jester*" and "*Toronto*" were painted across the eight-foot stern, but it was equally true these words were not only in the shadow of the stone bridge, but were also obscured by vegetable planters slung over the lower bar of the taffrail.

They'd fired their two shots and had gone away in the squealing car. Did the car, perhaps, return while I was searching and diving? Possible, but unlikely, I thought. Surely they would have shot again. They had already demonstrated a certain trigger-happy lack of professionalism.

But suppose, after all, that they had returned. *Jester* had been, for most of that time, not only in deep shadow on the upstream and shadowed side of the bridge, but also obscured because of the searchlight shining brightly from her. The light would have been a natural touch under the circumstances, a vessel looking for a swimmer. This searching would have also implied very strongly that the girl wasn't on the boat. Not only that, but the breeze had pivoted *Jester* around. The name and home port painted across the stern would not have been visible from the bridge for much of the time. Even glimpses of part of these words would be of minimal help. *Folderol Jester* and *Toronto* were unusual words, and there were twenty European languages to choose from in trying to reconstruct the vessel's name.

In thinking it over, I thought that they knew only that a barge was heading upstream toward Moissac New City, Toulouse and Carcassonne. This barge might, or might not, have recovered the girl. She could possibly have clung to it long enough to attract attention and get aboard. Or, she could have been forced under by the barge and drowned, mutilated by the propeller. In trying to view the incident from their perspective, a long, low and fairly wide vessel had passed just when she went off the bridge – a typical small barge.

The details of *Jester's* relatively slim central hull flanked by two lithe outriggers would not have been noted; particularly since the space separating the outriggers from the hull was decked over, and also further obscured by my rather hurried stowage of Bouchard's wine casks. These spilled lumpily over from the main hull onto the outrigger decks, secured with a crazy web of lashings over the dark blue plastic tarp. Even if the knife-shaped aft end of an aluminum outrigger had been spotted, I thought that it would most probably have been taken for part of a glistening wake.

What would they do? Since they had demonstrated ten days of persistence, it was unlikely that they would give up now. I imagined that they would divide up their forces. One man would stay down at Moissac Old city where, from any one of several vantage points, he could keep an eye on both the medieval market and on the old stone bridge just downstream from it. The other man might go upstream along the bend to the more modern wharves of the New City to see whether the girl was on board any of the boats moored there and perhaps to make discreet enquiries at the police station. They would read the newspapers for any mention of a body discovered in the river. Of course, the inherent assumption here was that there were only two men. How much personnel could *they* deploy?

Since I couldn't answer that question, I stuck to things I knew. They had seen a boat going upstream from the old bridge. Therefore, I figured that they might mentally discount any vessel heading back toward Moissac's market and the old bridge from upstream. At least, I hoped so.

Accordingly, I decided to do what I had always planned to do anyway. But now I also had to do it because, for the first time, I needed Joëlle's help. I would cross the Garonne over to Moissac's ancient market on the old stone quay but would proceed well upstream, nearly around the bend, before turning back for Moissac.

Jester cruised about ten minutes in the near-dark under the willows at a speed that produced only swirls in the muddy shallows. Then, the last withy tassels brushed over me at the wheel, and the sun, just topping the horizon, suddenly blinded me almost dead ahead. From my place at the wheel behind the wheelhouse, I nudged over so that the smokestack and its two flanking whistle tubes were between me and the sun. In the cover of these slim shadows I could see that the bank with its concrete retaining wall started curving away to my left. *Jester* glided beside the wall for perhaps another hundred yards until, looking back, I saw the last willow completely obscured the view astern. I spun the wheel hard to starboard, shielding my eyes and hoping that no barge was indeed coming downstream in mid-channel because it would be coming quickly.

For what safety I could contrive, I tugged at the whistle lanyard. Toot-**Toot**! My two-toned whistle sent a warning out over the Garonne and little puffs of steam shot upward, aspiring to grow up to be clouds like the ones overhead.

Landlubbers assume it is just a matter of lazy drifting downstream, like Huck Finn on his raft. The fact of the matter is, however, that boats must go faster downstream than the current in order to get any steerage way at all, and on a bend in a river you need good steering. But I had gambled that few vessels would be under way so early, and *Jester* was lucky. I could feel the motion of small waves, and hear the chuckle of a wake. Gradually, I began to see again as the sun swung around behind me. Feeding more steam to the engine, I saw *Jester's* shadow jiggling over molten water around the curve, but heading downstream now.

Presently, I could see the ancient stone wall of the Old City's quay and, of course, I could see the nine-arched old stone bridge again. To any observer on the bridge, it might seem as if *Jester* had suddenly appeared around the bend coming from the direction of the New City, Toulouse and Carcassonne.

After a couple minutes, I could make out that only two vessels were berthed at this hour, and neither was *La Poule Frite*. So, Bouchard had not been able to make it to Moissac, as he had thought barely possible, and the always more likely rendezvous at Carcassonne was still the plan. I also noticed one of the vessels looked exceedingly odd. I was intrigued.

After tying up at the new cast iron bollards – new being another relative term since they had been cast in a motif of opposite-jumping dolphins popular about 1870 – I strolled over toward one of the moored vessels. It had seemed, as I had approached the quay, an interesting craft. Gazing out over the river as I walked over medieval cobblestones, I saw a vessel coming upstream through the central arch of the bridge. Two others, just specks on the water, could be seen far upstream under the wispy steel bridges of the New City. Bound downstream for Moissac's old market? Or would they journey on past to Agen or Bordeaux?

I thought about calling Joëlle, but it seemed too early. The French phone system has always been notoriously unreliable, especially public phones, and recently reduced maintenance of telephone lines had not improved matters. Strangely enough, though, cellular service had not been noticeably affected. Only a few radio broadcasting stations were required to cover all of France and these could be maintained much more cheaply than miles of wire. I had thought carefully about future communications before I ever came to France, and had anticipated this state of affairs, and others, when building *Jester*.

Once Joëlle and I had met and got together in Narbonne, I'd insisted she have a cell phone too. Strangely, even before we got together, Joëlle could easily have afforded a cell phone on her own. But in that curiously fatalistic and frugal way of hers, she'd never thought about it. Often, when we lived in Narbonne for a while, she'd forget either to recharge it or to carry it. Now, however, the police and the government were encouraging the use of cell phones on television, radio and billboards.

The only problem was recharging them. When on *Jester*, this posed no difficulty. In our tiny Moissac apartment, though, we had to juggle electric priorities like everyone else. Hot water or heat? Television or stereo? Lights or cell phone? Few people could afford everything at once, like before, and it had become socially unacceptable to use more electricity than needed even if you could pay for it. Since communication meant more security along darker streets, phone recharging was a high priority with everyone, particularly women. After the initial crisis, even Joëlle had seen the sense of maintaining communication and recharged her phone faithfully. She remembered to carry it with her when she went out. She'd even begun to use it sometimes.

I came to the edge of the quay about fifty yards along from *Jester*, and looked down onto a neo-barge. It was basically the top one-third of a fibreglass transport truck trailer turned upside down. Near the back end of it, a Mercedes sleeper truck cab had been grafted to the hull. Just ahead of the cab's flat front and windshield was a high thick cylinder with a smokestack that was tall enough to clear the cab. Wood – driftwood, logs and cut-up scrap – was piled around this boiler. A plastic tarp had been pulled aside, and the damp wood underneath had begun to give off the slight mist of starting to dry in the sun. The truck's rear axles turned stern paddle wheels. These were just normal wheel rims with welded-in partitions. Whatever strident colours the truck's cab and trailer might once have been, the barge was now all white with red for trim and the mechanical accessories. It was a neat job.

One of these red mechanical accessories was a tow truck's derrick that had been bolted to the Mercedes' front bumper. A writhing bundle of hydraulic hoses disappeared into a covered-over front wheel well through a carefully plastic-edged hole. I had no doubt, from the sturdy attachment of the derrick and the glistening black well-cared-for look of the hoses, that the makeshift crane would work quite well. The present difficulty was equally apparent, however. The Garonne was now too low for the crane to reach up and around and drop a load on the quay.

A thick-planked gangway swayed down from the quay into the cargo-carrying front three-quarters of the hull. A bearded young man in denim cut-offs and sandals, with a bright yellow dolly in his hands, glanced up at me. His earrings glinted in the sun. He smiled and nodded an invitation when I gestured at the gang plank, but then my phone trilled.

My, my. Fumbling the phone out of my belt case, I smiled back at him and shrugged at him with the shrilling phone. He turned again to the neatly-stacked pile of large brown sacks, from which another plastic tarp had been folded neatly back. I also turned discreetly away from his work, and scanned the cobblestone expanse of the market plaza. Only two stalls had been completely set up, but three others were being raised. No one was loitering on this quay.

"Oui, allo."

"Tu es à Moissac maintenant?"

"Oui, ma chérie. L'orage, tu sais."

"Tu a besoin de quelque chose?" she asked.

"Seulement toi, ma belle. Seulement toi."

She laughed. "A bientôt. Deux heures."

And it was true, I reflected while I tried to stretch the phone back into its leather sheath, the storm had at least been associated with the delay. It was also true that, already possessing *Folderol Jester* and having the canal, I needed nothing but her. What I might *want* was another matter. Joëlle would be here in two hours, so I had time to think about that.

7

The barge's builder was a tinkerer after my own heart, and I suspected from the young man's decisive and determined actions that the inventor and builder had been himself. It wasn't difficult to perceive his present intent. He was now loading the dolly with a heavy looking soft brown sack. He was then going to pull the dolly up the gangplank with a hand ratchet winch known more familiarly as a "come-along." I had two aboard *Jester*. Few gadgets prove more useful on a boat.

I had good reasons not to appear to be loitering on the quay. This would attract attention. Far better to be a part of the quay's normal commercial life until the marketplace had filled up a bit more.

His come-along had not yet been fixed to the bollard, but a well-worn length of stout rope lay beside the winch near my feet. So, I eased my lumpy nylon backpack carefully to the cobbles, bent down and lashed the come-along's hook to the cast iron dolphins with two quick half-hitches.

He glanced up from his nearly loaded dolly, approved the half-hitches, and nodded a quick thank you. I picked up the come-along, and I nodded back. He heaved the floppy bag onto the dolly, settled it on the frame with a few muscular tugs at the corners, and rolled the dolly in line with the gangplank. He stepped aside, slapping puffs of dust off his hands. We then greeted each other by name. His was Raoul.

As I cranked the dolly up the gang plank, I saw Raoul go aft and reach between the boiler and the Mercedes bumper. He returned with a second dolly, a smaller one. He began loading that one while I pumped the first dolly up and onto the quay's cobblestones. As soon as it came up to me with the final jerk of the cable, I saw that this dolly was a first class specimen of its kind. Magnesium and steel, roller bearing pneumatic wheels. I was impressed, having a thing for fine equipment.

The sack itself contained unbleached Moroccan wheat flour, fifty kilos of it. Well, well. I was even more impressed. I began to clumsy the sack off the dolly and onto the quay. It was like lifting a big bag of water.

There are many things that can make French people despondent. One is not having one's wine. The casks on *Jester* would go some small way toward alleviating Carcassonne's thirst. Not that there was an actual shortage of wine anywhere in France. There was a shortage of choice, though. For some perverse reason, probably just that they are French, people in the southeast around Carcassonne and Narbonne prefer

Bordeaux from around Bordeaux in the southwest. People in the north prefer red wines from the Midi, while people in the Midi prefer cassis and sauternes from the north. In short, wherever French people live in France, which is mostly all over, they prefer wine from somewhere else. This used to promote a brisk domestic trade, and it will again, but the distribution system had been disrupted for a while.

Another thing that can make French people despondent is not having one's croissant and baguette. And the current lack of pastry was not just a lack of choice. There had been something of a real flour shortage since spring. Not, of course, in the major port cities where freighters from Canada and Argentina docked. There, sacks of wheat and flour probably filled warehouses. And there was no shortage in Paris, of course. Flour was rushed into Paris from Calais, Brest, Cherbourg, Bordeaux and Marseilles using trains, barges and even generous highway transport. What with the harsh fuel restraints and the lack of choice in wine, no sane government could deny croissants and baguettes to Parisians. Parisians had taken to the barricades with much less provocation, and revolutions had ignited over much more trivial matters. Just recall Marie Antoinette's contemptuous "Let them eat cake."

So, there was no real shortage of wheat or flour in France so far, but the crippled distribution system had allowed only a comparative trickle of it into the hinterland. Everyone in the Haute Garonne was suffering from acute pastry withdrawal, although the populace was still adequately fed in most basic respects.

I'd noticed the occasional sacks of flour being carted through Moissac streets during the late winter and early spring. They had come in on trains, I'd imagined, probably begged by Moissac bakers who had good friends in Bordeaux, Narbonne or Marseilles. Joëlle had sorely missed her daily fresh croissants and her twice-weekly fresh baguettes. This was more than habit. It was very nearly religious ritual for Joëlle and most French people. As for me, fresh croissants are too chewy and I can hardly tell a fresh baguette from a stale one.

I myself had tried without success last week in Bordeaux to find a small cargo of flour, say, three tons. I could have got twenty tons easily enough, and at a good price too, but nothing less. Since *Jester* could carry only about five tons, this didn't do much good without my own warehouse space. Rental warehouse space for small traders would be coming soon, but wasn't available yet.

This was the first real quantity of flour I'd seen in a while, and the first ever coming in by barge. "Combien le kilo?" I shouted down.

"Ici...? Quatre-vingt dix," came the answer, with a wolfish grin.

Jesus! Three times the Bordeaux price five days ago. And I had no doubt that some bakers and housewives of Moissac would pay it. At those prices, each sack was worth 4,500 francs, or about $650 US. I was really lifting gold, and the flour seemed almost as heavy.

Working two dollies with dedication, it took us an hour to transfer fifty bags from the barge to the quay. Several times when I stood up to pump the empty dollies back down, I noticed movement through the Mercedes' windshield, and then curtains were modestly closed for a while. I must have been wrestling a sack up onto the waist high pile on the quay when the woman came out of the truck cab, because I suddenly noticed her help him lift the last bag onto the dolly. Our final burden, however, was an old-fashioned balance scale on iron wheels.

I jerked it up the gangplank while Raoul's wife Christine, a tired-looking young woman in well-filled jeans and a heavily sagging red halter-top, bent over to guide it. She held a wooden scoop in one hand, and a fat jogging purse lolled on her crotch with each upward step. Christine's long blonde hair was flowing in the river breeze, sometimes obscuring her face and sometimes revealing glints of multiple earrings.

When the scale was safely on the quay, I looked up from her cleavage to scan the plaza, wiping my dripping chin with a sweaty forearm. I heard her unsnap the winch cable from the scale, and I winced with all the sudden banging and clattering as she pushed it over the old cobblestones around to the market side of the pile of sacks. There were now at least fifty more stalls and a lot more bustle in the market. Most of the retail activity gathered under the high defensive wall where a huge arch through it led into the Old City, leaving the waterfront perimeter of the quay for incoming wholesale merchandise in barge-load quantities.

The train station was just inside the wall near the arch and so the market spilled through into nearby city streets. People now jostled through the arch, coming and going. And it was still early. Perceiving a stack of what looked like, and was, sacks of flour, some people were already trotting our way, bouncing hand carts or dollies over the cobbles.

There was too much commotion in the market now to have the faintest hope of spotting a possible watcher. I retreated toward the edge of the quay, lifting my backpack out of any possible danger of being trampled. Raoul vaulted from the side of the barge up onto the quay beside me, and for a moment or two we both watched people crowding around the Moroccan flour. Then we sat down with our backs to a scene that grew ever more hectic, to judge by the babble.

8

Raoul and I sat on the edge of the quay, with our legs dangling above the barge and our sweat drying into flour paste in the cooling breeze off the river. We talked under a blue sky and small puffy clouds, occasionally glancing over our shoulders at Christine selling flour a few yards away. Bakers and stall operators generally bought from one to five sacks, and every once in a while Raoul and I would be called upon to load a hand cart, wheelbarrow or dolly. But Christine also retailed from an open bag using a wooden scoop and the scale's bucket. The few early-bird housewives held their own plastic bags wide to help her, like starving fledglings. Later shoppers would have to buy from other stall owners and would pay an even higher price.

A medieval marketplace with merchant stalls should not necessarily convey the idea of regressive general poverty, although the economy had admittedly suffered a grievous blow. North American-style supermarkets and shopping malls – *grandes surfaces*, 'great expanses' – had been a relatively recent innovation in France, and had always been regarded with slight distaste even by self-conscious customers who patronised them because of one-stop-shopping convenience. The French have always extolled the virtue of buying fresh groceries daily from specialists in meat, fish, vegetables, cheeses, fruit and breads. The market has been an institution for several millennia. One day each week was considered a special market day, a weekly farmers' market, as North Americans might have it, when more merchandise than usual flooded in and became available to consumers.

Every European town used to have its special market day, and many still do, although most have become just anaemic tourist attractions. In England, especially, where everything seems more concentrated, one town of a cluster of villages might win the honour of being designated the region's communal market centre. On modern British road maps, for example, Market Harborough is still distinguished from South, North, East, West and Upper and Lower Harborough for this medieval reason.

Moissac is at the confluence of the Garonne and Tarn rivers. Although the Tarn is technically a tributary of the Garonne, it is really a much longer river that wends its way far into the heartland of France. Moissac's ancient market has been served by the Garonne and Tarn rivers since the end of the Ice Age about 12,000 years ago. Romans supposedly built the first stone quay about AD 30, and traces of it can still be seen. Moissac's market day, Saturday, was mentioned in a seventh century Merovingian almanac. Navigation was improved when the Canal du Midi was constructed in the 1680s and the railway followed the canal into the Old City in 1847.

Moissac Old Market went into very brief decline only during the era of highway transport. A modern food terminal had been constructed in the New City during the early 1960s. For the past forty-odd years, the old market had been, successively: increasingly ignored, then remembered and patronised sentimentally so that open-air restaurants again flourished – and was finally regarded as trendy, with glassed-in restaurants and a high proportion of upscale goods nestled in weekly stalls backed against the city's defensive ramparts. The locale had become quaint and the view over the river was considered romantic.

Today was Saturday, market day, and the quay was not particularly trendy, quaint or romantic. No one seemed to care about the view. It was once again just a teeming expanse of ageless activity. With the reduction of highway transport and the rebirth of rail and canal transport, it was once more the only market in Moissac, Old or New. Of course, there were still a few supermarkets. But their shelves held increasingly fewer products, and mostly only packaged and canned goods. Even supermarket managers were coming to the Old Market in order to replenish their stock. Here and there on the quay were tiny quarter-tonne Innocenti, Fiat and Citroën trucks that had beeped their way through the wall's archway. Either they were owned by upscale shoppers disdainful of disapproval, or more probably they belonged to store operators in the New City and its suburbs. We also counted three of the new Evolution automobiles that could do service as a mini-van; and a couple of Smarts.

Raoul and I were quite interested in these toy trucks because of their potential along the canals. These tiny trucks had created a new sub-economy all their own. They had smaller engines than most motorcycles. Their cabs could barely squeeze in a driver and a passenger side-by-side, and they could also carry up to maybe five hundred pounds as a flat-bed or diminutive pick-up. So loaded, an Innocenti three-wheeler in good condition could go thirty miles per hour on a level road. Fiat and Citroën four-wheelers could usually better this velocity. Typically, the cargo bed could be covered by a canvas top stretched over steel hoops.

During the post-war 1950s they had been very numerous in Europe, but were quickly superseded by larger vehicles as the volume and pace of business increased, fuelled by burgeoning population. By the 1980s, they were rare sights on the road because even when new they could not meet modern safety standards and they were much too slow for modern traffic. In cities these tiny vehicles could still be seen abandoned at the back of driveways, but even more often in rural areas they rusted beside barns.

A few Innocenti three-wheelers had even come to North America where they had been used almost exclusively for cute pizza delivery. I told Raoul that in the late 1990s I had looked for one in vain while *Jester* was under construction, but by then they had been driven completely off Canadian and American roads. I had been forced to modify a boat trailer in order to make *Jester's* on-board vehicle, and this had turned out better in the long run.

There are few vehicles tougher than a Citroën 2CV or 'deux chevaux' – two horses – a laughable two cylinder truck, with its pod headlights popping above the fenders like frog eyes. One still holds the automotive record for longest continuous operation, some 250,000 non-stop miles with the engine never once shut off. I had written a humorous newspaper article about that. There are few vehicles more frugal with fuel than an Innocenti three-wheeler. Many of these forsaken and rusted old mini-trucks could be coaxed to run and their simple little engines suited the new times. Not nearly enough new Smarts or Evolutions had been manufactured before the energy crisis, or could be manufactured now. So, the old small vehicles were getting on the road again all over Europe. An industry had developed to fix up these derelict little vehicles and sell them.

In rural areas, their lightweight chassis were often pulled by horses or oxen. In Agen two days ago, I had seen a Fiat 500 partly loaded with jars of milk. A man walked beside it and turned the steering wheel through the side window – which didn't necessarily mean that the Fiat wouldn't run on gasoline. It had been pulled by a calf and two Great Pyrenees dogs, but presumably the man helped them to pull uphill.

Naturally, Raoul and I discussed the weather because of the unusual violence of last night's storm. Unlike Mariko and me, however, Raoul and Christine had tied up at the quay before the storm had broken over Moissac. From Raoul's account, there had been some powerful gusts and choppy water that had bounced them around half the night and then had kept them awake by slapping against the stone wall until almost dawn. From the sound of it, we had been better off under our tree.

Being between the Massif Central to the north and the Pyrenees to the south, the valley of the Garonne has always been a battleground for contending wind and storm systems, and so the weather along the Garonne can be highly variable. As the valley narrows to the Garonne's source on the watershed between the Atlantic and the Mediterranean, weather becomes more changeable yet. Moissac is at the Atlantic end of this watershed region and Carcassonne is at the Mediterranean end of it. The Canal du Midi had originally been dug to connect the Atlantic at Bordeaux on the Garonne River with the Mediterranean at Narbonne on the Aude River.

So, the heart of the Canal du Midi connects Moissac, Toulouse and Carcassonne on the highland watershed between the two river systems.

Later, the canal had been extended from Narbonne to Marseilles using the string of étangs, or 'ponds' immediately inland from the Mediterranean coast. Later still, all the canals of France had been connected together, and then integrated with the canal systems of Germany, Belgium, the Netherlands and most other European countries. By about 1950 it was theoretically possible, if not politically easy, to travel from Brittany to the Caspian Sea. Now more than a half-century later it was definitely possible and much easier politically.

Up on the watershed connected by the Canal du Midi, the Départements of Lot-et-Garonne, Tarn-et-Garonne and Haute Garonne boast neither the Atlantic's commerce and coastal fisheries, nor the Mediterranean's sunshine and coastal fisheries. They also lack rich, deep earth for intensive modern agribusiness. But there is no local shortage of food, thanks to the many small family farms. They produce a modest surplus that fills local markets. These three upland Départements are not densely populated. They are economically depressed areas and so it is much cheaper to live there. At the same time, though, they too possess centuries of history and ancient stonework, just like the rest of Europe.

Lot-et-Garonne, Tarn-et-Garonne and Haute Garonne are perched between two different worlds. And yet the distance to the Atlantic or the Mediterranean is very small by North American standards, just over a hundred miles either way, with a beautiful canal linking them. Liking boats and seeing the way things seemed to be going, I had spent the money from my unexpected literary success to have *Jester* completed more sumptuously than I had previously thought possible. I had been able to buy the computer equipment. And to install my futuristic contingencies that had been part of my German hospital fantasy.

I had targeted the middle of the Canal du Midi as a good place to be in the first decades of the new millennium for anyone with a general European cultural background. Had I been an Afro-American, I might have chosen the Niger, Congo, the Intercoastal Waterway or the Mississippi. Had I been Asian, I might have chosen the Mekong River system. In short, I thought that an energy crisis would probably reverse the trend of cultural globalization, except in communication. Ordinary people would be more comfortable within their native cultural milieu.

After the trucks, the weather and the Haute Garonne, Raoul and I discussed the barge and the Moroccan flour because it was still causing subdued excitement behind us. However, the beginning of Raoul and Christine's recent life had actually started eight months earlier and the cargo of flour was only its most recent episode. Raoul and Christine typified the present situation – "the best of times and the worst of times" – as Charles Dickens had written, more or less, but maybe the other way around.

A couple of years ago, Raoul and Christine had begun the first of many subsequent urgent discussions. As a married team of independent truckers operating out of Bordeaux, they had once participated in the first traffic-blocking protests that had brought France, Germany and especially Great Britain to a halt back in September of 2000. In France and Germany, the governments immediately lowered taxes on fuel in order to reduce operating costs for truckers and farmers. In Great Britain, Prime Minister Tony Blair had at first refused to make similar tax concessions in order to show that Britain wasn't like other European governments that caved in to pressure. Then he had quietly followed the French and German initiatives once British protests had been quelled by police. Raoul and Christine had resumed their long-haul business, mostly from Bordeaux to Marseilles, barely making a living at it over the next eight years. Although they had married when very young, and although Chistine's desire had always been to have a family, she and Raoul had both realized that children would have to wait until the world settled down into *something* more stable, whatever that proved to be.

Thankfully, Raoul told me, Christine was still young and she still had the biological time for children. Maybe the barge and Raoul's plans, he gestured at the mutilated Mercedez rig below, would buy her that fulfilment. This threatened to start me thinking about Joëlle, but thankfully Raoul's account continued without interruption.

"Even back then, the Autoroute des 2 Mers was getting in rough shape. Less traffic, less roadwork. Cracks and a few holes. It was bumpy and you had to drive even slower than just to save fuel. If you valued your teeth. Would you believe eight hours from Bordeaux to the Narbonne bypass?"

The 'Highway of Two Seas' was... had been?... the modern equivalent of the older Canal du Midi, connecting Atlantic Bordeaux and Mediterranean Narbonne by four lanes of superhighway. It boasted the usual laughable French so-called speed limit, and was accounted a five-hour run for conservative truckers, less for most other truckers.

"All during late September and early October of 2000," Raoul explains, "we never stopped for a day or so, like before. Couldn't afford the time. Just turn around in Marseilles, and turn around in Bordeaux. Me and Christine took turns driving and sleeping. Back and forth. We mostly ate on the road, in the truck." That difficult time lasted almost eight years. Christine sometimes had cramps, and so they were used to taking it easy for a couple of days. Not that month, or for many long months to come. "The poor kid hardly had time to change her tampon."

Weeks later, in late 2000, the OPEC summit in Caracas had surprised Wall Street pundits by reducing production by 800,000 barrels a day and by hiking the price per barrel. This move endangered the growth of global economy, and even reduced the value of OPEC's own investments in the developed West. Therefore, sophisticated economists could not understand the counter-productive Caracas announcement. They had chalked it up to Arab political instability and usual irresponsibility. It apparently never occurred to Wall Street's financial experts that many countries were fed up with globalization, a euphemism for 'Western', mostly American, control of the world's economy.

Bill Clinton's continued occupation of the White House back then hadn't helped at that time. Whenever he had needed diversionary headlines during Monica Lewinski's scandalous revelations, he had dropped a cruise missile on some Arab country. That had earned Clinton brownie points and approval ratings in mainstream American press like *The New York Times* – and further underscored the tragedy of Israel for the Western World. OPEC would never forget that miscarriage of justice, although they might have been able to forgive it – if only Clinton hadn't dropped missiles on the Sudan and Afghanistan. OPEC had never forgiven Bill Clinton, and Arabs had been enraged. In order to maintain their positions and social stability, Arab politicians had been forced to encourage 'terrorism' since their countries lacked U.S. cruise missiles with which to deliver bombs. As 'rogue' countries, they also struck back with OPEC.

And the United States had lost even more credibility and influence because of the George W. Bush versus Al Gore presidential election scandal and confrontation in Florida during November 2000. Social cohesion in the West was crumbling.

With winter coming on, the West had been forced to dig into stockpiled strategic petroleum reserves in order to offset the shortage and price of home heating oil. Experts were confident both of eventual price relief and recovery of petroleum production back to pre-crisis levels, but neither ever quite materialised. In the meantime, European and North American coal deposits, which had been almost forgotten, began to be worked again.

September 11, 2001 at about 9:00 in the morning was a date and time that is still remembered, more or less, as starting the real and ongoing crisis. It was, of course, the unforgettable day when supposedly Arab terrorists from Afghanistan had destroyed New York's World Trade Center by crashing two jet airliners into the twin towers. The Pentagon itself had been hit by another hijacked jetliner within another hour.

The infamous American "War on Terrorism" began with the bombing and invasion of Afghanistan in early 2002 and then the invasion of Iraq in 2003 – with its occupation that's still ongoing after eight years of attrition of daily American casualties. The American and British publics, and the entire Western world along with them, were learning the true cost of maintaining Israel in a place, where scholarship was increasingly demonstrating, it should never have been created. OPEC raised its prices and decreased oil production in an attempt to punish the West even as oil deposits in Alaska's "protected" Arctic Wildlife Refuge had been opened up for exploitation. And almost-forgotten coal deposits in North America and Western Europe had rather desperately begun to be worked again.

This had alleviated the immediate heating problem – over protests by environmentalists – because some home furnaces could burn coal, or be easily converted from oil and gas, and most electrical generating plants could also be converted from oil to coal. But coal did not solve the immediate automotive crisis and the highway distribution of goods. Given the price of gasoline and diesel fuel, only the large companies could profitably keep on truckin', augmented by military convoys. Independent truckers like Raoul and Christine got the occasional run, but operated at a loss.

Raoul and Christine were realists. And after seven years of marginal existence, not living, they began the first of those urgent late-night discussions that were to change their lives. Unlike some of their colleagues, they suspected that things were never going to return to "normal" – now something so far in the past that few could remember it. They had made the decision to cannibalize their rig while they still had the money and time to do it.

"At places along the autoroute you can see the canal down in the valley. At first," Raoul admitted, "I didn't really know what it was, but I had sometimes noticed barges going along it." Christine had gone to the library to find out about the Canal du Midi. "We never knew it went between Bordeaux and Marseilles," he said. "Our route."

After they learned about the Canal du Midi, they got the idea of trading the 18-wheeler for a canal barge, but they soon discovered that canal barges had become almost extinct because of railroads and trucking. The few barges left had mostly been converted into houseboats. In any case, no one would trade a barge for a half-owned transport truck, not even a long-haul sleeper cab Mercedes.

"Then, I got this crazy idea," Raoul laughed and rubbed his hair. "Really awesome. But we had no choice," he said seriously. "Christine and me don't want to work for anyone else. We're different. Loners, in a way… I mean, we have friends, but…"

From books Christine got out of the library, Raoul thought he could turn the truck into a barge. Christine had also researched navigation rules and barge regulations, but Raoul had rightly figured that the authorities would not be too fussy if a pair of truckers supported themselves, stayed off welfare and moved merchandise. At least, not for a while.

First, Raoul had found an old home furnace for heating water radiators. Then, "I had a new cam ground for a two-stroke and piped steam through the engine using the old furnace. I really wasn't risking much, was I? I mean, I could take out the two-stroke cam and put the engine back together again and be no worse off than before," Raoul said.

I explained that I had used exactly the same idea with an old motorcycle engine for my on-board vehicle, but using compressed air provided by the boat's steam engine. "How much pressure is the boiler good for," I asked, looking at the riveted plates. It must have been made around 1920.

He shrugged. "I filled it with compressed air and found leaks using water bubbles. I welded the joints, and all around the rivets. It has two new safety valves. I run it at about a hundred pounds. That's enough."

"Don't you get a lot of condensation in the cylinders?"

"Not if I keep the steam hot enough," he grinned. "I learned that right off. Now I whip the head off every week and wipe the cylinder walls down with oil. It works."

It was not a very efficient steam engine, not with the steam having to pass through convoluted channels and automotive valves. The diesel had a relatively long stroke by modern internal combustion standards, but nowhere near the piston stroke that would use steam most efficiently. "It produces maybe twenty or thirty horsepower, I figure," Raoul said. Nonetheless, it actually worked.

Canal water is always level and also presents less friction than paved roads or steel rails. One man, for example, can tow a barge carrying sixty tons – getting it moving is the hard part. Once he knew that the steam engine actually worked, however inefficiently, Raoul had made the barge by cutting off the top of his fibreglass trailer, turning it upside down, and then putting the cab and boiler inside it. There were a lot of details to iron out because Raoul had made the conversion very carefully, with the idea of being able, with a great deal of work, to return the rig back into a truck if things ever returned to normal. Christine had sewed the sails and awnings. Raoul had designed a mast and sail system, but they had never used it so far. She had contrived a stove from a barbecue and she had made planters to hang over the side – just as I had done with *Jester*. She had also been in charge of gathering and preparing all the charts, ropes, warps and marine gear that Raoul had estimated they would need.

Things like nylon tie-downs, dollies and come-alongs were common to both trucking and barging. The conversion had taken them six months, and Christine had got a job as a waitress in a bar to conserve their savings. Raoul was a dedicated and careful workman and he would not rush the job.

In the spring, Raoul had put temporary axles under the finished hull and another trucker had towed it twenty blocks through Bordeaux to a road leading to the water. "That was the tricky part," Raoul said, "going through Bordeaux. Too many small streets and sharp turns. I made her in a truck repair shop near our place, down by the train station east of the Hotel Atlantique. Do you know Bordeaux?"

"Not that part of it. I stick closer to the river." I meant the Gironde. Bordeaux means 'by the waters'. Plural. Three rivers are involved, and navigation is complicated.

"Five hours through Bordeaux. But we got to the river." I assumed that he meant the Garonne. "It's been good to us."

Considering that Raoul and Christine had not planned ahead back when things were easier and less costly to do, and had improvised under adverse conditions, they had not done badly. Their barge – which they had not yet named, by the way – was, of course, much less efficient and much less comfortable than *Folderol Jester*. For instance, Raoul's boiler was outside and exposed on the deck. Even if he decided to burn coal oil instead of wood, he still had to tend the boiler out in the open, and this could be uncomfortable in bad weather. In heavy rain, even wood under a tarp could become too damp to burn. Also, they had to cook on deck, under an awning if necessary. But they actually enjoyed the life, and this was their third venture out of Bordeaux.

In spite of the ad lib nature of their barge and business, they had had several advantages that I had not. First, they spoke French fluently. Second, as truckers along an accustomed route, they knew exactly what merchandise had always been carried inland from Bordeaux. Third, their fellow truckers and warehouse contacts had told them what merchandise was available, where and at what price. A tip of this kind had alerted them to a small shipment of Moroccan flour. And fourth, of course, in theory at least, Raoul's barge could carry about twice as much cargo as *Jester*, although *much* more slowly.

Even with their steam engine's failings, their barge could safely carry about ten tons of cargo at a top speed of about 10 kilometres per hour, as Raoul put it, but they usually cruised slower. Call it a long week between Bordeaux and Moissac.

The flour had cost 20 francs per kilo on the dock at Royan as it was being unloaded from a rusty Moroccan coastal steamer because Raoul had loaded it from the dock into the barge himself. Just a thousand francs for each bag - about $142. Since the pile of sacks on the Moissac quay was almost gone, and would be before noon, they would make roughly $25,000, less their operating expenses and investor shares. This was about $13,000 net on the two and a half tonnes of flour, and there had also been some miscellaneous merchandise sold on the way in Villeneuve-sur-Lot up the Lot River.

Of course, such delightfully unconscionable profiteering could not continue forever. Raoul was thinking about putting some of the money into other converted barges to build a part-owned fleet, but there were pitfalls in this. Christine was for fixing their own barge first. After only three ventures between Bordeaux and Moissac, including the side trip up the Lot River, they could envision getting out of their Bordeaux apartment and getting a waterfront house somewhere.

"The key to success in this business is a secure mooring and secure warehouse space," Raoul insisted. "I saw some empty buildings, old derelict canal factories and warehouses, between Marmande and Agen. I want to rent some space before too many other people get the same idea. That's the way to go." I tended to agree with him, remembering the twenty tons of inexpensive flour that I could have bought if I had only had a warehouse in which to store it.

Although I had begun to watch the time, I was always interested in product information and potential opportunities. I had to be. It would be a few years yet before there would be a solid market for new books. Before I left them, I sketched out a steam engine like *Jester's*. If Raoul could ever get it built, it would save a lot of fuel.

I also suggested a landing craft type ramp for their barge. A smaller version of this steam engine, or even any small two-stroke, using compressed air in scuba or welding tanks, could power a small utility vehicle, something like the miniature flat-beds and pick-ups we'd been seeing in the marketplace. Such a vehicle could come aboard on the ramp and greatly expedite loading and unloading. If loaded itself when it came aboard for the last time, it would waste little cargo space.

"Yeah. I didn't think of the water level dropping," Raoul laughed. "Highways hardly ever sink lower."

"But it's not only that," I said. "Between Narbonne and Marseilles, there are plenty of places around the étangs without wharves at all. But you can get fantastic lobsters there."

"How would you get them to market?" Raoul asked.

"I used tanks of water. Have to pump air through the water to keep 'em alive – about three days if they're kept out of the direct sun. Have to rig a tarp over the tanks. But the profits anywhere inland are worth the effort. They'll live long enough to reach Carcassonne and Toulouse. Or Avignon and Lyon if you buy them in the Camargue. But you need a vehicle to carry the lobster tanks. And a drive-on ramp."

These were some features from *Folderol Jester* and Raoul was extremely interested in them. He naturally wanted to see these things himself, if possible, but I explained that Bouchard's wine obscured the vehicle and made access inconvenient. I promised to look them up when I was next in Bordeaux, if they also happened to be there at the time, but we'd probably meet again along the river before that. We exchanged phone numbers, and I wished them luck.

As I stood up, brushing dried flour from my clothes and arms, Raoul called out to Christine. Although I protested, he went over and folded the top of the jute sack and handed it to me. I accepted about twenty kilos of flour… over $200 worth at Raoul's prices. Joëlle could lay this on a baker and get fresh croissants and baguettes for six months.

I was about to walk away when an idea came to me. I grinned. "I don't know about trucks," I said, "but sailors believe it's bad luck to be on a boat without a name… What about *Mer-Cedez*?"

Raoul thought for a split second, and then started laughing. Christine giggled. "Yeah, yeah, Man," he said, clapping me on the shoulder, "that's about it." Very roughly translated *Mer-Cedez* could mean 'water ("sea"), give us a break'.

With the flour in one hand and the bulging backpack in the other, I wended my way awkwardly back toward *Jester*, just to have a look. There seemed to be no activity on her, and no unusual activity around her. I turned away and began to waddle toward our usual Moissac market restaurant, *Le Port Romain*.

9

Although it was still a few minutes early and Joëlle might well be a few minutes late, I first went over to *Le Port Romain*, beside the archway in the city's great wall. Glassed-in for much of the early summer because of the cool river winds and the frequent storms this year, it was wide open to the elements now. Joëlle's distinctive tricycle was nowhere to be seen, but, of course, she could have chosen to walk.

Tall glass panels had been rolled back and the interior was filled with warm breezes from the river and slanting light from the young sun. It was not very crowded because it was upscale trendy and the prices were steep, but I couldn't see Joëlle through these rolled-back windows amid the greenery of potted palms in terra cotta urns and ferns hanging from artfully broken amphora. Our usual place was just inside beside the glass so that I could keep an eye on *Jester* whenever we came here. *Jester* had a berth on the quay when I wasn't actually working on the canal.

Our habitual table wasn't taken and Joëlle wasn't sitting at it. Of course, she could have been powdering her nose. But, just as I was considering this possibility, Françoise, banking between tables with two cups of café au lait, caught a glimpse of me through the wide opening and shook her head no.

I stepped away, somewhat uncertain about what to do. I'd brought some presents back from Bordeaux, but Mère Lalie's paté was not among them. Looking for paté in the marketplace would be awkward, carrying the backpack and the sack of flour. They seemed to be getting heavier because of unloading Raoul's barge. I didn't know the management of *Le Port Romain* well enough to ask about leaving them there and besides, I didn't trust anyone with the flour. However, I did have a very great interest in trying to discover anyone who might be watching the quay. Browsing the stalls would be a good way of surveying the crowd. The sun was well up by now and the place was busy. I therefore picked up my burdens from the cobblestones where I had put them for a brief respite.

I'd hardly taken a couple of steps before the restaurant's stereo, now activated for the morning shopping crowd, began broadcasting Joe Dassin's mid-1970s hit *Champs Elysées*. It didn't blare out over the quay; *Le Port Romain's* clientele was too well-mannered for that. Dassin just seeped through the opening overlooking the crowd and cobblestones as a distinct and subtle background of melancholia for a lost, brighter time. The song was sufficiently passé, except for *Le Port Romain's* mature crowd. Including me? Dassin's *Champs Elysées* forcibly brought me back to Mariko O'Shaugnessey's Tectosages, and many other things. That was the crux of the matter, right?

My immediate priorities changed when the thought of Mariko came to mind. Instead of sallying forth immediately in search of paté, I looked around for a display of ladies' intimate apparel. Soon, I had packed a package of small-sized multi-coloured bikini briefs into a side compartment of my backpack. When I zippered it closed, I forgot about Mariko and concentrated on Joëlle...

Whereas most of the experts confess ignorance about the ancient megalithic civilisation that had preceded the Tectosages, some people claim to know all about it. I met my first Elysian in a Narbonne coffee house called Cyrano's which is across the Boulevard Gambetta from the post office. Joëlle claimed to carry previous life memories, including some from the megalithic civilization of southern France.

Somewhat amused at first that the New Age had even established a foothold in France after conquering North America, I had listened with polite interest to her version of the Tectosages.

"Les Tectosages ne sont pas vraiment celtique," she had insisted seriously. The wise builders were not actually Celts, although they had suffered the imposition of Celtic language and genes from their Danube conquerors. They were Elysians, and the myth of the Elysian Fields was simply a garbled memory of their introduction of Neolithic agriculture, orchards and domesticated cattle and sheep into Europe.

Aside from bringing the seeds, no pun intended, of Western civilization, they brought the tradition of megalithic construction and of building giant earthworks.

Elysians had probably come from Atlantis where they had developed not only Neolithic arts and fertility religion, but also mathematics.

They were a relatively peaceful people and were matriarchal worshippers of the Earth Mother. Had I ever read Dr. Marija Gimbutas's *Civilization of the Goddess*? Their culture was conquered by the invading patriarchal Celts, but reverence for the Earth Mother has persisted in various disguises – such as Mary-worship in Christianity, and especially in coastal areas of Europe.

This was all standard New Age lore.

But Joëlle had departed from it by emphasising that the Elysians, although they were at first orchard and bee keepers, and then farmers and later herders, had above all been a maritime people. They had come from Atlantis and had settled on European coasts and along the rivers. They had reached the Mediterranean by using the Garonne-Aude waterway, the route of the later Canal du Midi. They settled more densely around Narbonne than other places and were remembered as the Elysians of the most ancient European myths. From Narbonne, they had carried their civilisation across the Mediterranean. They had island-hopped to the Middle East, carrying their Neolithic arts, their megalithic tradition and their livestock with them.

"The Elysians had boats. They liked boats. Just like you," she had said. Joëlle was very young, in her early twenties and barely out of college where she had studied international commerce and computers. She had something of an Earth Mother figure herself. Her historical reconstruction was generally familiar to me as the usual North American New Age litany, but Joëlle was not starry-eyed. On the contrary, she had the clearest and most direct grey eyes I have ever encountered.

However, while remaining clear, her eyes could also occasionally focus elsewhere into some place or some time that removed her from her present surroundings. At such times her conversation would trail off and her eyes reflected a rather sombre depth that really did suggest a burden of past life experiences. She would become dissociated, and it could happen very suddenly. When this had first occurred with me, I had wondered if she suffered from a mild form of brain damage, epilepsy or schizophrenia. I could sympathize with brain damage. Later, though, I had begun to wonder whether these neat clinical labels were less adequate than ancient humanity's understanding of the same affliction.

But, when she was fully here and now, or when she was brought back by my saying: "Joëlle…?" her straightforward style of conversation made disconcerting counter-points between psychic insights and carbon dates. I also never forgot that she was sufficiently here and now to hold a demanding and responsible position as an analyst with Narbonne's municipal government.

She had been born in Lot-et-Garonne, and she had demonstrated with plausible genealogies that her family, the Lauriols, had been settled along the Garonne for at least a thousand years. The Lauriols were obviously not a restless breed. She herself had never travelled far from her birthplace of Tonneins, near the confluence of the Lot and Garonne rivers. Joëlle Lauriol had come all the way to Narbonne, almost two hundred and fifty kilometres, only because of a data processing job that couldn't be duplicated closer to home in Agen or Moissac.

'L'auriol' means halo. And, although she had never claimed it, it was plain that Joëlle considered herself someone with a special burden and a special sanctity, a kind of deathless spirit of the Haute Garonne that was continually reborn into countless ordinary lives.

"The Haute Garonne was a special place for the Elysians," she had insisted, "even though most of them didn't live there, but around Narbonne – 'mais dans le pays Narbonnais.' It was the transition between their old lost home of Atlantis to the west and their new home. How do you say… the place where rivers flow different ways…?"

"Watershed."

"Watershed. It was the watershed between their old remembered home in Atlantis… Heaven… and their new world of the Mediterranean. Earth. It was a special place between heaven and earth, where I was born." She did very closely resemble the rather Rubenesque female figures that allegorical French sculptors of the 1700s and 1800s had employed to represent the 'Spirit of the Nile' and so on. I later brought Joëlle a postcard from Bordeaux where, almost unbelievably, she had never been. One of the female Girondins, who was sporting voluptuously in the city's famous fountain, was the spitting image of Joëlle's own buxom self.

Naturally, I had not learned all this over just one afternoon at Cyrano's. It was easy to be with her because she spoke fluent English, the language of international e-business, when I had to fall back on it. I was also oddly attracted to her, once I realised that her direct eyes, her matter of fact speech and her respect for hard data belied the too-familiar New Age perspective… although her mental lapses sometimes made me uncomfortable. Over the course of several encounters with Joëlle, my own perspective began to shift. Perhaps the New Age had not originally been a North American phenomenon, after all. Maybe it was a transplanted and garbled version, lacking everyday cultural nutrition in the New World, of what Joëlle had never doubted as being historical fact.

As I was introduced to some of her acquaintances, I had learned that many people in the Narbonne area, or the 'Narbonnais', believed in their Elysians. Joëlle once led me through Narbonne's library to a collection of obscure locally authored novels. Written about the turn of the last century, these Narbonnais writers had elaborated on the Elysian theme in a way that had proved too breathy to survive as literature in competition with Baudelaire, Flaubert and Anatole France. But these novels predated the New Age by almost a century and proved that the Narbonnais had had a long and genuine tradition as the original Elysian Fields. "Oh, Champs Elysées…"

It was never primarily a sexual attraction for me, although we had shared some intimacy in the beginning. As I had a chance to know her better when she began to spend some nights aboard *Jester*, she frequently had dreams that made her call out in fear or merely talk and sometimes even chuckle. She admitted that her dreams could sometimes be called nightmares, but she stressed that some were also beautiful and serene.

These dreams were always vivid and featured the same geographic place, although its features changed over time. At one time, for instance, this place had been overlooking the sea, while at another it had been along 'a' river – but which river was never in any doubt. Joëlle insisted that she'd had these dreams as long as she could remember. I began to suspect that some other reality might actually weigh upon her.

I began to believe that Joëlle really could be something of a geographical and cultural spirit, or at least I had begun to take the Elysians more seriously. On weekends, Joëlle would sometimes lead me to one of the several nearby archaeological sites. We had visited the barrows and earthworks I had seen when first coming into Narbonne along the étang, and we had also gone to Ensérune and Peche Maho. All of them were Elysian sites, according to Joëlle. I felt, unaccountably, that we all ought to treasure the ruins and other remnants of the Elysians. This feeling transferred itself to Joëlle. In some subtle but powerful way, I felt responsible for her.

It was not exactly a relationship between adults, but more of a parent-child relationship. However, the parent-child characteristics cut both ways. Given her age, she was something like a daughter to me. And, considering her self-confessed timeless spirit, also like a mother. I had never known either. Joëlle therefore quickly claimed two portions of my affection, although, as everyone knows, these relationships can be an emotional burden… both ways.

She could readily understand sexual and romantic urgency, and her response could be affectionate and often even abandoned. I even began to suspect that sex, because few things are more emotionally and physically here and now, could sometimes be a welcome respite from that other world that claimed a good part of her. She had the usual feminine lack of physical inhibitions that can intimidate many men who would never admit their discomfort with it.

Joëlle could also be sexually knowledgeable and deft, a sophistication that amazed me in someone who had lived such a limited life in Lot-et-Garonne that she'd never been to Bordeaux, and to whom Narbonne seemed far away. Yet, she told me that she had never had a relationship with a man before. I had reason to believe her.

But it had gradually dawned on me that her occasional displays of sexual virtuosity had an artificial quality. It was not faked or contrived or learned from books, but it was also not properly a part of her. I truly began to suspect that she could call up sexual knowledge and response from aeons of experience embodied in both genders. That may also be why the difference in our ages, more than a decade, has never bothered her so far as I know. That span of time was nothing compared to the spectrum she seemed to inhabit. As for the incarnated Joëlle Lauriol of this new millennium, she could really just as well have been a nun.

Since the daughterly and motherly affection between us already possessed uncomfortably incestuous overtones, and since I had never had much sexual interest in her anyway, we had rapidly evolved toward an asexual relationship. It was much more profound than friendship, and it was not what is usually called platonic because there was no conscious commitment to sexless principles. It just unfolded that way.

One late summer weekend in Narbonne, not long before the September 2000 oil crisis, we had rented a car and had driven down to the now famous village of Rennes-le-Château about a hundred airline kilometres south of Narbonne. It was considerably further by winding Pyrenees Mountain roads.

Joëlle had naturally given me a pamphlet about the site. She wanted to show me the church and its now-infamous gravestones. I learned from the pamphlet, though, that the church was a fairly recent thing – as things go in the part of the world, that is. It had been built around AD 1050 on a much older megalithic sacred site once dedicated to Venus back in Greco-Roman times, but that was a mere figurative yesterday in the Narbonnais. Long before Venus, the site had been sacred to a succession of much older pre-Celtic fertility goddesses. Among the spate of recent books about Rennes-le-Château, at least two had suggested that the astonishing geometric figures centred on the village, and delineated by megalithic monuments at least seven thousand years old, actually depicted symbols associated with Isis. But this would have been long before any conventionally accepted Ancient Egyptian reference to Isis. Joëlle insisted that Rennes-le-Château had probably been one of the first sacred sites established by the Elysians in the Narbonnais when they had arrived as refugees from Atlantis. According to her, this would have been about 10,000 years ago at the end of the last Ice Age.

I had followed her sturdy figure up the steep streets of the hilltop village and into the little graveyard of the village church. A scraggly line of wind-bent poplars sheltered its dead on the very top of the hill. She had sat blithely down on a low tombstone that suited her height, her shirt pockets pulsing heavily with exertion. She wiped her brow and then rubbed her hand on her shorts. She grinned and pointed. "L'église la, elle est nommée Marie Magaleña. Regarde la porte…" I had nodded and walked over to the church's door.

'Locus iste terribilis' read the Latin inscription in stone above the door. This place is terrible. Joëlle recounted how the eccentric Abbé Saunière had had this inscription cut into the stone above the door shortly after he had come into immense and unexplained wealth. This mystery of Rennes-le-Château is just one of many that, together, has made the village the subject of many books and television documentaries. One 1990s book, *The Tomb of God*, had even argued that the body of Jesus was buried beneath a nearby mountain in these Pyrenees foothills.

On catching her breath, Joëlle had joined me beside the door.

"This place is terrible…" I had said thoughtfully in English as I she came up beside me.

"Il était absolument correct," she had replied.

We had spent an enjoyable two hours in the church, but the decorations seemed blasphemous. For example, a carved devil held the font for what Joëlle explained was 'Holy Water'. I'd heard of this, of course, as a Catholic thing, and Joëlle had then explained what Holy Water was. She had regarded the devil himself offering the Holy Water a highly amusing touch in Saunière's church.

But, like many modern people who had no true depth of religion, I found the blasphemous church to be vaguely disturbing. But the sky remained clear and the potential for thunderbolts out of the blue was, I had figured, minimal. Joëlle had laughed at my superstitious nature.

A few weeks after our visit to Rennes-le-Château, the oil crisis had burst upon the Western World. Almost immediately afterwards, violence between Israelis and Palestinians reached a new height that had scuttled the 'peace initiative' that Clinton sought to leave as a legacy of his Administration – which was really only an attempt to cement recognition of Israel as a legitimate state among the Arab nations. When the Middle East heated up with America's war in Afghanistan and then Iraq in retaliation for the September 11, 2001 World Trade Center disaster, me, I had figured that it was high time to retreat to the Haute Garonne.

Because of the crisis and the immediate onset of cost-cutting measures, Joëlle's contract with municipal Narbonne had also been unexpectedly terminated at that time. The town government had decided to place emphasis on employing long-established local residents who had children. But she received a fairly good severance for the breach, just as a similar job came up in Moissac, a place I had earmarked even before coming to France. It was all quite odd. After discussing the situation, we had decided that we might as well relocate to Moissac together. *Jester* had moved us up the canal.

We'd found a tiny and curiously arranged two bedroom apartment on the ground floor of a charming medieval warren. The address had been considered somewhat trendy at the time. This jumble of habitation piled up against the Old City's massive defensive ramparts even gave us a tiny walled-in courtyard off the living room. A wrought iron gate in the courtyard's thick but crumbling wall opened directly onto a quiet old street sheltering under the Old City's defensive battlements.

The place had suited both our greatly differing requirements. It was only a short block from a major bus route over the river to the municipal complex in the New City where Joëlle's new office was, and only about a kilometre along the wall from the riverside quay. From the courtyard gate, we could even see the huge archway through the medieval wall that led out onto the quay. Many little shops could be seen a long curving block away, crowded between the railway station and the arch. The ornate wrought iron streetlights had once been gaslights, but had since been converted to electricity. We were enchanted with the place.

Although the lease would have been steep for either of us alone, it was comfortably within our combined financial resources. Joëlle was earning money, while I had some left from the success of *War Crimes*.

As French truckers continued to demonstrate, sometimes violently, against the rising cost of fuel, a quiet return to canal commerce began to open up opportunities that had lain dormant for a century. And it was high time for me to start earning money, too, since my savings were dwindling. I had only played around with the occasional cargo of lobsters back in Narbonne, and that was mostly just to give a paying excuse to see the major canal cities like Marseilles and Toulouse. But I had designed *Jester* for serious work in precisely this social situation and I was eager to put us to the test of real life again. I had never considered being a writer and a book author 'real'.

Through Joëlle's uncle Hervé, manager of a Moissac supermarket, I began to get contracts to carry non-perishable goods. At first, this had been a private and discreet matter consisting mainly of canned goods from the chain's Bordeaux food terminal. Hervé's single supermarket had suddenly become much less affected by delayed truck deliveries than other Moissac stores, while I had learned on the job that *Jester* had been designed and built correctly as a neo-barge. *Jester* proved to be the success I had hoped.

Later, as the oil crisis deepened over the next eight or nine years, and especially during the unusually cold previous winter, the cargoes and customers had become more varied. I'd even carried a shipment for *Provigo Midi* last year, a regional chain of supermarkets that technically competed with Hervé's in Moissac, but mainly served the surrounding area. Hervé himself had arranged this because he feared for the people in the smaller towns away from the river and railway.

Almost inevitably, Joëlle had assisted with my business administration and did the accounting, and she also gave strategic planning advice. She had been trained for this and was employed by Moissac's municipal government as an analyst, just as she had been in Narbonne. We had settled down in Moissac. So, it was true that the Tectosages and Elysians had eased my adaptation to France and had helped in establishing a life along the canal.

My failure to find Mère Lalie's paté in Bordeaux had seemed no great loss at the time, since baguettes had not then been readily available anyway. However, standing as I was with a weighty sack of incipient fresh baguettes by the dozen, the missing paté assumed unforgivable proportions. Paté and baguettes go together like a horse and carriage, love and marriage… And, as Joëlle sometimes casually remarked, we'd now been really together for over seven years…

We're not talking paté de foie gras here. That's goose liver paté that mainly Parisians and pretentious foreigners eat. Joëlle's paté, and the paté of most French people, was pig liver paté that had been invented in the Haute Garonne, and had spread to other highland regions, especially to the hills of Brittany. And who has ever seen a goose grazing on upland meadows? The *sangliers*, not geese, had started it all.

Sangliers. When I first came to Moissac with Joëlle, her uncle Hervé had invited me to go out hunting for the famous sanglier. Now, my French being the way it is, combined with Hervé's somewhat lazy southern accent, I thought he'd said *sangria*. I was a bit puzzled, but I could think of few things more delightful than capturing bottles of Spanish wine as they presumably rolled down the Pyrenees Mountains to infiltrate, duty-free, into France. Given the customs protection afforded to France's domestic wine industry, I could see how the *sangria sauvage*, or wild sangria, must be fairly rare. I thought that this hunting was just a cute euphemism for local smuggling across the Pyrenees border, a time-honoured occupation, after all. Naturally, I had fallen in with the joke.

When I told Hervé that I had a couple of landing nets for fishing aboard *Jester* that might serve for intercepting wild sangria if we saw any, and would also be handy for carrying them home, he and Joëlle had looked at me rather oddly.

But they, out of courtesy on their part, had been trying to ignore my atrocious pronunciation.

When I saw Hervé sally forth with a shotgun of fearsome bore, I found it curious. Who would shatter sangria instead of trying to take them uninjured? I figured it was time for a long talk with Joëlle.

There were, it turned out, still sanglier up in the Pyrenees pine forests of the Haute Garonne. These were the last French examples of Europe's wild boars, just as a few still inhabited Germany's Schwartzenwald or 'Black Forest'. Black Forest ham, and all that.

The people of the Haute Garonne had also found a way of preserving the meat of their own wild boars as ham. Probably as early as 2000 BC, they had discovered a way of making it keep over the winter by a combination of light smoking with pine wood and air-drying in the Pyrenees wind – just like Parma ham.

Much better known to the general public as a gourmet delicacy, Parma ham is made the age-old Haute Garonne way. The distinctive taste of both, and I prefer Haute Garonne to Parma ham, is just curtailed decomposition.

The people of the Haute Garonne had later graduated from hams to discovering a way of preserving even pigs' livers. Paté. Me, I think from the taste that it amounted only to ensuring enough decomposition so that even competing bacteria became poisoned. This technique was extended to seal the fate of geese in lowland areas – hence paté de foie gras.

My attention returned to the here and now. I could sometimes see *Jester* across the cobblestones as people ebbed and flowed in the marketplace. But, although I'd been taught skills in careful surveillance, and in hard schools at that, I'd seen no too-frequently recurring figure.

It was coming on for high summer and so, in local farmers' stalls, the winter's preserved foods were mostly sold out while the fresh had not yet been harvested. There were hams, sausages and cheeses hanging from strings and nets, but they looked a bit dried out to me. There were barrels filled with dried apples and other fruit, but I preferred canned fruit until fresh became available. Maybe someday soon we would all learn to like dried fruits, but I wanted to postpone the lesson as long as I could afford to. There were home-preserved vegetables in oil or vinegar, and I felt the same way about them.

Joëlle often bought canned goods coming in on the trains, and frozen when she could get it. Since she was Hervé's niece, we were more fortunate than most people. But our apartment refrigerator had severely limited freezing capacity, so Joëlle grew bean sprouts, a superb and rapid source of always fresh vegetable vitamins.

I was really looking for paté, but somewhat half-heartedly. I visited one stall, across the quay, which had jars filled with what looked like, and must have been, local home-made paté. But the jars were of different sizes, and the contents seemed to have a greenish tinge. Maybe it was just the light off the Garonne. Call me a wuss, squeamish if you like, but in the matter of paté I preferred Joëlle to have the benefits of modern sterilization and even irradiation while it was still available. Later, there would be plenty of opportunity to perish from botulism, salmonella and peritonitis. I couldn't see any uniform and familiar jars of Mère Lalie, a brand I had taken to buying simply because Joëlle.

The stalls that were doing the most business at this time of year seemed to stock clothing. There were racks of dresses and stacks of jeans. I also saw piles of shoe boxes. These had started to come in through Marseilles from Serbia and Croatia early in the spring. Marcel Bouchard and I had discussed the wisdom of shipping these shoes inland. However, we didn't have a ready market for them. Also, the price and quality were so low, and the cargo so bulky, that we preferred to carry wine. More profit for the volume of available cargo space. Marcel also thought that shoes from local leather would start to come onto the market. If confronted with the choice, French people would buy French products and even pay a bit more, so long as the quality and styling were about equal. I did see a couple of leather goods stalls, but these displayed mostly belts, vests, jackets and hats. Shoes were a bit more complicated and would appear later, if Bouchard was right.

Formerly, there had been a brisk traffic in stereo equipment and computer accessories, but this had dwindled from the look of it. However, there was still traffic in new CD and tape releases by recording artists. The government had taken some steps to subsidize French artists and also the recording and production of CDs as a morale booster, but I was hazy on the details of the policy. However, it was ominous to see that the supply of newly manufactured appliances had decreased quite noticeably from last year. Slower distribution and sales had begun to inhibit production. Time is money, and especially cash flow.

One thing interested me a lot. There were several establishments selling bicycles. Last summer there had been only one, and it had dealt mostly in new machines. Someone had also firmly grasped the marketing fact that bicycles are of limited practicality when human-power must increasingly be used to move goods. Cargo-carrying tricycles had always enjoyed a secure place in Far Eastern economies, and they would now play an increasing role in the West.

I had my own ideas about tricycles, and they had been incorporated into Joëlle's machine. The basic engineering challenge with a tricycle is how can it lean around corners so that the rider can naturally maintain balance? I was interested to see that the tricycle vendor on the quay had taken the obvious and easy way out.

First, just to dispense with them, there were also a few bicycle trailers on display, but these are a cumbersome solution to the problem. Bicycle trailers have never caught on as a way of moving merchandise.

Second, the actual cargo-carrying tricycles being offered featured their carrying capacity between two wheels at the front and used a single rear bicycle wheel for power. The vendor had cobbled together tricycles of this kind from scrap bicycle parts. However, care had been taken and the finish wasn't bad. A small crowd examined these vehicles, and I figured that sales would be rewarding. There was nothing else immediately available for a shopper who had to carry weekly purchases from, say, Moissac's market back home to a suburb five miles away.

However, front-end carrying capacity made for a clumsy tricycle. The more it carried, the harder steering it became. Coasting downhill on a loaded tricycle of this sort could be a terrifying experience because its braking was inadequate for various reasons. If there were brakes on the front wheels, the rider could be catapulted over the handlebars. And a brake on just the rear wheel wasn't enough. Especially on cobblestones, and many French streets are cobbled.

There was nothing for it, really, but to bite the bullet and make the tricycle carry things between the two rear wheels. That meant a suspension system for the two rear wheels that could lean around corners with the rider. To do it right was a surprisingly difficult engineering challenge and a surprisingly expensive one. I saw nothing on the quay comparable to Joëlle's tricycle.

Having methodically examined the market on a stall-by-stall basis, and having seen no one I could suspect, I concluded that there was probably no surveillance on the quay. After all, *they* might be just as tired as Mariko from the stress of the last ten days. She was sleeping like the proverbial log, and they might well be following her example.

A loud beep blared behind me and the bag of flour bumped in my hand at the same time. Startled, jerking and twisting all together, I turned to find myself looking down at something that resembled a very large and aggressive frog. But its bug eyes resolved themselves into 2CV pod headlights, and its warts into splotches of brown primer on a bilious green paint job. Its gnashing jaw was really a wobbling bumper that was only two inches from my shins. It put-putted at me menacingly and beeped again. I moved out of the way.

As it shuddered on toward the great archway through the wall with the gears going ribbet whenever the driver crunched them, I read *Provigo Midi* painted on the bodywork. Memories and premonitions were alike roiled up by this regional chain of small supermarkets. Stacked in the rear truck bed, among other things, were a few boxes labelled with Mère Lalie's rather gruesomely smiling face. I'd missed her in Bordeaux, and now again on my own home quay.

With the incident of the pushy frog in mind, and deciding to retreat from oblivious mainstream humanity, I dropped anchor in *Le Port Romain* after all. I settled myself at our usual table with my back to the wall and the colourful quay spread out before me though the rolled-back windows. As before with Raoul, I noticed a few other diminutive vehicles in the marketplace and they were mostly old ones. Noticeably more than last year.

Françoise unceremoniously clattered my usual cup of café au lait down on the table with a "Bonjour, Marc" so cheery and brisk that she obviously had no time to chat. I opened the paper tube and dumped large brown sugar crystals into the cup. They needed careful stirring before they would mix with coffee.

Mère Lalie had confided to me, as she had smiled goodbye from the back of her ridiculous truck, that we had only survived the first punch, but that subsequent rounds of the energy confrontation would become a battle of attrition. There were too many of us, and something would be done about it. Mère Lalie's paté hailed from Brittany where some five thousand pig factories worked day and night to supply Europe's demand for pork products, Mère Lalie's among them. These pork plants were powered by electricity as much as by hogs.

Only round-the-clock lighting stimulated piglet growth to meet the demand of the new millennium's hungry population. Electricity powered the electric processing machines that converted pigs into cello-wrapped pork chops, hams, bacon, loin steaks and jars of paté. All this food had normally been distributed by transport trucks. As electricity and highway transport became attenuated, so must Mère Lalie's smile diminish. Her abattoirs would successively shut down, and the supply of paté would slow to a trickle. It was just a matter of time and, duplicated in all sectors of agribusiness, would sooner or later mean famine. Would we hold the cultural line at 1800, 1900 or 1950? Or would we fall all the way back to medieval Moissac?

Watching the comical pick-ups on the quay, and seeing the pedestrians jostling around them, I saw these figurative automotive frogs bouncing over cobblestones as they were inundated by a figurative flow of humanity around them. The vehicles' insistent ribbets and beeps were therefore muted.

But I heard humanity becoming muted. I reflected that holding the line at the era of these old toy trucks, the 1950s, wouldn't be too bad. Only two-thirds of the population would have to die.

10

"Bonjour, mon ami."

I looked up to see Joëlle smiling down at me, back-lit in the wide opening looking out onto the quay and the river. Her hair seemed shorter and lighter than I remembered it from only a couple of weeks ago. It was like young wheat blowing in the river breeze and flowing golden in the sun. I smiled and mouthed her a kiss. Usually, though, I had hugged her.

"You had your hair done," I said in English as she pulled her chair out from the table. English was our sign that a serious conversation was in the offing since I couldn't manage serious French. I didn't remember the dress, either, a floor length red floral print, which – as she sat down – revealed thigh-high slashes just below the familiar jogging purse. "And bought a new dress," I added, as she loosened the laces of a rather medieval bodice. I wondered if she'd bought it at a shop in town or in one of the clothing booths I could see over her shoulder. Were even dress designers also unconsciously anticipating the future?

It had become something of a ritual that Joëlle would get her hair done, or buy a little something for herself, whenever I came home from a trip. It was supposed to be a treat for me, but I had really started the custom to combat her habitual frugality that could come close to asceticism. I had thought about it and had concluded that this near-asceticism was really an indication of that other world's domination of her life. In an attempt to encourage here-and-nowness, I had suggested these shopping sprees as a homecoming surprise for me. Choosing a hair style or a dress demands some present tense focus. I had also insisted on paying for this aspect of our relationship, one of the ways in which I compensated Joëlle for her very real assistance. Also, even her Moissac job was now becoming more precarious day by day.

Joëlle had interpreted all this as my desire for a somewhat sexy homecoming after my presumably celibate canal voyages. In this, she was somewhat off the mark, but I didn't try to explain. Consequently, since clothes or hair styles didn't much matter to her, she generally chose what she thought I might find sexy.

"Do you like it?" She at last fumbled the tied laces undone from the medieval bodice and buxom bounty threatened to spill onto the table. This made things more difficult.

"Very much. Both… the hair and the dress, I mean."

Françoise brought two tiny cups of café au lait automatically, and removed my empty while transferring the untouched biscuit to the new saucer. In France, little butter biscuits or chocolates generally come with each café au lait. I leaned over and began to untie the backpack on the floor beside my chair. As she informed me of the latest layoffs at work, small treasures came up, one by one, and most of them were enriched by the burnt sienna tile of *Le Port Romain's* table top.

"Garçonne," breathed Joëlle. "You were able to find some."

"Two bottles… and one of Opium." Although we were not speaking of narcotics, we might as well have been, considering the cost. Garçonne by Gemey and Opium by Yves St-Laurent, both of Paris, were Joëlle's favourite perfumes, and they had become increasingly harder to get.

Garçonne, meaning roughly 'tomboy' but with slightly greater feminine connotations, was freshly astringent with more than a hint of mischief.

Opium was her second choice because it was a trifle over-musky. Garçonne suited Joëlle very well most of the time, while Opium served for rare occasions.

"Mon dieu… Jesus," she said, remembering our agreement. "How much did…"

"Never mind… Honey." And I placed two large jars of Anjou honey beside the perfume on the table. The amber bottles of perfume had turned honey-coloured in the reflected sienna light off the tile, while the honey itself turned topaz. Anjou honey is what is called buckwheat honey in North America – made from a mixture of early wheat flower nectar and meadow wildflower nectar – and it is a deep glowing bronze colour. Joëlle loved it. People in Anjou naturally preferred the pale golden clover honey from the Haute Garonne.

The perfume and honey was followed by a bottle of Kalhua coffee liqueur, two bottles of very good Bordeaux and several packages of American-made Prima mini-pads that had cushioned all the bottles. But I kept one package in the bottom of the backpack.

"You found them!" Joëlle enthused, squeezing a soft package to her even softer chest.

"I looked." Finally, I rummaged for the thick sealed envelope of francs and tossed it on the table. "Twenty-one thousand, six eighty." I said. But I sometimes miscounted. "You'd better check it." It was a little over $3,000 U.S.

Joëlle cocked an eyebrow. "A good trip," she said, while she fished in her jogging purse and finally tossed a bankbook on the table.

"Just so-so," I responded. Raoul's profiteering with Moroccan flour was still too fresh in my mind.

I had time to re-pack the bottles and packages on the table top into a canvas bag I'd folded in the bottom of the backpack. I left the lumpy bag on the table and studied the bankbook, while Joëlle counted francs. She ordered café au lait from Françoise, and pain au chocolate for herself.

Joëlle looked after my banking and accounting, as well as her own and ours. I noted the general flow of transactions in the book, but contented myself with the final balance. Since coming to Moissac, and especially since meeting Bouchard early in the spring a year ago, I was making about twenty thousand francs every two weeks or ten days. Call it $3,000 U.S., less operating costs. Of course, winter was very different. Even southern French canals could freeze over, for a day or two at rare intervals, but in any case miserable weather naturally slowed progress. *Jester's* rather high weather-protected wheelhouse gave me greater comfort than most bargees, along with better visibility because of the windows and electric-powered front wiper, so I was slowed less than others. But winter barging could still be miserable.

Between us, Bouchard and I moved a fair amount of wine between Marseilles and Bordeaux, a route that pandered to the entire south's tastes. We transferred cargoes at Carcassonne. We had established a regular route, and had regular customers. *Too regular?* But punctuality is the soul of commerce.

I was pleased with my bank balance, and slid the little book back across the table. Joëlle reached for it automatically and worked it down into her now thicker purse. A discussion, or at least the end of one, necessarily intruded upon my preoccupation with the quay outside.

"Vieux de deux jours," Françoise warned. As far as I was concerned, two day old croissants were better than fresh ones and almost anything was better than chocolate ones. But then, I wasn't concerned. I looked over in time to see Joëlle shrug in that enduring Gallic way that could accept anything from the siege of Paris by Attila's Huns in AD 453 to stale croissants in *Le Port Romain* AD 2011.

"That reminds me," I said and lifted the sack of flour from the other side of my chair. Françoise and Joëlle stared, and then Françoise whirled and fled. I swung the sack gently beside the table toward the side of Joëlle's chair. It landed on the marine motif floor with a soft thud that obscured most of a mock-ruined mosaic octopus.

She scuffed her chair sideways and twisted around in it to bend down closer. One red leather shoe with a charmingly upturned medieval toe that matched her dress poked through one of the side slashes. The fabric fell away as the muscles of her thigh flexed. She'd gone whole hog on the outfit.

"Wow," I said.

"You always said that a medieval look might suit me."

"It does."

"Either I'm the lady of the castle… or only a h-efty h-elf," she said. Was that her way of summing up our relationship?

Joëlle pointed. "Where on earth did you get that?" Joëlle whispered.

She was looking down, re-reading the label through the thin filter of white dust motes dancing and swirling and spiralling down in the sunbeams.

"On the dock. Just a while ago."

Blue octopus tentacles were hardly powdered at all before Françoise was back with the Manager, whom I vaguely recognised, and an obvious chef with his muffin hat. For a while, I actually thought that the chef was going to wrestle the bag from Joëlle, but she held on. Out of the voluble French excitement came her distinct words, "How much did you pay?" It was not now so much that she remembered to speak in English, it just came naturally as a convenient commercial code.

"Nothing. But it was thirty francs a kilo in Bordeaux last week. The chap I helped unload was selling it on the dock for ninety."

"Is any left?"

"I doubt it."

She turned back to the fray and firmly said "Cent vingt." She said it with a straight face. A hundred and twenty francs for a kilo – about $8 a pound U.S. I admired her gall, or Gaul. The sale, I believe, involved not only cash but free fresh croissants at *Le Port Romain* over some future period, plus baguettes later in the day. Joëlle was a modern girl… er, woman now… and didn't bake. She couldn't have baked in the tiny oven of our Moissac apartment stove anyway. The confusion ended with the bag being taken in triumph by the chef. He stalked back to his lair, holding the sack by its neck as he might have held a plump pheasant by its legs. The transaction was lengthy and gave me time to ponder.

I shrugged to myself and decided just to take the direct approach.

After the incident had simmered down with some laughing words between Joëlle and Françoise, and after the now complementary café au lait and chocolate croissant had actually materialised, Joëlle's grey eyes looked steadily across the table. She looked at the lumpy canvas bag on the table between us. "So, what's up?" she asked.

11

I looked into Joëlle's grey eyes. "I'm going away for a while, I think."
"Not just a run up to Marseilles, then," she said. It was a statement, not a question.

"No."

Joëlle spooned froth off her coffee, and nibbled her biscuit thoughtfully. She finally smiled. "It's been coming for a while."

"What do you mean?"

"You've been getting restless...I could tell." She paused. "You're not wholly domestic, Marc."

"Oh."

Her smile deepened, and her eyes crinkled mischievously, like any young woman gossiping with a friend. She leaned slightly across the table. "A woman...?"

I nodded. "There's a woman involved. Yes."

She leaned back in her chair, thinking, and unconsciously began slowly to tighten up her bodice. "So... you want to collect your things...?" She was referring to a clutter of personal files and nautical gear that, along with her own boxes of genealogical files and many books, had made my bedroom even smaller. This was a fair way of storing our possessions, however. I was in Moissac only at intervals whereas she lived there all the time and had to rest and dress for work.

"Not just yet," I said. "Besides, I just handed over twenty-two thousand francs. That should tell you something."

"So, it is not like *that*...Then...?"

"I don't know."

"Oh..." She nodded and sipped thoughtfully. "That's good. If you want my advice, Marc... as a good friend who knows you... take it slow. What will be, will be. Is she aboard *Jester*?"

I nodded.

"So you won't be coming home... to the apartment... right now." It was a gentle statement.

"No." The problem was also that I couldn't explain very much. Mariko had not given me permission to discuss the parchment with anyone. Also, there was danger involved and I didn't want to put Joëlle in harm's way. And also, of course, I was attracted to Mariko in a way that I wasn't attracted to Joëlle.

Joëlle was studying me with grey eyes that absorbed all grey truths.

"Is she beautiful?"

"Not particularly." But then I remembered that she had been grey and grainy with exhaustion, except for that flush of apricot after the warmth, safety and hot meal. "Not now, at any rate... But I think she could be..."

"Ah."

"And exotic. And also in a lot of trouble."

She laughed softly. "Now, that's quite a lot of temptation, if I know Marc Rennsalaer," she said. "And I do. Better than you." She paused for some moments. "Do you want to talk about it?"

I was silent while I took in her eyes, her face, her newly-cut hair and the bodice of her new dress – now tightened a bit, but not closed. I couldn't truthfully say that she was more than mildly attractive by my standards, and probably even by most men's standards. Her figure was too full for her height, her eyes could seem dispassionate and the bridge of her nose was a bit sharp and challenging. Her mouth was finely moulded, if very definitely determined. Her chin could still be called delicate, but was more than just a little determined as well. No, Joëlle could not be called beautiful at all, but then why should she be?

Neither is the Haute Garonne beautiful compared to the tempestuous Atlantic or the seductive Mediterranean. And I remembered that I had rejected both as places to live, long before I had ever met either Joëlle or Mariko, in favour of the Haute Garonne. There was something timeless about the uplands where self-sown wheat had always naturally flourished, just like the river wind was fluttering Joëlle's hair now.

But there was equally the challenge of Atlantic unpredictability and the romance of the languorous Mediterranean. That was beauty. I laughed softly to myself, shook misgivings and mild guilt aside, and truly enjoyed a mouthful of coffee. What would be, would be... And always had been. Curiously enough, I winked at her.

"The problem is, Joey, I *can't* talk about it. This trouble is no joke. They've been following her for days. We were shot at," I said in a lowered voice. I put my finger to my lips and shook my head to stifle any possible exclamation.

Her eyes widened. But not in disbelief because I had never given her cause to doubt me.

I nodded. "That's why I can't explain much. I don't know much..."

"All right."

"And you might also be in danger, for all I know. If they trace you through me. And that could happen... if they manage to identify *Jester*. That's one reason why I don't want to go home just now. If anyone is watching me, Joëlle, I don't want to lead them to our place."

She didn't ask what other reasons there might be for not wanting to go home. She sighed her understanding. "Who are *they*?" she asked.

"Well, that's the question, isn't it? I wish we knew."

She nodded slowly, then once more and briskly. "Can I help...?"

"Yes. You can. That's why I came here, Joey."

Although my appearances were now regularly scheduled, in a general way, much could happen on rivers and canals to scramble a timetable. I had had to phone Joëlle several times previously about a change in my estimated time of arrival. Or, even a change in plan, like once when I had to travel on to Carcassonne without even stopping at Moissac. She had taken a train to meet me for the weekend. In short, I could have avoided her easily enough.

She was remembering all this. "Yes, I see," she said.

"I badly need some information... I can't think of anyone but you who might have it quickly. It's been too choppy for the Internet, what with the storm last night and the breeze today." I sipped thoughtfully before I continued. "That church at Rennes-le-Château... Remember...?"

She nodded.

"It was dedicated to Mary Magdalene, right?" I was more than a little hazy about who Mary Magdalene was, knowing only that she had been a character in the Bible and a bit more from what Mariko had said. Joëlle had been raised as a good Catholic, even if her Christianity was now apparently much less than nominal. But even a fallen Catholic could be counted on to know the Bible.

"Ye...ess." The question obviously surprised her, within the context of our discussion, but my tone made it clear that I was not attempting to change the subject. "But it had been dedicated to Aphrodite when the Greeks were there, and then to Venus when the Romans occupied the Narbonnais and to Isis long before that."

"Can you tell me everything you know about Mary Magdalene?"

"I think I just did, Marc," she said with a quick smile. Then, she looked down into her lap, and then gazed off into some middle distance where I couldn't follow. But she returned quickly enough. "That's a very big question. You don't know what you're asking, and I don't know what you're really asking."

"I came because I figure you must know the Bible, being raised Catholic and all."

She smiled at me. "Oh, *that*. That part is easy enough... According to the New Testament, Mary Magdalene was afflicted with demons..."

"Seven devils...?"

She nodded. "Priests have interpreted the devils as harlotry, or driving her to it, but the Bible never actually said that... Anyway, after Jesus exorcised them, the devils, she became a devoted disciple. She washed his feet with her hair. She anointed him with oil... expensive oil, and some of the other disciples complained about that. She was at the Crucifixion, and it was to Mary Magdalene that Jesus first revealed himself after the Resurrection. That's about it. That's about all the Bible says about her."

"Was she Jesus' most devoted disciple?" I wanted to check Mariko's story out.

"In the Bible?" She toyed with her spoon, and finally stirred with it. "That's hard to say. There's a figure called 'the beloved disciple' mentioned in the Bible," she emphasised the phrase, "but I was *taught*..." the emphasis again, along with a wry smile "...that the most beloved disciple was John." She sipped her coffee thoughtfully. "But there are good reasons to think that it was really Mary Magdalene."

"My favourite haloed Elysian," I said, looking around. There was no one at the two neighbouring tables or anywhere else who seemed remotely interested in us, but I almost whispered anyway. "Could Mary Magdalene have written a gospel... or anything?"

"Certainly," Joëlle replied after some deliberation, "or at least possibly. Mary Magdalene, if she really existed as described in the New Testament, was closely associated with New Testament Jesus – if he ever existed as described. She could have written a gospel herself, assuming that she could write, that is. Female literacy wasn't common back then. But, being a figure of some status with Jesus, she could certainly have dictated a gospel to a scribe." She paused and sipped, and then her eyes crinkled in a mischievous smile. "Now, *that* would be a gospel worth reading." Her intonation said everything that Mariko had said in words.

"That's too bad...In a way," I said. I was thinking, but was also scanning the expanse of the marketplace over Joëlle's shoulder.

The possibility that Joëlle had just made much more remote was that Mariko had simply fabricated her entire story about finding the parchment.

Sure, I'd seen the small page of jumbled script when she'd patted it dry. But Mariko had said she was a linguist. If this was true, then she could have had a piece of parchment – vellum – that had absolutely nothing to do with why the men were after her. Her briefcase could still have held something else that the men had really wanted. Or wanted destroyed. Something, perhaps, that Mariko had stolen. Maybe more correctly, something *else* that Mariko O'Shaugnessey had stolen.

Mostly because of Mariko's potential stunning and exotic looks, a compromising love letter had immediately sprung to my mind. She had already admitted to an affair with her Oxford professor, although I'd never heard of academics hiring hit men. Still, if there had been one affair, there might have been others. Say that the briefcase had held an embarrassing revelation relating to, for example, a British cabinet minister? Or, even a prince? That would explain the men's eagerness to shoot at her, so long as the briefcase would go to the bottom of the Garonne at the same time.

But if it was actually possible for Mary Magdalene to have authored a gospel, and so the parchment alone had been the true objective of the men, then Mariko was in possibly even worse trouble. And so was I. That could also explain the men's trigger-happy demeanour. They wanted her dead, so long as the briefcase was lost along with her. She had found something from the Glastonbury church, and had had some chance to study it. She enjoyed at least something of an academic reputation, or had a... er... mentor who did, and therefore might get some attention for a shocking biblical revelation.

On the other hand, of course, being so ready to shoot might just indicate a certain lack of professionalism. I'd been considering their enthusiasm for shooting. It was a very important aspect of the situation because Mariko had said these men began following her in England. True, England had suffered erosion of traditional values like the rest of the developed West. Nonetheless, the criminal use of firearms was still much rarer in England than elsewhere in Europe or North America. Even British agents had preferred a car accident to shooting Princess Di and Dodi Al Faid, if such rumours were founded and I don't know that they were. This suggested English tradition was still honoured, after a fashion. Was this a reliable indicator that Mariko's men were not English? That the group they represented was not English? I doubted it.

But it wasn't at all difficult to think of at least one organization that might be interested in suppressing a Mary Magdalene gospel, and it was large, wealthy and ruthless. I might not know much about what was specifically within the Bible's covers, but I had read a few newspapers. Like everyone else, I knew of the Vatican's vehement objections to releasing the results of the Dead Sea Scroll studies until the translations could be sanitized. Mariko had said that a Mary Magdalene gospel might shed new light on the life of Jesus. Joëlle had just broadly hinted the same thing. Perhaps at least one organization wanted to keep that light extinguished. Judging from the Banco Ambrosiano murders, the Vatican had ways to extinguish things very thoroughly. The Mafia and the Union Corse. Those allegations of murder had proved to be very well founded indeed, despite the first indignant denials by cardinals and even popes.

And there might even be other organizations that might also be interested in a Mary Magdalene gospel, groups that I couldn't think of or imagine... I was lost in thought.

"Marc," I heard Joëlle say. "Come back."

When I focussed on her again, she said: "Too bad...?" And she was obviously repeating the question.

I nodded. "In a way." I paused. "It means that I'm probably able to trust her," I smiled. It also meant it might have been a very big mistake to come to Moissac and meet with Joëlle. The organization that had sprung so readily to mind had plenty of personnel and resources. But, it was too late to worry about that now. I had to hope that only two men had been assigned to Mariko and that events had taken them by surprise.

"That is Mary Magdalene as far as the Bible is concerned," Joëlle said in a way that was meant to close the conversation.

But I didn't want to go away for an extended period – and perhaps forever, emotionally – on that note. "That reminds me," I said, shoving my newly formed fears as far away as I could. "Before we leave this subject… what does Mary Magdalene mean?"

Joëlle paused. "The name Mary means basically 'of the sea'," she emphasised the phrase. "'Magdalene' is supposed to mean that this particular Mary came from a place called Magdala. I don't know where Magdala is. I was taught that Magdala might have been Mediggo, a place famous for its strong fortifications. It was supposed to be somewhere in Palestine. I do know that Mary Magdalene's crown always looks like stone battlements. Maybe they stand for Mediggo." She sipped, looking across her cup and waiting.

"Crown?"

She shrugged. "A Catholic thing. Some Catholic artists depicted her with a crown in their paintings. In sculptures too. Just like the Virgin Mary is sometimes shown with a crown and is often called 'The Queen of Heaven.'"

"That's another thing," I said. "I get all these Marys mixed up."

"You're not the only one."

"There's the Virgin Mary, Mary Magdalene…"

"And Mary of Bethany."

"Another one? They're all in the Bible?"

"And that's just in the New Testament… the… Jesus part," she added for my benefit.

"It's crazy," I said. "Too many Marys in one story."

"Others before you have commented on that," she said mildly. But if it's any consolation, most theologians think that Mary Magdalene and Mary of Bethany were the same person."

"Why confuse the issue by using two names in the Bible for the same woman?"

"To confuse the issue."

Remembering the hints of Mariko and Joëlle, I thought that I was starting to get the idea. "To disguise the fact that Mary Magdalene was so important. Or this other Mary, not Virgin Mary."

"Mary of Bethany."

"That's her."

Joëlle gazed upward… thinking. She came back to earth and smiled softly. "They say that behind every great man there's a great woman. Jesus was a certainly a great man and he had a hard job. It makes sense that he had a loving woman to help him. Doesn't it? I think that the celibate priests tried to confuse the truth by editing too many Marys into the New Testament." She paused. She licked froth from her spoon.

"Just *a* woman? What about a wife?"

She smiled and nodded yes. "That's what I believe. Mary would have been a good name for her, the best name for her… whatever her real name may have been. It suited the story. Just like his mother had to be a Mary too, whatever her real name may have been. It suited the story."

Several thoughts were running through my head at once. I shook it to clear it of unwanted fears only because I now had worse ones. Mariko's gunmen. So, get thee behind me, Blasphemy. "What you're saying, when all is said and done, is that Jesus may have been a consort… for…" I shrugged helplessly, "…Marys."

She regarded me seriously. She nodded a concession, and smiled. "You know," she said, "that was a brave statement for someone who has a big streak of unconscious male chauvinism."

"Joëlle… I never say or do anything that's remotely – "

"I said *unconscious*," she emphasised.

I didn't want to pursue this "Then, the… ah… divinity may have been hers."

She nodded. "Even the Church admits that the Holy Spirit… Holy Ghost… is female. Sancta Sophia."

"And that means," I mused thoughtfully, "that there could have been children." I'd thought of this when Mariko had mentioned the possibility that Jesus and Mary Magdalene had been married, but Mariko had been so tired that I hadn't wanted to prolong our conversation.

"That's the whole idea, isn't it?" Was this an observation on our relationship, or just more objectivity? I decided not to investigate this too closely.

"But, essentially," I continued, the children would have been hers – naturally, of course, because she carried them and birthed them – but also in the sense of inheritance and…"

"A matriarchal lineage is what you're trying to express, I think."

"Yes, I guess it is."

"Others before you have made that observation as well, Marc."

"They have? I should have known."

"Ever heard of the Holy Grail?"

"Jesus, Joey… the Holy Grail…?" I couldn't mask my scepticism. Or sarcasm.

"You just stumbled on it yourself. Though I never would have expected it," she finished.

"This can't be real…"

"What bank do we use?"

I was taken by surprise, and watched Joëlle fumble in her jogging purse. Was she ending things between us? I shrugged. What would be, would be. "I don't remember," I said. The same bank we used in Narbonne. Your bank."

"That's right." She tossed the bankbook across the table for the second time within an hour. "Take a look," she said.

Banque du Puy de Parseval. I remembered the bank on Boulevard Gambetta, a small building not far from the Canal de la Robine… number 8… 8A? Joëlle had recommended it. I had waited at Cyrano's while Joey had opened an account for me, and also one for us. I had given her an impressive number of francs to deposit in my account. And to distribute in hers and ours according to a long discussion featuring pieces of paper and columns of figures.

I had idly wondered, while drinking café au lait in Cyrano's, whether I would ever see her again. But she had returned and had fumbled bank-books from the same jogging purse she was wearing now. Since then, I had only looked at the entries and balances. I had never added and subtracted the columns.

"The Bank of Perceval's Well," I said in disbelief. "Gimme a break." I knew vaguely that Perceval had featured in the Holy Grail stories. I had no idea what role he had supposedly played in them. "But that's just a name, Joëlle."

"Of course it is," she agreed, glancing at her watch. "On the other hand, Dear, you might ask why the French for "Holy Grail" is still *San Graal* to this day, or 'holy blood' in pronunciation. A bloodline or lineage. And you might wonder why this little Midi bank is located in Languedoc, just where the Cathars fought the Church… and where the Elysians had lived so long before. Perceval had to learn to ask the right questions, too." She smiled sweetly as I slid the bank-book back across the table to her. "Shouldn't you be getting back to *Jester*?"

"Right."

"Did all this help?" she asked seriously.

"I don't know. Maybe it's too soon to say. But thank you." I reverted to business, agreeing that I needed to get back to *Jester*. I just asked her to keep especially alert when she went out, and to make very sure to lock the doors when she was home. I stressed that she should keep an eye out for any suspicious characters hanging around… now that I would be away for a while. I also arranged to keep in contact on a regular schedule, and this was a marked departure from our usual mode of operation. I was about to stand up when I remembered.

"Oh, I almost forgot." I fished the scrap of paper with Raoul's phone number out of my shirt pocket. I handed it to her. She scanned it, and then pushed it down into her purse along with the bankbook. She was used to filing things for me, and she had never lost anything so far despite her casual acceptance and storage of data. "That's the guy with the flour. I want to keep in touch with him." I stood.

"Sure," she said, rising with me and arranging the purse on her hip. She zipped it closed.

"Your bike outside?"

"Yes... and the chain's loose."

"I'll tend to it." I turned to leave the restaurant, picking up the nearly empty backpack and the canvas bag. Joëlle went to settle the bill... or get the money. I hadn't followed the fine print of the previous transaction.

I came down *Le Port Romain's* few steps very slowly, as if entranced with the view, as indeed I was. I'd noticed nothing noteworthy out in the market for the hour or so that we had talked. But after Joëlle's confirmation that a Mary Magdalene gospel was indeed a possibility, I was determined to be even more observant. The battlements of the old wall towered behind the restaurant, and I could see them now that I was down by the bike rack. No one could be seen looking between the crenellations up above.

The front wheel was locked into the rack beside *Le Port Romain's* door. I unlocked the anti-theft bar and also the steel box between the two rear wheels of her tricycle. The lock-bar slotted into the frame behind the seat to form a back rest. I reached inside the box for the small tool kit and the pump and wiggled the canvas bag down into the box. It was a bit of a struggle and I perceived that a thick magazine was obstructing the bag's progress. After I removed it – *L'Almanach du Languedoc* – the bag fitted easily down in the bottom of the storage box. I curled the magazine back down into the storage compartment on top of the canvas bag.

I was inordinately proud of that tricycle. It had been a present to Joëlle in Narbonne almost seven years ago. Fussing with it, and around it, gave me an opportunity to scan the immediate area while being partly obscured myself. I hoped that adjusting a tricycle would seem a natural part of the scene and, of course, kneeling beside it let me peek through its spoke wheels.

Basically, it was a post World War II Velocette moped, at least fifty years old, and one of the most unlikely motorized contrivances ever made by man. I'd seen it abandoned in a Narbonne garage and, just intrigued at first with its Rube Goldberg design, had bought it for seventy francs, about $10 U.S. I had been fairly warned that it didn't work.

A 35cc gas engine was hinged on top of the sturdy fender to straddle the front wheel, magneto on one side and a similar-sized gasoline tank on the other. The engine turned a cylindrical grindstone that pressed onto the top of the front tire. The idea was that you could use it as a bicycle with the motor pivoted up completely off the wheel. To enjoy motorised riding, you pivoted the engine down, and killed the compression by pulling a lever that opened a valve in the cylinder head. When the motor was turning over by pedalling, you let go of the lever and gave compression to the cylinder. In theory, the motor would start, and the revolving grindstone would turn the front wheel by friction. So much was clear from my examination of the ancient artefact. I started fixing it up, just for fun, while I was first in Narbonne getting used to France.

Incredibly, the thing worked when it was cleaned up and put back together. You could only get about twenty miles per hour out of it on a level road with a fair wind. You had to pedal uphill to help the engine. But, it seemed to work quite well – within its limits. Amazingly, the stone did not noticeably wear the tire away. Even more to my amazement, I learned that Velocettes had been manufactured up until the late 1990's and that spare parts were easily available throughout France.

By the time I had discovered all this, I had met Joëlle and thought of her waiting for buses. And even then she had to walk a fair distance to work anyway. Narbonne had never boasted a good public transit system. But I doubted, from my knowledge of her, that she had the balance and co-ordination to want a bicycle. She wasn't an athletic girl; she'd just been born with a sturdy body. So, I had a 10-speed tricycle welded up, a tricycle built for two. It was the real thing with an independent rear suspension for cornering. It had a roomy waterproof and lockable compartment for shopping, whose top was the second tandem seat. The second handlebar could be reversed for a single rider's back rest, and served also for an anti-theft lock bar. It had cost a small fortune.

Because I had noticed that Joëlle often wore full-length dresses and skirts, I had contrived a truly all-enclosed chain guard. I had taken immense care with the candy apple maroon paint job – I knew that red was her favourite colour – and had added good-sized mirrors and a brass squeeze-bulb horn for safety.

I had presented it to her by contriving to meet her at its natal garage, and she had loved it. We had often pedalled it together around Narbonne. With two aboard, the motorised speed was reduced by about half. Since she didn't have a safe place to keep it at home, she kept it aboard *Jester* whose berth was not far from her flat. Indeed, the tricycle was part of the evolution of our starting to live together. *Jester* had carried the tricycle up to Moissac, along with all our other possessions, when circumstances had dictated our relocation.

Its rear wheels had not quite fitted through our courtyard's gateway, but this had been remedied with a little judicious chipping away at the already crumbling walls. And this had also given me the excuse to replace the sagging wrought iron gate with a new and much stronger steel one that actually had two working hinges, not to mention a lock. This new gate was also supported by new cement reinforced by rods driven into the walls and by wire mesh. No ordinary thief could get through the gate without literally demolishing the stonework walls to either side. Of course, a thief could climb over the walls if he was determined to risk the broken glass cemented into the top. During the unusually harsh winter last year, when there had been snow on the ground for more than a month, Joëlle had wheeled her tricycle through the French windows into the living room, which left little living room.

Normal gas consumption was about half a litre a week. We could easily afford this, but Joey tended toward automatic frugality that was, to my mind, counter-productive. Tinkering around last March, however, I found, after some experimentation, that it would run on a mixture of coal oil and cognac. It ran even better on coal oil and grain alcohol, which was again being produced locally and was much cheaper. Of course, you had to keep the fuel well mixed, but that was no problem on cobblestones. I didn't tell Joëlle about the alcohol mixture. Since she liked cognac, she had found a way of rationalising the use of cognac dregs in glasses. Frugality.

The chain was indeed a bit loose. I had adjusted it and oiled it for her, had pumped up the tires a bit and was finishing up by checking the tire pressure when Joëlle came out of *Le Port Romain*. "You should watch the tire pressure, Joey… Easier to pedal."

Coming down the steps to stand beside the tricycle, she espied the curled-up magazine in the storage compartment. "I brought this for you," she said, taking it out. I stood up and replaced the toolbox, closing the compartment's top. I peered over her shoulder at *L'Almanach du Languedoc* as she riffled pages. "An article about very early Neolithic sites near Narbonne."

"Elysians."

"Certainly," she smiled.

I took the magazine, noting the page of the article. "My favourite Elysian," I said. "Please remember to keep your eyes open. And make sure to keep our telephone schedule." After a somewhat awkward time involving pecked kisses and a sibling-like embrace, she swung aboard her tricycle. I didn't want to say too much with all the people passing nearby. Who knew might overhear? "You take care, Joey. Remember, I'll keep in touch," I said.

"You take care," she responded quietly. "And you remember…"

"What?"

"Knights herrant spend their nights herring," she grinned. Nights herrant, nights herring? But then I factored in her French pronunciation, and I got the idea. I slapped her on the bum, but gently. She bent over the handlebars and the tires scuffed away over the now dusty cobblestones.

The last I saw of her for a very long time were brown muscular thighs pumping through the long slits of her new red dress. Her brass squeeze-horn reverberated insistently under the archway into the city.

Part Two

"...Hades, Persephone,
Hermes, steward of death,
Eternal Wrath and Furies,
Children of gods,
Who see all murderers
And all adulterous thieves, come soon!
Be near me, and avenge
My father's death, and bring
My brother home."

Sophocles: *Electra*

12

Mist boiled off the Canal du Midi like steam from a roiling cauldron. Only thicker. It was altogether too good to be wasted. *Jester* chuckled along at five knots, perhaps a touch too fast in this poor visibility, but I was gambling that no one else might be inclined to travel in this early fog. A swift glance at the moisture-beaded face of my Seiko told me, however, that I'd have to start being more careful pretty soon. Almost seven, and the canal's locks opened at that hour of the morning. Whatever vessels might choose to venture out into the canal before this fog lifted would begin locking through at that time. Of course, there might also be many vessels, like *Jester* herself, presently on the summit level and under way now.

The canal intertwines with the Garonne in a way that is much too complicated to explain to anyone without a chart in front of them. Sometimes, the canal route uses the river itself, and sometimes there's an artificial cut that snakes away from the river through the countryside. When the canal leaves the river, it is always to avoid some obstacle. On the Haute Garonne, these obstacles are invariably rapids. A canal boat makes up for this fall of water level by negotiating locks.

I had made good time from Moissac, even though I'd had to pass up through seventeen locks just to get to Toulouse, and up another three to reach the summit level at Castelnaudary. There was a 40-kilometre stretch of level water from there to Carcassonne where the Canal du Midi would drop abruptly through twenty locks to reach the level of the Mediterranean just west of Narbonne. A spur line called the Canal de la Robine continued on into the very centre of Narbonne, from which, after a few kilometres, one could reach the sea at Narbonne Plage... 'Narbonne Beach'. The Canal du Midi itself continued on to Béziers, and from there one could travel to Marseilles.

If one didn't fancy the bustle and underworld of Marseilles, ascending the Rhône to Chalons north of Lyons would lead to a canal connecting with the Saône River and northern France. Continuing up the Rhône would lead into Switzerland where a canal connects with the Rhine. An ordinary canal barge could reach most major cities in Europe, while a vessel like *Folderol Jester* could also sail throughout the Mediterranean, with a cautious weather eye, and could even coast the Atlantic seaboard.

Mariko had not been able to help with the locks, having been asleep for most of the day-and-a-half since I had met up with Joëlle. I have seldom seen anyone sleep so deeply, and at times I was a bit worried. But her breathing had always been regular and her colour was good.

She was young, and I concluded that she needed only to make up for ten days of physical and mental exhaustion. She had awakened at intervals to shower and to have some onion soup and cheese toast that I kept preparing and warming on the galley stove. Other than that, she'd sprawled on the bunk and hadn't stirred with my comings and goings.

So, I had worked the locks myself, and that had probably been more efficient anyway. That is to say that I assisted the war veterans to work the locks. These poor fellows were often missing an arm or a leg, but nonetheless hobbled around deftly. They worked with a will and seemed cheerful on the whole. Being a lockmaster on the Canal du Midi was a more pleasant life than many available alternatives. It was the custom to give the lockmaster three cigarettes per lock. Sometimes there was a flight of three locks or more under one lockmaster if a significant difference in water level had to be overcome within a short distance. Nine cigarettes or more. Presumably this custom was meant to hasten the demise of lockmasters so that others on the waiting list could have their turn. The French can be humanistic, in a pragmatic way.

Jester's blunt bow, with the cut-water panels folded back, barged into the grey curtain. The wind of our passage sent uncanny wraith shapes of torn mist writhing slowly, slowly back toward me at the wheel. I reflected that we seem to have been lucky. No one had paid *Jester* any attention, so far as I could tell. I had seen nothing sinister back at the Moissac market, and Joëlle had not called to report anything or anyone unusual around the apartment.

Nonetheless, I had pushed *Jester* outward bound from Moissac, stopping to sleep only for a few hours at St. Jory west of Toulouse – and that is a long afternoon's haul from Moissac – and again at Castelnaudary last night.

Maybe I was wrong, but I considered it safer to stop at small places, so I had pushed on to avoid berthing at Toulouse. The old wharves at Toulouse, said to be of first Roman and then Visigothic origin, served a rather unsavoury part of town where many twisting streets and alleys ran down to the docks. The quays there were badly lighted.

On the other hand, the smaller canal towns like St. Jory and Castelnaudary are not located along highways at all, but at places out in the countryside where the canal departs from the river. Some highway maps didn't think these towns worth depicting. I was hoping to use Mariko's nautical diversion as effectively as possible. They would have to get canal charts if they wanted to know all the places that *Jester* could hide.

St. Jory's quay was not lighted at all, and several barges were already moored there when *Jester* had arrived. And, while Cantelnaudary's wharf possessed three lights, only one road served it. Barges had been berthed there, too. Both places had boasted many frogs to sing me to sleep. I figured that the frogs might stop singing if anyone disturbed them. I tended, even in sleep, to register such things, and I was fond of frogs. In East Timor, they had saved my life twice. Frogs are just about the best watchdogs there are. They stop singing at the least tread on their muddy turf and saturated land is a good conductor of vibrations. Water is even better. In Indonesia, I discovered that I could sleep safely so long as the frogs were singing and woke up very quickly when they stopped.

Castelnaudary was at the western, or Atlantic, end of what is called 'the summit level' of the Canal du Midi. One will recall from observation, if not from basic physics classes, that water always seeks a level, and that water always flows downhill. These two basic facts being the deciding ones in canal surveying and building, the early engineers, such as the brilliant if nearly-illiterate Brindley in late 17th Century England, had always tried their best to make the summit level as long and as "fullsumme," as Brindley put it, as possible. This meant no water-using locks for as long a stretch as possible.

Unfortunately, though, reality and Murphy's Law being what they are, the summit level of any canal is always on the top of a watershed. It is on top of a ridge, or on top of hills, that make water decide to flow one direction or another. This is usually a very restricted geographic area and, in addition, one to which no water naturally flows. It all flows down and away. And yet this very part of the canal had to be the one which acted as a reservoir to hold all the water that would operate the canal locks during the entire navigational season.

As with so many things that the Chinese supposedly invented, and the canal lock was one of them, they didn't do a lot with it. They never solved the vexing problem of the summit level, so they restricted their canals to lowlands.

In China, when the water on the summit level disappeared, well, the navigation season came to a muddy halt. When the idea of the canal lock percolated into Europe from embryonic China trade in the early 15th Century, Europeans turned their aggressive, technological brains toward the challenge of the summit level. The summit level problem had inspired Oriental engineers, with more brains but considerably less aggression, to appreciate the celestially-dictated harmony of life. To everything there is a season, and in July or August the canals become mudslides. So the Oriental engineers thought, and so, too, more or less, Pete Seeger sang during the 1960s rebirth of Western Man's cosmic consciousness.

Just as the Europeans had transformed Chinese-invented gunpowder into a propellant for ever increasingly efficient and deadly cannons, when the Chinese had only used it for firecrackers and gloriously erratic military rockets, Europeans turned their brains toward the conquest of the summit level problem.

James Edward Brindley in England, and Jean-Pierre Auguste Testard Montrofier in France, got the same bright idea at the same time, although the French had bigger rivers and more water with which to work. Why not find an artificial summit level somewhat below the actual top of the watershed?

So, Brindley and Montrofier surveyed canal routes that clung to the upper slopes of a watershed, choosing their contour level with great care to involve the least work. This contour might be many, many miles in length, and this was all to the good. Eventually the canal went *around*, not *over*, the actual highest point of the watershed.

If, as sometimes happened, a ridge of rock at the top of a pass blocked the proposed route; they would tunnel through rather than reduce the length of the canal's summit level. The contour was chosen, at some appropriate and level altitude, so that the canal could also be made as wide as possible, to hold more water. Then, too, with clever surveying, little lakes and reservoirs could be contrived where the canal walls transformed some valleys and ravines into cul-de-sacs. Best of all, the rainfall onto the very top of the watershed would fill the hill streams and mountain burns, and they could be made to flow into either the widened canal itself or into the subsidiary lakes and reservoirs connected with it.

The water supply problem of the summit level had been solved. Montrofier in France, with bigger rivers and more water, could afford summit levels that were not too contour-convoluting, like a strand of spaghetti arranged snakewise around one height of a range of hills. Brindley in England, with much smaller rivers and much less water at his disposal, had had to resort to extremely serpentine summit levels in order to amass sufficient water to operate the locks at each end of his canals.

On one particular stretch of the Kennet and Avon Canal, near Market Harborough, the canal is so serpentine that it is said that you can travel twenty miles and still keep approaching, and receding from, the spire of the same church. Brindley's canals did get to their destinations eventually. But the average horse-drawn barge speed of about two miles per hour over an average day of twelve hours, combined with lengthy routes dictated by Brindley's contour-canals, explains why aggressive European technology, once unleashed, developed railways in order to deliver merchandise faster than canal barges. Railways killed canal traffic, just as motorways and the reliable transport truck had almost killed the trains. Until now.

Progress, you see... except that asphalt covers more and more food-growing land every year in the so-called civilized world, whereas canals took little space and irrigated the surrounding fields to enhance natural organic productivity. Some of the late 17th century yields per acre from canal-side fields still stand as records, even compared with yields from modern chemical fertilisers. Emissions from internal combustion engines, like carbon monoxide, put a damper on plant growth while carbon dioxide emissions from canal water plants and algae stimulate neighbouring agricultural crops. And, of course, there was the eventual problem with diesel trains and trucks of using fuel based on someone else's oil. Maybe terrestrial, if not celestial, harmony must draw its line somewhere between Oriental and Occidental perspectives.

This engineering retrospective explains why I considered us lucky. Nothing sinister had happened since Mariko had jumped off the Moissac bridge. From Castelnaudary toward Carcassonne gave us forty kilometres of Montrofier's summit level. No locks, and so no need to risk going ashore at all. Not only that, but the summit level canal was fairly wide in order to contain water. Therefore, I could stay out of the centre shipping channel at night and still have room to anchor *Jester* well away from the shore. Since I would have to get a little more and better sleep at some point, this summit level promised to be something of a respite. And, although Montrofier had employed a relatively straight summit level here, one clinging to the northern foothills of the Pyrenees, and had used a hundred-meter wide canal to act as a reservoir, he had also engineered charming little lakes and coves running southward into the foothills every few kilometres.

These were duly and excellently drawn on the canal navigational charts, and most of them were thicker with little crosses than a churchyard, meaning lots of rocks, and thus *Folderol Jester* could lose herself in several of these watery cul-de-sacs if prudence dictated. But none of these little lakes and coves showed on most highway maps. Mariko's pursuers would have to turn all nautical to find us, if I chose to play the game that way. Some of these lakes created in the Pyrenees foothills boasted tasty bream and trout, while others were the last reputed haunts of the giant Garonne sturgeon.

Also, I loved this high country. Geography changed before your eyes on the summit level. Starting out in the northern-looking evergreen trees and crags around Castelnaudary, you could actually see ahead the white limestone peaks that extend all the way to Carcassonne. These limestone hills are covered with typical Mediterranean maquis.

Therefore, after finding *La Poule Frite* and offloading Bouchard's wine casks, there could be some time for a lost week or so among the Pyrenees foothills, the sparkling little lakes and the excellent fishing. The water would be warm for swimming, too. I would have time to learn more about Mariko O'Shaugnessey. And her parchment, of course. We could plan further moves. I'd already given some thought to this.

The muffled slapping from *Jester's* blunt bow increased in volume, and the hull began to see-saw gently and ponderously. We were into waves of some sort, not simply the bare ripples of a fog-shrouded channel. I throttled back quickly, and in a few moments the clumsy stern of a big Rhine tanker barge loomed out of the fog ahead. *Die Lorelei,* Aachen. Hull down and heavy laden, she was probably carrying chemicals bound for the refineries at Marseilles, to judge from the prominent sign amidships. I couldn't read this because my angle was too oblique and the fog was too thick, but only hazardous material warranted such a sign at all. It seemed as though she was pushing half the canal ahead of her in a huge bow wave, and sucking the rest of the canal along behind her with monstrous quarter waves. In short, she made a large displacement of water and a hell of a wake.

I throttled *Jester* back even more, tucking in behind the barge's rather hausfrau-ish behind. I ingested her crew's breakfast of coffee, smoked herring, sauerbraten and fresh, hot bauernbrot, by osmosis, as the domestic smells were carried softly back to my nose by obliging wraith-stewards in their rather dull grey uniforms of ragged fog. A surrogate breakfast, as it were, was perhaps better than none. Perhaps.

Die Lorelei shouldered through the fog like a pudgy, determined housewife through a mass of shoppers, and the rent she tore in the mist was about a hundred metres in length. I edged *Jester* into this opened seam of semi-clear fog, tucking close in behind the Aachen barge, and not keeping too much distance at that, so that our passage tore the mist as one vessel rather than as two. Just ahead of *Lorelei* the mist rose as a dark, grey wall. And just behind *Jester* it closed together again. There was no great length of disturbed, torn fog in which a shore observer on the canal-side roads might chance to see *Jester*. It would take great luck to get a glimpse of us in our hundred-meter window of ghostly vision out in the navigation channel, and then one might well conclude that *Lorelei* was towing another barge. That was how close I was keeping *Jester* to *Lorelei's* stern.

So, I reasoned. And, while doing so I heard the hatch slide open with that little bit of extra zip and smoothness conferred by the lubrication of foggy moisture. Mariko's head appeared in the open hatchway, but she didn't look around for me. She stared at something, concentrating and rocking gently, but uncertainly, as *Jester* frolicked ponderously in *Lorelei's* substantial wake.

I saw that Mariko had made an attempt to fix her hair into a ponytail, though her cut was really unsuited for that. Hair at the front couldn't be pulled back far enough to become part of the tail, but quivered beside her temples and cheeks in the breeze of our slow speed. The rest was also too short. The result was a short bob-tail behind her head. The effect reminded me of the appendage of some rare and wild Central Asian pony once considered extinct but recently sighted somewhere in Mongolia. You come across things like that in the papers every now and then.

But I knew women well enough, at least, to keep this sort of *National Geographic* perspective to myself. I watched as arms and hands emerged from the hatchway to place my large, square skillet on the deck. Inside were a thermos cup and a small plate. She shoved it toward me on the moisture-beaded deck, finally looked up and grinned. Her eyes were bright, but some fatigue still lingered in the corners.

"It was the only tray I could find," she said.

"Fine," I nodded. The cup proved to have excellent coffee in it, creamed and sugared the way she'd seen me do it two nights ago during the *saucisses à la Catalane*. The thick plastic Melmac plate held two croissants filled, I soon discovered, with Black Forest ham, Havarti cheese and fried egg.

She scrambled up out of the hatch and perched herself beside me on the break of the poop. The Jordache jeans again. She'd slept in them the first night, but then later I'd seen her sprawled out in her original white blouse and a blue pair of the new briefs I had bought in Moissac. She hugged one leg up against her chest in the clammy world, and let the other dangle down on to the glistening wet and lumpy plastic tarp that covered the casks. As I munched, I saw her Adidas toe drawing idle patterns in the wetness on the tarpaulin.

"Thanks for the breakfast," I said as soon as I had swallowed, brandishing a half-gone croissant.

Mariko nodded. "You're welcome. The least I could do."

"Good to have a real bite. I've been having a surrogate breakfast for the past few minutes." I gestured toward *Lorelei's* broad stern, and saw Mariko wrinkle her nose with a good whiff. Then I saw her smile. She closed her eyes and sniffed seriously.

"Kippers and fresh bread...? And something else... "

"Sauerbraten, I think," I said.

"Ye... ess... " She drew it out in a carefully considered way. "Yes. I do think you're right."

Then I remembered. "Mariko, I'd like you to have a look at that brass rail back there." I hooked a thumb over my shoulder. She slithered up and walked gingerly over the restless deck, but I didn't allow my eyes to follow because I wanted to pay close attention to *Lorelei's* position. Mariko was back at the rail for some little time before I heard her Adidas soles squeak cautiously back over the deck. She brushed down beside me, and I flicked a brief glance away from *Lorelei's* fat bottom to see Mariko, head down, thoughtfully rubbing her thumb and a grey-smudged forefinger together.

"See it?" I asked, once more watching the water froth up alongside the rudder blade of the barge ahead, seeing the dark smoke of *Lorelei's* throbbing diesel.

"Yes."

"A bullet, Mariko. Ricochet. A bright scar on my shiny brass rail."

"I know. I believed it before, you know. I know it now, Marc. It left a smear of lead on the brass." She held up her smudged forefinger and thumb. Peering closely for just a second, I saw tiny grains of grey metal glinting in the whorl grooves of her fingerprint.

There did not seem to be anything more to say on that subject. I swallowed my last tasty morsel of croissant, and then injected another dollop of rich, wonderful coffee through the no-spill slot. A beautiful burn down the throat. A satisfying thump of the heart.

"Did you read that stuff about *Folderol Jester*?" I asked idly. I didn't think that she had viewed the CD yet. It was still stacked among others and the collection seemed undisturbed. After leaving her the note at Moissac, I had rummaged in the bookshelf beside my settee-bunk. I found the thin sheaf of paper quickly enough and had left it beside one of the computers. It was an abridged account of the CD, and it had lain there, untouched, all day yesterday and last night. It outlined a lot, but not all, about my boat's design and capabilities.

"I read it through while I was making breakfast," she said.

"That *Jester* material," I mused casually, "wasn't just boyish pride."

I sensed her looking up at me, but I couldn't spare a glance because we were heading into one of Montrofier's gentle curves and *Lorelei's* deep-vee wakes, one from her blunt bows and one from her ample buttocks, were challenging *Jester's* own bow with a changing angle and increased heaving. I turned the wheel a bit to keep us directly astern in the relatively flat froth and foam of *Lorelei's* prop.

"It... your boat... is very clever," she said. Mariko obviously didn't know what I was getting at. Perhaps she was still a bit groggy.

"You actually read that stuff...?"

"I skimmed it. I speed-read, you know. Good comprehension."

"Hmmm."

As if searching around for an example with which to prove her speed reading prowess, she said: "Very clever. Especially the folding of everything, and the folding up of the... outriggers... to allow cruising on the narrow English canals... and the folding down of them to give stability on the wider European canals... and coastal waters."

"Hmmm," I said. I started to believe that she'd actually read it all.

Continuing somewhat hesitantly, an intelligent person trying to find something to say in what clearly seemed to be incongruous circumstances, she proved that she had read the material I'd given her. "I never realised that the English canals were so narrow," she said. "Imagine. Just eight feet wide. Poor Brindley. Trying to save water."

"Hmmm," I remarked.

"So, I read about your damned boat," she said impatiently. "The least I could do for being rescued. The vellum's... "

"Being rescued," I finished for her.

"Yes. And your breakfast!"

"Is that the only reason you read that boat stuff?" I asked mildly.

"Well, no," she said.

"Then... *why*?"

"Because I can't get a handle on you, Marc Rennsalaer. Thales of Miletus. Tiffinagh. A boat bum and *saucisses à la Catalane*. And... and..."

"And?"

"And... you said that you had been a soldier."

"Hmmm," I said.

"And I don't think you do things by accident. Everything seems planned out."

"You... think I'm somehow involved with your parchment?"

"N... No... How could you be? I just *fell* onto this boat."

"True."

"Then, why *did* you give me all that boat stuff to read?" she asked. "And I read it, all of it, as a courtesy to you... and because I think you don't do things by accident. And... and... I tried to think of something nice to say about your cleverness, this boat being able to do so many things, like going on the canals of Britain."

"The canals of Britain," I said like a stentorian narrator on *Aerial Britain*, "are not merely filled with water, they are filled with history."

Mariko sighed. "And what does *that* mean?"

"Well, for one thing, it means that the Kennet and Avon canal really begins in Christchurch, you know – if you count the Avon River as part of it – and wends its way through a lot of Somerset and Dorset. In fact, Mariko, it wends pretty close to Glastonbury."

"Oh..." A pause. "Oh," again.

"Yes," I continued. "And judging from what you told me, that little box holding the parchment had once been sealed with molten lead. Over the years, and it would take a hell of a lot of years, this molten lead corroded until it had no strength to speak of. The seal broke when the stones of the altar shifted and put some oblique pressure on the box."

"Oh, so now, the rest of the parchment is exposed to air for the first time in centuries?" Mariko asked.

"Yes."

"And...?"

"If it isn't recovered and preserved fairly quickly, it will... disintegrate," I explained.

"I knew that."

"I'm sure you did."

Mariko was silent for a long time, letting the implications of it all sink in. Then she said: "You're willing to go to Glastonbury, with me, in this boat, and... recover... the whole thing?"

"Steal," I said. "It actually belongs to the National Trust. Just like your little scrap of it."

"But... but... *Why?*" There was a significantly long lacuna in the conversation, as she might have put it.

Finally, Mariko rejoined the conversation with a comment: "You could get killed. I mean, I think they were going to kill me. They shot at you... or, shot at your boat, anyway... So... *Why?*"

"Say... that I'm just curious," I said, and it didn't sound convincing even to myself, so I pressed on: "I'm curious about why a scrap of parchment is valuable enough to kill for. To shoot at people for. I'm curious to know who's doing the shooting."

"I don't believe that can be all there is to it."

"Maybe not."

"Don't you have responsibilities? A wife..."

"I have responsibilities, but they're not pressing." I paused. "No wife. I do have a good... friend. That's one of the reasons I want to help recover... steal... the rest of the manuscript. But she is only one of the reasons why I'm willing to go to Glastonbury."

I could feel her looking at me, but she said nothing.

"Consider this, Mariko. They followed you and they tried to abduct you. They didn't hesitate to shoot at you. Now... what happens if they manage to identify my boat?"

"If I leave the boat, then there's no reason for them to harm you or... your friend."

"Really? Think again. They couldn't have known for certain that you had found anything, or what it might be, and yet they were willing to stalk and kill. What if you had had a chance to tell someone else about it, or even to make a copy for safekeeping somewhere?"

"I see," she said after a long pause.

"The only way out of this is through it."

"I'm sorry, Marc Rennsalaer."

"I want to be honest, though, Mariko O'Shaugnessey…now that we're being formal."

She waited, and pulled her other knee up to her chest. She was studying the mist and dew runnels on the tarp.

"I'm also curious about you, not only about the parchment."

"Oh." A lengthy silence. "And what about your… friend."

"We're not married Mariko. But we are, truly, good friends. What will be, will be," I said. "As a matter of fact, those were her words."

"So… you told her about me and the parchment?"

"Yes and no. Well, sort of. That's why I had to go into Moissac. I told her about you, but I didn't mention your name, and I asked some questions about Mary Magdalene. I didn't mention the parchment."

"Oh."

"I didn't tell her enough to put her in any danger… I hope." I changed the subject. "You really seem to have read that boat stuff…"

"Of course. I said I did."

"Well… Mariko… I gave you the expurgated version."

13

Again, I felt her looking up at me. But, at the same time, I thought that I heard a chainsaw ashore. Then, thinking again, I thought that doubtful after all. French people have never taken to chainsaws. I placed the pulsing buzzing. Finally. It was a powerful boat breasting over waves. A very powerful boat. It was difficult to locate the sound in the fog. Ahead of us? Behind us? But the sound itself began to be quite definite, and I could begin to make out the slaps of a high-speed hull over waves.

The chart of the summit level of the Canal du Midi was folded to the correct section under the plastic sheet near the wheel. A quick glance told me that one of Montrofier's little reservoirs, the Lac des Doigts, *should* be just abaft the beam to starboard. The glance also told me that the narrow entrance to this lake was not only shallow, but obstructed with rocks, and probably, drowned tree stumps.

"After reflection," Mariko began, "I think it better if I simply turn the parchment over to the National Heritage people. That will be better for everyone. I will go back to being a meek little… protégé, and…"

"Please be quiet."

"Just drop me at Carcassonne. I know you mean well, but I will get a train and go back to Moissac for my passport and clothes…And…"

"Shut *up!*"

The chainsaw sound, or the high-powered boat going over waves, was off to port. And, although deep vee wakes make many rebounds from shores as narrow as this canal, I suspected that the still-distant high-powered boat was surfing over *Lorelei's* wakes and rebounds, and was coming up astern, off to port out further in the channel, and hidden from me by the fog.

What idiot would surf a motorboat over waves *in the fog?*

Of course, there *are* such idiots everywhere. But then I heard, or thought I heard, the angry buzzing of the boat's engine relax ever so slightly. It flashed through my mind that the boat, having located the moving source of a wake, was stalking along a bow or quarter wave, more slowly now, but still at a fair clip. Very suddenly, I knew that I didn't want this boat to see us. And it was converging on *Lorelei*.

Mariko was so shocked by my vehemence and my rudeness that she only now began to react. She started to stand up. I pressed my free hand to her thigh with enough force to sit her down again. I felt the resistance in her muscles. *"Listen,"* I hissed. I felt the resistance decrease and felt her relapse into a hunch so that I removed by hand.

I remember doing several things simultaneously. I killed the steam flow to the pistons, and pulled back on the lever that opened and closed the impeller's ducts so that thrust astern was directed forward. Then, I fed a little more steam to the pistons, gently, and looked aloft. *Jester* glided to a gentle halt and then began to move astern. I spun the wheel.

Mist closed over us and *Lorelei's* full shape receded into the fog ahead. It seemed to me, looking up, that I could discern the top of the fog. Was a little light percolating down? When the sun topped the Pyrenees to the south, I thought the fog would burn off pretty quickly.

A quick glance at my Seiko: seven-thirty. Another glance up at the smokestack showed a dirty smudge of smoke mixing with the upper levels of the mist. Coal oil doesn't burn cleanly. Was there enough smoke to betray our position? I doubted our smoke could be seen from a speedboat, which would be in the lower and thicker layer of fog closer to the water's surface... *but what about aerial surveillance?* – and the thought just stabbed me from nowhere: How far could I rely on Mariko?

I bent down to Mariko's ear. It was small, dainty and elfin. Scantily fuzzed and golden, like a peach slice. A peach slice enmeshed in a quivering web of dark tendrils. I whispered deliberately: "Mariko, did you read that boat stuff carefully enough to remember how to switch from oil to Calor gas?" I used the European name for propane, although both terms were used in the sheaf of paper I'd given her.

Her eyes widened in alarm, since I had also grasped her arm. But she shifted her gaze to some inner or remembered focus. When she looked at me again, she nodded. "I think so," she whispered back.

"Then do it. Don't slam any metal doors." I smiled, she nodded. She ducked from beside me and I saw her scrabbling backwards down the hatch. I looked up at the stack. Presently the dark smoke ceased drifting from it. I glanced down at one of the dials under the plastic cover atop the wheelhouse. The needle soon jumped from zero to 150 psi. So much for the main valve. Would Mariko remember, though, to crack the secondary feed valve just barely, and light the propane jet with the butane wand clipped to the bulkhead, before turning up the secondary feed? If she forgot, or failed to think it through even if she'd forgotten... well, there would be difficulties...

Since I couldn't do anything useful but rely on Mariko's considerable intelligence, I consulted the chart carefully. The entrance to the little lake should be directly abeam to starboard, now, or maybe a few tens of meters astern if my running mental fixes had been sloppy. Reversing slowly as we were, I turned the wheel a little to port and watched *Jester's* bow arc slowly to starboard.

The mist-muted burst of automatic fire came a split second before the flash, and the flash came an instant before the roar. Instinct gave me just time to grab the top of the wheelhouse, because the blast came with the roar. Reflex, once honed by training but now rusty, was bending me down behind the wheelhouse when the world turned hot and orange.

Heat seared my exposed hand on top of the wheelhouse, just as I saw the pane of protective Lucite warp and curl away from its hinges to fly past my face. I noted, intrigued, that the folded chart of the canal beneath the Lucite stayed neatly in its place for a fraction of a second before it was whirled upward, unfolding as it went, and burst into flame just over my head. Part of the blue tarpaulin bulged up, a huge balloon-tumour swelling from *Jester's* deck and I saw, in incongruous slow motion, the plastic fibre-weave stretching away from brass grommets and simultaneously wrinkling in melt from the heat.

Oh, God, I thought, it's going to fold back and engulf me in hot shrink-wrap. But no. Some of the ropes held. Only a sheet-sized piece of tarp flapped up and away, clearing the wheelhouse with just one brief snag when the writhing plastic flame fluttered in my face and I could smell the sweet sickness of melting polymers. Then, the blast was over.

But I knew that more was to follow.

I stood up and made for the hatchway. *Try to get below.* But Mariko had pre-empted my move. Her head was coming upward, just as I wanted to scrabble downward. There was nothing to do but clamp my hand on top of her head and push her back down. Her face swivelled up, wide-eyed and panicked. "But I did it right!" she screamed, before I shoved her down and slid the hatch cover closed. I snicked the latch. She pounded on the hatch. "Don't! Please! I did it right!" She shrieked it out: "I did it right!" But her screams were muffled now.

Off the port bow, flames roiled upward in a glowing globe of eye-burning light and heat. As I glimpsed this with hand-shielded eyes, it began to take on a mushroom shape. For one stunned instant, it flashed through my mind that it was a nuclear explosion of some sort, and then I snapped back to the remembrance that any explosion of intense heat took on the same form.

What I feared, and why I wanted to get below, was the inevitable rain of debris. Bits and pieces carried up by the explosion would begin to come down again. As I couldn't go below, I knelt behind the wheelhouse and snuggled up to it. I reached for the wheel with a hand devoid of hair, but with bright red skin, and not much evidence of other damage.

Jester's bow had swung through about ninety degrees. We were pointed toward the Pyrenees, toward the south, and hopefully pointed toward the entrance to the lake. I slammed *Jester* into forward and felt her shudder gently to a stop, then begin creeping forward in the mist. I fed just a little more steam to the pistons. I looked up at the stack. Yes, she had done it right. No smoke at all came from the clean-burning propane, just a ripple of heated air.

Then things started to fall, and some were heavy judging from the splashes. But, reasonably, I considered it highly unlikely that I would be hit by anything. My person constituted a very small target in a very great area of potential fallout. And, as events transpired, not even *Jester* received a direct hit from anything, although there were some loud splashes close aboard, and not a few hollow-sounding thunks. I worried about these thunks more than the splashes because they bespoke something very heavy, but without much surface area or volume, falling at a great speed. Metal bits and pieces. They could punch a hole in the bottom of a hull... or in the top of a skull.

The southern bank of the canal loomed suddenly out of the fog, and I scanned it with eager eyes. There seemed to be a stretch of bank where the fog refused to clear, just off the starboard bow almost dead ahead. I took this to be the entrance to the lake. I felt toward it with a light hand on the wheel and throttled back. *Jester* lost way until we were running dead slow. I was thankful that neither *Jester's* steam engine nor the impeller drive made any sound at all, for I now heard the buzzing of the motorboat again. There was no pulsation to the sound, now, because there were no large waves to surmount. I glanced back at *Jester's* wake. Her smooth central hull left but a flattened swath of subdued water at this speed, while the knife-sharp outriggers left only lazy, soft swirls like languorous curls off a canoe paddle.

I approached the section of fog along the bank with bare steerage way. I scrambled up, unlatched and opened the hatch, and reached down to turn on the Eagle 5000 sonar. Mariko was huddled on the floor, sobbing. She looked up when I opened the hatch, but she didn't move and said nothing. Red, wet eyes stared at me.

"Stay put, girl," I said gently. Then, remembering, I smiled. "Yes, Mariko, you did it right."

By standing behind the wheelhouse, and not cringing in its lee, I could both grasp the wheel and look through the hatchway to view various displays. Radar and sonar screens dominated, but the radar screens were dead since the masts had been lowered to negotiate the old stone bridges along the canal. By standing thus, I could also reach all the necessary knobs and levers. Some of these were within the wheelhouse, but some were extension units fixed to the outside of it. I preferred to steer from deck, but could operate *Jester* from within the weather-proof wheelhouse if necessary. Indeed, this dual steerage capability without duplication of the more expensive and delicate equipment, was more evidence of my cleverness...

Stupidly, my mind was congratulating myself on this, and being alive. So clever. And I was watching the still-bright mushroom of fire whorling and convoluting itself high into the atmosphere, and also watching the Eagle 5000's illuminated screen telling me about steadily shallower water as we approached the lake entrance. Something large splashed wetly very close aboard. It was more of a big flap than a splash, like a big hooked fish cascading water.

Then I remembered that there had been many instances of people surviving blasts even though they had been blown fifty or a hundred yards. Since we were hardly moving anyway, I looked and saw a floppy-looking object in the middle of a widening circle of lazy ripples, but wisps of mist still obscured the surface. Nonetheless, it looked like a broad back covered by a Tee shirt.

I scrambled out onto the port outrigger deck and reached down to grasp the white and red thing as we drifted by it. It looked like cloth, but it was surprisingly heavy. I gave it a jerk to yank it from the water. It came up, roiling around erratically until the thick and hairy section of headless torso slipped out of the cloth and disappeared into the depths. But I still pulled at it and saw a section of arm slide out of a sleeve like something difficult being excreted from a distended anus. Before the arm plopped into the water and spiralled into the depths, I saw that it had no hand, and had been wrenched off raggedly at the shoulder.

I would have dropped the white rag except that my muscles had seized up when my brain registered that it was, indeed, a torso and arm that had slipped out and away. I backed away, and stood up slowly, holding a wet and slimy mass in my cramped hand like the ruin of a rabbit in the talons of a hawk. I resisted the temptation to fling it off and scream. Instead, I forced myself to unclutch my hand and use the other to spread out the cloth, for by now I had truly recognised it as being part of a Tee shirt.

In a muted yellow, obviously trying to pass for gold, was the coy form of a naked lady perched side-saddle on a rock. She might have reminded me of Copenhagen's famous mermaid if she'd been much less teutonically endowed and if these had not been aggressively thrust toward the viewer in unlikely shapeliness, given their size. Beneath her long webbed toes, about where her rock had its waterline, Germanic characters spelled out *Lorelei*. Beneath that, but in businesslike Latin letters: "Aachen, Deutschland." The cloth had been white, but was now mottled scarlet. I bent down and rinsed it in the water as thoroughly as time permitted, but this was mere seconds. The blood was acceptable under the circumstances, but I didn't want Mariko to see the smears of hair-covered flesh that had been mashed into the cotton weave.

14

The mind does curious things under stress.

I remember thinking about the French and how they had always been an innovative people. Indeed, if they are asked, they will modestly inform you that they invented *all* of the important things of Western Civilisation. And if they're not asked.

But not even the most dedicated Francophobe can deny that one area for the exercise of boundless French ingenuity in contributing to Western culture is, and has been, contriving numerous and unlikely ways of catching fish.

On the smaller rivers of Languedoc and Provence there are large and curious wooden pylons, made of neatly trimmed and de-barked upright logs, constructed opposite each other on either bank. These pylons can easily be twenty to thirty feet high. If a recreational boater is lucky and observant, he will see the cables and ropes, rigged in a complex web, slanting down into the river before he runs afoul of them. If he does become ensnared, he will curse himself as he tries to free his craft from the confusion of ropes and will be fluently abused with rich French invective from both banks of the river at the same time.

Enmeshed or not, if he is curious, our hypothetical recreational boater will sooner or later enquire what this large and complex contraption is. Are the pylons intended for power or telephone lines being strung across the river with the ropes and tackle? No. Are the pylons a railway trestle in process of construction, or a local road bridge being built? Again, no.

Sooner or later he will learn that the pylons and ropes allow a large, square net to be hauled up from the bottom of the river, where most of the time it lays flat and spread out on the river bed. The net is raised whenever one of the fishermen on shore has reason to believe that a fish may be swimming above the net. This reason may be wrong. Or, as frequently happens, the reasoning was correct, but the fish swam elsewhere before the cumbersome net could be raised.

One naturally supposes that such a large net, and such elaborate apparatus for raising it, would be intended for large victims – such as the now nearly mythical Garonne *esturgeon*. But again, *non*. I have seen many such nets raised enthusiastically for the capture of a three-pound shad, and have seen many three-pound shad escape their fate. One wonders why the original elaborate and difficult construction of the pylons, the allocation of hundreds of metres of rope and tackle, and the ongoing maintenance of the contrivance can ever have been considered worth it. One wonders if these fishermen have families to support with their activities. One feels a certain pity, if so.

Or, again. When Frenchmen reached Indochina in the 18th century, anglers among them became intrigued with the Oriental art of kite fishing. Now, Southeast Asians had developed this technique for fishing well offshore, in the sea, when a high surf was running and fishing boats could not live in the waves. Centuries of Oriental observation had revealed the fact that at times of high surf, during storms at certain phases of the moon, normally pelagic fish came inshore to feed on smaller fry that were swept onshore in huge and helpless congregations by the waves. Big tuna, giant wrass, pompano, barracuda and sharks all indulged in a feeding frenzy just outside the surf line where the breakers gathered themselves to curl ashore.

Since boats could not be launched to catch these big fish, someone thought of flying kites out above the breakers with baited lines dangling and skipping on the frothing surf like small fish trying to escape by leaping. This method of fishing proved productive. The big fish were there, their size brought the kites into splashdown when they hit the bait, but the kites were cheap and expendable.

Frenchmen brought this technique back to France, particularly southern France, for use on the Garonne and Aude rivers, where the idea was, and remains, to place a fishing line further out in the current. It is easy to imagine the time and dexterity needed to change bait. It is hard to see how the fisherman can possibly know if he gets a bite – for fishermen here are not dealing with the large and voracious sharks and tunas of the South China Sea. It is difficult to see how a fish, if one is ever caught, could possibly be landed by this method. But that may be the answer, in a way. After watching for hours, I've never seen anything caught by kite-fishing in southern France.

My own favourite French fishing innovation is the *birol*. It is a rectangular frame covered with netting. A shaft is attached across the middle of the rectangle so that it can revolve around this central shaft-axis. Think of a two-bladed paddle-wheel covered with net, and you'll get the idea. Okay. The theory of a *birol* is that it is attached across the middle of a rather flat boat. As the boat moves through the water, the *birol* revolves – just like a paddle-wheel – and any fish within its reach are scooped up by this rotary action. The fisherman, secure aboard his flat-hulled craft, can simply reach into the *birol* net as it emerges from the water and conveniently remove any flapping fish that the net has collected.

A century ago, during the later 1800s and early 1900s, *birols* became very popular and equally refined. First, flat-hulled scows were made to have one or more *birols* on both sides. Then, as the second last century closed, the scows were often fitted with dubious steam engines of local design and fabrication. Then, in the early 20th century, *two* such steam engines were often fitted to the basic fishing craft: one to propel the scow itself, and one to rotate the flanking *birol(s)* by a fearsome system of chains and gears cannibalised from the newly and uproariously popular bicycle.

I've always been fascinated with *birols*. One intuits, rather than reasons, that they must have been efficient at their basic job of catching fish, otherwise why so much time, ingenuity and money devoted to their refinement and fabrication? *Birols* – and by now the word has been applied to the class of fishing vessels carrying these nets, and not just to the revolving nets themselves – still exist on the Garonne River, the Aude River. And on the Canal du Midi which links them, and which links the Atlantic coast of France with the Mediterranean coast.

Nonetheless, although I have seen *birols* in action along these waterways, I confess that I've never seen a fish of any species ever caught by one.

I'm not the only person to have been fascinated by the mystery of the *birol*. Pierre Vital, in his obscure and locally published book, *Requiem pour une Garonne Défunte*, illustrates his work with several turn-of-the-last-century sepia post-card photos of quite elaborate *birols* then operating on the Gironde, Garonne, Canal du Midi and the Aude. Vital, too, had been fascinated by the crazy nature of the whole *birol* concept. He tried to find photographs of exceptional catches of fish harvested by these unlikely vessels, but he failed.

And he also failed, I think, to state his own suspicion... and mine. That *birols*, per se, were never meant to catch fish. They existed as a sort of Gallic version of a Sufi parable. A lesson that the *process* is more important than the *result*; that the *journey* more important than the *destination*, and so on. Zen and the art of angling.

In short, the awful and brutal insight intruded into one's consciousness that *birols* exist(ed) only to ignite the terrifying suspicion that existential philosophers might be right. Perhaps post-war, both I and II, ennui did glimpse the terrible truth that life has no especial and absolute *purpose*. After years of shrugging at Sartre, not to mention Heidegger, well, the existence of *birols* kinda shook my cynicism toward existentialism. Birols seemed to *be* existence without purpose. And how can that be? I could live without God in life, perhaps, as both Jean Paul Sartre and Martin Heidegger have told us that we must, but could I live without purpose?

Naturally, I didn't allow these aspects of French fishing to affect my actions at the time. Nor was that final existential cry of anguish and despair truly born in, and torn from, my brain and being as *Jester* thumped her way into Lac des Doigts. These thoughts and associations just flitted around my consciousness, a mental defence against *Lorelei's* apparently purposeless fate, as I aimed the boat into that stretch of denser fog that I took to be the entrance. I was much too busy looking at the sonar's illuminated LCD screen, which showed the warning flash of three *feet-feet-feet* of water beneath us.

The Eagle 5000 had been born in a Silicon Valley factory, and was consequently ignorant of meters. It knew fathoms, but went into that scary flashing mode of *feet-feet-feet* when its panicked transducer ran out of them.

Aside from the generalized lack of water at the entrance of the lake, the transducer heard of solid objects much closer to the surface. Now, some of these had indeed been marked on the chart. Rocks. But, of course, the chart had recently flapped to fiery freedom in the blast, exploding past my head like a distressed pigeon with highly combustible flatulence, or like an exuberant phoenix in the throes of rebirth. Whatever the nature of its intestinal or existential anguish, well, it was no use to me.

But some of these objects had not been noted on the chart, and so I suspected that they were deadheads. This term did not refer to persons devoid of philosophical speculations, but to dead trees and logs, nearly in a completely waterlogged state, the drier end of which could still float and seek the surface. This is a North American term, and a frequent one on waterways used for floating timber down to pulp mills. On British Columbia coasts and rivers, logs four and five feet in diameter float vertically with the cut end just breaking the surface. They drift slowly, their mass is several tons, and they can make a mess out of the family cruiser that encounters them. I had read about the B.C. deadheads.

Here, I didn't expect to encounter deadheads anywhere near as large as those off the B.C. coast. Still, a drowned Pyrenees pine could, perhaps, dent *Jester's* steel skin.

So, in spite of the urgency that was crushing my stomach with blunt fingers, I went softly through the foggy entrance. My chief anxiety was the possibility of getting *Jester* aground on rocks, or on a bunch of logs, so firmly that she'd still be stuck when the fog lifted.

The transducer was mounted in the exact centre of the middle hull's bottom, and its 20-degree cone of search was directed somewhat forward and not directly downward. I had some warning of solid objects ahead, and had three hulls and two spaces with which to avoid them. So, we got through, but not without some worrying and reverberating booms from the main hull. And not without each outrigger being canted up, with the barest squeaks of protest from sheet aluminum and steel tubes, at one point or another in the heart-thumping fifty meters.

I had enough power in *Jester's* steam engine, and no prop to foul, so that I could have powered over anything but a solid grounding. This would have reduced the sounds and time of anguish, but only at the cost of creating a very large wake – and I had good reasons, I was starting to suspect, for avoiding the creation of a large wake. Especially one that would traverse the entire canal in a straight line pointing directly back to its source.

I could still hear the buzzing boat, though much more distantly now, as it quested the lockless summit level. And I could still hear that burst of automatic gunfire in my head. The roar and flame of *Lorelei's* demise had not diminished all that much in my memory, either.

Once into the Lac des Doigts, the water deepened reassuringly and there were immediately fewer obstructions to scare the transducer. It stopped flashing *feet-feet-feet* at me. At least, mostly. The entrance obstructions, including the silt which had collected the deadheads, were not caused by any current in the normal scheme of things. No stream or river fed the lake to empty its overflow into the Canal du Midi. It was all the work of seasonal rainfall. This ran down the Pyrenees slopes around the lake and created a seasonal drift toward the only exit into the canal. I had encountered the mess caused by the rain of last winter and this spring. I figured that the body of the lake, including its fingers running far up into flooded ravines, might be relatively open water and, very possibly, surprisingly deep in places where Montrofier's little reservoir had flooded a canyon.

Being right-handed, my natural instinct, once within the lake, was to bear to starboard and head for the little finger of this Pyrenees lake which, palm up, was spreading a left hand to God. Of course, God had not existed since Martin Heidegger said so after World War I, an opinion confirmed by Jean Paul Sartre, his pupil, after World War II. So, on impulse, I decided to bear to port, to the left, and seek for the thumb of this lake, which was surprisingly faithful to anatomy, according to the departed, but not forgotten, chart.

Glancing aloft, I saw that the mist was definitely less dense not many feet above *Jester,* although fog steamed off the water's surface as thickly as ever. For some reason, the thought of having nothing over us bothered me considerably.

I worked my way through the narrow, but very deep, bend of a crooked thumb and came out into more open water. As far as I could tell in the mist, the slightly oblong and spatulate pad of a rather generous thumb. Its gently rounded extremity lapped on the sandy shore of a bowl-shaped dell. This little valley gradually became both steeper and more elongated as it became a ravine rising toward the tree-line. I didn't see this at the time, of course, because of the surface mist on the water, but the local topography explained the *birol* that was rather insecurely tethered to *maquis* on the curving little beach. As soon as I saw the vessel and its *birol* nets laid out ashore, I knew that this particular *birol*, at least, had a purpose. Could I safely disregard Heidegger and Sartre?

I disengaged the engine from the impeller. *Jester* lost way rapidly and her bow nudged onto the sandy beach with a comfortable little crunch not far from the somnolent *birol*. I valved back the propane, or Calor, just enough to keep *Jester's* boiler on simmer and the engine turning over. Without pausing to give succour to Mariko for the moment, I scrabbled the length of the boat and hopped over the bows onto firm, damp sand. Not forgetting seamanship completely, I reached back to grab a coil of mooring line and, unwinding it as I went, I scuffed up the beach to where the gnarled pines formed a ragged rank of vegetative assertion. I threw a quick half hitch around the largest and most gnarled trunk I could locate with a quick look.

Then, it was back to the partly beached *birol*.

When the rather ramshackle cabin door opened to my impatient knocking, the *birol,* after exactly six minutes of parley in their fluent but strangely quaint French, and my modern but terrible French, proved to be owned and crewed by one old man and another exceedingly ancient one. François, *père*. Roland, *fils*. My negotiations, after literally moments of conversational exploration, focussed on the *fils*. Roland's speech was less quaint. Also, he could still hear... at least, better than his father. They offered me a bite of their breakfast, in progress: *vin rouge*, most of a crusty *baguette,* and three delicious-looking bream that had been nailed to a rough and resinous pine plank and were grilling in front of the open iron door of their old wood stove. The fillets glistened with hot oil, garlic and onions. The pine-scented fish smelled heavenly, but the memory of *Lorelei's* Tee-shirt was too recent to permit indulgence.

Part of the negotiations involved my guarantee that they would have *vin rouge* for weeks to come. This provoked nodding all around and even a tooth-scanty grin when François peered determinedly through a hazy window to see for himself the comfortable, rounded shapes under what was left of the tarp. I returned, followed by much good will, to *Jester*.

15

Clambering back over *Jester's* bow and onto the fore deck, I glanced up and beheld a pathetic tableau. While I'd been aboard the *birol*, Mariko had obviously recovered sufficiently to hunch and roll herself up off the wheelhouse floor and to haul herself up the companionway steps. She had climbed out onto the poop deck. I caught the last of this motion, and her slow bending toward the rag of Tee-shirt. I had not wanted her to see it this way, without me to somehow soften the impact, but I wasn't in the best shape myself. I found that my throat had tightened up so that I couldn't even call out to her, as a distraction, until I could reach her.

And I couldn't reach her because my knees seemed both shaky and locked at the same time. I could only watch as she retrieved the bloody rag, looked intently at it, and then, still clutching it but letting it fall in a limp hand to her hip, walked stiffly to the rail. I saw her chest heave, and then she literally spewed whatever she'd had for breakfast about three feet. Dropping *Lorelei's* memorabilia to the deck, both hands grabbed at her stomach as if to hold it inside of her by main force, but she spurted lumps and liquid again. But not so far.

By that time, I was moving and stripping off my flannel shirt. Before leaping over the confusion of casks onto the higher level of the poop deck, I paused to bend over *Jester's* side while I was still on the lower level of the forward hull. Nonetheless, it was two feet down to the water so I had to bend over the side to soak the flannel thoroughly. I heard, but couldn't witness, Mariko's third voiding. It worried me because it ended on a high-pitched gurgle that would become a hysterical scream when she could get enough breath for it through the wet, burning bile in her throat. She was wheezing and choking up to it.

Not bothering to wring the dripping shirt, I scrambled over those damned barrels. They were slippery with moisture, of course, but also now even more treacherous with a coating of melted plastic. This had no strength, and it sloughed off both the wood surface of the casks and also off the soles of my Nikes when I tried to get traction. At last I got to Mariko at the poop rail and cradled her head... and tried to wash the sickness from her face. Tried. But she whirled toward me and buried her fingers in my chest. Her nails were sharp, and she was past caring about anything but something to grasp. Hard. Her eyes fluttered open and stared up, wide and mostly white.

"Why?" It was a soft and distant whisper that contrasted curiously with the here, now and forever desperation of her fingers in my chest. "*Why?*" This was louder. The next one would be a scream.

So, ignoring the pain in my chest, since I knew she wouldn't relax her grip for anything in the world just now, I wrapped my arms around hers somewhat awkwardly and continued stroking the mess off her face with the wet shirt. I used the opportunity to upturn her face, and gently keep her mouth from opening, so that she would have to breathe through her nose. And so she couldn't scream. Her eyes closed, too, and this was good. I stroked her eyelids with a piece of the wet flannel, and I noticed then that blisters had begun to bubble up on my right hand.

Her eyes opened again. Her cheeks glistened with wet runnels, whether from the wet cloth or her own tears I couldn't tell. Probably both. She focussed on me, still distant and puzzled, though. "Why?" It was strong, but wondering.

"I don't know, Mariko."

"No... ?" she questioned, like a puzzled child.

"Well..." I hesitated, "... I do have a hateful thought."

She looked down, then, and stared at her fingers clinched in my flesh. But she didn't know them for her own for a moment or two. Slowly, she unclenched them. She closed her eyes again, as if denying the deep scratches that her own fingernails had made.

"I'm sorry... " she mumbled; her arms dropped limply to her side.

I took the opportunity to clasp her firmly to me, since she was shaking, while I finished sponging off her face and front of her jersey.

"Why... then?"

"Not now. We have to work fast." I tipped her chin up with a gently knuckled fore-finger. Her eyes were steady. "Do you trust me, Mariko?"

She hesitated, but she nodded tentatively after a long second.

"Good. We have to work now. I need your help. Talk later, okay?"

She nodded a bit more briskly, and I stood away from her, draping the shirt over the rail. "Right, then. Down in the cabin, in the clothes closet, there's a pair of khaki pants, you know, Mariko ...army type pants with green and olive splotches...?" I looked at her and she nodded again. She was in such shock, though, that her face held no expression at all. "Please go get them for me. Come back as fast as you can." I wanted to keep her busy. "Okay?" She bobbed a nod and went to scrabble back down the hatch.

Jester carries four masts. They are basically identical. They're circular tapered tubes, many layers of rolled-up glass cloth thoroughly impregnated with slow-curing epoxy resin. For their size, they are not heavy. They are very, very strong. These masts fit down and into steel tubes of the appropriate diameter. The masts are light enough to lift and set into their tube steps if there is little or no wind, and it helps if there is another person stabilising things by using the halyards and stays to guy the masts as they are lifted up. I would have to do the lifting. I would put Mariko on the lines.

I had always generally kept these masts lowered in order to pass under some of the medieval bridges of the canal. But now I needed them. The actual masts were all identical, but the mizzens, at the extreme aft end of Jester's squarish stern, were higher than the mains because of the higher hull at the rear and also because of the addition of Decca radar fittings to their tops. These two radars were also identical, but the fittings were different heights so that the beams from the two radars could not interfere with each other. My Deccas were good for about ten miles, not top of the line, but adequate for most purposes.

Decca radars are protected by streamlined oblong plastic and steel weatherproof covers about the size and shape of a florist box intended for a dozen long-stemmed roses. These boxes revolve by motors built into the masthead fitting. The motors are powered by the boat's electrical system. Before we set up the mizzens, I cut the legs off the camouflage pants that Mariko had fetched for me. Using tarred marline, I wrapped one pant leg around each radar cover, being careful not to leave any loose cloth that could get caught in the rotating mechanism. It took us ten minutes after I had wrapped the antennas for us to get the mizzens vertical in their tubular steps, and for me to double check that the two radar antennas were revolving freely.

Mariko was not at all interested, although I kept chatting about the whys and wherefores of everything as I worked. She stared into space, and I didn't like that.

Each radar had its separate screen visible from the hatch in the wheelhouse. Mostly, of course, I used radar for getting a handle on weather in the offing, for coastal navigation, and for some warning of other craft in bad visibility. But my radar had also been planned with other uses in mind. Radar blips could be selected and isolated, and their identity fed one of the Toshiba laptops down below. Or, the Toshiba could be brought up to the wheelhouse. Because the masts were eight feet apart, and because the Toshiba knew trigonometry quite well because of its math module, the exact distance to any target could be triangulated to the nearest few feet.

So much for the mizzen masts, the ones at the rear of the boat. I wanted to better our ten minutes with the main masts, the ones closer to the middle of the boat.

For reasons of my own, which will become apparent, the starboard main mast carried a standard, but high-quality, yachting-type digital wind speed indicator. The port main mast carried a standard yachting wind direction indicator. Digital output from these could also fed into the Toshiba. I considered these mast-top digital instruments so small that they need not be wrapped with what remained of my camouflage scraps. So Mariko and I got the main masts up and stayed in just six minutes. We were improving as a team, but she had said not a word.

Things timed out about right because, by the time all four masts were vertical and secure, and their halyards dangling, I saw that François and Roland had already adorned their first rectangular *birol* net with specimens of flora comprising the local *maquis*. Heavy on the stunted pine, a sprinkling of mulberry bushes, a bit of cactus and just a touch of palmetto palm.

I waved to them, and they splashed out to *Jester*. They balanced a corner of the rectangular net frame on *Jester's* forward hull rail until Mariko and I scrambled over to lend a hand. The four of us, after François and Roland swung aboard, clumsied the net lengthwise up onto the poop. There, vegetable side up, we affixed halyards from all four masts and hauled away. Soon, and it was great fun co-ordinating the hauling with my French and Mariko's limited strength, the *birol* net hung level over our heads some fifteen feet above the poop deck. Mariko bent over to shake bits of down-raining pine bark from her Przhevalskytail. Also, a few mulberry leaves. Luckily, no cactus fell out of the net; the prickles on their leaves probably snagged them.

"Vite, vitez-vous," I said. "Un autre."

Roland gave me a blank stare, then a slow grin, a shake of the head. He grabbed François's undershirt where it was not weakened by any large hole, and turned the ancient man from his disconcertingly youthful appraisal of Mariko. They shimmied over *Jester's* side rail like hesitant, slow-motioned, cheating pole vaulters. They slogged ashore where they began working vegetation into the second *birol* net laid out on the sand.

I had made it clear, I hoped, that three *birol* nets were to be prepared in this way, since the nets were about eight feet wide and more than twice as long. *Jester* was fifty feet long with her bow cut-water panels folded back, as they were now. I had rigged the first net to take account of this with some overhang astern. Since the nets were only about fifteen feet above the deck, I hoped no one would be able to peek under them.

By nine o'clock, all three nets were suspended above *Jester*, and there was a little front overhang as well. During this time, though, sounds of sirens, motors and the occasional shout had wafted through the fog to us from the direction of the canal channel or canal banks. I also heard the distant whapping of chopper blades, but only briefly, and then it went away.

I squinted upwards and assessed our work critically. The foremost net angled a little downward toward the bow because its forward end was attached to stays which slanted down from the main masts in the central part of the boat. But, I thought, this probably would not matter much. From the air either no one would be likely to notice, or the irregularity would be taken for natural topography. Land is seldom level. But I had made sure that this forward net had pine boughs of distinctly unequal size and length in order to disguise and confuse matters.

What to do with the outriggers? They were of symmetrical shape. Man made. But for all that, their decks extended only four feet from *Jester's* main hull, and I was very tempted to just disguise them a bit with local *maquis* shoved between Bouchard's barrels on the deck. But then I remembered *Lorelei*, and the fact that I had underestimated the gravity of the situation before. So, I set myself and Mariko to the work of hauling them up using the halyards of opposite-side masts. There were a few strut-support bolts to undo first, and some of these cost some profanity because our encounters with the rocks on entering the lake had sprung some fittings just enough to bind the bolts annoyingly.

Also, of course, before we could pivot an outrigger and its deck up, I had to lift some casks up to Mariko. We made a tidier pile amidships, and I left a narrow corridor bounded by upturned casks along one side.

If the masts had been down, the outriggers could have been pivoted completely inboard so as to be beneath the camouflage nets. Inboard outriggers allowed *Jester* to cope with the narrow English canals since the masts had to be down anyway. English bridges had even less vertical clearance than those on the Canal du Midi. As it was, though, with the masts having to be up in order to suspend the nets, the best we could do was bring the outriggers up snug against the masts and lash them there. I had designed *Jester* to be flexible for many situations, but not this one. The profile of the outrigger floats now being exposed to an aerial view out from under the nets, Mariko and I covered them as well as we could with pine boughs brought by Roland. François had returned to the serious business of repairing the netting on the fourth *birol* laid out on the sand.

By nine thirty I was quite satisfied, and just in time too, because the sun then topped the high Southeast peaks with a sudden flare down onto our little lake as if someone – God? – had turned up a rheostat. The mist had already thinned and lowered considerably while we worked. It would not last long now. I smiled at Roland, and nodded. "Un moment, Roland," I said. I gestured to Mariko and she followed me to the pile of casks, a pile now somewhat higher since the casks on the outrigger deck had been manhandled quickly onto the central hull. I didn't really need Mariko's help to manage these casks, since they were not full-sized barrels, but I wanted to tire her out. We rolled and swivelled three casks over to the rail. Roland's eyes brightened, but he looked up in a question.

He raised a hand with two fingers. I shook my head, smiled, and raised three fingers. Roland brightened considerably then.

Mariko and I rolled the casks up the inner side of the hull and up onto the rail where we balanced them for a moment before shoving them well overboard. They landed with quite a splash, but bobbed to the surface with enough flotation to make little egg-shaped wooden islands. When there were three little wobbling and bobbing islands, Roland herded them toward the *birol* boat like a soccer forward.

Mariko was beaded with perspiration and she looked much better for it. Her complexion was no longer the lime-yellow of an under-ripe grapefruit, but rising toward overheated apricot. The sun, now fully on the job, was putting a glow on her cheeks even as it sucked up the top layer of fog. Mariko smiled, and I grinned back. Up above, jigsaw puzzle pieces of startlingly blue sky showed through the last wisps of mist and even through chinks in the foliage. This turned our eyes toward the north and the canal where a thick column of black smoke could be seen climbing into the blue. This sight made us very serious again. Mariko regarded me levelly, she brushed damp hair from her face.

"Why?" It was said gently enough, but also demanded an answer with a distinct edge from a clear throat. She could not be angry with me, I knew. She was angry at the world. It was an impotent, futile hatred and therefore potentially harmful to her.

"Mariko," I began hesitantly, "... I can't be absolutely certain, you know, but I don't think it was just an accident. I heard gunfire before *Lorelei* blew up."

"But... that barge... wasn't connected with me!" She ended on a high, frantic note and clamped her hands to her head as if to hold it together, to preserve sanity.

I stepped close to her and gently unclamped the hands. She looked at me fearfully. "I know it wasn't connected with you, Honey," I said slowly and softly. I continued against the twitching gaze of terrified eyes. "They... *they*... got a fast boat. Cruised the canal until... until *they* found a barge they were looking for."

"*A* barge...?"

I nodded. "*Any* barge that was... well... right, any barge carrying something volatile. The *Lorelei* was from Aachen, in the Ruhr, carrying chemicals – that's obvious now – and *they* wanted to blow it up."

A look of relief flitted across her face. "Terrorists. A coincidence."

I shook my head. "I don't think so, Mariko..."

"But... *why*?"

I grasped her hunched shoulders and pulled her against my chest. I had to say it, but I didn't have to look her in the eye. "I think... Mariko... just to close the canal for a while... so they can search for you with all canal traffic stopped." I felt her starting to sob, so I went on while I could. "You see…Mariko… with all the canal traffic stopped, and under the confusion of police and emergency and media response, they can maybe find you easier."

"But… *How* can they find me?" she sobbed it out. "I don't *understand…* "

"Helicopter, I think."

She pulled away, and I let her go. Her genuine puzzlement was winning over the incipient hysteria. That was all to the good, I thought. She looked up and around. She looked up again. It seemed as though she was seeing the *birol* nets for the first time, as though she suddenly realized she'd helped put them there with her own effort, as though she suddenly realized my urgency of the past two hours and the thoughts behind it. She brusquely and deftly brushed her hair back – a very good sign with any woman. Her hand came down from her temple to rest on her hip, and was almost immediately copied by her other hand. She glanced up again, squinting at the foliage suspended in the nets. Then her chin dropped and she studied the deck. "*Helicopter!*"

"Well… " I said. "Think about it. There will be police helicopters. Maybe ambulance helicopters… if there are any in this part of France. There will be media helicopters from every major television network in Europe… It… it wouldn't be too difficult to insert just one more chopper into all that air traffic."

She was quick, that one. Her face came up wearing a wry smile. "Do you realize what you're saying?"

"Yes."

"You're crazy," she said, pleasantly enough.

"I sincerely hope so," I answered. I felt drained, and the day had hardly unfolded. And I hurt, not much, but a bit. My right hand burned in a way that I was finding difficult to ignore. My chest burned, too, but not so badly, where Mariko's nails had curled the skin away. "I sincerely hope so," I repeated.

Mariko looked up, then. She searched my face, and then scanned me up and down. She seemed to notice certain things for the first time. Her "Oh… " was just a whisper. Then she said "I see" very distinctly. She turned away, quite callously, I thought at the time. She hesitated for a moment, looking toward the thick smudge of black smoke that now towered over us, before I clearly heard her Adidas soles squeaking down the companionway steps.

I come from a generation modern enough to maintain that a man may weep without losing his masculinity. And to hell with social norms anyway. So, I sat down on the break of the poop and let the wetness trickle down my cheeks. I alternately watched François down on the beach doing an age-old job at his net. His gnarled hands were as strong and natural as any Pyrenees pine. And then I would glance up to witness the spread of the dark cloud that threatened to shadow much of our lives.

Presently, I heard doppler squeaking again. Something warm squeezed next to me and took up my right hand. Simultaneously, something cold and hard touched my chest. Since my right hand was held, my left came up in reflex about the time that my head swivelled away from the cloud and down to Mariko's eyes. They smiled at the same time that my startled left hand closed around the beaded can at my chest. Coors.

I raised the can for a tentative sip on a still-queasy stomach. She raised my right hand slightly and started to pat thick ointment gently over the blisters. She must have found the tube of Solarcaine. "Only the lowest types drink beer before noon," I said.

"Veddy probably."

It was then that we both heard the distant sound of a helicopter. It circled the smoke column like a curious dragonfly. I could see that it was an ancient bubble-Bell two-seater. Obsolete, but nothing better had ever flown for camera work. It was not good for much else, nowadays.

"Dear God," Mariko breathed.

"Relax. That's just media. Real media."

Marc...?"

"Yeah."

"What will we do if you're right? If... others... come...?"

"We can do a few things, Mariko. And we'll do them soon. I promise. After that... "

"What?"

"Well, after we do all we can, Mariko, I want to have a close look at that *birol* there." I gestured toward François, the old boat and the beach. "I think it had a purpose, after all. I think that maybe Heidegger was wrong."

I turned to smile at her, but she didn't even look up. She was busy wrapping gauze around my blistered hand. "All right," she said.

16

It didn't take long for Mariko to bandage my right hand, and also to attend similarly to the scratches on my chest, sponging it clean with a towel that was not only warmly wet, but also far more antiseptic than my flannel shirt had been. She applied Solarcaine. She applied gauze pads loosely and secured them with Elastoplast tape.

During this time, I noted two things. First, I heard other distant aircraft engines converging on our general area like flies buzzing to carrion. Second, for all her kindness, the Coors had been a mistake, so I set it aside three-quarters full and really savoured the sensations of my innards writhing.

When she'd finished with me, Mariko deftly dropped her medicaments into a zippered plastic bag – it must have been in the briefcase, and I presumed it also contained feminine curiosities – and arose briskly. But I placed a restraining, gauzed hand on the denim stretching over her thigh. She sat down again. She zipped the bag.

"Yes...?" She enquired.

"Mariko... as... as a scholar, you want to find out about the parchment. You want to... *recover*... " I couldn't help smiling wryly "... the rest of the manuscript."

She nodded.

"And... as a friend, and as someone who has similar historical interests, well, I would like to help you all I can. But..." I paused, looking at the column and billow of smoke, then glanced at her. I was surprised to see a look of weary resignation on her face. I honestly think she expected me to say *au revoir*, and wish her well, because of the circumstances. Maybe I should have... She waited for it to come. "But," I continued, "as human beings, when it comes to the last extremity, the bottom line, we have but one expectation on us."

I patted her thigh in a brotherly way, and stood up. She arose, too, staring a question up at me.

"And what is that?"

I nodded toward the smoke. "*To take two, just two – one for you and one for me – of* those *bastards with us.*" It came out viciously, and for an instant I feared I had horrified such a refined soul. I watched her eyes alternating between my face and the column of smoke. After a few moments, I added. "Of course, that's only in the last extremity. Ideally, I'd like to take more."

"Is that… possible, Marc?"

"Oh, yes, Mariko O'Shaugnessey." I smiled down at her.

"Even so, it's better if I just go back and turn the parchment over to the Heritage people," she said.

"Go ahead."

"You'll stay here and… and… fight them?"

I nodded. "Yep." I looked down into her puzzled face. "It's not bravado, Mariko… At least I don't think it is… We touched on it before, out in the canal. With people like that on the loose, if I'm right, that is, no one's safety can be guaranteed even if you do return the parchment … and me, I don't want to share the world with people like that. They scare me too much, you see, Mariko O'Shaugnessey. They need exterminating."

"We should go to the police."

"And tell them what, Mariko? Even if they put us in protective custody on the strength of your story, which I doubt, they would just take a statement from us and sooner or later put us out on the street again. Probably sooner. And I can't see us – or my friend – lasting very long."

"But we can't do anything about… them."

"I can. I told you that I gave you the expurgated version."

"Oh." She was silent for a few moments. "But that's illegal… Surely it must be."

"So is shooting at you. And me," I added. "Not to mention blowing up a barge." I jerked my head toward the smoke. "If one can't rely on the police, then one must rely on oneself. If they come for us like I think they will, then I don't have much choice. Neither do you."

"I can go to the police, tell the truth and then everything will be all right."

"Maybe," I conceded, "but I wouldn't like to bet on it. Not with people like that. And do you want to? Do you want to go back to being a little… protégé … a convenience?"

"No," she barely whispered it. "But I am afraid…"

"You've been afraid for ten days. I am afraid too, now, if it is any consolation." I tried to smile.

She gazed up at me. "Longer," she said. "I've been afraid for years."

"So, Mariko O'Shaugnessey, which is worse? Being afraid, or being tired of being afraid."

"You were a soldier. So it is easy for you to think like that."

"Once, Mariko, I did think like that because I was a soldier. But, like you, I've been afraid of the world for a long time now. My question applied to myself just as much as to you."

"If you're willing to stay and fight if necessary… you seem to have answered it."

"I have. But it has taken a long time."

"Why … now?"

"You."

"I don't want to be responsible for that, Marc Rennsalaer."

"And for a… friend. But mostly just for myself." Then I laughed. "But it's not so dramatic, as all that, Mariko. We won't have to fight if they don't come after us as I think they will. I may be wrong, you know. We don't have to do anything… illegal… unless they do it first. If nothing happens, we'll just follow our plan of going on to Glastonbury."

She thought about this. "I do not want to keep feeling afraid. I would prefer to chance finding out what will happen."

"All right, Mariko, but if I turn out to be right, then it will be too late to back out. Too late to go to the police for protection. So, you make up your mind."

She nodded uncertainly and I would not have bet on her decision. What she did surprised me. She put her arms around me and hugged me tightly and briefly. Then she stepped back, and smiled grimly. "I'll stay," she said, "if that is acceptable to you. And, if you are right, we will take at least two with us… if you show me how, that is."

I had reckoned without that awful mixture of Celt and Oriental. Boudicca and the warrior code of Bushido. You know, careening chariots with whirling scythe-blades on the wheels mixed with life falling as gently as a cherry blossom. Dust and blood, blood and petals, and all that. I glanced at her, found her smiling grimly and also gazing with slit eyes at the smoke. She turned to look at me, and her smile thankfully became more softened. Her eyelids lifted, but with modesty. Maybe she wasn't Celt or Oriental, but just a woman weary of being a shadow. She was crying softly, but she nodded briskly. "We'll take at least two, then."

"God can ask no more," I said piously, gazing toward heaven. "Mariko, my ready abandonment out there," I pointed back to the canal, "even so temporary as it was, to Jean Paul and Martin, weighs heavily on my soul. For solace I've cleaved more closely unto Soren Kierkegaard."

She sniffled a laugh through her tears, a gay tinkle of wind-chimes. "I like you, Marc Rennsalaer," she said.

Mariko turned immediately to head below, presumably to return the medicines to their place, but I prevailed on her to remain on the poop for just a few minutes while I myself made a short excursion to the cabin. I watched her as she turned away toward the panorama that the rising mist was revealing. Her shoes squeaked over to the rail, she re-arranged my shirt over it so that it would dry more quickly in the climbing sun.

Ridges rose toward the south, each a little higher than the last, until jagged, snow-capped serres and peaks on the southern horizon threatened the sky like bared teeth.

But, closer to hand, the foothill ridges were more rounded, and often into an abrupt sugar-loaf mountain, or "pog," as the locals called them. These were sometimes high enough to be bare rock on top, but more often were clothed by *maquis* right to the skyline.

Among the palmetto palms, stunted pine, mulberry and small cork-oaks, smaller herbs thrived at ground level. Many of these had become spices and seasonings known to most kitchens of the Western World, for they had originated here and had been spread across Europe wherever Gauls and more modern Frenchmen had gone with their love of cooking. Oregano, sage, mint, parsley and thyme all grew on the slopes of the hills rising above the Lac de Doigts. Also, the small and purple Provençal garlic, with its lively but sweetly distinct taste variation on the general garlic theme, supposedly sometimes grew this far to the west, in the Languedoc and Roussillon.

As the sun topped the Pyrenees, it stirred the morning breeze. This cleared out what was left of the fog and mist very quickly, and also wafted these pungent kitchen smells down onto *Jester*. I left her gazing out over these northern foothills of the Pyrenees and the true mountains well to the south. While Mariko breathed the delicately spiced air at the rail, I disappeared downwards through the wheelhouse hatch.

17

As with so many things about *Jester*, the steps from the wheelhouse down into the cabin were not simply what they appeared to be.

Jester had a two-foot deep keel which ran the entire length of the rear hull. This twenty-five foot rear hull contained the rather cramped accommodations, engine room, wheelhouse and so on. Most keels are narrow but there's no law that says they have to be. So long as the front edge is reasonably sharp and streamlined so that the keel cuts into the water beneath the boat, well, it can gradually widen out.

An eccentric naval architect named Philip C. Bolger in his book *30 Odd Boats*, featured several craft in which special problems or requirements gave him the idea of widening a keel sufficiently for it to become a long narrow floor. The hull could then remain relatively low and still provide standing headroom along a central corridor.

I had stolen this concept for *Jester* – once I had discovered in Germany that Bolger had stolen it from the Indonesians. As I have explained, *Folderol Jester* was a type of vessel called an *orembai* in ancient Java, Sumatra, Borneo and the Philippines. It was a deliberate hybrid created to have much of the cargo capacity of a Chinese junk and most of the speed of a Polynesian multihull. I'd seen my first *orembai* in Brunei, a part of Borneo, and others around Timor. They had been one of my few pleasant memories of these islands.

Just as American servicemen in the Pacific during World War II had seen Polynesian catamarans and trimarans and had brought the so-called multihull revolution to the Western World's yachting, so Marc Rennsalaer had seen *orembais* in a putative part of Indonesia. The difference was that no revolution in Western yachting had so far taken place. *Jester*, so far as I knew, was the only example of the breed outside of the Sulu and Arafura Seas.

In trying to express the traditional *orembai* in modern materials, I had discovered that the key factor of the *orembai's* versatility had been this wide keel. It served both as a floor for central headroom and also for flotation to get the larger central hull up out of the water and barely floating upon it. Lightly loaded, an *orembai* was a trimaran. Heavily loaded, it became a Chinese junk. Ancient Indonesians had pioneered the wide keel long before Bolger did. My only original contribution was to contrive a folding *orembai* by taking advantage of the strength of modern materials and welding.

For me, this wide keel provided yet another convenience – but no doubt some wily Sulu Sea skipper had discovered the same thing centuries ago.

The keel extended the entire length of the rear hull, half the total length of *Jester*. All along this length it provided flotation, but only from the sleeping cabin aft did it provide a floor and standing headroom. Forward of the cabin, and to the front end of the rear hull, the keel extended under the wheelhouse floor. And, in this part of the boat, the raised wheelhouse provided the headroom. The keel, therefore, extended a few feet forward with no functions except providing flotation and lateral resistance – and to form a roomy secret compartment.

Access to this compartment was provided by the steps down into the cabin. The steps were hinged and could be lifted up. These cabin steps had been made in the style of the rest of the tiny cabin, mahogany-and-brass with burgundy carpet. My little parody of the yachty saloon. The steps were mahogany veneer over exceedingly strong triple-pass welded steel plate of the keel itself. The mahogany of the steps was carpeted with a centre strip of plush burgundy.

A discreet slit where the carpet rounded under the second step's overhang was closed by velcro tabs. Uncrackle the velcro, widen the soft, plush burgundy aperture and the knowledgeable would see the gleam of a lock's small disc recessed in a hole through the veneer down into solid steel. If one had a key to fit the lock, the solid-seeming steps would lift, as a lid, and any treasure within would be revealed in the secret compartment.

The compartment was roomy at two feet high and wide and about four feet in length. It was smooth, hard steel, welded to absolute waterproof like the rest of the hull, sprayed with molten zinc during manufacture, and cosmetically covered inside with white epoxy resin. Given its essentially cavern-like character, I had fitted a small ceiling light, which would reflect adequately off the white inner surface.

Entering my cache had once given me much sensual pleasure. The modesty of the entire disguise made me smug. The peeking under the step edges to find the slight irregularity in the plush, denoting the slit, had seemed naughty. The rip of velcro recalled to mind the insubstantial nature of small, delicate panties. The widening of the burgundy plush slit forcefully reminded me of intimate places where girl parts, under certain conditions, are apt to be rosy and swollen. The penetration of the lock was a thrill. The revelation of treasure within somehow seemed, well, symbolic.

My valuables did not completely fill this compartment, and its light subdued off into shadows. Yes, these more obscure and less accessible further reaches of my cache flung the challenge, gauntlet-like, at my male psyche: after the superficial pleasures, could female depths truly be plumbed? What dark and primal things might lurk in the shadowed void...? When I had completed my boat's safe, long after the workmen had completed *Jester's* basic fabrication, I felt well satisfied. My secret compartment provided me with both superficial titillation and Freudian miasma whenever I delved into it. And who could ask for more?

But, nonetheless, my pleasure in my secret safe had slowly diminished. There was anguish wondering whether this bespoke an increasingly age-blah id. This self doubt was not much mitigated by my reading of Sartre and Heidegger during my time on the Canal du Midi. But it had dawned on me in Narbonne one day, after reading financial statements from my London agent, that my pleasure had transmuted into mild trepidation because of my steadily dwindling bank balances. Shrinking of funds is, in some ways, an incipiently inhibited id. So, we had relocated to Moissac and I'd gone seriously to work along the canal.

I thought it likely that urgency and the fear of death might also depress an id, so I wasn't particularly surprised when I felt but the smallest glimmer of lechery when I peeked beneath the steps, ripped the Velcro asunder and parted the plush.

My diminishing treasure was finally exposed, but at least it was my own and no one knew about this treasure but me. Not even Joëlle knew about my secret cache, although she probably suspected one. She had never enquired, of course.

I thought that it would be a good idea, the way things seemed to be going, to check my store of emergency funds, in spite of the possibly id-flattening potential of this exercise. Aside from my account in the Bank of Perceval's Well, which now had a very comfortable balance, I had some hidden sheafs of German Marks, American Dollars, French Francs, Swiss Francs and British Pounds. The sheafs might be thin, but the denominations comprising them were large. I also had a small collection of Krugerrands, and fifteen one-ounce wafers of Canadian gold.

I counted all this, computing the value of the Krugerrands and wafers according to the latest gold price I had happened to notice, which was at least two weeks ago. I decided that with all the resources at my disposal, including two pristine credit cards, there was still enough for most contingencies I might encounter. Gold had skyrocketed in value since the onset of the oil crisis, while most Western currencies had become softer. I tucked the sheaf of French Francs into my pocket against the probability of more or less immediate need.

I found and grasped my Walther PPK and a couple of 9mm clips for it. I didn't bother with the Braun silencer. Stretching my arm somewhat further in, I reached the handle-sight of the AR-15. I took two of the five banana clips for it. This was the genuine, old, unadorned and unimproved AR-15 designed by Eugene Stoner back in the late 1950s. For my money, it remains the best assault rifle ever made, a design which was not enhanced at all by various fancy modifications that various armies had grafted onto it.

Stoner, a combat U.S. Marine before turning gun designer for the Armalite company – hence the original AR designation – knew three things about military rifles and riflemen. First, although military so-called experts had always valued relatively large calibre weapons that could hit and kill men at a range of a mile or more, Stoner knew from combat experience that most real-life engagements took place at ranges of 400 yards or less. Second, again from his own experience, Stoner knew that riflemen liked to have plenty of ammunition and yet the heavy traditional military calibres meant that a soldier could only carry a limited number of rounds into battle. Third, the sheer weight of the heavy rifles and the heavy ammunition contributed to rapid fatigue, perhaps the most important factor affecting combat efficiency and combat casualties.

Working for Armalite, and given a free hand, Eugene Stoner single-handedly revolutionised the military rifle. First, he had created a new cartridge for an old and venerable calibre – the familiar .22 or 5.56mm. But Stoner's cartridge wasn't for plinking at cans or zapping rats. With a heavier projectile and a relatively large and dramatically-necked case, Stoner's '22' had a muzzle velocity of 990 meters per second, 3250 feet per second. At this terrific speed, the 55-grain bullet possessed enormous striking power.

At 450 yards, it was hideously lethal because a hit on a forearm, for instance, could tear a man's entire arm away from his shoulder. You could die almost instantly from sheer shock, or more slowly, but still quickly, by blood loss that no field medic could staunch. A hit in the thorax meant a literal explosion of the body, and heads splattered like ripe melons. At closer ranges the effects were worse. But at ranges much over 450 yards, well, the AR-15 was almost useless. Its accuracy was a joke. Its light bullet, losing velocity rapidly past 450 yards, had all the impact of a thrown sponge.

But a soldier could carry a lot of ammunition into battle because Stoner's cartridge was about half the size and weight of conventional military cartridges. And a soldier needed a lot of ammunition because the original AR-15 could fire 600 rounds per minute on full automatic. This was a higher rate of fire than some field machine guns of the era.

The rifle itself was a marvel of lightweight construction. Stoner had used then-new high-density plastics where he could. This, plus the short barrel intended for the 450-yard range, resulted in a rifle that weighed only 2.88 kilos – 6.3 pounds. Conventional army experts were, of course, not too impressed with the AR-15. No one bought it for several years.

Then, in 1961, the United States Air Force adopted it as a 'survival rifle' for downed aircrews. It spread to USAF security units and one of these went to Vietnam in 1963. It didn't take long for the South Vietnamese Army to appreciate the AR-15. The average Asian soldier was barely five feet tall. He weighed just 100 pounds. The traditional Western-style rifles with which they had been equipped were unsuitable, and the AR-15 seemed, and was, tailor made. Armalite started receiving large orders from the South Vietnamese government. The Viet Cong liked it too, and the North Vietnamese and the Chinese Communists stole, captured or bought from South Vietnamese entrepreneurs as many as they could lay their hands on. It became the weapon of choice for the U.S. Army Special Forces, commonly called the Green Berets.

Mariko, for example, with five minutes of simple instruction, could become, for all practical purposes – i.e. ranges up to 400 yards – just as deadly as a trained soldier... with an AR-15. It was lightweight enough for her to aim and handle comfortably. Most other weapons would knock her flat with recoil, and she would run out of ammunition quickly with the amount that I could hide aboard Jester. Indeed, I collected the AR-15 and clips from my secret compartment with Mariko in mind. The Walther PPK was for me in a last extremity, but I planned to be more useful before it came down to the last stand.

I also dragged my two heavy brass boxes from the cache, and gathered up my old RC – radio control – model airplane console, closed down the step lids, and locked them. There in the cabin, I shrugged into my Walther's shoulder holster, tucked the automatic into the soft leather, and put my last flannel shirt on in order to cover this personal armament.

On my way through the wheelhouse, I stuck the AR-15 to the bulkhead with its taped-on ceramic magnets, an innovation of my own devising, and stacked the bananas on the floor by the butt of the plastic stock. The two air hoses with their squeeze-valves – just like you might encounter in any gas station – dangled on the wall from their ceramic magnets and I gathered them up as I clambered out of the wheelhouse.

Mariko turned from the rail as I came out on deck, looked at the hoses and boxes in my hands, but she said nothing. She pointed. "Two more helicopters," she said.

I sighed, and placed the boxes gingerly on the poop deck beside the wheelhouse. Then I ducked back into the wheelhouse and grabbed the straps of binocular cases from their hook. Emerging on deck again, I handed the Bausch and Lomb pair to Mariko and slung the Zeiss pair around my neck.

"I could never learn to look through these things," Mariko commented, a touch helplessly in my view. "There's always two images mixed up beside each other... and on top of each other... "

"There's a dial on the right eyepiece," I said. "Find it? Okay, the idea is to hold the binoculars up to your eyes – don't squint – and turn the dial until all becomes clear." I waited.

"These things weren't made for Oriental eyes... "

"Strange," I mused, "how Admiral Yamamoto never seemed to have any trouble."

I peered through the Zeiss 10 X 50s, which may have dated from Rommel's time, and the Sud Aéronautique Kestrel III leaped at me through the lenses in all its orange-and-silver painted glory. It whirled, banked and dived with the grace and dedication of its namesake around and alongside the coiling mass of smoke. I could see the old bubble-Bell still noodling about. Two more helicopters...? The Zeisses had the range, focus and clarity... but Mariko's 7 X 35s had the greater field of view.

"Oh...!" she said, followed by an intake of breath. "Ooh! Beautiful!"

"Great", I said. "You said there were two more helicopters. We know about the bubble-Bell. I see the orange and silver Kestrel. Gee, Mariko, am I ever curious about number three."

"It's a long way off, now. It was a curious hump-backed browny-green thing."

"A long way...? *Which* way, Mariko?"

"Back along the canal where we were."

"Ah," I said, and swung Carl Zeiss's lenses back toward Castelnaudary, about three miles west. "Low or high?" I enquired mildly.

"Low," she said. "Very low." A brief silence. "This is wonderful! I can see!... Marc... there are birds, big birds, 'way up in the sky!"

"Lammergaiers," I said.

"What...?"

"Lammergaiers," I repeated, but much more distinctly, emphasising each syllable.

"Oh. Lam-mer-gai-ers," she tried it. "What are they? Eagles?"

"Vultures," I answered. "Of the buteo family. Supposed to be the largest birds in Europe. Native to the Pyrenees, also native to the mountains of Italy, Switzerland, Greece, the Balkans, and some of the larger Mediterranean islands."

"Vultures... Oh." She sounded disappointed. "But... there are so many... one, two, three... four... no, five... What are they here for?"

But I didn't answer. The good Zeiss lenses had framed it low on the western horizon. A curious, hump-backed thing, indeed. And it was browny-green. Now, it is a strange thing about us Americans that we must believe that we have made everything better. Especially military things. Our military victories, and they are not nearly so many as our unequalled media propaganda machine has tried to convince us of, have been won by quantity and productivity, not by quality and excellence. The Sherman tank, for example, was no match for the Russian T-33 and mere breakfast for German Tigers. Were any P-40 or Hellcat pilots really eager to go up against a Mitsubishi Zero? The Canadian Avro Arrow fighter plane made McDonald's Phantom F-4s look pretty slow – and that was twenty years before Phantoms became operational. For that matter, Israeli pilots much preferred Dassault Mirages and Mystères, both French-built, to the Phantoms that the United States shoved down Israeli throats. For Israeli pilots, Phantom F-4s were called 'flying coffins'. They'd earned the same epithet among U.S. pilots in Vietnam.

So it is with attack helicopters. Americans hear a lot about the Apache and its Hellfire missiles. That's nice. What American has ever heard of Sweden's Sleipnir IV attack helicopter equipped with Mjolnir III missiles? Built by Saab. Sleipnir, the 'slippery one', the legendary eight-legged steed of Odin, that could cross over land or water with supernatural speed and agility. Mjolnir, the Hammer of Thor – Thor tended to throw it when he became angry and Mjolnir never missed.

Me? Well, I wouldn't like to be the Apache pilot in a duel with a Saab Sleipnir. I'd seen early model Sleipnirs in Somalia, where the rebels had a couple in their mixed bag of equipment that also included a few early Apaches. The Saab choppers made the Apaches seem a bit silly. I heard that in Afghanistan, the Saabs slipped around the massive Soviet Tupolev attack helicopters like flies around a cow, and even those old Mjolnir missiles could afflict the Soviet cows with instant and acute dropsy.

Zeiss lenses were showing me a Sleipnir now, albeit almost at the limit of definition. It must have been a little west of Castelnaudary by the time I picked it up, a respectable speed since Mariko had first commented on the two helicopters just a couple of minutes earlier and since the Saab helicopter was just cruising lazily. The Sleipnir IV was banking to come back eastward along the canal.

The funny looking hump-back that Mariko had described held two Saab turbo-jet engines. As un-American as it was, the Sleipnir IV did not nestle its Mjolnir missiles in gentlemanly external pods that were obviously military hardware, as both the American Apache and the Russian Tupolev so conveniently did. The Mjolnirs were in streamlined tubes in that funny looking hump-back, just below the rotor, so that one just couldn't tell whether any specific Sleipnir IV was carrying missiles or not.

I'd heard that a few of the top European news agencies had bought Sleipnirs for television work. The missile tubes could be modified for cameras – there was a military variant for reconnaissance anyway – and the chopper's speed and agility gave these agencies an edge in getting videotape on the air. Apparently, the expense was worth it.

As the Sleipnir grew larger in the lenses, I could begin to see that it was green and brown. Not *quite* a camouflage pattern, but a wavy diagonal green band or stripe around the humped fuselage that was a rather drably brown at each end. The chopper grew larger until I could make out white words in rather small and demure Latin script: Norddeutsch Kreuzzuger Zeitblatt... roughly, because my German had never been fluent and was now rusty, 'North German Crusader's Times Herald'. Hmmm. In my experience, media was usually promotion oriented. Lots of glitz. Trendy logos. Large words of identification. Like the **TV5** Kestrel.

Then, having enjoyed at least one success as an author, and having therefore been exposed to a bit of media promotion, interviews and wire stories, I'd heard of the major Western networks and news agencies. AP, UPI, Reuters, BBC, Nippon TV, NBC, ABC, CBS, Global, Turner, France's TV5 and so on. I boasted even some slight acquaintance with producers and broadcasters of TV series that had featured me and my book – or, more often, had talked about doing so. Greystone Productions and its German co-producers, Britain's Grenada, Bram Roos, Germany's Der Spiegel media, and even Euronovo, a co-operative venture of Italian, French, German, Dutch and Scandinavian television.

But never once had I heard of the North German Crusader Times Herald.

"Mariko... ". I lowered the Zeisses and turned to her. She was looking high up above. Lammergaiers. But she lowered the binoculars instantly and faced me. "Mariko. How are your computer skills?"

"Veddy good," she said evenly.

"Okay. When you take that stuff back down," I gestured to the zippered bag that she still held in her hand, "try to bring up Nord-deutsch Zeit-blatt Kreuz-zuger," I pronounced this very slowly and carefully, but she nodded easily, "on the Internet. Print from the screen if there's anything... and not too much," I amended. "Then find the CD-ROM of *Jane's Attack Helicopters*. Jane's... J-A-N-E, like the girl's name. Possessive." She nodded. "Go to Sleipnir... S-L-E-I-P-N-I-R... Models four and later... maybe there's a new one I don't know..." she nodded, "... and print from the screen the bit on specifications and customers. I want hard copies."

She nodded, and since I raised the Zeisses to frame the approaching chopper again, she squeaked toward the wheelhouse hatchway.

I remembered, and lowered the binoculars. "Oh... One more thing... *Jane's* again. Military small arms. AR-15.. but it might be under M-16... print out the specifications and operating instructions." I smiled and said to her: "That's for you. Study it."

"Anything else...?"

I considered this. How much could she digest at once? On the other hand, time was pressing and it might prove crucial. "In the diskette file box labelled 'Folderol Jester', hidden somewhere in the bottom of the pile, you'll find, I hope, a diskette labelled 'PC Fire Control and Other Defences'. Read the 'PC Fire Control' part, no need for the 'Other Defences' right now. Print out if you have to. But learn it, Mariko."

"I'll find out what 'PC' means...?"

I nodded, trying to keep track of Odin's slippery steed. It was slipping in and out of clouds, behind hills and trees on the north side of the canal. It did not seem at all focussed on the scene of the tragedy.

"Am I to take it that I am the fire control officer?"

"You got it."

She disappeared down into the wheelhouse.

I went aft between the mizzen masts to align the satellite dish. This was possible in the thumb of Lac des Doigts. It was so narrow that even a Pyrenees breeze raised only ripples, whereas on the longer fingers extending into the foothills, the longer fetch could produce waves that would have jiggled *Jester*.

18

Mariko disappeared downwards, placing her binoculars carefully on top of the wheelhouse as she went, and the Sleipnir disappeared toward Carcassonne while keeping north of the canal.

Since both Mariko and the chopper were gone, I decided that I might as well do what I could while I had the chance. Not wanting to scuff my thin teak deck, I lifted the two boxes the three feet up to the base of the smokestack.

The smokestack, too, was not merely what it seemed to be. To be sure, it *was* a smokestack. A real one. A handsome one. Presently it was an eight-foot tall, eight-inch diameter gleaming brass tube, highly and proudly polished, and ornately frilled around the top. It arose from the middle of the wheelhouse just behind the hatch, dead on the centreline of the boat. It was therefore was out of the way of sails set behind it and to either side on the mizzens in the extreme stern. It would telescope down to just above the height of the wheelhouse, a measure necessary to clear those low, British, bridges on Brindley's narrow canals. In France, I could generally keep the stack eight feet up, and this kept smoke and hot air out of eyes in most situations of wind and speed. Smoke got to it from the offset boiler via the tube steel frame of the wheelhouse itself.

This telescoping smokestack had been inordinately expensive to fabricate because it had to be strong enough to serve as the mount for two pneumatic cannons. These were in plain view – the best way to hide anything – but disguised as tall riverboat whistles on either side of the smokestack. These were two-inch diameter brass tubes, highly polished. At their base, where they emerged from the top of the wheelhouse along with the thicker smokestack, they carried brass fittings for steam or air.

And, indeed, most of the time, the boiler's automatic safety valves, and the manual steam release valve, exhausted through these slim brass tubes. They had whistle inserts pressed into their upper ends, inserts that could be removed with the twist of a brass knob. I could, and frequently did, use my two-toned whistle. I had been travelling the Canal du Midi for almost six years by now, and my whistles were known from Bordeaux to Narbonne. Even the Canal Police patrol boats would sometimes wave at me to get a return two-toned whistle and puffs of steam from the brass Mississippi River Boat style stacks. *Toot*-**Toot!**

Joining these two slim tubes to the central smokestack was a large and ornate brass plate. This plate could rotate around the smokestack on a brass collar. It was stamped with '*Folderol Jester*', and some letters were completely cut out in the manner of a stencil. The intaglio was gaily painted with red, black and yellow letters.

The truth was that the lower ends of the slim two-inch tubes were barely connected to the wheelhouse at all. A twist of a clamp would loosen their bases so that they could pivot up on the brass plate with hinges. In this case, the tubes were pivoted as pneumatic cannon barrels, while the partly intaglioed brass connecting plate formed effective shield against small arms. The whistle tubes could be aimed by sighting through the first 'o' in *Folderol* and the last 'e' in *Jester*. These, at least, were true cut-outs.

The base of each slim tube boasted a rectangular fitting – you could regard them as support flanges for the whistle-tubes if you were so inclined. My two brass boxes from the secret cache fitted snugly into these rectangular flanges. Each box held five finned, spindle-shaped projectiles, each weighing precisely 300 grams, each filled with 200 grams of home-mixed nitrate explosive extracted from garden fertilizer. A .22 casing in the nose of each projectile served for a contact detonator. Each projectile had four triangular fins attached to its tapering rear end. The trailing edge of each fin had been carefully bent just 20 degrees to the right. These projectiles had been hand-crafted back in Canada.

With a sufficient amount of steam or air pressure, the finned projectiles emerged from their tubes like tiny spinning American footballs thrown by diminutive Brett Favres or John Elways. However, the fact that each little football had two strips of high-density felt epoxied around its circumference, and the fact that a lot of steam or air pressure could be released into these seven-foot tubes, meant that these footballs could traverse the length of five Rose Bowls. A maximum range of about half a kilometre. Explosion on impact would demolish something the size of a city bus.

Compared to a firearm, the breech action of the automatic feed was simple. It was based on the usual pressure blow-back system taken from near the muzzle of the tubes. This pressure would untwist a sliding breech-tube by blow-back force, and another projectile would roll in. A soft spring closed the breech again. Things were simplified as there did not have to be any provision for the ejection of spent cartridge casings.

With *Jester's* boiler rated for 1000 psi – pounds per square inch – though I normally used less than 500, it seemed a shame to waste this pressure. And, originally, I had intended to use steam for my little cannons. But then I had decided to operate my on-board vehicle with compressed air, an idea pioneered by Guy Negre's Evolution automobile then in prototype development. I therefore needed an air compressor and pressure tanks in which to store the compressed air. This would also be handy for possible diving and salvage work.

Thinking about it very carefully, I couldn't imagine any possible situation in which I would be using either the cannons or the vehicle simultaneously with diving and salvage work. Therefore, I decided to save much space by not having any compressed air storage tanks inside *Jester* herself. It was compressed directly into and stored in the on-board vehicle's tanks. These were just a collection of scuba tanks connected together under a false floor of the vehicle's cargo bed. One or more tanks could be removed for diving if necessary. But the total capacity of compressed air storage was very great with no usage of *Jester's* limited hull space. The valving was a bit complex, but all the fittings were standard off-the-shelf units. I therefore had a choice of steam or air pressure for the pneumatic cannons.

Shortly before I had folded *Jester's* front hull over the rear one to become her own container and had her shipped across the Atlantic as deck cargo, I had conducted trials out in the St. Lawrence estuary. Part of this testing involved the pneumatic cannons. I discovered that each launch of a projectile lowered the boiler steam pressure considerably, and I would generally need steam for propulsion in any cannon-shooting situation. The air compressor, by contrast, would gradually give me 2,000 psi, or more, in the tanks. Pneumatic power didn't reduce propulsion, and there was much more of it. So, I now disconnected the steam for the whistles and connected the air hoses for the cannons.

For the present, I climbed on top of the wheelhouse and just removed the whistle inserts from the ends of the cannon tubes. I then checked that the projectile magazines were secured securely into the breech flanges and I loosened the base clamps of the tubes. But I didn't actually pivot the tubes away from vertical. That could be done in a literal instant. In the meantime, *Jester* would look almost exactly the same to François and Roland. Only the addition of the brass magazine boxes atop the wheelhouse had altered *Jester's* appearance. A minor detail and, given the lack of observation among most people, one that would never be noticed unless they had been given some clue. Mariko had seen the brass magazines when I had brought them topside, and she would certainly notice them in their new positions. I rather hoped so. But I sincerely hoped that circumstances would permit *Jester* to remain looking more or less the same to the less observant.

Fire control could be very simple. Sight through the intaglio cut-outs and squeeze a service station air valve.

However, fire control for my pneumatic cannons could also be highly sophisticated, involving a Tasco electrical telescope mount on the smokestack collar that would swivel the cannons according to computer calculations. Data from the radars on the mizzen masts gave the distance to target, while wind speed and direction from atop the main masts supplied corrections. A thermostat's mercury switch ensured that *Jester* was level before the cannons would fire.

I'd planned for the contingency I might be elsewhere on deck when I might have to use the cannons, so I had rigged a mechanical switch that could be activated by the model airplane radio control console. My idea was to use the sophisticated fire control, but to let Mariko shoot the cannons herself. I could use the remote console if she balked.

These pneumatic cannons had been installed on *Jester*, not to mention a few other innovations, because I had anticipated a not-too-distant future when authority might collapse – or when authority might become tyranny. So far, the energy crisis had been handled with the preservation of democratic social cohesion in Western countries. But that could either change very quickly or evolve very slowly.

I had always given some thought to *security*, since even in the mid-1990s yacht burglary had already become a serious concern for boaters in some places, but as *Jester* later neared completion it had seemed prudent to give some thought to actual *defence*. If my hunches were right, I would need to survive in a vastly different world. It was then that I decided actually to develop and mount the pneumatic cannons. And, I admit, I devoted much time and money to this. Among other things, in a changed world I couldn't discount the possibility that I might find it convenient to turn pirate myself.

So, it seemed a little puzzling that my careful preparations were now being used as a defence against old-fashioned crime provoked by an ancient parchment.

Smoke was still high in the sky, though it was thinning out now and pluming toward the north and east. A separate and much smaller smudge was coming from the direction of Carcassonne. I had been hearing hoots from a ship's horn for some time. I supposed that this would be a canal tug, possibly stationed in Carcassonne, although I'd never noticed a tug there. But, now that I thought of it, it would make sense to headquarter a canal tug on the summit level where it could easily go in either direction. That's why the headquarters of the Canal Police were in Carcassonne, after all, or so I had always supposed.

Die Lorelei would not have sunk. Could not have sunk was more to the point. The channel was only about ten feet deep. The barge would have gone to the bottom, but her cabin and wheelhouse would have remained above the surface – if they remained at all, that is. It should be possible to insert plastic salvage bags under the deck, or tie them alongside, and then inflate them. Once floating off the bottom, a tug could get a cable on her, or around her hull, perhaps with the aid of Navy divers, and tow her as far as Carcassonne. Just 40 kilometres. Once there, the wreck could be put into dry dock or just broken up. She would be out of the channel, at least, and the Canal du Midi could open to barge traffic once again. But now, I figured, only official craft were being locked through. I also suspected that there might well be some official concern about what sort of hazardous chemicals *Lorelei* had been carrying.

Scanning the skies around, I saw that two light planes had joined the flying circus. I couldn't see the bubble Bell, but it would probably be back. The *Kestrel* was still circling the immediate vicinity of the *Lorelei's* demise. Such dedication at the scene of the tragedy, not to mention the paint, made me virtually certain that this helicopter was media-owned. The Sleipnir was another matter.

And of it, I could at first see no sign. It was then that I had that unpleasant tingling up the spine that I remembered from various unpleasant places. A sudden and startling whacking of blades clattered into our little ravine in the foothills, giving my heart a sickening lurch. A brown-headed dragonfly of large size lifted over the ridge that rose above the little finger of Lac des Doigts and swooped over the water toward us with a roar of turbo-jets and a great thwacking of blades. I ducked, even though I imagined that the Sleipnir kept to the legal minimum altitude of a few hundred feet.

It zoomed over us and away, lifting up gracefully to clear the ridge that cradled the thumb of water, leaving two thin trails of smoke from its twin jets. It disappeared in the direction of Carcassonne. I saw Roland burst out of the *birol's* cabin door just in time to see the last of the chopper cresting the ridge and vanishing behind it. He raised a fist and shouted something inaudible over the howl of the departing helicopter. Then he turned away, happened to see me, grinned sheepishly and waved. I waved in return as he went back into the cabin. Still on the sand of the little curved beach, and still at his task, François never looked up.

I thought for sure that the Sleipnir*'s* sudden, shocking and awful commotion would bring Mariko up on deck, just as it had brought Roland from his cabin, but after a few moments, when she didn't appear, I bent my head toward the open hatch. I heard the discreet whirring of the LaserJet 1100 printing away. Mariko, it seemed, was made of stern stuff. As she seemed busy and unperturbed, and since I was no longer busy but quite perturbed, I decided to carry out my intent of taking a close look at the *birol*. The time seemed propitious since Roland had just shown himself to be awake, active and friendly. And, for all I knew, their *birol* might well be the oldest one still operating on the Garonne. It *looked* old. Perhaps it had even featured in one of Vital's turn-of-the-last-century sepia photos.

19

Accordingly, of the two pairs of binoculars available to me on the wheelhouse top, I took the wider-angle ones that Mariko had used, and walked thankfully along the little corridor that we had contrived with Bouchard's accursed, but three fewer, casks.

Once on the beach through the landing-craft style ramp-door, out from under our camouflage *birol* nets, the nearly-summer sun of Languedoc, now arching toward noon, suddenly seared me like a breath from a blast furnace. I actually stumbled coming out of the shadow of the net and into the glare of the beach, but not from the sun's impact, though it was palpable enough. I had unconsciously remembered the firm, damp sand of the cool, misty morning and was not quite prepared for the soft Sahara my foot gritted into.

A quick scan with the 7 X 35 eyepieces sweaty-wet on my cheeks showed the Sleipnir, rotor disc flashing silver in the sun, banking out to the south and east against the Pyrenees. She was coming back in our general direction, but I suspected that she would not be so rude as to fly directly over us again. At least, not for a decent while.

Twenty-five long paces – I was counting – from *Jester*, I stepped up onto the *birol's* flat shallow hull. It was just a float, really. Like a large section of dock, just as flat and angular, but some minimal effort had been made to give it a boatish shape. It looked like a flat iron with a large box on top. The hull was surprisingly large, about fifty feet long and maybe fifteen feet wide. As I knocked at the door, I saw that there must be a lot of the cabin I had not yet seen, and also that there must be another door somewhere. A grinning, shadowed Roland materialised in the doorway of the darkened interior. I stepped aside as he opened the screen door.

"Bonjour, Monsieur Vin," he said. He gestured upward. "Maudit oiseau", he growled. Then, opening the screen door wide. "Mais, entrez dans..." I was amused at being called Mister Wine, agreed the helicopter was a bird accursed and accepted the invitation to go inside.

"Merci bien," I said, but hesitated. I turned to look at François sitting beside the net and slowly tying cord around the frame. He had half the frame to go, hundreds of knots. I glanced at the blazing sun. "Il fait très chaud," I said. "L'ancien, il a besoin d'un chapeau?" I noted it was getting very hot outside and wondered if the old man needed a hat.

Roland, surprised at my question, stooped to stare toward the old man's mahogany-coloured bald head shining in the sun. He shrugged, puzzled. "Je ne sais pas" ("I don't know"), he said. I shrugged too, and followed Roland inside. I told him that he had a very fine *birol*, and that I was interested in *birols*. Roland appreciated my interest, for it quickly became clear that he loved the thing. Gradually, as I drew Roland out, I learned much about *birols* in general, and this one in particular. Strangely, however, the vessel appeared never to have been given a name – or, maybe, Roland and his father had lived on it so long that they were too familiar with it to use the name. Or, perhaps, they had forgotten it.

Roland said that it had been built in 1881, but, of course, had been repaired and so virtually rebuilt several times since. She'd been launched at Narbonne. And, but yes, it had caught many, many fish. Especially giant sturgeons, but they were nearly gone now. Perhaps, higher up the Tarn River, a few might still remain...

Slowly, we got around to what was uppermost in my mind. She had a steam engine, this *birol*. Oh, you understand, a diesel had been installed in 1936, but then the Germans came a few years later. And during the war there was no fuel... But, thankfully, the old man had kept the *moteur à vapeur,* the steam engine, in a neighbour's barn. Many others had not kept the old steam engines once diesels had become available. But they themselves had been lucky. The steam engine could run on many things.

If I understood correctly, they had even used fish oil sometimes – or, rather, actually burned heaps of little, dried fishes. They were small, these fishes, the size of Roland's massive old pocket watch, but one could net thousands of them in the tidal waters of the Gironde and Aude. They were good for nothing, Roland said, these fishes, until someone discovered that they would burn well if dried in the sun. So, they'd had fuel for the *moteur à vapeur* the Germans didn't want and couldn't use.

I decided that these little fishes must be some sort of menhaden, or like the gaspereau of North America. I hadn't known there was any similar oily species in southern France, but I made a mental note to add a small-meshed net to my herring seine. This was the sort of local information that is rarely covered in encyclopaedias.

They were left alone, during the war. They survived, although many did not. Roland never mentioned his mother except to say that she had died just after the Germans went away.

François, he had never replaced the diesel – which was also still stored in the same barn because for many years he thought that Russians might come, like the Germans had come, and take all the fuel. From what he'd heard, Roland thought that this still might be possible. Besides, now they were both old and it would be much work to change the engine. But the *moteur à vapeur* was very, very good, although it was not so convenient in many ways. Roland had made the motion of inserting a key and turning it. "Pas de vroom", he said, chuckling. Indeed, I had never heard of a better name for a steam engine. And yes, they kept the boiler on simmer because it was easier to raise steam to pressure if a little fire was always kept. Or, at least, a bed of hot embers.

I very much wanted to see this pas-de-vroom. An 1880 steam engine from southern France was likely to be a thing of beauty, not to mention certain eccentricity of design, but just as I was about to ask this, I heard Mariko call my name. I was relieved that her tone was querying, but not desperately urgent.

Smiling a bit ruefully, and shrugging, I rose from my hardwood, hard-back, and just plain *hard,* chair. Roland did the same as I stood up. These chairs, just two of them, were now hard against adjoining walls whereas this morning they had closely flanked the cast iron wood stove, a small but voluptuous pot-bellied thing, that was still emanating heat. Its fire was out, but its embers smouldered. It recalled to mind one of those shapeless, vaguely female, Upper Palaeolithic 'Venus figurines' saving her stuff for the next fertility rite. What with the sun and this stove, the room was overly warm – but not anything like the shadeless beach.

In the act of getting up, noticing the chairs, and then truly noticing the stove, I realised that the chairs were genuine rosewood. The stove had been cast about the same time as the *moteur* à *vapeur,* judging by the carefully rendered lion's paws that did service as the feet. Looking more closely at the thing I'd taken for the only table in the room, I saw it for a neglected spinet. Madame was gone, maybe, but had never been forgotten. As I made for the door, I saw also that the faded and filthy curtains had once been delicate chintz, or more properly since this was a French-made vessel, *chinoise.*

There had been a woman's hand and spirit at work on this old *birol.* A woman of some refinement, so the spinet argued, who had softened the work of fishing, in a supposedly cruder age, with *chinoisie.* Who had supplied the grace of music on starlit Pyrenees summer nights while she had played in her bustles, *décolleté* and petticoats. And who, no doubt, had brought warmth and passion to winter nights when the *birol* was shore bound by the infamous French *Mistral.*

She would have had courage to have chosen this life, too, and I had no doubt that Roland had been born aboard this *birol,* perhaps at some anchorage as secluded as our lake. An ancient life, and a difficult one, but also a graceful one with the spirit of a good Madame over it all...

Then and there, reconstructing their lives from the artefacts that remained, I made a decision...

"Marc...?"

I pushed the door open, and saw Mariko pacing the poop and scanning the *maquis* with a questing head. Her right hand held some paper. I waved and called out, "Un moment... ah... just a moment, Mariko." When she turned toward the sound, I waved. She waved back, and settled herself on the break of the poop with the great rounded hinges beneath her knees. Again, she flexed one leg up and let the other dangle to play footsie with the casks. Long legs.

"Une belle poule," Roland said behind me. Freely translated, 'a good-looking chick', and the same slang that had induced Bouchard to name his barge *La Poule Frite* – 'The Fried Chickie', meaning a stressed-out or sexually aroused young woman.

"Très certainement," I said. His words had given me an idea.

"Roland... Voulez-vous gagner de l'argent?" I supposed from their lifestyle and from the natural nature of their breakfast earlier in the morning that they subsisted well enough with little actual cash, but might welcome some hard currency.

"Oui... ", he said cautiously

"Connaissez-vous *La Poule Frite?*" This was a stupid question. All the boat people on the canal knew *La Poule Frite.*

But Roland just nodded. "Marcel Bouchard... Il part de Carcassonne demain, ou en après-midi, vers Narbonne,." he said. I couldn't figure out how Roland could possibly know that Marcel was presently in Carcassonne, but could be expected to leave for Narbonne tomorrow afternoon. There was no radio or other electronic device aboard the *birol.*

I had encountered this sort of knowledge during the months I'd spent in the south of France. The boat people seemed to know, and were very seldom mistaken, just where any other boat was at any given time and where it was going. Most of the time, I attributed this to the incessant amount of gossip and news that was shouted across the water whenever one barge encountered another. But sometimes the knowledge couldn't be explained so easily.

A dialogue flashed through my mind. American anthropologists in Haiti. They had noticed that when the men of a mountain village went down into town to sell produce at the weekly market, the village women would frequently go to a particular tree and talk to it. The anthropologists asked what they were doing, and the women explained. They told the tree what they wanted their men to buy for them down in the village, once the men had sold their products and had cash. Little things. An arm's length of red ribbon. A quarter-kilo of flour. Two plantains. A coconut, or three re-straightened Bobby Pins. Things like that. And the anthropologists kept track and discovered that most of the time the men returned with these items. Things that the women had thought of after the men had left. The anthropologists were amazed, and a little spooked.

'How does it work?' they had asked one of the women. 'I don't know,' she answered, 'but if we had a telephone, it would be better.'

So, I didn't doubt Roland's knowledge stated in such an offhand manner. I myself merely *thought* that Bouchard would be in Carcassonne about now, because I had his wine, after all, and was supposed to meet him today or tomorrow at the last *écluse* on the summit level.

"Roland," I asked thoughtfully, "combien des gens savoir que j'apporte de vin pour Marcel Bouchard?" I hoped it was not common knowledge that I carried wine for Bouchard. Although the French police are lenient with French residents, especially in times like these, a special permit was needed to carry wine. In theory. My transgressions could make things awkward if anyone wanted to exploit them.

"Tout le monde," he said.

Everyone...? So, my activities were common canal knowledge. I sighed. "Hmmm. Et les policiers...?"

"Mais... *certainement*..." He seemed shocked.

"Right," I said, and delved into my pocket for my wad of French francs. I peeled and counted off *cinq cent* as Roland watched with interest. Handing the bills into his hand, and shoving the remainder down deeply into my pocket, I told Roland to take François and find *La Poule Frite*. "Tell Bouchard that if he wants his wine, *bien sur* he'd better meet me tomorrow at the last lock on the summit level. If he's not there at *quinze heures* in the afternoon, then I'll dump the casks in the canal. The police can have fun collecting them."

"Pardon," Roland looked puzzled. "Le vin... où, exactement... ?"

Where? Why would Roland want to know where I planned to dump the casks? That was unimportant. "À la dernière écluse, the last lock on the summit level," I said emphatically and impatiently... before I had truly computed the mild tone of Roland's question.

I looked into a pair of too-old and too-innocent eyes. The old dog, he'd pretended not to understand *my* French. It occurred to me that the threats should be modified if I wanted Bouchard there at *quinze heures*...

"L'oubliez, Roland. Forget that." I rubbed my chin in thought. "Tell him that I'll just take the wine back to... ah... Toulouse... that's it... and he can pick it up there."

Roland's eyes dulled a bit. "Oui, certainement," he said in a subdued way. "Et... de plus...?"

"Oui, Roland... Dites-vous à Bouchard, s'il vous plaît , que j'ai besoin de la salon de Josephine." I needed Josie's beauty salon for Mariko, not me. I supposed that Roland knew that.

"Annette," he said.

"Annette?"

"Oui... la nouvelle... le semaine dernière." Annette? I had no way of knowing that Marcel Bouchard had got a new girlfriend just last week. I'd been trying to keep up with other rapidly changing events.

"Okay," I said. "Dites-vous à Bouchard apporter Annette avec him," I finished. Marcel Bouchard was an obsessive man... or a canny one. He had a small *esthétique* in the large cabin of *La Poule Frite*. It had originated with an earlier female companion who had been a hair stylist. The salon remained, but the first hairdresser had long gone. Strangely, Bouchard's subsequent companions had all been hair stylists. This brought income that was not at all insubstantial. There were plenty of unemployed *esthéticiennes* in the canal towns between Bordeaux and Narbonne. Plenty of canal barges were family operated and yet no one, other than Bouchard, had thought of a floating salon to serve the many boat women working the Garonne and Aude.

"Merci, Roland." I was about to leave the vessel when Roland asked a question.

"Et nos birols, Monsieur...?" He pointed upward, and toward *Jester*.

"Pardon, Roland... Ici," I pointed toward François, "sur la plage comme avant. Demain matin. Aussi avec les herbes et bois en haut." It would take less time and work for me and Mariko just to lower the *birol* nets, and struggle them ashore, without having to pick the foliage out of them. Also, leaving their vegetable disguise on top might fool beachcombers.

This seemed to satisfy Roland. He smiled and nodded, then looked up at the sun. Was it past the meridian? "Nous y allons immédiatement," he said carefully so that I would clearly understand.

"Bon." I jumped off the hull and scrunched through the sand toward *Jester*. I stopped to scan the sky with the Bausch & Lombs, even though this gave the sand enough time to send its heat into my Nikes. I couldn't swear it, but maybe I saw the Sleipnir to the west, slanting down toward Toulouse.

20

Mariko stood up as I threaded the corridor of casks and stepped up onto the poop. She smiled, somewhat tiredly, I thought. I glanced at the papers in her hand. They were already smudged a bit with sweat.

"Yes..." she said, sounding bemused, as if she'd forgotten. "All right," this was brisk, businesslike. "In order, then. First, there's nothing on the Internet about the *Norddeutsch Kreuzzuger Zeitblatt.* However... I tried a long shot, as you Americans say... "

"Some Americans."

"I e-mailed a query to a colleague at Armagh University, and to another colleague at Oxford. Both places have sociology departments. Both keep track of the IRA and any other organizations mentioned in connection with it..." She waited, so I nodded. She smiled and patted the poop deck beside her. "Sit down, Marc. You look hot and worried."

"I am," I answered, and sat down.

"Oxford came through with one clipping, Armagh was better with two clippings." She handed me paper. "But the gist is that the *Norddeutch Kreuzugger Zeitblatt* – you read the name correctly."

"But the words were painted in a funny way, staggered, sort of."

"... has been mentioned thrice as..."

"*Thrice...?* C'mon, Mariko. Gimme a break."

She patted my thigh, and smiled mischievously, and left her hand there. "All right. Three times... as the... ah... official publication of an organization called *Die Kruezzugers von dem Graal.*" She emphasized this. "Crusaders of the Grail," she translated.

"Got it."

"They've been described as a mystical and militant neo-Nazi group which has, on occasion, supplied arms to the IRA. Mostly Swedish munitions." She said this last with some surprise. "I always rather thought that Sweden was a peace-loving Democratic Socialist state," she mused. "Perhaps there's some mistake here."

I laughed. "You're sweet," I said. I felt her fingers on my thigh flutter, as if about to be withdrawn. Like a spooked butterfly taking wing from a thistle on which it had inadvertently landed. But then the fingers tightened, even squeezed, in challenge.

"Well...?" she asked. "What about all of Sweden's progressive social legislation, policies and programs?"

"Admirable," I answered. "Truly. But probably only possible economically because Sweden is, given its relatively small population, the world's largest per capita arms manufacturer. A big percentage of its GNP."

"You're joking!"

"Ask Saab and Oerlikon the next time you're in their boardrooms."

"Speaking of Saab..." she mused, shuffling papers. "I thought they were Czech," she said meanwhile. "Honestly."

"All right."

"Here," she said proudly. She handed me some more paper, and replaced the hand on my thigh. "The Sleipnir material." She paused, added a page, "And the Mjolnir data." She replaced her hand again. Another emphasis.

My, time flies. While I had been doing a lot of things to get from Canada to France, Saab had several times updated the Sleipnir. We were now at Model VI with F and G improvements and retrofits. The silhouettes and photos confirmed that we had seen a IV. It didn't much matter, however, just which of the variants I had seen through the Zeiss lenses. All Sleipnirs since Model IIID had carried HUD (head up display) for IFR (infra-red) heat sensors. In glancing at the published specs for this, I learned that it could distinguish the heat from a single human body to an accuracy of ten feet from an altitude of 500 feet.

Hmmm. I thought it more than likely, then, that the Sleipnir that had overflown us so definitively would have been able to distinguish *Jester's* boiler on simmer from the *birol's* boiler, also kept on simmer. A roughly measured thirty yards separated them.

Speaking of the *birol*, and just thinking about it made me glance up, I was surprised to see that Roland was shoving it off the beach. His *"immédiatement"* had meant something. I had not really expected their departure before mid-afternoon – given the heat, and the certainty that it would ameliorate later – but my Seiko assured me that it was not quite one o'clock.

"They're leaving!" Mariko exclaimed. Then she said, after a second, "But you said that the canal would be closed. How can they leave?"

"The shipping channel will be closed, Mariko," I replied. "But that *birol* draws only about six inches. They will travel along the edge of the canal."

"Won't the police stop them and search, or ask questions?"

"Possibly, but I doubt it. I just learned that it's been on the canal since the 1880s. I imagine police are fairly familiar with it by now. The very old man is stone deaf, and the old man can't hear too well either."

"Yes, I see."

Mariko lifted her right hand off my thigh to wave. Roland waved back when the *birol* had slid off the sand and was truly afloat. Then he hopped nimbly aboard the departing craft and disappeared behind the angle of the deck house. I had no doubt that he was venturing into the lair of the pas-de-vroom to feed steam to the pistons I had unfortunately never seen, to stoke the 1880-style boiler I could only imagine. François waved also from the huge steering wheel in front of the deck house – no weather protection there – and added a toothless, but wolfish for all that, grin toward Mariko. She waved again, the innocent. She replaced that hand on my leg. Emphasis. *Trust?* Perhaps... well... only *need*.

But... but... my memory protested. Was it not true that experts like Dr. Wayne W. Dyer, author of *Your Erroneous Zones*, had warned us in no uncertain terms that a mature, fulfilling and satisfying male-female relationship could only be forged with no hint of *need*, or *obligation*?

Rather, the optimum relationship must be that of two needless and selfishly, gloriously independent people. I *did* wonder, when absorbing Dyer's paen to emotional independence, why any such person of one gender would bother with the sheer physical messiness of joining with a person of the other gender. Surely, these independent and non-co-dependent persons could not *need* sex, by definition, or really want to put up with the perceptions, aspirations, foibles or puzzling genitalia of *any* other individual. They would glory forever in themselves. If they felt, not *needed*, sexuality, well, they could always masturbate.

As Mariko's fingers settled comfortably onto my thigh again, a small voice in my co-dependent self reminded me that Jean Paul and Martin had, perhaps, led me astray. Did not the *fact* of a departing *birol* prove this? And not only that, but a birol that had been proved to have had a *purpose*? And so, therefore, experts such as Dr. Wayne W. Dyer might also lead a questing soul astray. Another small voice, or perhaps the very same one, whispered to my needful self: "Take what you can get, boy!" and "What the hell!" As the *birol* left a gentle curving wake to starboard, heading for the exit of the lake, the satisfying peace of self-acceptance slipped over me.

"...the PCFC, as you call it, for the pneumatic cannons is just as clever," Mariko continued. "I learned the procedure – even went through an exercise or two – and I can be a Fire Control Officer. Or, FCO, as you Americans might say."

"Some Americans."

"Right." She paused. "Can I ask a question? With no intent to be insulting?"

"Sure."

"Why are Americans obsessed with letter designations... like PCFC, for example... and, worse, actual acronyms, like... like...?"

"S-W-A-T. Special Weapons Attack Team. Swat," I supplied.

"Yes."

"A national trait – just like an obsession with tea, for example."

"Right. Just one thing, however, if I may say so... " She paused, as if uncertain to speak her mind. When I didn't respond, she continued. "But there seems to be no provision for the Personal Computer Fire Control... PCFC, that is... *altitude* of a target. It appears that the whole thing was intended for boats on water. Of course," she amended, "I suppose it would be possible to be out in the water and shoot at something up on a hill. Manually, that is, and it would probably be reasonably effective. But the radars don't really give a very accurate indication of an object's height above water..." She stopped for a few moments, but went on. "I took a peek at the motorised Tasco equatorial telescope siting mechanism. It could fix on a high-altitude object, of course, but it wouldn't track quickly enough for an..."

"For an aircraft," I finished for her.

"Quite so."

"Well, yes, Mariko," I said, "in the world I envisioned there would be no... er... flying machines. Balloons, maybe."

"I know," she said, surprising me. I looked at her, and found her studying my face when I turned. She brushed her hair back, a swift and distracted movement, and looked away. "The name 'Rennsalaer' rang a bell, a small one, from the beginning. So, I tried you on the Internet. Some reviews, of course – and that long interview cover feature in *Saturday Night*. And there was that cover-advertised write-up in *People*. I've heard of your book, Marc, vaguely, but I confess I've never read it."

I sighed. "Dear me," I said. "You'd be surprised how many times I've heard those words from attractive women. It's a shame, really," I mused, "because they're not properly impressed with me from the beginning. They have to get to know me before they become... ah... admirers. And that takes time."

Mariko laughed, and I felt her hand give my thigh a little squeeze. I felt her head suddenly resting on my shoulder, so I put my arm around hers. I gave her a friendly little nudge toward me.

"On the other hand, Mariko, helicopters are just about the slowest flying machines there are. They set down very slowly, you know."

"Hmmm. About the AR-15," she continued, "I read all about it. How it works. You left it downstairs..."

"Below."

"...Below. So, I figured you did that for a reason. I checked it out, and worked it. One of the banana clips is loaded, by the way, but the breech is empty. Safety on. I brought the other banana up here." She twitched her shoulder in the appropriate direction. "It's at the foot of the smokestack, hidden by the cannon magazines. When do we bring the laptop up?"

"Later." I slowly curled my arm to glance at my Seiko, and this embrace of Mariko's neck brought her cheek gently against mine. She nuzzled me ever so tentatively. One-thirty, and damp wisps of her hair were tickling my ear. "Plenty of time."

"Marc...? It has become obvious to me that you were been thinking about a lot of things while I've only been reacting emotionally. We wouldn't even be alive and in this lake without a great deal of fine calculation... What do you think is going to happen...?"

"Yes, well, that *is* the question, isn't it?" I paused for a while, thinking. "Let's predict the future from the little that we know, and more that we suspect." Rubbing her cheek softly with my stubble helped me think. "You went off the bridge into the river. A barge, and they cannot know which one, was going by. It might have rescued you because you clung to it long enough to get attention. Or you might have drowned. Or you and the barge might have missed each other, and maybe you swam ashore. They can't *know*, you see. And they can't know what became of the briefcase." I paused, and felt her nod and nuzzle, tickling my ear. "Okay. But they do know it is *possible* that you are on a barge. And they absolutely know that the barge was heading upstream. That is, toward the summit level between Castelnaudary and Carcassonne."

"Therefore," said Mariko, "they allotted a reasonable window of time for a barge to go from Moissac to the summit level. And then sealed it off."

I nodded agreement. "Now, how to find you? The speedboat could try to search the summit level. But air would be better, a helicopter, and there would be plenty flying around for police, media, air ambulances and so on. Like I said earlier, it would not be difficult to put one more choppers, appropriately disguised and plausible, into that air traffic. First, it could overfly the entire length of summit level in minutes and simultaneously video tape every vessel on this part of the canal. Second, it would begin to go further afield to check out the little lakes and reservoirs. Third, if it had the equipment, it could do infra-red scans. With luck, Mariko, and good equipment, they could get a body count of everyone on every barge."

"Infra-red scans?"

"Heat sensors. That tally could be checked against known crew lists. Lloyd's has a canal registry on the Internet. Arrivals, departures, cargo and crew lists. They could have a fair chance of pinpointing vessels with too many bodies aboard. There would be several of these, because there are always stowaways – girlfriends and unreported last-minute guests – aboard boats, but it would reduce the number of boats to be checked."

"You thought of all this going into the lake?" She was silent for a moment, remembering. "While I was sobbing on the floor down there."

"You had a right to be sobbing," I said evenly. "Anyway, when I saw the *birol* – that's a kind of local fishing boat – I thought that their nets," I gestured upward, "might hide us from a chopper. If we could get them rigged before the fog lifted."

"We did," she said.

"We did, indeed," I agreed.

"So... we may be safe."

I gazed the length of *Jester*, and then let my eyes scan the *maquis* on the beautiful, scented hills covered with a gorgeous blue sky. "Possible, but I rather doubt it, I think." I hurried on to replace vague anxiety with specific problems. A mind can deal with problems. "I *did* think in terms of a military-type helicopter, Mariko. I even thought about infrared. That's why I ran *Jester* up so close to the *birol* – the fishing boat. As soon as I saw her, I knew she was an antique. I didn't notice any diesel exhaust pipe, but I did see a central smokestack. The old ones had steam engines. A steam boiler is most always kept warm by a banked fire. We have propane and oil on *Jester*, but when we're stopped I close down to simmer, as I call it. Still, it is a lot of heat. I thought maybe I could confuse infra-red by berthing close to another steam engine on simmer, once I suspected that the *birol* had steam."

"But... " It was very quietly said.

"But I didn't expect a Sleipnir, that's all. They're equipped with maybe the best infrared in the business. As an extra. They're also sold to a couple of news agencies, but I didn't think that news agencies would purchase any military IFR package, and so I still thought we would be okay. Especially under this camouflage. And with the fishing boat in plain view as protective colouration."

I glanced down at the sheaf of papers and then started thumbing through them. There's no obligation for a manufacturer to list its customers in *Jane's*. No informed reader takes such claims very seriously even if clients are listed. Nonetheless, I was interested. I wasn't surprised to learn that the Federal Republic of Germany had purchased several dozen Sleipnirs over the years, most recently the latest model.

But I strongly doubted that the German government would let used Sleipnirs be sold as military surplus, and especially not with military IFR packages included. Germany had enough trouble with terrorists and security. Then, I noticed that a South African client, not the government, had purchased four late-model Sleipnirs within the past three years. Strange, given the Mandala government's previous insistence on the development of South Africa's domestic aircraft industry. But everyone familiar with the arms business knew that a South African purchase of truly exotic military hardware usually meant that it was destined for Israel eventually. Not always, of course, but usually.

And Israel could definitely use Sleipnirs instead of its U.S. Apache and Comanche helicopters, but it could use many more than just four. A small scale Israeli purchase of exotic hardware usually meant that it was earmarked for the Mossad, Israel's highly efficient and much feared secret service that operates all over the world. But would even the Mossad co-operate with a neo-Nazi organization?

The more I thought about it, the more terrifying that thought became. Not overt "co-operation," of course, but "infiltration." And the Mossad would certainly do that, possibly with a Sleipnir as bait for some major neo-Nazi group. That was the Mossad's job. But where was that line between "co-operation" and "infiltration" to be drawn? Infiltrators have to co-operate to some extent. Now that I thought about it, Israel had a vested interest in preserving the orthodox status quo of an originally Jewish Jesus with the New Testament's story being set in "Palestine." After all, nominal American Christians had supported the creation of Israel through the United Nations in 1947 and had supported Israel militarily to the tune of about $10-million per day since 1948. Israel had just as much interest in preserving orthodox Christianity as the Vatican. This realization made me even more frightened than I already was.

I registered Mariko's voice. "But now that we know that our... friends... are a terrorist organization," she surmised, "you have to assume a near military model with good infrared."

"The best, in fact, in a Sleipnir." I tried to say it matter-of-factly. I stood up and stretched. I remained standing to unkink my legs, and also I had a slightly larger horizon and field of view. Light planes and a couple of media helicopters, including a new old bubble-Bell by its paint, circled around the canal. I looked toward Toulouse, and all around. No Sleipnir. I looked down at Mariko. "You know," I mused, "you and I have difficulties with communications." I stopped, as she looked a question up at me. "We have differences of nomenclature and the meaning of labels," I added.

"Yes...?" she said, but cautiously. She also stood up.

"The point is, Mariko, that I wished to hell that we *were* dealing with terrorists – and it is dangerous for both of us if you delude yourself that we are."

She was confused and angry. Just what I wanted. *"Wished we were dealing with terrorists! They're ruthless, they're unpredictable, they don't care who gets in the way! What could possibly be worse?"* It had been said vehemently. She had to turn her back on me in sheer helpless exasperation.

"All very true," I agreed mildly. "But one thing about terrorists is that they're fighting for a cause that can be realized. Once it *starts* to be acknowledged, the head terrorists become statesmen like Yasser Arafat or even Prime Ministers like Menachem Begin. Natanyahu and Ariel Sharon. They were all 'terrorists' once. And boy, once they become statesmen, are they ever hard on their dimmer-witted former terrorist colleagues who cannot perceive that their cause has been victorious in some way or another." I stopped as she seemed to be turning slightly toward me. "One man's terrorist is another man's patriot. Or, for that matter, today's terrorist may well be, and often has been, tomorrow's statesman. The term is very fluid, Mariko. It means little to me."

She had faced me, again, now. She looked up, and her mouth twitched into a shy corner-smile that could be taken as a peace-feeler.

"As for your question... *What could be worse?*" I continued. "Well, that's exactly what we are up against."

Mariko looked up at that. Her eyes widened from their tentatively friendly crinkle.

"Mystical *paramilitary* is worse. They do all the things that *terrorists* do with one big difference. Their cause can never be victorious in this world because their objectives can never be achieved in political or in economic terms. They can never transmute into statesmen because they can never achieve a state. Their goals are not of this world, they are spiritual." I paused. "And so, therefore, they are absolutely ruthless because even world opinion means nothing to them."

"Religious fanaticism."

"Combined with rigorous military organization."

"Like... like... the Inquisition," she said.

"Right. Now, describe the Inquisition if there had been helicopters, tanks, machine guns, gas chambers and all that good stuff."

"Nazi Germany," she whispered. Then it hit her. "My God, Marc, the Grail Crusaders are supposed to be a mystical neo-Nazi organization... "

"By George, I think she's got it!" I exclaimed, mimicking Colonel Pickering in *My Fair Lady*. There was a pause while I tried to think how to summarize. "Mariko, don't confuse your *terrorist* with the *mystical soldier*. Most of the Paddy O'Flanagans in the IRA will become clerks, gas bar attendants or sales representatives once their political goals even begin to be seriously viewed with serious policies to change things. Except for the few psychopaths, and there are always a few, who will be eliminated by the IRA faster than by anyone else. But mystical soldiers *are* psycho-paths... there's never any going back for your Dominican Inquisitor, your Nazi *Ubermensch* or your North German Grail

Crusader… whatever the hell that means. There's no place on earth for them to go, or to reach."

She thought about this, and bit her lip. She looked up.

"And, if you clear your mind of all preconceptions and maybe ingrained loyalties, you could well add Israel to that list along with Dominican Inquisitors and Nazi *Ubermensch*."

I saw her eyes widen again, then flare, but she bit back a quick and automatic retort. Finally, she nodded slowly. "Israel *is* more of an ideal than a geopolitical state." There was a rueful ghost of a smile. "But do you think that Israel could be involved with a group of neo-Nazis?"

"I don't know, Mariko. It *is* possible, I suppose. Geopolitics makes strange bedfellows. I sincerely hope not because the Israeli Mossad – its secret service – is about the most professional, efficient and ruthless organization in the world. The nasty thought came to me because the Israeli secret service is about the only organization outside of overt government with enough money to buy Sleipnirs. And four were bought through South Africa. When it comes to certain purchases, Mariko, that's understood as a euphemism for Israel." I handed her the papers and pointed to the list of Sleipnir purchasers.

"Yes", she finally nodded. "I do know about that much-criticized trade pact from articles in *The Manchester Guardian*."

"And if you think about it very carefully, Mariko, Israel has just as much to lose as the Vatican by any threat to orthodox Christianity."

After a few seconds, she said. "Perhaps that is why the Israeli government assisted Vatican experts in stalling about the release of the Dead Sea Scrolls translations."

"I think she's got it."

Mariko looked puzzled. "All right, Marc. Let's grant all that, as crazy as it may seem… But why would a neo-Nazi group conceive of itself as Grail Crusaders?"

I shrugged and stretched again, scanning the horizon along the canal. "Everyone wants to associate themselves with so-called goodness, Mariko. The problem is that the definition of what's good, honest and true may change over the centuries. It always has, in fact."

"I'm afraid again," she almost whispered.

"That makes two of us."

"What can we expect?" This was stronger.

We were back to the original question of the symposium but, perhaps, with greater insight. The spiral of conceptions, and all that.

"Even if they have missiles, machine guns or grenades they can drop, and they do, I don't *think* they will use them. One explosion is enough. More would cause talk. They are organized. They have *some* discipline. They have enough money for a Sleipnir, so I *know* that they have significant financial resources, organization, discipline and infrastructure. The *Lorelei* could be explained as an accident of carrying hazardous cargo, especially if there is not much wreckage to examine, but not two acts of pyrotechnic violence within a kilometre. They'll do what I've said, I think. They may overfly us a couple of times this afternoon. If they have IFR, and I must *assume* they do, then they will then know for certain, if they didn't before, that something is wrong – because the obvious heat source, the *birol*, is no longer here."

"Why did they leave, do you know?"

"I sent Roland on an errand, Mariko. It may help us, it will certainly help them. This isn't their problem."

Mariko nodded. "I see. Yes, of course, you're right."

"So. When they overfly again, see the *birol* gone, but the heat source remaining, they must investigate. No missiles, no machine guns or grenades from the air. They will land, and a few men will hop out to check it out. Obviously, with all this air traffic, they must come for us after dark. No telling the time. They may have a lot of things to check out, you know, and I refuse to believe that such a flimsy media cover could hide the operation of *two* choppers from routine police curiosity."

"So, Marc Rennsalaer, we just wait for them to come in the night..." She started to sniffle a bit. I ignored this.

I looked around and waved my arm. "This is something like a little bowl, Mariko. A little isolated bowl of hills with ridges running in it. And, so far as I can see, there's only one place to set a chopper down." I pointed toward the beach where the *birol* had been and where Francois had worked in the sun. "Now a helicopter, if it hovered or landed there, would be on *Jester's* level. Like a boat on water. No problem about altitude. But, in any case, it's point blank range, Mariko."

I watched Mariko as she looked at the situation. Slowly, she began to smile, but it was grim. "That's what I meant." I paused. "We have a chance to bring that chopper down. With luck, that is. But, in a way, the advantage of surprise is very much on our side. They will not expect that capability and they will not expect that resolve."

She wiped her eyes with a corner of her Jersey, revealing the lower part of one rounded breast. I was glad to see that it was not constrained by her workaday bra. It was bare and unfettered. Celtic women had always gone into battle like that. She sniffed again, looked up and tried a bright smile. "And... with luck," she said, "there might not be any survivors to tell about us."

I had considered this myself. "That is at least possible... with luck. But I doubt it. You see, Mariko, I've underestimated their ruthlessness and their planning. I tend to think they will radio back to someone before they check out any vessel and also afterwards."

"So, they'll have our position… even if we destroy the helicopter."

I grinned. "But they won't have the chopper, will they? They won't have a good description of *Jester*, either. They can't see her now, and they can't get a gook look if they land here after dark. And we can always change our position. Back to square one."

"What about the speedboat?"

"The canal will be crawling with police for a couple of days and I do not think that the cops will have much patience for a speedboat out there. Besides, at a pinch, *Jester* can take out a speedboat too. Easier."

"What will we do, Marc…?" She sat down on the edge of the poop deck again and pulled her knees up.

I assumed that she was asking about the longer future, some final resolution. "Like I said earlier, Mariko, I think we have to go to Glastonbury and get the rest of the parchment. If possible, it should be made very public somehow. That way, the danger will truly be over."

She sat there, rocking gently to herself, working it out. She finally nodded yes to herself, looked up and tried a small smile. "Well, then. What do we do while awaiting the wolves?"

I stretched again, as casually as I could do it. "Me, I'm for lunch. Then maybe a nap. Then, Mariko, I think I'd like have a look at the cause of all this. I'd like to have a good look at that parchment."

21

They came much later than I had thought they would.

And, in a way, as I realised when I had time to think about it, this fact alone made things turn out better for us than I could have reasonably expected. Their tardy arrival meant that their interest in the Lac des Doigts was considered a low priority compared with other data they had gathered.

Perhaps they came because of an IFR contact, which I had to assume. Or perhaps they had glimpsed *Jester* below the camouflage nets, which I considered unlikely. Or, maybe they simply wanted to check out the *birol* they had seen, the men and tracks on the beach. I was never to know why they came. By the time they got around to us the crew must have been tired.

But, initially, their late arrival caught me less than bright-eyed and bushy-tailed. Mariko and I had brought the settees' foam mattresses up on deck. After a while we stretched out on them. For a time, we looked at the bright Pyrenees stars visible over the shimmering grey-white peaks to the south. Our only other light was the pulsating green glow from the wheelhouse where the Decca radar screens swept their beams round and round. The Toshiba was nestled in its wheelhouse shelf, all hooked up, but somnolent. The pneumatic cannons were horizontal, poking through the bullet shield, and their muzzles seemed to quiver with the slightly fishy scent of the beach. This was merely a trick of the pulsating green light on polished brass.

Mariko explained, in detail, that it was not difficult to be an academic's protégé. One merely had to be a scrupulous student whenever one was in public. Since she had always been a scrupulous student, this had never been difficult. No hint of the liaison had ever reached the professor's wife and colleagues, so far as she knew. As for these colleagues, it was necessary only to dress rather primly and to be so obsessed with linguistics that no one could imagine her capable of anything else. That had been easy, too, for it had been very nearly true. As for sex, every week or two she had only to lay back and spread her legs. He had not been demanding and had not required much response. Indeed, response had seemed mildly off-putting to him.

Then, Mariko had switched to Ireland, father, mother and growing roses. Somehow, and I still don't know how, I just fell asleep while Mariko was telling me about her family's greenhouses near Cork. This was all the more surprising since we were on our backs and holding hands, so there was visual, auditory and tactile stimulation. Maybe I had just lost my edge.

Anyway, the thwacking of the chopper's blades, and the underlying moan of turbojets, fitted seamlessly into a dream in which Somalia featured. But this wasn't all that surprising since the mountains are similarly barren, the vegetation similar and Somalia had also boasted some helicopters. I opened my eyes the instant Mariko's hand clamped my shoulder, but for a moment this didn't help. As it chanced, bright Aldeberan blazed above jagged Pyrenees teeth... just as it had blazed above Somalian peaks years before. I wasn't certain that I wasn't dreaming still.

"Damn you! Wake up!" She shook me. Hard. And that did it.

Rolling off the foam, and coming up with the AR-15 ready in one hand and the RC console in the other, the undoubtedly real thwacking and moaning came to my ears. It registered even then that the chopper was throttling back, was circling our little ridge-rimmed bowl, but at first I couldn't see it because it was low among the hills and in shadow against a *maquis* background.

"Two o'clock low," Mariko hissed from near the hatchway.

Two o'clock low...? Where had Mariko picked *that* up? I glanced at her, saw her opening and awakening the Toshiba in the hatchway, and decided firmly that green illumination did nothing for Oriental skin tones. Nonetheless, the helicopter was – or had been – at two o'clock low. I picked it up easily by the time I snatched my eyes back from Mariko. But it didn't throttle back and feather its blades as if to set down. I know that sound. She was going around again, as if puzzled.

And well she might be. *Jester's* steam engine was quietly ticking over at about 50 revs, necessary to charge the batteries that the Deccas were discharging, and for compressing air. And, now, for the Toshiba. Soon, maybe, for all the electrical innards of the cannons. As I've said, I intended to use personal computer fire control if Mariko balked... PCFC... and the cannons were even now tracking the chopper. But Mariko was waltzing eagerly around the wheelhouse behind the shield. There was probably a strong IFR signal, and perhaps two radar signatures as well, and all coming from a patch of *maquis*. I could well understand their befuddlement.

I scrabbled behind the pile of casks with the AR-15 and the radio control console, noting en passant that Mariko was doing exactly what we'd planned and rehearsed. She was staying directly behind the cannon's shield with her hands on the red switches. She had the best-protected place on deck... so long as the enemy was in front of the barrels, that is.

With the chopper circling around again, I wanted to make sure that I could see what it was doing. If it did anything hostile, I'd decided to open up with the cannons and the AR-15. This chopper didn't sound like a police helicopter and so it had no business thwacking around at night. Its very low altitude was also illegal. But, so long as it didn't do anything nasty, like shooting small arms at us, we'd just wait for it to land on the little beach in front of Mariko's air cannons.

Mariko's expression, as I glimpsed it from time to time, conveyed an eagerness that I found odd. She was scared, I could see that from the way her teeth clamped her lip. But she was also keyed up beneath the fear. Her eyes were bright and wide whenever the Decca beams glinted off them. But her cheeks also reflected wetly. She was afraid and excited at the same time. Women. Me, I was just scared.

As the helicopter banked to port to come around us on the canal side, it cleared the hills and swung out over the spit of land that separated our lagoon from the channel. This low horizon glowed with the soft sheen of unseen village lights and streetlights across the canal. I caught a silhouette and knew it for the Sleipnir. Good. This confirmed that it wasn't a police helicopter.

"Mariko, what time is it?" I didn't want to take my eyes off the Sleipnir for an instant.

"Two-thirty a.m.," she stage-whispered. And with the chopper making all that racket? That's when the surprise hit me that they were so late getting around to us. "I'm ready, Marc," she hissed.

"Hmmm. I can see that."

The Sleipnir was banking round our stern and would soon be back against the hills and *maquis,* but by now my eyes were fully opened, as it were, and I'd acquired some night vision. When glancing at Mariko, I'd been careful not to look directly at the brightest part of any glow. This time, I didn't lose the chopper against the background. During this dark-side half of the circle though, I made out the dim light inside her through her cabin windows. A tasteful, very subdued amber aura emanated from the instrument panels. Studies had shown that this colour, not green, actually tired the eyes less. It also affected night vision less – green tends to induce its complementary colour, red, when you look away from it into the dark. You can't beat Scandinavians for applied research.

The moan lessened, and the whacking quite suddenly became a much softer swish. I followed the shadow, peeking up from under the nets, to make sure that it was canting around toward the beach. The sand shone pale gold in the starlight, and I saw that Aldeberan actually cast a wraith shadow of a twisted pine undulating over the little hummocks. Presently, these little dunes started to dissipate before my eyes, and little glints of sand, flicking starlight, whirled down and outward in billows.

I took this moment to get prone on the poop deck, well clear of Mariko, with the AR-15 pointing between a rounded vee in the piled casks toward the descending helicopter. Stoner's flat black finish precluded any reflection. I settled the console beneath my left hand.

I glanced over toward Mariko. "Steady, Honey..." I said, as calmly as I could. We'd gone over the fact that for morality's sake, not to mention legal ones, we had to make absolutely certain that armed men got out of the helicopter before we shot at anything.

The Sleipnir settled slowly, terribly slowly, it seemed, into a thickening cloud of boiling sand that glittered and flicked pale silver in Aldeberan's sheen. I noticed a brief increase in the amber glow, as the door slid back and spilled it out onto the beach. Just as quickly, though, it was eclipsed by man-forms jostling toward us. I discerned thin, rigid shadows wavering upwards diagonally from them. They wavered more as they jumped from the chopper. I heard the scrunches as their feet hit the sand. But I was unable to count them. Now, they would have seen *Jester's* hull beneath the nets and through the sand storm of their landing.

"Police! Descendez! Les mains en l'air!" It was French, but the accent was thick. Also, I had good reason to doubt that any French cop would be so rude to a darkened boat at that hour. We had not even seen any police from our little lake and had certainly not offered any provocation or reason to arouse suspicion. The dark blobs were standing, still, but I could no longer see those diagonal, thin shadows. I could see the white words on the side of the Sleipnir. Staggered kinda funny.

"Was wollen sie?" I asked, for I truly *was* curious about what they wanted so badly. "Wir sprechen nur ein wienig?" And it was also true that I did want to talk a little... but from a distance. They were standing in the same way, one man more or less behind the other, as I could see from the amber glow seeping out of the chopper's cargo doors. It bothered me mightily that a Sleipnir could carry six soldiers, and I was counting just two men in addition to a form...or *two*?... at the console.

"Kommen sie herunter," a voice said. "Come down here," another voice repeated, in English. Apparently they had placed my accent, and my German, never good, was rusty.

"Nein," I replied evenly.

"Haben sie eine Madschen zum bot?" I waited, and the other voice repeated it in English. "Is there a girl aboard? Oriental looking?" Were only two men on the beach?

I heard Mariko's intake of breath. "Easy, Sweetie," I whispered. "Nein," I called out. "No girl here."

"We intend to find out," that second voice said. "We'll come by force if necessary."

"Ja, wir kommen, Yankee."

"Are you guys refugees from old war movies?" I actually heard a chuckle. From number two, obviously. "You need asylum," I added as an afterthought. Mariko giggled, but very softly.

"Just give us the girl, or let us see for ourselves that there is no girl aboard, and we'll leave you in peace."

"You'll rest in peace if you don't clear out," I answered. "You're not French police, Dumkopf. And I have a gun. Don't take one tiny step toward this boat." I heard some muttering, and one gutteral exclamation. I honestly thought it was 'Schweinhund,' but I doubted that even then. The flashes and ker-blams came almost simultaneously. I heard a heavy whine, more like a buzz, whizzing off either the cannon shield or the wheelhouse.

You don't fool around in combat. So, I just said "Fire!" to Mariko. She said, much later, that I had sounded quite calm. Naturally, I didn't believe her.

I heard the phutt-phutting of her cannons and so I ignored the RC console. All hell broke loose around the Sleipnir. The first phutt was followed by a terrific flash against a hill behind the chopper. I'd lost my night vision in that flash, but not my memory of where the man-forms had been. I opened up with Stoner's brainchild. The range was less than forty yards.

Funny thing about an AR-15. It doesn't sound like the ker-blam of any other gun. It has a rough, terminal-sounding and explosive cough. At six hundred rounds per minute, though, it sounds almost exactly like one of those pneumatic drills that mechanics use to tighten your tire's lug nuts. Almost. Much louder. And it bucks in your hands mightily each time, but not traumatically. The shadows in the bare amber glow assumed all sorts of grotesque positions before I could see them no longer. I stood up, but stayed crouched. I could make out shapes on the beach.

The Sleipnir flowered into orange and red incandescence before my eyes. Forget about night vision. Incredibly, though, I heard the moaning increase. I honestly thought that it came from Odin's steed, now mortally wounded. A great thwacking sound. Valkyrie wing-beats. Very slow, but that chopper actually lifted up. Another flash of orange and red, and a pillow of hot air reeled me back, but Sleipnir lifted off anyway. It banked away, and was very easy to see, because it trailed flames. Another flash, a roar, and thump of heat, but that came from a not-so-distant ridge of rock behind the beach.

"Okay, Mariko. For God's sake stop."

I watched the flame soar gracefully up and into the southern sky. It didn't sound right, though, as it closed range with Aldeberan. But it topped the nearest shimmering ridge and plummeted down below, beyond my vision. It seemed an inordinately long time later before the southern sky flared, and Pyrenees teeth bared whitely just for an instant. There was surprisingly small thunder in the distance.

As arranged, I bent to the deck and slid the AR-15 toward the wheelhouse. I was on the move, and drawing the Walther from beneath my shirt, before the distant rumble had faded into poignant echoes. Not forgetting to keep to the corridor made of Bouchard's casks – how could I? – I was along the foredeck and had scrambled over *Jester's* drawn-up ramp before I really knew what I was doing. My feet hit the sand, scrunching comfortably, just about the time that a flash, but a small and focussed one, ruined my night vision for good. The Walther bucked in my hand before I knew I'd pulled the trigger. A shadow was flung back like a floppy spider. Then I had sand in my mouth, and the shrieking agony of a hot poker shoved slowly into my calf. The only solace, and it wasn't much right then, was the cool water lapping over my toes. Presently, I heard coughing, *loud* coughing. It went on. And on. Some mechanic changing a lot of tires.

22

Now, as strange as it seems to me, I think I dozed off again. I do not think, to this day, that I passed out. The pain in my calf was just excruciating, not actually unbearable. And it seemed to diminish to bearable, much as though you'd jerked your hand away from a red-hot element that would, however, leave a nasty burn welt. Cool water had filled my shoes.

On the other hand, in spite of my previous adventures, I'd never actually been shot before. So, perhaps I did pass out from some sort of shock. I know only that I went right back into that dream of mountains and Aldeberan. And it could not have been for all that long.

I awakened quite suddenly, and saw Mariko very clearly bending over my legs. She had turned the searchlight on, but we were in the shadows of *Jester's* hull. The light glimmered on her cheek. I noticed that Aldeberan had not moved much. I casually flexed the knee of my good leg up, feeling my right heel gouge a little furrow in the sand as I did. The sand felt more intimate than against the padded heels of the Nikes, so I glanced at my knee and saw, with some surprise, that it was bare. I met Mariko's eyes because she had turned toward me at my abrupt movement.

"Keep still," she said, and smiled. I knew *that* because faint light glittered off very white teeth. I felt tugging on my left calf, and it occurred to me to wonder why there was no pain until my eyes flicked around and saw the white box, also glimmering in the assorted starlight and aided considerably by the glow bouncing off *Jester's* white hull. That explained it. She had used an ampoule of Novocaine. Maybe more. The tugging became insistent, and I saw her dextrous hand pull a ribbon of Elastoplast tight while the other hand, just as dextrously, snipped it with a click of scissors. She returned the scissors and tape to the box. She rummaged around.

"You have a well-stocked First Aid kit," she said, brandishing a condom.

"How do you know how to use it?"

"I read labels and instructions."

"Hmmm." I put my hands behind my head. I truly felt very good. I watched her tidy up the contents of the box. She looked around on the sand and even added the spent Novocaine ampoule. So, there was no urgency. There was no panic.

"How much of the second banana clip did you... use?" I asked.

"All of it," she answered, veddy casually.

"I see," I said. At point blank range, from *Jester's* gunwale? Dear, sweet God. Well, I could think of nothing more productive to do than close my eyes for a moment, trying to forget about that carnage, but, of course imaging it all the more vividly. So, I gave that up and opened my eyes again. It suddenly came to me how cold, diamond-like and distant those Pyrenees stars looked. I must have still been somewhat dozy because it came to me only then that I was more than a little cold, and that I was shivering. The reason for this, and that came to me rather slowly, too, was that I had nothing on except the flannel shirt. I glanced down at myself to verify this, discovering that it was true.

I saw, also, that I had a more than substantial erection, given the rather incongruous circumstances. Or, I thought it was incongruous, because at that moment Mariko snicked the First Aid box closed, and clicked its clamps shut at the same time with deft and definite co-operation of both hands. She turned to find me looking at myself. As she gazed at me, I began to feel my erection, too. Tissue stretched more tightly than many times before, and a heavy throbbing that not only rocked my penis gently above my abdomen, but argued, I noted, no damage to my cardio-vascular system. My brain registered, too, testicles weighing hot and heavy, swollen, in the valley of my uneven thighs.

Mariko looked at me, and her eyes crinkled mischievously at my suddenly embarrassed expression. She smiled. Slowly. "A perfectly normal reaction, Mister Rennsalaer," she said, but not quite clinically. "After excitement and stimulation, particularly after a potentially life-threatening experience, and especially after one combined with painful physical trauma, males nearly always react sexually. And they do so acutely just before the moment of death... even quite aged males... decades older than you," she finished.

In my still dozy state, now combined with the pleasant embarrassment of her looking at me, I wasn't quite sure whether she was giving me good news or bad news. "El momento de la veridad," I said. My tongue generally murdered Spanish less brutally than it bludgeoned French.

She giggled, giving me the information that was intriguing me. Part of it. The rest followed clinically. "Not likely, Mister Rennsalaer, in at least *one* sense in which the Spanish use that term." She paused. Gee, it was great to be involved with a linguist... "No mortidad," she said. "Just a bit of inside calf muscle torn through and, I suppose, *away*, if you understand."

"I think I have it."

"No tib or fib trauma... breaks..."

"Got it. How do you know this stuff?"

"My roomy at Armagh was in medicine. I helped her quizz for exams... No pulsating bleeding indicative of a traumatised femoral artery, although it *does* bifurcate below the knee – I just forget the names of them then."

"I see," I said.

"And no loss of pulse, or blood-pressure due to shock," she said.

"How do you know that?"

She smiled slowly again. She nodded toward my throbbing penis, and cocked an eyebrow. "That seems obvious from that indicator there."

Rather surprisingly, though, she stood up. But, even more surprisingly, this was only because it was easier for her to peel the horizontally-striped Jersey over her head. Rather full, but not actually *Rubenesque*, upturned and pleasantly peaked breasts jiggled ever so briefly in the light's reflection. I had expected... imagined?... I had not had much time for such speculations, but they somehow had wriggled through on occasion, darker Oriental nipples. Perhaps suffused with pink and red epidermal embers in excitement.

What jiggled as she flung the jersey away were large gilded aureols, squeezed into spun gold whorls by the pressure of arousal, and surmounted with finger-thick cylinders of pure, rich gold. These might have held low and sputtering small candles, for, so far as I could tell, the golden skin glowed from within.

My throbbing increased, and she could see that. She smiled, and posed in the starlight, for just an instant. "What is seldom mentioned," she continued almost clinically, although the professional rendition was becoming somewhat disrupted by irregular breathing, "is that females after trauma experience analogous reactions. Swollen nipples..." She paused in the starlight.

"I got it," I said.

"... and an... exfoliation... of... of... lubrication from..." The pauses were caused mostly by her shucking of the Jordache jeans. The jeans were followed by blue nylon briefs, showing that she had appreciated the multi-coloured briefs discreetly left for her only two... or three?... days previously. She swayed toward me, hips canting with every step, in the soft sand. "And rhythmic contractions of various internal organs..." Orientals are the most glabrous, to use a scientific term, of all existing human 'racial' types. Mariko had no pubic hair, merely a deep... *deep*... cleft in a soft-fuzzed mound, like a particularly juicy peach. The moisture content could not reasonably be doubted because even in the shadows there was enough illumination to show that her thighs glistened.

She stood over me and turned slowly one way and then the other so that I could get a good look. She raised her elbows as she put her hands behind her neck and arched her back so that her ribs stretched under taut flesh and her breasts quivered heavily.

"Damn!" She'd discovered the ponytail. She must have removed the elastic because her hair soon fell past her shoulders. She shook it into place. "Let's try that again," she said.

So, she turned and stretched upward again, but this time she looked down demurely with closed eyes, turned her head slightly to hide one downcast eye behind the fringe of hair and bit her lip in a superb exhibition of helpless, apprehensive vulnerability. She reminded me of merchandise I once almost bought at a slave auction in Somalia.

She knelt slowly beside me, holding her hands back as long as she could. Then she shifted next to me and rolled the condom on. She had obviously been undoing more than her ponytail. She straddled me, folding her long legs so that her knees were snuggled against the sides of my chest, and squeezing. I saw just how long those legs were.

"Be gentle with me, Mariko," I said, "I'm injured... "

She giggled.

With a confident hand, she manipulated the swollen and pulsing head of my penis to the right place. Like an artist, she lowered herself slowly, very slowly, so that I felt all the sensation of her peach-lips parting. Reluctantly, so it seemed to me. And I felt strongly, naughtily and deliciously invasive.

"El momento de la veridad," she whispered. The moment of truth, as the Spaniards say, when the brave bull is about to be skewered by the stiff and rigid matador. Of course, to do this, the matador must enter the deadly circle of the horns.

But I found the entrance closed against me. She applied the pressure of her body and, slowly, reluctantly it seemed to me, the soft and moist gates into her parted to the throbbing and eager invader. She shoved down, a little push, and the distended, swollen foreguard penetrated the outer defences. She sobbed, and wriggled, and she thrust her hips backward, thrusting her breasts forward at the same time, until I could reach up to grasp, and pull them to my mouth, and suck the nipples into swollen pacifiers.

But she never surrendered. With muscle discipline within her, the invader fought for every single millimetre of moist conquest. Occasionally, Mariko counter-attacked with determined muscle closure on the way up into her. And she did it superbly. Her interior muscles were so strong, and so responsive to her will, that she might well have actually been able to squeeze me out of her. But of course, she never intended that. It was a see-saw contest scripted for her to lose. But not before her resistance had subjected the invader to the maximum possible stimulation. And herself.

At times, I became so eager to have her, and just to get release from the unbearable sensations, that I grasped her hips with my hands and tried to force her down on me to get it over with. But she was by now sweaty, and slippery, and she would twist her hips suddenly so that my fingers slipped from her curves and, instead, gouged smooth furrows in her thighs as she would rise up and away. This started the moist, frantic internal battle all over again. And, in addition, sweetened it with visual stimulus. For, with her knees flexed so that she hovered above me, I saw that her interior struggles undulated her golden abdomen, from her navel to that clefted peach, in waves of helpless response. And, as she clamped her hands over mine, to force my hands from her swollen flesh rising between my fingers, and the furrowed flesh dimpling beneath them, her arm and chest muscles tightened with effort, letting her breasts sway and dance heavily.

By the time the foreguard reached her final citadel, at *exactly* the time that my unbearably throbbing penis snuggled into the dimple of her cervix, I exploded. The searing heat of me caused a sudden capitulation, and it was a shudder that caused Mariko's writhing torso to pull away, her breasts briefly heaving frantically in the glimmer, before she bent back to me and bury her hot molten-gold candlesticks in my chest. And I had thought that those candles had guttered.

I held her until her shuddering stopped, and until I felt my invader contracting and receding from a citadel that had been stormed and conquered, yes, but had somehow absorbed and nullified the invader.

After a while, she sat back and smiled. "Pretty good jig-jig, heya GI Joe...?" she said, and giggled. Linguists. Women.

"Your... er... mentor must have been in pretty good shape, Mariko O'Shaugnessey."

"I never did that with him," she responded. "He wouldn't have liked it." She paused and smiled. "*That* I discovered myself."

"I'm honoured that you decided to share it."

She rolled moistly from me and sucked my now-inadequate and much more tentative penis from her. I noticed that Aldeberan was blazing less fiercely. Knowing astronomy, I did not chalk this up the lesser amounts of helium being transformed into hydrogen in the few minutes we'd been on the sand, but to the advent of dawn. "What time is it, Mariko?" I asked.

She glanced at her watch, which was drowned and useless, but which she had retained. The only thing she had retained. But her memory conjured up continual digital reminders from the Toshiba's screen. "I guess," she said, "about three-thirty." She yawned.

They say that a man's work is from sun to sun, but a woman's work is never done. She had had a full day of domestic chores. Making breakfast for a strange man on a strange boat. Surviving an explosion and thinking she'd been locked down in a sinking boat. Downloading all that stuff from the computer. Finding out that she was most probably being hunted by a neo-Nazi organization for reasons unknown, with the possible assistance of the Vatican and even the Israeli Mossad. Shooting down an attack helicopter with cannons. Blasting two thugs to mincemeat with her AR-15. Playing Florence Nightingale with my leg. Raping me. Well, I could see with my discerning eye that this O'Shaugnessey rose was wilting.

My knowledge of women, little good though it appeared to be most of the time, had at least impressed one absolute datum on my mind: After orgasm, and Mariko had arranged that, women invariably *go to sleep*. Men may be restless, preoccupied with intimations of mortality whispered by 'la petite mort', but women will snore.

She yawned again. And I could see a droop from her eyelids that had no relation to epicanthic characteristics. She was kneeling side saddle in the sand, supporting herself with a braced, straight arm. Her chin dropped, and her breasts drooped – one exhausted and dissipated geisha. She was absolutely gorgeous.

I reluctantly stopped looking at her, and rolled over onto my knees. This caused me to remember the injury my left calf had sustained, and I waited for the pain but it didn't come. Great! I bounced to my feet, or at least my genitals did, and Mariko giggled again. She was getting giddy. I felt very, very good except for one small emotional corner of dissatisfaction. An unfulfilled yearning. No, urgent necessity. I wanted to rape her in retaliation.

23

Being the modern man that I am, I resisted the urge to "rape" Mariko and I instead shuffled unsteadily the few steps to her and extended my right arm down to help her up.

But then I noticed the new bandage on my burned right hand. I had ripped the old one off when I had slid the AR-15 back toward Mariko, while running forward and knowing I'd have to draw the Walther from beneath my left arm. The sudden squeeze on the pistol's trigger, and the convulsive grip of the hand when the Walther kicked, had been enough to burst the fat blisters and crack open broiled skin.

Mariko must have attended to the hand while she had waited for the Novocaine to numb my calf. I was glad she'd done things in that order... and I noticed that this new bandage was a more practical affair than the first one. She seemed resigned to the fact that my right hand was going to be used, so she had just taped a very smooth and firm bandage around my palm, to cover the worst of the burn on the back of my hand, and had left the red fingers free. These fingers resembled newly ground sausages more than anything else, sausages only recently packed into sheaves of clear skin. But they worked, and she had accepted that they would probably have to work some more.

Mariko looked up at me, took my newly and alternatively extended left hand, and I hauled her to her feet. She fell against me gently, and I pressed her to me with my left arm. All this on top of the previous ten days. "C'mon, Kid," I said. "We've got to get you to bed."

"But... but... there's so much to do, Marc... " She waved vaguely up the beach. "We can't just leave those bodies there. Causes talk." She giggled and tried a grin up at me. "And those nets," she pointed slackly above *Jester*, "what about those...?"

"I have several notions, Mariko. The police will be here any time, I think... should have been here already, maybe. I'll take care of things. Let's get you to bed." So, muffling a soft protest by squeezing her head into my shoulder as I lifted her up, I swung her knees over the side of *Jester* to save her a scramble over the rail, and she pivoted her feet gracefully down. I was bending to collect her Adidas shoes, the Jordache jeans and the striped Jersey. After looking a bit in the shadows from the hull, I finally found her nylon panties in my own shadow, and moist and musty-pine scented they were, too. I handed these up to her.

"Okay, Mariko," I smiled and I hoped she could see it in the faint light. "Make sure you don't drop any of that stuff on deck. Just go below and flake out, Love. Don't worry."

She nodded sleepily, and tried to cover her yawn with one of the hands that clasped the clothing to her chest. She turned away, and I came to the rail, rested my chin and watched her walk carefully along the foredeck. *Long* legs. And a bum like another, larger and plumper peach with a rosy-gold infolding cleft.

Me, I had a plan... the best that I figured I could do under the circumstances. I scanned the beach and found the AR-15 where she'd thrown it. Sand poured out of the muzzle, and trickled out of the breech – it was open to accept the next round which had never came from the empty banana magazine.

I went over to the two bodies. They were a mess. They seemed to have some sort of uniform-like clothing on, but I couldn't see in the dark. I looked around, and finally found the Schmeisser machine pistols. *Three* of them? Two had the long-barrel attachments I had seen when the men had tumbled from the chopper, but the third had just the short pistol barrel. I did not touch them, of course, but this third gun meant that I might be able to keep the AR-15... if I hurried.

Therefore, I quickly did what I had to do first. I found the jeans that Mariko had partly cut away, and then had slipped off of me. Using the scissors from the First Aid box, I amputated them into cut-offs and put them on. I took the jean scraps and the First Aid box to a convenient spot on the beach – not too close to the bodies, and leaving enough room for a helipad. I crossed the jean legs to mark the place of my fire, and moved the First Aid box to a place that would be within the firelight when it came. I opened the box's top, and made messy what Mariko had packed so carefully. I even found the used and empty Novocaine ampoule, which she had replaced so as not to leave trash on the beach, and I placed this deeply dimpled clear plastic tube on top of things so that it would twinkle in the firelight.

I vaulted over *Jester's* rail, negotiated the narrow detour around Bouchard's wine, and arrived on the poop. It didn't take long to find the other, first, banana clip. I put it by the hatch with the gun while I took the few minutes to up-end the cannons, replacing the whistle inserts first, and to connect the normal steam hoses to the boiler. I left the foam mattresses on the deck.

Gathering up the AR-15, the extra banana clip and the two boxes, and noticing that Mariko had attended to the delicate Toshiba by turning it off and closing its top, I fumbled my way down the wheelhouse steps and through the waterproof bulkhead door into the cabin. Mariko was showering, and I could hear occasional splashes of water that seemed odd, until I recognised the sound for wringing of heavy, saturated material. She was washing out the Jordache jeans and the Jersey. Yes, they would have sand in them.

Her activity gave me time to open my cache, and stuff the rifle, the extra clip for it, and the two still-weighty boxes down inside. Making a decision reluctantly, I shrugged first out of my flannel shirt, and then out of the shoulder holster. I wrapped the PPK up in the leather straps, I nestled it into the cache. I didn't feel right without it, but then I would shortly be meeting police. The way things were on the beach, well, it was a good chance I'd be searched. Not good to have an unlicensed firearm in one's possession... on the other hand, if I hadn't had some unlicensed pyrotechnics in my possession, Mariko and I would not now be possessing anything except spiritual natures – and had anyone *proved* that that was best?

I closed and locked the cache. From a cabinet near the head of my bunk, I collected my folding camera tripod, my old Hassleblad 500C outfit, and my *Birds of Southern Europe*. I also hid the cache key in its nest deep in the cabinet's veneer.

Now I took these articles back through the wheelhouse en route for the poop, and heard the shower sounds stop while I was closing the bulkhead door. In the wheelhouse briefly, I reached up and fitted the two toggles into protruding perforated brass tabs above my head. These, when the toggles were through their holes, locked the cannon tubes down to the wheelhouse top independently of the brass knobs outside. Now, the tubes could not be pivoted from vertical short of bending them or wrenching them from their mounting on the wheelhouse roof.

I climbed up the steps and onto the poop. There, I took time to set up the tripod and put a long Hasselblad lens onto it. Then I let a couple of extra Hasselblad backs fall carefully onto the foam mattress, added two unopened boxes of 120 professional colour film. As an artistic touch, I opened the end of one of the boxes, and let the roll come half out. More artistry – and time – when I took the trouble to find "Lammergaier" in the index, flip to the proper pages, and placed the splayed-open book face down on deck beside the mattresses.

I headed back along *Jester's* deck, this time wondering how much trouble Bouchard's casks were going to cause, but decided not to vault over *Jester's* rail. This time, I lowered the six-and-a-half-foot wide landing-craft type of ramp from *Jester's* blunt bow. It was raised and lowered by a boat trailer winch, and unwinding it consumed about ninety seconds.

Running off the ramp... and now starting to notice a throbbing in my left leg... I made for the line of *maquis*. Choosing smaller pines I could uproot by hand, I gathered a bundle and piled them on the beach on top of the crossed jean legs. I had left enough room for a helicopter to land, but the fire wouldn't endanger the sprawled bodies. I lit the pile quickly from waterproof Australian matches that I always carry around my neck in a plated brass water-tight cylinder. The dry pine flared instantly, and I went back for another bundle of *maquis*.

When these were dumped on, the flames rose in a bright orange spire. The bonfire also lit up the sand on the beach. This could be seen for miles, from the air. Not more than five minutes later, I was gratified to hear the sound of a helicopter in the far distance. I went for another easy load of *maquis*, adding fuel to the flames. Then I ran aboard *Jester*, up to the poop. I turned the light in the wheelhouse up to maximum illumination, and left the Deccas turning.

Taking the searchlight from its mount, I beamed S-O-S to all quarters of the sky. After a minute or so, the approaching helicopter, which I could now see carried proper flying lights and a strobe, flashed its landing lights on and off. It wasn't far away now, and I was illuminated by *Jester's* re-mounted searchlight. I limped my way back to the bow of *Jester*. And, since I was being watched by trained and shrewd eyes that I dared not underestimate, I didn't limp *much* more than I felt like doing.

I ran out over the ramp and onto the beach just as the helicopter set gently down on the almost exactly where the Sleipnir had been. I was standing by the fire, waving, and I *was* relieved... in a way... that this chopper was blue and had "POLICE" written on it in nice, big letters. Shielding my eyes against the sand blowing up all around, I waited for them to step out of the four-seater *Kestrel*.

Disconcertingly, one of the gendarmes carried one of the new Gasconnade assault rifles, normally reserved for French commandos and based on Stoner's cartridge without the lunatic additions to the rifle, and the other carried a shotgun of considerable bore that I didn't recognise. These weapons were not actually pointing *at* me, though, just nearby. That, at least, was a distinct improvement over the previous encounter.

Following the uniformed gendarmes was a middle-aged man in plain clothes. He kept his face down, ducking needlessly from the rotors and also to shield his eyes from the settling sand with a hat that he was firmly clamping down over his head.

When plain clothes man raised his eyes, finally, and blinked the grit out of them, I recognised him as a very weary Inspector Bernard Gabereau. He was head of the Carcassonne office of the Canal Police.

We had met a few times along the canal, and also once because *Jester* had been at the right place at the right time to rescue an impromptu raft crewed by one French Tom Sawyer, one Huck Finn, and a Becky. A sudden storm had come up while they drifted, and the wind had pushed them three kilometres toward Carcassonne and around a bend. Emergency calls, and that sort of thing.

Jester, coming around the same bend seconds after hearing the police distress call, just came alongside the raft and the kids scrambled aboard. I even took their raft in tow, since Captain Tom had expressed the intention of going down with it.

The kids were pleased at being on a real steamboat. Becky toot-**tooted** all the way to Inspector Gabereau's office. I therefore knew that Gabereau spoke English quite well.

He stopped and graced me with a small, cautious smile when he recognized me. "Bonjour… Monsieur Rennsalaer… n'est-ce pas?"

"Oui," I said wearily. "Inspecteur Gabereau, well, vous avez beaucoup de trouble."

24

Gabereau gazed toward the two bodies on the beach, took off his hat and flapped it against his thigh to puff the sand and dust out of it. The two gendarmes had gone immediately to the sprawled forms as soon as it became apparent that Gabereau knew me and was not particularly anxious about it. French gendarmes carry curious little flashlights and they viewed the corpses with these. But not for long. A muffled "Mon Dieu" came to our ears.

"Dead?" Gabereau asked me.

"Very," I answered. "Several times over, in fact."

As the gendarmes stood up, not saying much, but turning somewhat helplessly toward Gabereau, the Inspector started to trudge tiredly in their direction. "Trouble," the Inspector grumbled it.

"Ah... excuse me, Inspector," I said quietly. He turned back, looked me up and down. "When I said you have lots of trouble, I wasn't referring only to the barge. Or them," I gestured up the beach. He waited, so I went on. "I was thinking rather of the helicopter that exploded just over that ridge there." I pointed. "I thought you'd know. Surely, someone's reported it by now?"

"Not yet," he said. This time he turned away and went over to his men and the bodies.

In the firelight, I'd seen a lumpish thing a bit further long the beach, nearer where the *birol* had been. I limped over to it. It proved to be a substantial half-log, and the smell of this morning's – *yesterday morning's* – grilling bream came to me. If there was one half-log, well, there might be two, I reasoned. Somewhat surprised, I actually saw it a few feet away half-buried in the sand. I picked one up in each hand, and limped back into the circle of firelight. As I planted them, working them into the sand, I noticed the young gendarme with the Gasconnade watching me suspiciously. Suddenly a wave of both anger and exhaustion swept over me, so I pointedly ignored him as I sat down on one of the half-logs.

My crimes were puny, and committed in self-defence, compared to the crimes against Mariko and me. And if we had gone to the police with our story and fears, we would have been patronized and laughed at, and we'd have got no protection at all. My anger was building, not subsiding, and I decided to retain it as a good companion with Gabereau. I spat into the fire, a little toward the young gendarme with his play-toy. He jerked and scrunched in the sand, glaring at me. He took a step toward me.

"Allez, mon enfant," I said tiredly, "voulez-vous le manger, votre fusil?" I flicked a hand at his assault rifle. "Allez, mon garçon." I'd offered to feed him his assault rifle, and he didn't like it. He realized that he couldn't do anything without Gabereau's orders, so he stopped. But he didn't like it, and he never knew that he was lucky.

The half-log was a foot high, maybe, and it teetered in the sand, but with my legs stretched out toward the fire, the log and I made a tripod that was stable enough. Gabereau had ducked his head into the helicopter's door. He was bent at a curious angle such that I could imagine him talking into the radio's microphone, and thumbing the button occasionally to hear a response. I could hear the soft mumbling interspersed with sizzles of static.

The chopper whined down, as I knew it must, for Gabereau was obliged to call in an ambulance helicopter and a full homicide crew. The Inspector bent even further. I could almost see him hooking the microphone in place, as he ducked back out of the doorway. Drooping blades look lower than they really are. The gendarme said something brusque and edgy to Gabereau, but the motor was still whining down into a death moan and I couldn't catch the words. Also, like many people poor at a language, I could converse – well, almost – so long as responses were appropriately simple and slow. Most people were kind to me. But I had a hard time following the rapid repartee between natives. I saw Gabereau walk over to him, say a few words, dole out a weary chuckle, and slap the boy's shoulder. I saw dust puff with this. Gabereau walked my way, saw the half-log upended for him, and sank down gingerly. Like me, he extended his splayed feet to the fire, although his were shod with polished leather. Not disreputable fabric and plastic. Wet fabric.

"He's young," Gabereau observed.

"But does he want to grow older...?" I mused.

"Now, now," said the Inspector. "I'm tired, too." He paused, flapped his hat again, and placed it on his lap. "Just came in. A farmer reported a small plane crashing and burning. Took him a while to get to a phone."

I glanced at my Seiko. "It took him an hour and twenty minutes, Inspector. The time of death – for all concerned – was three-thirty a.m., near enough. I didn't check the time *immediately*." I saw Gabereau take a notebook from inside his coat. He began to scribble. Still pencils? With tape recorders?

Gabereau wrote this down in his notebook balanced beside his hat on his thigh. In the process, he looked up to gauge the firelight and adjust his notebook a little. He noticed my bandaged calf, if he hadn't before. I know he'd noticed my hand and chest. "Gunshot?" he asked. "Want a ride back to a hospital?" He waved toward the corpses. "They can wait, you know."

I knew that gunshot wounds had to be reported. On the other hand, I didn't want to be *caught* in a lie if I couldn't talk us out of the worst complications. So, I shrugged. "Maybe it was a direct hit, Inspector... but more likely a ricochet. Maybe just a chunk of flying rock. I don't know, but it won't kill me."

"I wouldn't think so," he said. He'd swivelled to look over toward, at and into the open First Aid box. He stretched to pick up the squished ampoule of Novocaine. He held this up, returned it, and then wrote in his notebook.

"All prescription, Inspector. The prescriptions are all clipped to the inside of the lid. I'm supposed to try to replace certain things on a schedule. Like the penicillin. Limited shelf life and all that."

"Canadian... " He was writing again. Then he closed the book, and half turned to look at me. "So," he said, "tell me a story."

Accordingly, I told him that I'd come down last night – night before last, that is – from Castelnaudary. I was trying to find this place because I'd heard of it. Folks said you could sometimes see lammergaiers here, although they were supposed to be restricted to the real Pyrenees to the south. And since I was writing a book about life along the canal, well, and so on. Arriving at the lake before navigation stopped at nine...

"Naturally."

I'd noticed the *birol* ashore, but not much of it because the light had faded in a squally storm. We... I began to inject the 'we' here, but he didn't comment on it then... didn't see any lights aboard the *birol*, either, and it looked buttoned up. We assumed the crew had turned in. We called it a day, too.

"Why the interest in this *birol*, Monsieur Rennsalaer?"

"It seemed to be a very old one, Inspector. I thought maybe it was in Vital's book. If I could get a good photo of it – in the morning, of course, when there was light – I could show a solid example of a hundred year old lifestyle preserved here. I thought to juxtapose Pierre Vital's turn-of-the-century black and white photo with a modern colour photo of the same boat... if, of course, it had appeared in Vital's work."

"What made you think that it had?"

"Just something about its shape, the bow and the house, rang a bell, that's all. Maybe I'm wrong... I still don't know, for that matter," I said. "Also, Inspector, I could see that she was steam-powered. I was interested in a local design of the late 19th century."

"All right," Gabereau said. "Now I understand."

Anyway, I continued with my tale, by seven-thirty the next morning – this morning – there was thick fog. I saw that the *birol* nets were stacked on shore looking as though the crew had chosen this beach to mend them. Since there was fog anyway, I couldn't take any immediate photos of the *birol*. But I thought that the fog might burn off pretty soon, as soon as the sun topped the ridge to the south, and I had an idea about lammergaiers. I went ashore, and onto the *birol*. The crew... an old man named Roland and a much older one named François...

"Ah, yes, the old *Amaranthe,*" Gabereau said.

"*Amaranthe.* That's her name? They never mentioned it, you know."

"Seldom do." The Inspector sighed. "That was the grande dame's name. François's wife, Roland's mother. She had all the brains on that *birol*. During the war, I was told, she carried messages, and sometimes supplies, for the Resistance using the boat's wanderings as a cover. François and Roland never knew, they say." Gabereau looked up at me, a slight smile of remembrance playing on his face. Not for me.

But I caught his eye. "You know, Inspector Gabereau, I wouldn't bet on that at all." He cocked an eyebrow. "Maybe François and Roland were her cover, if you know what I mean." He nodded, slowly. "Ever been aboard the *Amaranthe*?" I asked. He shook his head. "It's a museum, Inspector. Decrepit, but a time capsule for all that. The lady's hand has been preserved. Being a detective, I guess you'll see more than I did. You might take a look at the spinet, in the corner – there may be papers in there. Memoirs, Resistance documents. I wouldn't know, but I wouldn't be surprised."

He scribbled again in his notebook. "Is that so? I shall have to pay a visit now, at any rate, to get statements from François and Roland... The spinet, you said...?"

My narrative continued with my proposition to Roland – I explained that François was stone deaf, so far as I could tell – to transform the *birol* nets into camouflage nets for *Jester*. Lammergaiers are high-flying birds, like all vultures, but they can come low if they're not spooked. My idea was to camouflage *Jester* with three of the nets while they worked on the fourth. We'd change nets every so often so that the repairs could keep going on. That way, the birds might fly lower, particularly if I caught a fish, or, better, found a dead one and put it out in the *maquis* as bait. Within convenient and photogenic camera range, of course.

"All this trouble just to photograph a bird?"

"They're supposed to be very rare, Inspector, although there are clearly many more than the experts believe. They do nest and roost in virtually inaccessible places, however. There are only two or three genuine close-range photographs known. From these, it appears that there may be two species. Any close-up I could get would be a coup for my own book, but might also be valuable – I assured him I was talking cash – in a scientific and environmental sense. The Sierra Club, or the World Wildlife Fund, might pay up to $1,000, American, for a good, close-up photo.

Gabereau was impressed, and agreed that the effort seemed worth it. But he had a doubt... "Your boat, Mister Rennsalaer, *Jester,* she would be camouflaged by the *birol's* nets, but the *Amaranthe* would not be so disguised. And François and Roland would be in plain view on the beach, working on a net. Would not that frighten these birds?"

"Not necessarily at all," I replied with the genuine emphasis of knowledge and experience. "Birds are generally quite intelligent, Inspector. The *Amaranthe* frequently comes here, as few boats do, and François and Roland have worked on this beach many times before, for many years. By now, the lammergaiers might well have accepted them."

Gabereau looked sceptical, and this naturally tended to make him doubt the truth of all I was saying, all that I had said – and would say. In spite of the hour and my creeping exhaustion, and in spite of the fact that this was a small and irrelevant aside to my whole story, I had to make him at least *accept* it.

"Inspector..." I began. "Did you ever hunt crows... rooks, I think they call them here... when you were a boy?"

"Yes. Yes, I did." I could hear the warmth of past times in his voice.

"Did any older man, maybe your father, tell you to try to disguise your gun as a stick? Maybe a walking stick, by hiding the rifle stock under your coat...?"

"Yes... yes, I remember something about that. But not my father, he didn't hunt. Some old farmer... What was his name?"

"It is widely believed that rooks can distinguish the shape of a rifle's stock and breech from the shape of an ordinary stick."

"Yes, Rennsalaer, it's coming back. I did it, but I don't believe it. Do you believe it?"

"Not entirely, Gabereau. I suppose that one rook out of ten would be that smart, maybe only one of twenty. But that's all it takes. When *that* rook takes off cawing, the rest of the flock goes with him."

"True. That is so."

"The same with the lammergaiers, but reversed," I said. I wanted to get back to the story before I fell asleep into the fire. Also, I noticed, the sky was much lighter behind the ridge. The sun would top the lowland horizon soon in the true dawn, though the sun would not climb above our local ridge until hours later. I didn't dare look at my Seiko. Gabereau, by contrast, knowing that he had to remain awake for a while yet, seemed to use me and my story as a distraction from nodding off. I had to stop this. "The older birds, the leaders, would know the *Amaranthe*. If they did not fear, and came down, then the rest would follow. There were five birds, we counted them, and we had a good chance for at least one good photo... *but it was the explosion that spooked them*." I emphasised this.

"Ah, yes," Gabereau said wearily, as if unwilling to get back to it. "What time was that?"

"Seven-thirty, near enough," I said. But I hurried on, as if trying to impart information in spite of my physical and mental state. "But the explosion wasn't what got me, Inspector." I was gratified that *that* statement brought his eyes to focus on my face. "This place is a funny little configuration of hills and ridges. Bad acoustics. Then, there was the fog. Still thick when the explosion came. So, it was muffled. Just a dull boom here." Gaspereau nodded. "It was what I heard just before the explosion that's of interest in the... ah... light of later events. I heard a powerful speedboat out in the canal – its higher-pitched sound carried into here, and just before the explosion I heard automatic fire. Heavy calibre stuff."

"Before the explosion?"

"Yes, definitely. But almost simultaneously with it."

"In the same place?"

"As far as I could tell, yes. The boat's engine came very near to the explosion out there. The shots came from near the boom."

"Did the shots come from the boat?"

"Well, that's the question, isn't it?" I shook my head. "I cannot swear to that, Inspector, obviously. I couldn't see anything from here anyway, and there was fog."

He nodded, flexing his writing thigh. This caused his hat to topple off and, when he bent to reach for it, his notebook fell, too. I picked it up and handed it to him. "Merci," he said absently.

"Bernard..." I tried this, but also just as absently, as if I was thinking to myself. He didn't react to the familiarity, but I could sense no stiffening. "Someone else besides me must have heard that boat and the shots," I mused.

I saw him nod almost imperceptibly, and shake his head just as marginally. Finally. "Yes... yes... A woman walking to work on the north canal bank reported the same thing. A speedboat in the fog, and shots, just before the explosion."

"And...?"

He shrugged. "We discounted it... Hers was the only such report before yours."

I doubted that. "There must be others who heard the same thing... If an effort was made to find them."

He shrugged. "We... the police..." and I noted that he widened the burden of responsibility here "... saw it as an accidental explosion, Mar – ... Rennsalaer."

"Oh."

"The *Lorelei* – the barge," he amended, and too late, so he shrugged, "was carrying liquid hydrogen for Marseilles. You know what that means. Any little leak. Any little spark. Leaks of cargo, particularly gas under pressure, are frequent. Sparks are virtually continuous. Static electricity, common in fog, jumps from one metal part of the ship to another. Then, there's always careless smoking. They were also cooking breakfast at the time."

"I heard the shots, Inspector. I heard the boat. I'll swear to that if you like... "

"Thanks, Marc... this time there was no caught correction... Your testimony can be accepted as... ah... expert, in such matters." He was trying a little wry humour to cover the slip into familiarity. But I needed a bit more banter to carry me though.

"Don't give me that 'thanks', Gabereau. We both know that I'll have to testify, if you want me to, and now we know what I'll have to say... we also both know that it complicates things... ah ... messily."

"Damned right, Rennsalaer. *Merde*." He spat it out.

"Not necessarily all shit," I said. He looked up. "There's some information that you should know... first. It'll put you on top of things, Bernard." I said it casually, and hoped it didn't sound over-played. His career worry must be that a supposed accident on his piece of watery turf, the canal, might not be an accident. It might well be sabotage, or an act of "terrorism"... as Mariko might have put it, and had, once hopefully, put it. And the problem with these developments, from Inspector Bernard Gabereau's point of view, was that he, the chief of the canal police, would not know about the complications before Interpol and the Sûreté briefed him.

This would not make him seem *incompetent*, maybe, since a canal cop isn't expected to sniff out international intrigue from a few scraps... but he'd be regarded as just a good, plodding canal cop. One that could be replaced if need arose, or just drowned in the normal ebb and flow of promotion and retirement. Another pallid body found in the tide of bureaucracy. But, to provide new and useful facts, plus not-so-obvious identifications, would place him in a superior league. A man to be remembered if someone needed a good man to police *all* the French canals. Or, a canal specialist for the Sûreté, or Interpol.

With the Soviet bloc open, and canals from the Atlantic to the Caspian, and all of them potential routes for smuggling anything from blue jeans to misplaced ex-Soviet nuclear warheads, such a position might well be in the planning stages now – or could be advocated.

Gabereau was looking at me, hungrily, I thought. Was the firelight *glinting* off his eyes? But I decided to keep it slow, in spite of my exhaustion, and in character to the end. My story continued with the observation that when the fog lifted, the column of smoke was easy to see. The official-seeming noises from the canal had wafted our way. It was obvious, at least to me, that a boat was burning out in the channel. The lammergaiers were spooked for the day, but if things cleared up, they might yet venture lower tomorrow. So, I tentatively arranged to keep the nets. It cost me an extra cask of Bouchard's wine. Here, I decided to give Gabereau a small upper hand. He duly chuckled.

"How many?"

"Originally two, then three."

But the point was that I couldn't view lammergaiers. And I didn't want to photograph the *Amaranthe* without all four *birols*, in order to match her configuration with the old photos in Vital's book. Gabereau nodded quickly, and I sensed his impatience. "Well, Bernard, I decided to look at helicopters instead," I said. "I'm pretty good at it, you know." He was flipping open his notebook, licking a pencil.

"There was a joker in your air traffic." He nodded, so I just went on and told him about the Sleipnir attack helicopter, its colour scheme, cost and capabilities.

"I saw it, once or twice," he said. "German newspaper." He paused. "I don't know much about helicopters... Don't like them," he added as an afterthought.

"Norddeutsch Kreuzzug Zeitblatt," I intoned carefully while he wrote. "Tell Interpol to check that newspaper out in connection with neo-Nazi groups." He scribbled. "Also, Inspector Gabereau, no small newspaper – and I never heard mention of *that* one, could afford a Sleipnir chopper. Get a man on it, Bernard, and you'll see what I mean. Made by Saab. Sweden."

I explained that I'd been curious about seeing this kind of chopper, belonging to such an organisation, cruising around over the explosion site. I mentioned that it had overflown this little cul-de-sac a couple of times during the afternoon. It saw the *birol,* I knew, because it flew over at least once before I sent Roland away to arrange a rendezvous with Bouchard. It was the same helicopter that had gone down two hours ago.

Gabereau looked up at that. "You're sure?"

"Absolutely certain."

He knew my background. I was sure that the French police had a full and accurate file on me, and that this dossier must have been passed on to the appropriate local authority wherever I was residing in France.

"Now, Inspector Gabereau, I don't mean to suggest that I was *suspicious* of anything. But I knew a barge had blown up. I knew that a potentially lethal helicopter was in the air – and everyone just assumed it was media. I knew that a supposedly neo-Nazi organization owned it, and no paper like that should be able to afford it, and I knew that it had overflown this beach. Several times. When the *birol* left, well, here was a place to set down. Not far from the site of the explosion – if they needed to look for anything. I didn't *suspect* anything, but I was edgy. To make a long story shorter, I slept on deck."

"What happened, Marc?"

"I wish I knew for sure," I said. There was genuine tiredness was in my voice, at least. I hoped that some of it would pass for regret. I told him that I had sent the girl below for safety's sake – by now, we both knew that half of my 'we' was of the female gender – but I'd somehow fallen to sleep on deck. Much later I was awakened by a helicopter not far above *Jester*. I jumped up, naturally, and ran to the bows where, because one of the *birol* nets had had to be suspended somewhat slanted, I thought that I might be able to get a peek at the helicopter.

My first assumption was that it would probably turn out to be a police chopper just routinely checking things out in the vicinity of the explosion.

"In which case," Inspector Gabereau commented wryly, "your disguised boat would seem inordinately odd."

I stopped, as if this thought had only just occurred to me. Since I was truly tired, I used a long and quite legitimate sigh instead of trying to chuckle it off. "Yeah... it sure would," I agreed. But, after the briefest of pauses, I went doggedly on... And I told him how I had climbed up onto the rail, holding the forestay for support, and tried to peek up, and around, the netting by leaning out away from the hull.

The helicopter wasn't dead steady. It hovered, but it also sort of rocked from side-to-side – like a falling leaf that didn't fall – and I gestured this. In that way, I got a glimpse of the profile of it, near enough, so I knew it for a Sleipnir. Also, although I couldn't actually read the letters on the side of the chopper, they were the same size and pattern as those of the *Norddeutsch Kreuzzug Zeitblatt* painted in demure white on the afternoon's helicopter.

"Was it the same helicopter?"

"I cannot swear to that, Inspector. It was the same type of helicopter, though. They're not all that common, Gabereau, and very expensive. Ask Saab."

"And then... ?"

"Well, then... I don't know. Men – and here I gestured toward the bodies – were on the beach."

"On the beach?"

I nodded, and bent my head 'way back, stretching my neck and turning it from side to side. Vertebrae made clicking noises. "That's right. On the beach. My impression, though, is that they'd just got there. I think they came from that hill there. I pointed to the high, but rounded and climbable rocky side of a ridge. It had been behind the Sleipnir before, was now behind the police helicopter. Mariko's misses had probably scorched it, but it wasn't light enough to tell.

"And then?"

"Well, I think the men looked up at the chopper for a moment, seemed agitated, and they just opened up. Heavy stuff," I said. "Automatic."

"Schmeissers," said Gabereau.

"I know. I saw 'em."

"What then?"

This was important, because I didn't want to get caught out of sequence. "Okay," I said, "I was surprised – I don't *think* I saw their guns until they started firing – and I damned near let go of the stay. Almost instantly, the helicopter opened up, too. Lighter but more deadly stuff. This was right above me. Five point five-six. Here I stood up and fished one of the AR-15's spent casings from my left pocket of what had once been full-length jeans. I handed it to Gabereau.

"You shouldn't have touched any of the evidence, Mister Rennsalaer."

I sat down heavily, and impatiently. "Jesus! Gimme a break, Bernard. They're not exactly rare around here. They came raining down all around, through the netting. That one, I pointed to the shining brass cylinder in his palm, bounced off my shoulder. Into the boat. But don't worry. There's plenty more in the sand, in the water. All around." He was scribbling, so I shut up.

"How many rounds were fired?"

"Lots. Lots."

"Make an estimate."

"Don't know, Bernard. Look, all that noise just blasted my ears, I pointed – that kid there can give you a demonstration, his Gasconnade uses the same cartridge – then you'll understand. I fell off the stay, not entirely by accident... "

"Yes..." he said, "I can see why you'd want to fall off."

"Damned right. Wanted to get below *Jester's* bow. Somewhere low and sandy with steel over part of me." I paused. "To answer your question, maybe forty or fifty rounds. Your guys can find the casings... "

"And then?"

"The guys on the beach were finished... also, I *think*... but I can't be sure, that some rockets or grenades were fired. My head was down, Inspector, but there were flashes and explosions. Quite a party. I don't know..." I allowed my voice to trail off into a question.

"What is it?"

"I don't know if Schmeissers are equipped to launch a grenade. Never had much to do with 'em. Don't like machine pistols. Chopper could have had small rockets, I guess. I know that all sorts of gadgets were used in East Timor, Somalia and so on – things that Schmeisser or Armalite never heard of."

"Maybe a terrorist organization would make their own goodies," Gabereau suggested, and I was glad the thought had come from him.

"But, whatever they were shooting at each other, the helicopter got some of it. It took off and you could tell it didn't sound right. As soon as I could see it was really leaving, I looked up and saw it. It was easy to see because it was trailing fire. It managed to climb over that ridge there," I nodded toward it because I'd pointed before, "and it disappeared over the other side. But then there was an explosion, and a flare."

Gabereau got up abruptly and walked to the chopper, bent inside it again. I guessed that he was, first, querying the arrival of the summoned ambulance helicopter and homicide crew. Secondly, of course, he was feeding information as to the true nature of that 'crashed plane' that the farmer had reported, the make and probable model of the helicopter, its registration, the fact that the operators were a probable neo-Nazi outfit, the shoot-out on the beach.

All this, in context, put a different complexion on the explosion of the *Lorelei*. At borders, canal barges would have to be viewed more carefully, hazardous cargoes would have to be checked, barges on canals would have to be checked. Some analyst might start to work on what a 'terrorist' organization might want chemicals for... or why it should sabotage chemical shipments.

If I were Gabereau, well, I would take the trouble to be patched through to the Sûreté at the Quai d'Orsay *personally*. And to Interpol at The Hague, *personally*. Would I be so gauche as to awaken my regional superior, at this hour of the morning, with such tenuous matters? But, if these tenuous matters proved to be of international importance then skipping the chain of command, and its delays with inevitable *diffusion of credit* all along the links, could be justified by a mixture of respect and, yet, vague urgency. Nicely gauged, it could create a certain *memory*, in high places, for the discretion of Inspector Bernard Gabereau of the Carcassonne Office of the Canal Police.

If I knew the French, no one would be fooled by Gabereau's deference-with-urgency. It would be taken for the discreet Machiavellian ploy that it was. And *that* quality was prized above many others on the Quai d'Orsay. Had the virtues of this hitherto quiet Inspecteur been overlooked?

Judging from the length of time that Gabereau was 'in communication', I suspected that he was effecting *personal* communication with various places. And he'd do it better than I could hope to.

Finally, I got tired of waiting on my half-log. So, I went over to the First Aid box, more or less shut it, and clamped it under my arm. Limping with increasing pain, I trudged toward *Jester's* ramp-door that was gaining definition by the second in dawn light.

25

"Arrêtez!" And I heard the snick of a Gasconnade bolt being drawn back. "Posez la boîte, immédiatement." I wasn't about to drop the First Aid box and spill all my medical supplies into the sand. On the other hand, the situation made me nervous. The kid was already angry at me, possibly with justice. He was young and hormones were flowing. Most of all, I knew that mere gendarmes like him received only minimal instruction and practice on the deadlier toys. Gasconnades were deadly.

But I also knew two other things. First, he'd glowered for almost an hour while his superior and I were having a friendly-looking chat by the fire. Secondly, to give in to his psychological type was to start a game that might end with my forcible detention, and Mariko's, and I couldn't afford that.

I didn't think he'd fire *anyway*, not without Gabereau's order. But, to reduce the odds of this, I had to give him no room for bullying while offering no direct and personal insult. So, I just kept limping toward *Jester's* ramp, while making a point of changing the clamp of the First Aid box from under one arm to under the other. My back did feel funny, but I consoled myself with the thought that I would feel absolutely no pain. Not at that range. And this was a lot better than I was feeling now.

Reaching the poop, and I don't have to describe the inconvenience further, I went to the wheelhouse and aimed the spotlight with my hand. The beam came up out of the hull and onto the beach. "Attention les yeux," I called out, and I saw the boy raise his hand to shade his eyes.

Then I selected the wider beam, and bathed the whole tableau with light. The fire had burned 'way down. The *maquis* pine was full of resin, burns fairly quickly, and now even the thicker boughs and trunks I'd gathered were showing only the glowing embers. Bones of their martyrs. Mere tongues of flame fluttered up to sip a last taste of resinous blood. I aimed the widened beam to encompass the corpses, the *gendarmes*, and most of the helicopter. The incoming choppers would be able to see the place clearly enough.

"Merci, Marc," Gabereau called from still inside the helicopter.

Rummaging around, I found another ampoule of Novocaine in their compartment under the mess I'd made. I fumbled this out of its box, injected it into the bandaged area where it hurt the most, and squeezed mightily. Being neat, and male, I worked the ampoule with my fingers until it resembled a small, rolled and totally expended travel-size tube of toothpaste. Not like the crumpled thing that Mariko had left... By the time I had congratulated myself on this, I noticed that my right hand – or properly, fingers – had started to throb again. Sausages being re-ground.

Rummaging again, for Solarcaine, I came across a tube of Neosporin. Thinking that this might actually be better, or at least no worse, I was applying it when Gabereau joined me on the poop. He took in the camera on the tripod, the extra backs, the half-opened roll of film, and the bird book.

"Funny," he mused, "how books can fall open to the right page." He began to read about the habits of lammergaiers. He'd also taken in my physical and emotional state. "And, laying that way all night long, too..." He paused, pretending to read some more, or actually reading, from the extra spill of the searchlight. "Doesn't say here that lammergaiers are nocturnal."

But I'd pulled myself together. "Screw you!" I grimaced, and it was real. The Novocaine hadn't hit yet.

"So...?" he asked mildly.

"So, Gabereau, I was trying to get a shot of the helicopter... maybe a registration number. So, I left the camera and tripod out. The book got left, too. I was changing to better film, faster film, when the chopper came."

"Sorry, Marc." he said. It would have been nice if I could have believed the sympathy. He knelt down beside me, on the foam mattress, and methodically lifted expensive Hassleblad pieces out of the way. But he didn't actually sit down, like I was.

"And *she*, was going to point the light?" But it wasn't a question.

"That was the idea."

"But the helicopter came too late. You were both asleep... or in the throes of passion... " he let it trail, leering at the bandage on my chest.

"Oh, yeah, Gabereau. Real passion." I grimaced again, and it was *almost* totally real. "Ever seen a girl blasted awake by gunfire right above her head? In your dreams, maybe. They grab, Gabereau, at the first secure thing they can find... You might not have experienced that."

He was quiet for some time, after that. "Is she relevant? Can you tell me quickly?"

I nodded, after a few moments, as if getting relief from the Novocaine. "It's odd. Let me see. Friday night, that's right. Anyway, I was going under the Moissac bridge, the old one. She fell off in front of me. Really fell." I gazed at him with eyes that were meant to be glazed, and probably were. The truth, you see. He nodded.

"All right... okay."

"I fished her out," I continued, "and offered to set her on shore. But she wouldn't have it. She was scared."

"What had happened...?"

"Well, she *said*," I emphasised this, "that she'd been walking over the bridge when two men jumped out of a car. She struggled. She either jumped, or was pushed in the struggle, off the bridge."

"So she fell off, you had her, and she wouldn't be set ashore." His voice was gentle. I nodded. "Having no choice, you took her with you."

"She wouldn't even go back for her suitcase and passport. They were at some bed-and-breakfast in Moissac Old City. I don't know..." Gabereau was scribbling again.

"Did she say why she was attacked?"

"She thought it was just an abduction. Rape and mayhem, that sort of thing."

"Likely enough," Gabereau said with surprising vehemence, so I looked up from my misery. "Is she pretty?"

"I think she could be gorgeous, if you have a taste for the exotic. Half Japanese and half Irish." Gabereau cocked an eyebrow. "For the record, her name's Mariko O'Shaugnessey." I repeated this in syllables, while he scribbled. "Don't blame me," I added. "That's what she said."

"White slavery," Gabereau spat it out.

"You're putting me on. Now?"

"Now more than ever," he said. "A lot of young women still come to southern France in the summer," he said. "A few never get back home." I sensed a father's concern, and a lecture, coming on, so I didn't interrupt – I reverted to a worldly wise teenager. "Some of them wake up in Tunisia or Algeria or Dubai," he informed me, "strapped down in stirrups to a gynecological examination table. A doctor, generally trained in France, Germany, Switzerland or even the United States is busy swabbing them out. So that Mister Big has no danger of STDs or even a Candidia infection." He paused, but this was no time to interrupt. "Blood tests, and the best lab facilities. Oil money. If they have AIDS, of course they're just shot. If they're pretty enough, an effort will be made to cure siph or gonorrhea. So, Rennsalaer, if they're pretty enough, they all get the camel prod treatment."

"Gabereau... I don't want to know."

"Nobody does," he said.

"Straddled there, with their legs spread, they're told about African-Islamic circumcision... amputation of the labia, excision of the clitoris," he continued, "but they're assured that Mister Big wants something exotic, and Western. A whole woman, you understand."

"Gabereau... "

"So, they're spared mutilation... for the moment. But if they're pretty enough to save, and maybe cure, for Mister Big, Rennsalaer, they get the camel prod. All over. But especially the breasts, with focus on nipples. Then down the vulva – sometimes moistened by sterilized saline pads supplied by the United Nations's World Health Organisation – with much attention to the clitoris and the vaginal opening."

"Bernard, stop it."

He looked at me quite sanely. "After about an hour of this, she has stopped screaming and is just a gibbering wreck, but she can still hear. And she's told that if she doesn't absolutely please the Mister Big, doing every little thing he wants done, she'll have another dose of the oh-so-sterilized camel prod. In a modern clinic financed by the West's oil money, with heart and blood pressure monitored by the best equipment that oil can buy, so that she'll be taken right to the edge of death and sanity. But not over it. If she didn't behave before, Marc Rennsalaer, she will behave then."

"You know this. Don't you?"

"We've been able to recover a few. Sometimes, you see, Mister Big travels to Europe with his... his... *retinue*. All the national police, and Interpol, keep a list of missing kids – and boys go missing, too, of course, and sometimes we have a pretty good idea of which girl, or boy, is in which... *harem*. There have been discreet commando raids on hotels, mostly under the cover of supposed fire emergencies, and in the confusion we've sometimes grabbed some missing bodies. Bodies, Rennsalaer, because that's all they really are by then. A few make it back to their minds."

"Good sweet Jesus."

"I've been in on several raids against foreign yachts because sometimes Mister Big, if he's big enough, travels that way. So, we water flics have traded stories with land flics." He paused. "I don't want you to get the idea this is a sexist thing, Rennsalaer. There's Miz Bigs too, not so much in the Arab World, of course, but in the Far East. And both Mister and Miz Bigs tend to go both ways, if you know what I mean. And they have a taste for the exotic, you know." He paused, mused... "I remember this Dutch boy. A big blond boy, who spent two years as Miz Big's play toy in Bangkok. Big in the drug trade, she is, Marc, but puts her money into prestigious banks, as a shareholder, not a mere depositor.

Also *Big*," he emphasized the word, "in reputation as a creative sadist. Women are the worst at that sort of thing... when they go bad... "

"Please, Bernard. I'm feeling bad enough. Have a heart."

"Okay," he said. "I'll just say, and I'm sure you'll be happy to know, that the Dutch boy has begun to stop screaming every times he sees a female nurse... And think of it, Marc, he's only been treated in the clinic for three years... His doctors *do* wish he'd begin to speak again, though – even in Dutch."

"Jesus..." I was truly feeling much worse. "So... " I tried gently to get back to Mariko. "... you think it was just an abduction attempt? Not connected with, well, the rest?"

"Not at all," he said, surprising me. "It could well be connected somehow. We've known for a while that some terrorist groups finance their activities with white slavery along with drugs. A beautiful young girl will bring about $100,000. A beautiful and exotic one will bring twice that much. Boys bring a bit less, generally, except on special order... Miz Big Banker sometimes places these. There are plenty of gorgeous girls and boys in southern France in the summertime. Even now."

"You know best," I said. I also almost believed it.

"Can I talk with her?"

"She's sleeping, Inspector. Please... and I'm asking this sincerely... let her rest."

"You gave her a sedative?"

I shook my head. "She was just worn out. That was enough... after all the... ah... excitement she experienced. Moissac and here."

He was silent for a longish time, looking around the deck and appreciating, I think, the light of dawn blushing beyond the ridges. "What are we going to do?" he asked me.

"Inspector, that's up to you. You know that." I hesitated for a moment. "But if I have any say in the matter, I'd dearly love to go to sleep."

He heaved himself to his feet. "I guess I know where I can find you," he said. I nodded, bone weary. "Can you be at my office, Carcassonne, at seven this evening?"

"Sure."

"With the girl?"

"Sure."

"In the meantime, Marc Rennsalaer, we'll have to look around." He looked around then, and waved vaguely at the whole complication. This included *Jester's* deck.

"I think I can sleep though that," I said.

He nodded to me, and actually smiled at me, as tired as he must have been. Then he turned on his heels and began edging off the poop between the casks and the side rail. He laughed. "Seven this evening will give you time to meet with your Merchant of Vinasse," he said. He laughed, seeming to be immensely pleased with his terrible pun. Vinasse is the lowest quality of wine, almost vinegar. I figured that Marcel Bouchard would consider it a slur. One didn't carry vinasse in wooden casks. Or, did one?

I gathered up the bits of Hasselblad, and the bird book, and managed to stumble my way below. On the way, though, I slid the wheelhouse hatch shut, and locked it. Since the wheelhouse was made of steel, and its windows were polycarbonate, as I mentioned before, *Jester* buttoned up couldn't be opened from the outside unless someone had a welding torch and plenty of time. I locked the steel bulkhead door to the cabin as another, and equally strong, deterrent. Piling the Hassleblad bits on the top of my upper bunk, which had gradually become sort of a catch-all padded shelf, I noted that Mariko's privacy partition was pulled down.

I stripped off my cut-offs and my flannel shirt, flinging them on the top bunk near the camera parts and the bird book. I managed to have a shower without soaking the bandages completely. Not that I cared.

Six-thirty. But one thing could not wait even another minute. I took a half hour to send an e-mail to Joëlle's office. It was a long and urgent message. In English. But did she now trust me enough to do what I asked of her?

Finally pulling my own partition down, I set my mental alarm for ten o'clock. Blackness and quiet flooded over me. The luminous dial of my Seiko told me it was just seven a.m. and that was the last thing I saw for three hours – except, at some point, the brief image of violently rocking peach with a buzzing sound coming from deep from within its cleft.

Part Three

When one has good wine,
A graceful junk,
And a maiden's love –
Why envy the immortal gods?

Li Tsi Po

26

"See Carcassonne and die." So wrote the American adventurer and travel writer, Richard Halliburton, in 1932. He was referring, of course, to the exuberantly magnificent 19th century reconstruction of the entire old walled city by the eccentric French architect, Viollet-le-Duc.

Even in his own time, Viollet-le-Duc's conception of medieval architecture was criticized as being romantic and dramatic. If words like Disneyland and Hollywood had been in currency during the 1880s, they would have been lavishly used by his detractors. Reconstructed medieval Carcassonne is like stage sets for *The Hunchback of Notre Dame*, *Robin Hood* and *Prince Valiant* all dropped down in the middle of nowhere at the same time.

Carcassonne is at the very end of the Garonne-Aude watershed. Consequently, it can change hourly from the misty atmosphere of Atlantic weather to the opalescent light that rules over the Mediterranean. Mediterranean air masses are actually mostly dry because, in summer at least, the Saharan winds blow north from Africa. However, the light has a peculiar liquid quality due to the reflection and refraction of shades of subtle blues and greens from the Mediterranean Sea. Plenty of painters have seen Carcassonne, both before the reconstruction of its ruins and afterwards, but there are surprisingly few artistic representations of it.

The combination of both Atlantic and Mediterranean light probably seemed too deadly for artistic reputations.

Michelangelo Caravaggio, pioneer of the 'natural' school of Italian painting, who in some ways broke the last lingering chains of medieval formality that was submerged, but never quite drowned, in the Italian Renaissance, would have painted Carcassonne "realistically." And he would have depicted a muted, golden old town that was impossibly spectral with both Atlantic gloom and Mediterranean luminosity. He might well have painted what he was trying to free Italian painting from – an atavistic medieval allegory of the City of Man, half claimed by Satan, and also half City of God. Although Caravaggio's brush would have been true to the situation and city, his hypothetical painting of it would not, and could not, have looked natural at all. This is because Carcassonne doesn't look natural. Caravaggio's colleagues, of whom there were few because he was a footloose, drunken and violent man, would have considered him a traitor to the new school of naturalism he himself had helped to establish. Bad for his reputation.

Georges Seurat developed the technique of 'pointillism' in order to attempt to convey the psychological and physiological perceptive impression of a scene as it might appear to a subjective human viewer. Seurat sought to free himself from the obligation of depicting things naturally or objectively. He considered these terms meaningless since only an overseeing eye, perhaps the eye of God, could possibly see things that way. And even in Seurat's time, gossip from the German universities at Marburg and Freiburg had hinted that God might be dead.

Martin Heidegger, born three years before Seurat's death, was to confirm these rumours when he became Rector of Freiburg. So, Seurat had inklings of philosophical support for his technique of pointillism to reflect subjective impressions. There was nothing absolute, objective or 'natural' any longer. Reality was the sum total of subjective impressions of observers. Never officially a member of the French Impressionist School, he was nonetheless one of its primary precursors.

But Seurat's pointillism would have backfired at Carcassonne. With squalling columns of Atlantic rain sweeping across the Garonne-Aude valley, and with every droplet a prism and prison for Mediterranean light, pointillism alone could have approached the actual photographic reality of the scene. Carcassonne might have cost Seurat some of his stature as a proto-impressionist or, at least, a semi-impressionist. He would have painted ultra-realism with the best of pointillist intentions. Bad for his reputation.

Perhaps only the brush of a brilliant hack like Jean Honoré Fragonard could have done justice to Carcassonne. As a court painter, Fragonard was careful to depict jewels and brocade with exaggerated realism in order to proclaim the wealth, power and magnificence of his mostly pallid and incompetent clients. He would have therefore reproduced the magenta tapestry of a Carcassonne dawn faithfully, with its ruby flashes of fire on conical turret tops, without the emotional liability of being deeply moved. Fragonard could have painted Carcassonne without actually perceiving it.

While not trying to insult Halliburton by taking him too literally, personally I have never quite understood Halliburton's idea that after merely *seeing* Carcassonne, one could happily end one's life experience.

In my opinion, he should have written: "See Carcassonne and *live*." For Viollet-le-Duc's medieval fantasy-reconstruction managed to embrace the major tides of Western history that, by virtue of the city's geographical position, have flowed and ebbed through it. Carcassonne's appearance and existence whisper its history, but not loudly enough to be understood by most people without prompting from books.

Luckily, the Languedoc Tourist Bureau has prepared many pamphlets about various aspects of Carcassonne's history. They are prominently displayed at every lock from the summit level going down into the town. Visiting yacht people have always been avid customers of these publications, once they glimpse the medieval fantasy below them and to the south. This history is so ancient, complicated and evocative that it personifies in one improbable and dubious heap of battlements the saga of the entire Western World. A lifetime would not be enough to grasp this history firmly. Carcassonne has therefore held much fascination for writers of things other than pamphlets. Occasionally, some of these books are on sale at the locks too.

Aside from Richard Halliburton, Mary Stewart and Anya Seton have set all or most of at least one of their novels in Carcassonne. And these novels range from Arthurian legends to modern romance. This is entirely fitting.

Men have forgotten or distorted the stories, maybe, but Carcassonne's stone foundations, walls, battlements and twisted streets have not. These stones are also bones of the earth, which do not forget. Carcassonne has been defended, and it has fallen, under many banners.

Secrets and treasures congregate here, but they may all be connected if only one delved deeply enough. Each leaves its memory in Carcassonne.

The first insignia of Carcassonne may have been an Upper Palaeolithic totem. Perhaps a cave bear, but most probably a Venus figurine depicting the Great Goddess. At least, Joëlle and her Narbonnais friends had insisted upon it.

At the time, this had seemed fanciful to me. But with the *Almanach du Languedoc* still fluttering its pages on top of *Jester's* wheelhouse, I now wasn't so sure. Out of both courtesy to Joëlle and also out of interest, I had read the article that she had retrieved from her tricycle's storage compartment, off and on this morning, while steering along a calm and sparkling canal summit level for Carcassonne. It was a reprint of a decade-old news story about the Viols-le-Fort site, first excavated in August 1999 about a hundred kilometres north of Narbonne and an account of what had been discovered since – especially traces of undoubted alphabetic writing. The CNRS team – Centre Nationale des Recherches Scientifiques – had found the oldest known Neolithic site in the world. At some 10,000 BC, it was older than any Neolithic site in the Middle East.

No, the CNRS team had naturally not called this culture 'Elysian'. They had called it 'Cardial' after the remains of a shellfish that were common in the site. French people then, as now, had apparently prized oysters and mussels.

The Garonne-Aude waterway, and the modern Canal du Midi that links these two rivers, has always been the natural route across Europe from the Atlantic into the Mediterranean. It is by far the shortest route from the Atlantic into the Mediterranean. Now, *if* there was ever an ancient lost civilization out in the Atlantic, call it Atlantis for convenience, refugees from it might well have come to the Atlantic coast of France at the tumultuous close of the last so-called Ice Age.

Evidence is building, in the form of radio-carbon dates, that the cataclysm, which sank Atlantis, was part of a global change that also shifted the polar zones. If cultured refugees had then sought a place of gentle climate to preserve what remained of their civilization, and to "begin again," they might well have travelled the Garonne-Aude river system to the Mediterranean at Narbonne. Joëlle always said as much.

Did the Upper Palaeolithic Magdalenian Ice Age cultures – and is that designation *mere* coincidence – flanking this waterway receive scraps of knowledge, art and technology from these refugees? Because the Upper Palaeolithic Magdalenian cave paintings are so stunning, and Magdalenian artefacts are so common, modern prehistorians believe that Modern Man radiated out of the French caves. But perhaps the Magdalenian cave artists were just getting marginal cultural influences from refugee people who preserved their knowledge carefully and secretly. So, call them Elysians, if you wish, those first cultured residents around Carcassonne.

When the Celts invaded about 1500 BC, did one tribe, the Tectosages, discover or appropriate more than just scraps of this knowledge? Did they preserve a good part of it?

It is said that Thales of Miletus himself fled here about 600 BC and founded a philosophical community. Pythagoras arrived in Languedoc near Carcassonne about forty years later, about 560 BC, in order to study the secrets of mathematical proportions given to man by the gods. His disciples followed him to study the divine secrets, to preserve them and to enlarge upon mathematical truth.

But... is one permitted to wonder if these Ionian Greeks fled first to southern France and *then* learned of the secrets and treasures of the gods? History books have it the other way around, of course.

Mariko's lies about her Tectosages research had led me to one kernel of truth. You can't build wisely without mathematics. Buildings tend to fall down. And maybe the Tectosages built other things besides buildings – things not so solid, perhaps, but things a good deal more durable. Isn't it just possible that the famous Ionian Greek philosophers had learned their knowledge in Languedoc? That would seem to be the blasphemous truth because the precisely geometric earthworks and megaliths scattered around Carcassonne are at least three thousand years older than Thales of Miletus.

Rome annexed this part of Gaul in 127 BC and called it Septimania because it was intended as a colonial settlement for retired veterans of the Seventh Legion.

It is said that Mary Magdalene, Mary of Bethany, Joseph of Arimathaea and the Virgin Mary fled to Septimania after the Crucifixion of Jesus. I had heard of this legend since coming here. There is the Shrine of Les Saintes Maries – the 'Holy Marys' – near Marseilles, although I had never stopped to visit it. But I had read a pamphlet about it. Now, however, after Joëlle's comments and Mariko's, I was becoming curious. Legend has it that Mary left a tangible legacy in Provence and Languedoc.

British traditions insist that Joseph of Arimathaea finally journeyed on to Glastonbury with one of the Marys and founded the first church in all of Christendom there. Unfortunately, I had forgotten to ask Joëlle about Joseph of Arimathaea, and I'd had no chance since to read the New Testament…"the Jesus part," as she had put it.

Then, four centuries after the New Testament's Christ, in AD 410, the Visigothic chieftain Alaric, the barbarian who began the tradition of sacking Rome, took wagonloads of his Roman treasure around the Gulf of Lyon to Languedoc. Alaric himself had died while his Visigothic horde was still in Italy, but trusted chieftains had carried out his intent.

But veterans of the Seventh and their descendants proved to be no match for Visigothic cavalry. Although the old Roman legionary families were fiercely loyal to Rome, Septimania was overrun. Thus, in the region around Carcassonne, most of the loot from the world's richest and most acquisitive empire must be buried – somewhere. Very little of it has been found. Or, to be more correct, very few announcements of discovered treasure have been made.

And here, I did remember the curious and unexplained wealth of Abbé Saunière, village priest at the church of Mary Magdalene… hmmm… at Rennes-le-Château about one hundred airline kilometres south of Carcassonne. A curious folk tale persists that Alaric had wanted to hide the booty of Rome *in the country of God*. Perhaps he had figured that the Visigoths' loot would be safer there.

These upper Garonne and Aude valleys fanning out and down to the Mediterranean coast are, basically, the old Roman Province of Septimania. The name of the place lingered, though, and even gave its name to the Visigoths' huge black horses. *Septimanian horses* were famous throughout the Western World during the Dark Ages after the fall of Rome. They, alone of European horses descended from Ice Age tarpans, were large enough to carry the weight of armoured knights. This strain of great horses had first been bred on the steppes of Khazakhstan by distant ancestors of the Visigoths, people called Tocharians, about 2500 BC.

It is even said that King Arthur of Britain, as a young man sometime around AD 525 before he became Dux Bellorum, had journeyed to Septimania to buy horses. He had attended the annual Visigothic horse fair at the old Roman town of Narbo Martius, today's Narbonne. Arthur needed the large Visigothic breed for the heavy cavalry he planned to create in order to defend Britain.

Details cling to this story that are difficult to discount. Arthur could not afford to buy hundreds of large Septimanian horses to mount his heavy cavalry directly. He intended to cross them with the much smaller British hill ponies and gradually build up a herd of significantly larger horses which would, nonetheless, not be as big as the huge Septimanian ones. Therefore, in Narbo Martius he'd been careful to buy only mares. These big mares could be bred... covered? Is that the horsy term? ...by British hill pony stallions who possessed sufficient size, fortitude and will. But the reverse could not be true. British mares could not have given birth to large foals sired by Septimanian stallions.

This story is common knowledge in the Narbonnais.

It is also common folk knowledge in Britain. I remember reading that one English author had plotted the geographical position of all 'Black Horse Pubs' and 'Black Horse Inns' in Britain. Without exception, they were located en route between Cadbury Hill and one or another of Arthur's legendary battles. The townsfolk had crowded to watch the procession of Arthur's knights on their impressive black horses, and local pubs and inns had been named after the Dark Ages spectacle. These pub and inn names preserve memories that are about 1,500 years old. This newspaper article... or book review? had been crazy enough to lodge in my mind. Now, however, I was becoming mightily interested in it.

In Arthur's time, the banner over Carcassonne had probably been the scarlet battle flag of the first Frankish kings, part-Visigothic Merovingians, about AD 500-800. They were Arthur's contemporaries. Their pennant bore a depiction of three golden bees against a carnage-red background. It is said that the honey of Carcassonne's mystery derives from these bees, though few supposedly know why the secret is so honey-sweet.

It is not particularly strange that the best and most enduring self-images of the Western World were either preserved, or actually born, in this corner of southern France. Yes, the Ionian Greeks supposedly brought a dollop of civilization here when Rome was just a collection of huts. But after Rome became great, and was then laid low by barbarians, the Visigoths realized that they had broken the heart of Mediterranean civilization. The old story. The barbarian realizes that he has destroyed something greater than himself and so, in his own way, he sets out to eulogize what was lost.

Or, as St. Remy put it when he baptized pagan Merovingian Clovis, "Barbarian, destroy what you have worshipped and revere what you have destroyed." Then, St. Remy had said, "In hoc signo vinces"… "In this our sign of victory"… meaning Christ.

I knew this because, in my early days as a soldier, I was in hoc fairly frequently. Also, at this time I had smoked, and the most common cigarettes in Somalia were Pall Malls, which a Brit ex-SAS demolition expert had taught me to pronounce "Pell Mell." Pall Malls have *In hoc signo vinces* on the package. I'd been curious.

The grandeur that was Rome was exaggerated by those who had sacked the city, and out of this wistful barbaric aggrandizement came the best values that the Western World has had to offer. *Love of something greater than oneself, and the courage to defend it.* Ideals not often attained, but always sought.

Stories of love and courage have sustained our Western self-image for two thousand years. These stories have a special name. Romances. A tale of Rome, originally. Nowadays, romances are any story about love and courage and the preservation of great value.

Usually, but not always, modern romances are about a love relationship threatened by familial, social or psychological pressure, and it is considered a lowly genre by the literati. This expert opinion has not prevented this type of story from being by far the most popular among readers. Book and magazine publishers can attest to that. But even this supposedly lowly kind of story, by its very name, cannot escape the ancient aura of Rome. These tales still extol the best of the West, seldom achieved.

A thousand years after Alaric's Visigothic barbarians had conquered and settled in Septimania, their descendants started to eulogize their victim in ballads and songs.

Medieval troubadours of Languedoc and Provence began telling old Romance stories in a new way. Carcassonne was a center of troubadour poetry.

Poets wove their tales of love and courage around Rome, and around an obscure British war leader called Arthur who had become an Emperor of Rome. King Arthur. Their poems centered around Rome, the Tale of the Grail deriving from it, and King Arthur as its protector.

How did southern French poets even know about Arthur? Did some document survive until troubadour times? Was there a folk memory of Arthur's horse-buying trip to Septimania? Or did he do something more memorable in Languedoc than just buy horses? It is said that Arthur married Guinevere – "white aspect" in medieval French – but said to derive from Gwenhumara – "white owl" in Celtic.

The lady came from 'Wallis', supposedly Wales, but every barge skipper on the upper Rhône enters the country of Wallis around Lyon. It is called Valois in French, but is still Wallis in Switzerland. Did Arthur meet and marry a lady from Wallis while buying horses in Septimania? This local memory of King Arthur, and the Grail romances about him, is just another mystery hovering in the neighbourhood of Carcassonne.

And no, I had definitely not forgotten Joëlle's reference to the Holy Grail. Believers in this 'Holy Grail' were called Cathars. They lived in Provence and Languedoc. It was hard to remain ignorant of this fact since the Languedoc Tourist Bureau had plastered posters almost everywhere. These feature a ruin of some castle on a limestone hilltop near Carcassonne and the words 'Languedoc, Pays des Cathares'… Languedoc, Cathar Country.

This Provençal and Languedoc belief in the 'Holy Grail' had provoked a terrible religious war because Rome considered the 'Holy Grail' to be the worst heresy of all.

This war, raging between AD 1209 and 1244 is known as the Albigensian Crusade. The town of Albi just north of Carcassonne was a major centre of heretical belief.

The Cathars, or Albigensians, lost this brutal war, and this accounts for the ruins on the tourist posters. It also explains why Viollet-le-Duc had had to rebuild medieval Carcassonne. It had been thoroughly sacked by Vatican armies.

From the top lock before leaving the summit level to descend down into the Aude River at Carcassonne, one can see the valley of the Aude spilling out into the east. Directly below is, of course, Carcassonne itself.

Far away, in middle distance, is Narbonne – a whitish smudge against browny-green haze of *maquis*. Just as if someone had spilled sugar on an ochre place mat. Narbo Martius of the Romans, complete with a ruined amphitheatre, modern Narbonne boasts Roman columns in unlikely places, and baths.

And in the extreme distance, at a horizon made wiggly by heat waves on the plain, is the startling brilliant blue of the Mediterranean. Distance obscures the existence of brackish lakes inland from the sea, lakes through which canal barges may navigate up the coast. You can use inland waters all the way to the Rhône estuaries near Marseilles.

Even with all the recent excitement, I had never the less had a few quiet moments to reflect, mostly this morning during the five and a half hour trip from Lac des Doigts to Carcassonne.

As I gazed with new appreciation at the fairy tale turrets and battlements of Carcassonne from the deck of *La Poule Frite*, I wondered where the money to finance this mock-medieval extravagance had come from. I had decided that the Bank of Perseval's Well might very well have been involved.

Its head office was, of course, in Old Carcassonne. The bank was also the principal owner of Old Carcassonne's real estate and tourist concessions.

Since the 1880s, income from rentals and tourists had far eclipsed the cost of Viollet-le-Duc's folly. And few tourist souls had departed from Carcassonne unmoved by some vague, wistful and noble ideal. Thus, perhaps, does the Grail continue to work its magic in the Disneyland recesses of our materialistic minds.

27

"Doucement, Crétin!... Fils du bloody cochon!... Merde!... Doucement!" Marcel Bouchard's urgent profanity strangely did not detract from the Carcassonne scenery. It seemed even richer within the lusty medieval ambiance that the battlements and turrets cast over the vulgarly modern New City where, of course, such profanity was drably commonplace. And I could well appreciate Bouchard's anxiety. The last net of casks was being lowered into *La Poule Frite's* ample midsection, and Jean-Claude on the winch was letting the cable pull out too quickly over the revolving drum. As Bouchard shouted, I could see the man pull back on the brake lever with one hand, and on the cable with the other.

The net bounced to a stop in mid air. The boom swayed. Bouchard, down in the hold, waved his hand in come-hither motions alternating with traffic cop stop signals. The net jiggled down with the casks shifting around like a fertility symbol yet to be conceived in the fevered human brain – a scrotum full of jostling testicles being roiled by some urgent stimulus. It came to me then that I had under-rated Gabereau's skills as a *raconteur*. Vague, disturbing dreams, which I couldn't recall in detail, had made me edgy for a while this morning, too.

At last, the cargo net collapsed with multiple thumps into the bottom of the barge's hold. Bouchard jumped to loosen the hook that skewered grommets at all four corners, even as Jean-Claude flicked the two turns of cable free of the winch's drum and pushed his lever far forward to disengage the clutch. He scrambled down into *La Poule Frite's* belly to help Marcel with the job of stacking the casks securely.

Ordinarily, I also would have helped with this, and had done so many times before, but today I was absolved of dirty work by virtue of my attire. Since my leg was throbbing badly, I was more than happy to shirk. Marcel Bouchard himself, no less, had absolved me an hour ago when he had stepped aboard *Jester* and had looked up to see me on the poop beside the wheelhouse with *L'Almanach du Languedoc* and he had done the classic double-take.

"Ooh... la... *la...*," he'd said, flicking his hand as if to fling something nasty from his fingers. He walked around me, looking me up and down in mock admiration. "Regarde, Jean-Claude! Un vrai, grand capitaine, n'est-ce pas?" He had bobbed a deferential salute. But since he was almost as tall as me, and considerably thicker, I hadn't taken his deference all that seriously.

"Coupez-la. Vite, Mighty." Now, this may sound odd, even from me, but it was supposed to express "Cut that, quick, Matey" – in French-Australian. Bouchard had learned his English in a hard and underworld school, so to speak.

"Pourquoi the bleedin' shore rig, mon ami?" he had asked.

"Les flics, Bouchard," I answered. "Policiers."

He thought, and smiled. "Ah, oui, Mite. Les friggin' flics. Je sais..."

Forsaking the paradise that many seek, French Polynesia – and, one gathered, under some duress involving a large, extended family in close pursuit on account of an incipient new relative – Bouchard had signed aboard a decrepit Aussie coaster then in the port of Tubuai. This vessel usually only plied the coast between Perth and Darwin, touching at such world-renowned entrepots as Geraldton, Carnarvon, Port Headland and Broome. Not to mention Wyndham.

Cargo was cut cane, shark skins, mangrove poles, copra, bully beef and lungfish fertilizer. Every so often, if the skipper thought that the ex-collier might actually make it, they would venture out into the Pacific for good quality copra and palm oil. This could be worth the risk of going as far as Papeete or Tubuai. But, during Bouchard's three years aboard, the bucket had never gone further east than New Guinea and this had suited him fine. He claimed never to have been bored studying the endless panorama of the Great Sandy Desert. He was an optimist, and therefore happy for the opportunity of adding English and a smattering of Woojumera to his attainments.

I'd run into him years before in Dili on Timor, which is not far northwest of Western Australia. It was soon to become East Timor because of a revolutionary struggle I had been hired to assist. *Jindivik* had put into Dili with a load of shark skins for the Timor leather workers. From time immemorial, Timor artisans had produced high quality shark skin shoes and purses for Chinese mandarins. Now they produced the same products for mainland Chinese commissars and Hong Kong tycoons.

I had liked Bouchard in a cautious way. He'd explained that the name of the tiny freighter, *Jindivik*, was Australian aboriginal for 'the hunted one' and this designation also suited him just then. I had not been much surprised to meet up with him ten years later in Carcassonne. Boat people are globe-trotters.

From my vantage point on *La Poule Frite's* stern, which wasn't sufficiently higher than the main deck to be called a proper poop, I looked down onto *Jester* alongside and realized once more how small she really was. Without the cargo of casks amidship, *Jester's* configuration was again apparent and Ivory was clearly visible.

Whereas, the 250-ton *La Poule Frite* could still be called graceful because of her classical barge lines, the same could not be said of *Jester*. More than anything, she resembled two refrigerator ice trays arranged end-to-end with a massive hinge between them.

The rear ice tray was deeper and decked and constituted *Jester's* cabin. The front ice tray was just an empty shell with a false floor a foot off the bottom and filled with foam. It was just a rectangular hollow steel float with somewhat higher sides. Only I knew that the front ice tray could be pivoted up and over to cover the rear cabin like a steel shell. As for the outriggers, they were pivoted on the front hull's rail. When the front hull was covering the rear cabin, they were folded to rest on top of the hull's bottom that was now the top of a steel box. It was all quite simple really, but also subtly complicated, and had taken three months even to draw out on paper. Whenever I changed the dimension of one thing, everything else was affected and the whole boat had to be drawn all over again. But finally I had achieved not only plans, but a large-scale model that could be copied by a welding shop.

Only the strength of modern materials and welding had made the idea workable. I'd had the choice of having a much larger conventional boat or a pocket, folding *orembai*. Figuring to be alone, and not wanting to have any vessel that I couldn't easily manage single-handed, but still large enough to carry useful cargo, I'd chosen *Folderol Jester* and had used stainless steel and aluminum lavishly. I had been able to afford careful machining and tungsten welding. The resulting foldable neo-*orembai* could literally "sleep" four at a pinch and could accommodate two inconveniently. She had everything that one person needed to live aboard indefinitely – so long as one could go ashore now and then for variety, for stretching one's legs and for a feeling of space.

Jester had already saved me a great deal of money and was presently making money. After folding her over herself, I'd shipped her across the Atlantic as deck cargo on board a Panamanian freighter, which had called at Sept Isles in Canada for iron ore. *Moskito Venturer* had been bound for Marseilles where there are steel plants. For a price, the skipper had agreed to unfold *Jester* on deck, have the crew help secure the hulls together and have a derrick lift her into the Mediterranean off the Balearic Islands of Spain, but in international waters. This had saved me the time and challenge of sailing across the Atlantic. As I have already said, I had never aspired to be a blue water sailor.

Able to carry about five tons while providing me with a secure, if an extremely snug home at the same time, I had envisioned that *Jester* would be useful as a canal barge, at least in the beginning during a social transition period. Once things had stabilized at some cultural level short of the Palaeolithic, increasing canal usage would outclass *Jester's* limited carrying capacity. But then I planned to construct a wooden box of a barge that *Jester* could push – if I liked the life, that is, but needed some extra cargo capacity to compete at it. It was for this reason that I had sacrificed some of the limited space available for a larger-than-necessary steam engine and boiler. I might need extra pushing power.

But, of course, I might tire of barging. Also, by then, there might be a revived market for books. In this eventuality, the larger engine could provide more speed so that I could see the Mediterranean world a little more quickly. There was always a market for newspaper and magazine articles, including offbeat travel articles, though they didn't pay as much these days as before. I had figured, perhaps wrongly, that satellites in space would not be affected much by events on earth and had calculated that the Western World, at least, would preserve electronic communications to the very end. Therefore, I had planned *Jester* so that she could accommodate the best laptop computer system available in Y2K, and bring in the Internet by dish on calm water. This had given me a vastly larger library than any shelf that *Jester* had room for. I could also usefully employ a digital camera and therefore instantly illustrate and e-mail newspaper and magazine stories. So far, it appeared that I had been anticipating correctly. I had retained about 20 cherished books, real books with pages and covers, for reading by the light of an oil lantern.

The phone trilled in my blazer pocket.

"Oui."

"Joëlle." Her voice sounded guarded.

"Thank God," I said. "Where are you?"

"In a hotel. The 'Tarn et Garonne'." There was a pause. "I did what you said… and I've been watching the news. You were right. They're starting to report that sabotage may have been responsible for the blast."

"It was. Like I wrote, Joey, we were right behind that barge. In thick fog. I heard gunfire."

"*They* were after you?"

I didn't want to complicate matters for her. "I assume so." I also didn't want to stay on the phone too long. "Raoul?"

"He can't come until tomorrow morning. A friend brought some flour up from Bordeaux by truck. They have to unload it." She gave me Raoul's phone number. Afterwards, there was a significant pause. "Marc, I have only three days of sick leave, you know. And it is not good to use any sick leave these days."

"I know, Joey. Okay. I'll be in touch tomorrow. Maybe all this will blow over and you can go back home… and back to work," I added. "But, for now, please trust me, Joey."

"For now, Marc…"

We were saying awkward good-byes when Bouchard and Jean-Claude climbed out of *La Poule Frite's* wide deck hatch. Bouchard glanced up just as I was signing out. I waved the phone at him. "Why don't you break down and get one of these things?" I suggested for the umpteenth time. And that made me think of the *Amaranthe*. I gazed around, but the *birol* was nowhere in sight.

"Too easy to find me, Mite."

"That reminds me," I said, "where's Roland?"

Bouchard pointed to the canal toward Lac des Doigts. "They left early." I must have missed them in my preoccupation with *L'Almanach du Languedoc* during the cruise toward Carcassonne. On the other hand, they would certainly have hailed me if they had seen *Jester*. But then I recalled the grilling bream and, knowing that these tasty fish were denizens of weedy shorelines, I imagined that the *birol* had ventured into the reeds for a bit of dinner fishing. Being so low, the hull would have been easy to miss while the house might seem to have been on land. Still, this lapse in observation bothered me.

Bouchard grinned suddenly, and his head swivelled down from me to something closer. The grin broadened as Annette and Mariko came out of the companionway below me. I climbed down the worn wooden steps to join everyone on deck. Mariko was carrying a large garbage bag. "Clothes," she gestured. I looked at her, and up and down, but I couldn't find much to say. Mariko O'Shaugnessey had disappeared beneath a long strawberry blonde Farah Fawcett wig, red sunglasses with heart-shaped lenses, a pseudo-leather halter-top and a short matching black skirt. Prince Rupert would have coveted the higher-than-knee black boots into which black fishnet stockings disappeared. Mariko pirouetted slowly.

"Clothes...?" I said, stunned. "Right."

"I think I like you nearly speechless, Marc," she smiled with garish red lips. She turned away and sauntered to *La Poule Frite's* rail. Mariko bent with great exaggeration over the rail, giving a purposeful flash of black panties beneath the short skirt, and stretched down onto *Jester's* outrigger deck. She swayed toward the poop and the wheelhouse, edging beside Ivory, and looking around. Perhaps she had intended to keep on sauntering, but was sidetracked by seeing *Jester* empty and seeing Ivory for the first time. Small waves had begun to rock *Jester* just a little. A late afternoon breeze had sprung up, and it was fluttering the pages of *L'Almach du Languedoc* on top of the wheelhouse. "Mariko," I called out. "The magazine. Could you take it below, please?"

She nodded, picked it up and clambered awkwardly down, squeezing the plastic bag through the hatchway behind her. I turned back to Annette, Jean-Claude and Marcel. Bouchard and I had to settle our business and there were thanks due to Annette and Jean-Claude.

28

To be honest, I had been dreading the appointment with Inspector Gabereau. Although we had gone over my story in detail en route to Carcassonne, I was not at all sure that Mariko could lie convincingly under intensive questioning. For that matter, in spite of considerably more practice, I wasn't sure of my own abilities either.

However, surprises awaited us. A gendarme new to me simply presented us with two typed statements that had earlier been dictated by Gabereau from his notes. We were informed that Inspector Gabereau was at home, probably sleeping, after almost forty continual hours on duty. The statements were naturally in French, so we read them with great care. We made only a couple of changes and then we signed them.

Immediately after this, the gendarme presented Mariko with an envelope containing her passport. He also had her single suitcase. She had to sign for these too. They had been flown from Moissac to Carcassonne by police chopper – which meant that Gabereau had sent a minion almost immediately to seek out the pension and also to verify my story. Since they had apparently checked out to his satisfaction, Gabereau had obviously proceeded on to much more serious matters.

Mariko was delighted, and I was relieved. I told the gendarme that I would drop *Jester* down through Carcassonne in the morning and head for the étangs around Narbonne. There, I thought, we might rest a few days. I knew that Gabereau would have no trouble finding *Jester* there and this would give him a feeling of security if he wanted to question us further.

Now, I wanted to go down into Carcassonne to do some shopping. *Jester's* real disadvantage was an acute shortage of storage space, even for fuel. She would only carry food for two or three days. This had not seemed a disadvantage since, as I have already admitted, I had never had any inclination to become a blue water sailor making long oceanic passages. Along canals or along the coast, two or three days of independence from shore seemed more than sufficient. However, while we needed to buy provisions, I didn't feel like hauling Mariko's suitcase around with us in Carcassonne.

We walked the short distance back to *Jester*, now moored to the concrete retaining wall behind *La Poule Frite*, so that Mariko could stow the suitcase aboard.

"Ah…Mariko…while you're at it…?"

"Ye-ess…?"

"Would it be possible, now that you have your own clothes, to change into something less… ah… conspicuous?"

"Marc Rennsalaer! You're a prude!"

"Not necessarily," I equivocated. "Perhaps just not… avant garde."

Mariko laughed. "Of course, I'll change, if it makes you more comfortable…" But then she suddenly turned serious. "You know, Marc, as I think of it, it might not be a good idea for me to change clothes." She paused. "I brought only a few clothes from Oxford. The men have seen me in all of the ensembles. And one of them is also Oriental," she added.

I hadn't thought of that. "You're absolutely right. I'll learn to like avant garde." I fished *Jester's* key from my pocket. It had teeth for the tumblers and grooves for the electronic code. I hadn't given her my emergency spare that I kept hidden on the deck near the wheelhouse, and, of course, we'd had no time to have another key made. If that was ever to be in the cards.

In the brief time Mariko was below, I reflected that *avant-garde* wasn't exactly an appropriate description. The boots were 17th century refugees while the fishnets hailed from Toulouse Lautrec's Paris and the rest from Rudi Gernreich's 1970s New York. Maybe I *was* just prudish.

We walked down several flights of lock-side stone steps until we came to a street where we were able to attract a taxi. I wanted a 'grande surface', a shopping mall, and we were duly deposited at La Nouvelle Vague… the 'New Wave' complex of steel and glass. I gave Mariko a generous number of Bouchard's francs for shopping and went into the food supermarket, not a *Provigo Midi* and not one of Hervé's associates either. I noted that it was well stocked, but expensive. Having a rough list in my mind, I dumped mostly dehydrated stuff into the cart, and looked also for beer. No Coors, Canadian or Corona, so I took some Dutch brew called Pirate adorned with Long John Silver and a parrot.

I would much rather have done things the other way around, to have gone for dinner first and then to have gone shopping. Unfortunately, however, French malls generally closed at 9 p.m.

No one should miss reconstructed Carcassonne and I didn't want Mariko to miss it. We took another taxi from the mall because of our parcels and I asked the driver to make a tour of the Old City. It was exactly the right time for it, too, with the after-light of sunset tinting the dramatic battlements and turrets magenta, mauve and purple. Not only that, but the bats were coming out. These were not your small darting bats of more northerly climes that flit about for insects, but large fruit-eating bats sometimes called flying foxes. They can have a wingspread of two to three feet. They don't flit. They flap slowly and glide. They may look like pterodactyls, but they are perfectly harmless.

Carcassonne is home to thousands of these big bats because Viollet-le-Duc's too many overhanging balconies give them shady roosts during the day. At dusk they sally forth to forage in Narbonnais orchards. What with the brooding clouds streaked with sunset pyrotechnics and the prehistoric bat shapes soaring among the turrets and crenellations, it looked like an ancient mystical city under aerial assault by dragons. It was a scene from Tolkien or Lovecraft rendered visually by Gustave Doré or, much better, Frank Frazetta. *The Siege of Gondor,* or something like that.

I felt and heard Mariko's intake of breath and her slight shudder. "This is all veddy improbable," she observed. "Highly dramatic."

"It is, isn't it? That's because Carcassonne is more than a little unreal. Look at how we got here, for instance. An attempted abduction, a blown up barge and a blasted helicopter. Not exactly mundane."

"I take your point," Mariko said quietly. After a pause. "After what's happened to us, this is just an over-built Disneyland and the bats are large and harmless…*megachiroptera*, is it?"

"That's right. Fruit bats."

"You're certain they're harmless…?"

"I'm sure." I patted her thigh and peeked up out the window. "Still…Carcassonne is rather… ah… apocalyptic, Mariko," I conceded.

"I would have used 'Gothic', Marc," she said.

"Gothic scares me," I said.

I had asked the cabbie to take us to a place I had heard about but had never so far visited. *Le Cheval de Septimanie.* The Septimanian Horse. They were supposed to serve a local dish, *cassoulet*, that dates back to Roman times. According to reports, *Le Cheval de Septimanie* was exclusive by virtue of the quality and expense of its cuisine, but not because of any social pretensions. Many foreign yachtsmen and boat people, and some of them were, of course, quite wealthy in a casual and unsuspected way, had spread the restaurant's fame to a limited audience. Because of their descriptions, I figured that Mariko's attire would raise no eyebrows and it didn't. The décor, such as it was, was mock ruins and mounted barbarians somewhat crudely painted among them. Mariko's pseudo-leather garb and boots, if not the pink sunglasses, added a realistically three-dimensional touch to the motif of barbarian invasion. No one could complain about that.

Along with *cassoulet*, we had *gigot* – a wildly over-garnished saddle of lamb. I had tried to make this myself, once. And, while buying the ingredients, I had noticed that the garnishes reflected the Visigoths' migration from the Russian steppes to the Pyrenees. Crab apples from the Caucasus, almonds from Turkey, olives from Greece, pommidoro from Italy, garlic from Provence and finally oranges from the Narbonnais. All this was simmered into a sweet red wine sauce that could have derived from sacked and captured Greek Mavrodaphne or from 'Marsala' – wine named after Marseilles. Nowadays, *gigot* is usually roasted in an oven, but *Le Cheval de Septimanie* still took the trouble to braise it over charcoal. It had originally been skewered over barbarian fires. Basically, it was a kind of upscale Visigothic shish kebab for chieftains.

So, we ate something from both camps, as it were, Roman and Visigothic. Appropriate for Septimania, maybe and certainly appropriate in the atmosphere of huge candles with great wicks conveying the idea of nomadic campfires and torches amid the detritus of civilization. I'd also heard of a local, Carcassonne, red wine – *Domaine des Corbieres*. It isn't available everywhere, not even in some of Carcassonne's better restaurants, and I've never seen a bottle of it west of Toulouse.

We discussed the manuscript fragment over this eclectic, delicious dinner, dabbing glistening, flickering lamb fat from our mouths and fingers with serviettes that were almost as coarsely ochre as jute. This small page of parchment had been bothering me for some time. It was obviously the key to the entire matter... and I was starting to suspect the situation was more complex, more dangerous, than either Mariko or I had truly realised. I'd done a rough financial accounting, trying to reduce our predicament to something familiar; columns of dollars and cents. I was staggered at the time, money, manpower and sheer ruthlessness that had converged, apparently, on that small piece of manuscript.

Obviously, we had to get to the bottom of the mystery as quickly as possible. The only safety lay in making the parchment public knowledge as soon as we could steal it and as soon as Mariko could translate it. On the relaxing way to Carcassonne, I had outlined a plan during the times that Mariko ventured into the wheelhouse. We conversed through the hatch because I didn't want her visible on deck until we could disguise her appearance. This was both unfortunate and unfair. The day had been warm and gorgeous. The *cassoulet* and *gigot* in *Le Cheval de Septimanie* were in the nature of compensations – expensive ones.

And now, finishing up the last of them, she agreed that the best idea was what I had proposed. We would backtrack along the Canal du Midi to Bordeaux and cross the Bay of Biscay to Brittany. If she had wondered why I wanted to make another quick stop at Moissac on the way, she didn't ask. Since I didn't like the idea of navigating along the rocky and tidal coast of the Brittany peninsula, a lee shore to the treacherous North Atlantic, we'd enter the Vilaine River and take the inland canals through Rennes as far as possible. We would hop the Channel from Cherbourg. This would take us about a month, I'd figured out roughly this morning, if we really pushed. We discussed it again, agreed, and then paid our bill and left feeling very satisfied.

29

The Chinese call their gods 'the laughing immortals.' That being the case, I should have been hearing loud guffaws when we left the restaurant and not just crickets in the crenellations. Carcassonne changed all the plans we had just discussed, confirmed and endorsed, and possibly only Carcassonne could have done it.

Viollet-le-Duc's phantasmagoria had been both ambitious and expensive, but it was nonetheless limited in area. Confining itself strictly to the Old City within the ruined walls, the reconstruction had encompassed about a hundred acres. Viollet-le-Duc had been faithful to the city plan and so there were only two streets wide enough for two very narrow lanes of modern traffic. They crossed each other, dividing the city into quarters. In Viollet-le-Duc's day the main streets had accommodated the carriages of wealthy tourists, which could enter the town by four gates in the great wall. The other streets were all distinctly 'one way', a warren of twisting alleyways that could be threaded only by a careful and determined normal-sized car. An Innocenti three-wheeler had the edge in terms of motor vehicles. Bicycles and mopeds were even more popular in Carcassonne than in the rest of France.

We walked from *Le Cheval de Septimanie*, which was near the wall on one of the major streets, toward the intersection with the other thoroughfare in the centre, more or less, of the medieval town. That was where we expected to find a taxi because these days because they didn't cruise because of the high cost of gasoline. It was a matter of three or four medieval blocks or, regarded another way, a five minute walking tour of Quasimodo's neighbourhood. All modern traffic tended to park near the intersection because that was the only place that had any room for stationary vehicles. Only Carcassonne could have concentrated automobiles in one place so conveniently. Especially cars like a Mercedes 600 limousine. We were almost past its purring black hulk; it was idling – these days? – when Mariko's leggy stalk came to a halt.

"Dear God," she whispered. "Is the Pope here?"

I followed her gaze to the insignia on the front door. Crossed keys, the keys to the kingdom, the Vatican. I also noted the Mercedes was dusty and held a sleeping chauffeur. Muted Italian opera music came from within. A radio or, more likely, a stereo CD player. I grabbed her arm and hustled her along. "Don't you dare stop and stare," I whispered.

She nodded, and patted my hand on her arm nervously. "The Pope...?" she breathed.

"I doubt that, Mariko... But someone important. A legate. A Cardinal... and why *here... now.*" We went on past the Mercedes after Mariko's pause and I glanced back to confirm that it did, indeed, bear Vatican diplomatic plates. Our wonder increased when, behind the Mercedes, a big Citroen-Maserati was parked. It bore the livery of a major French airport limousine service. Its driver was not asleep, but he only had eyes for Mariko so I edged to the other side of her, hiding my face behind her cascading wig. "Keep going," I hissed, with my head bent as if nuzzling her cheek.

We turned the major corner and saw an empty taxi a few yards away. We walked toward it. By now I was looking around and had perceived that the limousines were parked in front of the largest building I had yet seen in Carcassonne, the 'Hotel du Languedoc'. With an exchange of Bouchard's francs through the window after a brief conversation, I ascertained that the cabbie wasn't waiting for anyone and was willing to spend all the time I could pay for. I opened the door and hustled Mariko into the taxi, passing our parcels in to her. I glanced at my watch. Just 11 p.m. The angle was such that we couldn't see much of the hotel now.

I could barely see that flanking the main door there was a tasteful extension of a lounge that spilled spear points of light through high Gothic windows out onto the pavement. But they were paled by much more light from the nearby modern glass front entrance. I had not noticed this before with my head hunched over behind Mariko's wig.

"Why the hell didn't you buy cigarettes before?" I said irritably, bending over Mariko in the open doorway and winking. She didn't smoke.

She hesitated for an instant, and it could have been taken for sullen indignation. "Don't worry," Mister, she said in heavily French-accented English, "you'll get plenty of what you want." She put the parcels on the floor impatiently.

"There," I pointed at the hotel. "You can get them in there." She scrabbled out, flashing thigh, to pose beside me on the curb.

Then I whispered in her ear as if nuzzling her again. "Mariko, they may be in the lounge. Are you up to trying to get a look at them?"

I could hear her intake of breath. But then I felt her body tense, and she nodded so that her hair ticked my nose.

She hesitated on the curb. "Only... I don't have any money." That was right. She'd returned what had been left of Bouchard's francs to me.

"Jeeze." I said loudly, fishing in my pocket.

"I won't be long, Lover," she said and gave me a wriggling hug. This put my mouth to her cheek for some moments, so I kissed her.

She sauntered brazenly across to the hotel and swayed seductively up the front steps. Not having to feign impatience, I edged a few steps closer to the corner. I saw through the glass entrance doors that the concierge was quick to intercept Mariko when she peered through into the lounge. The 'Languedoc' was much too classy to allow that kind of girl to work their lounge. As luck would have it, however, just as Mariko was being escorted to the desk and was being invited to stare at the available brands of cigarettes under the counter glass, I saw through the Gothic windows that four men stood up. They made their way briskly out of the lounge. They passed not ten feet behind Mariko in the foyer and she turned to appraise them. With her hand holding the purchased cigarettes resting against her cocked hip. She was at least partly enjoying the role. What had become of the mousy Oxford protégé?

The prospects could not have appeared very hopeful to her because the first man was an old one wearing a black clerical suit and a dog collar. The second was a big, blond and distinguished-looking gentleman who glanced at her with disdain visible even to me. She was ignored by the third man, who was speaking urgently to the second one.

But, as this talking pair passed her, I saw her body suddenly stiffen in its sultry pose and her hand come involuntarily up to her mouth. She had courage and managed to make it look like a coy hand-covered pout instead of a stifled scream. Only the fourth and youngest gave her an appreciative up and down, but she was too preoccupied to respond or notice. As the group jostled out through both glass entrance doors at once, I saw in the light this fourth man was the youthful gendarme with the Gasconnade I'd met. I turned quickly and walked back to the taxi.

Soon I heard the paced clicking of Mariko's boot heels, just a little faster than normal. I didn't try to meet her at the corner because I figured that the gendarme's eyes might well be following her. I lounged with my arms folded on the roof of the cab and my head turned away from the hotel as if with irritated impatience. She hugged me again as she came up to the cab. "See, Lover, no time at all," she cooed for the driver's benefit, but I could hear the flutter of fear in her voice. In my ear she whispered raggedly: "One of them was one of the men who have been following me, Marc… what are we to do?"

I patted her bum, hustled her back into the taxi and directed the driver to drop us at the foot of the lockside flight of steps. I looked like a true grand captain, right? It couldn't have been the first time that the cabbie had taken a yachtsman and a girl to those steps. All the way there, with one arm around her shoulders, I caressed Mariko thigh, which the driver could see when he glanced in his rear view mirror, and it gave her the excuse to cuddle up and moan softly. Only Mariko and I knew that her whimpers were real.

I remember paying the taxi off, but not running up the lock-side steps. I remember only that Mariko sobbed with every effort. I held her once we reached the canal and, while she wept softly, I scanned *Jester* over her shoulder. Even in the faint light reflecting up from the town, I could see no one on deck either fore or aft. I knew that no one could get below. *La Poule Frite* showed no lights, but I knew that Marcel slept lightly, as I did, and for fairly similar reasons.

"Marc…" she sniffled. "I'm tired, Marc."

"I know, Mariko."

"I can't run any longer." She was shaking with silent crying. She hesitated for a long moment. "I'll go to the police and take my chances."

I told her about the boy with the Gasconnade. She had not recognised *him*, of course.

"So… so… they know all about us…?"

I nodded.

"We… we… may as well give up." She wriggled into my chest, and it wasn't any act. "Oh, Marc… I'm so frightened."

I hugged her until she calmed down. Then I tipped her chin up and removed those horrible glasses. "And this is the girl who shot down a chopper and who ruthlessly raped a wounded man?"

She sniffled a little laugh.

"We're not finished yet, Girl," I said.

She nodded wearily. "If you say so."

"I do. Now let's get aboard."

Although navigation on the canal was technically forbidden after 9 p.m., this was a relative term. It was intended to apply to commercial barges of 250 tons or more travelling at commercial speeds.

It did not restrict canoes, skiffs and small yachts from using the canal at night, so long as they did it safely, but the law could be applied if the police found it convenient to do so.

Many French laws are similarly flexible, and people rely on centuries of civilization and common sense for judicious enforcement. This differs from the Anglo-Saxon concept of justice wherein everything must be written down. I preferred the French way because many social expectations are too subtle to be conveyed in words.

The very first item of business was to cast *Jester* free of the embankment and to nudge her out into the canal.

Even a few yards of deep water provides some protection from shore dangers. I did this while Mariko took the parcels below, trying to make no sound. I instructed her to put everything away as securely as possible and to look around for any loose items. I asked her to cram them somewhere, anywhere, that they wouldn't move. We showed no lights. As far as I could remember, the moon was supposed to rise in a couple of hours, but I was hazy on its phase – waxing or waning?

As soon as we had drifted clear of *La Poule Frite's* broad stern, I fed just a whisper of steam to the pistons. *Jester* turned slowly and the glimmer of Carcassonne wheeled lazily below.

When we were safely headed back toward Castelnaudary, I got on the phone for a long, urgent and extremely expensive conversation.

About half an hour later, Mariko came topside with the last cold Coors just as *Jester* was gliding into a wide gap in the reeds. She was dressed in the Jordache jeans and the jersey again. From this, I gathered that boat clothing had not been among the things she'd had brought from Oxford or in the garbage bag she had got from Annette.

Jester slid between reeds until her bow scraped up on concrete. The boat ramp was just a faint ghostly swath in the night ahead.

30

The moon had risen a little above the canal horizon when I heard the growl of a truck and seconds afterwards saw headlights shafting hesitantly around a bend and then toward us along the canal-side road. I risked a brief flash from the searchlight and the truck came on more confidently. I went out over *Jester's* bow, a true grand captain no longer, to meet Raoul and his friend from Bordeaux, Philippe.

I'd done what I could to get *Jester* ready. The main masts were up and Ivory was ashore and had been lengthened into a trailer. Nonetheless, it took the four of us two full hours before *Jester* was hitched behind the GMC diesel sleeper cab. The problem was that I had not folded *Jester* since the freighter had dropped her into the sea off Mallorca almost ten years before. True, the four beams under the hulls that slid forward into sockets were of the best stainless steel and had been lubricated regularly, but the growth of canal algae had still seized them up. It took Raoul and me, both hanging from the giant wrench, to crack them loose and even then retracting them with turns of the wrench was a struggle for two of us. Once that was done, lifting the front hull up between the mainmasts was easy by comparison. The big stainless hinges squealed, but they worked.

Raoul and Philippe were impressed by the way that the raised wheelhouse fitted into a corresponding rectangular cutout in the forward float. Ivory's wheels straddled this aperture when it was on board. Since the wheelhouse was a bit higher than the keel was deep, it protruded above it enough to slide the hatch open. *Jester* when folded could be a travel trailer with an inconvenient front entrance. Then we backed Ivory down under *Jester's* rear hull. From inside *Jester*, one could look down out of the wheelhouse front window and see the trailer hitch projecting from the front of Ivory.

Originally, this window had been ordinary safety glass. But during the trailering test back in Canada, a stone had been flung up from the towing truck's wheels and had shattered it. Live and learn. I had replaced the glass with polycarbonate. This plastic, the kind that separates the driver from passengers in many North American taxicabs, would withstand a shotgun blast at close range. Unfortunately, though, it was not quite as clear as glass and so the view through it was just a bit hazy.

It was close on to 1:30 in the morning when we had finally lowered the mainmasts again and Philippe's truck slowly and carefully jerked *Jester* up the ramp from the water. We all piled out except for Mariko, who had agreed to take the top bunk in the sleeper cab. We three men gave everything a final check while *Jester* slowly stopped dripping. It may have been a versatile design, but it was also a complicated one. It was easy to miss some crucial detail. So we went over all the bolts and nylon tie-downs carefully. I was particularly concerned about Ivory's tires. The vehicle had two axles and four tires, but they were technically overloaded with *Jester's* weight. Not by much. We made everything safe, but because were looking at the wheels, axles and the hitch, we forgot to notice the planter boxes, now above our heads, across the stern.

By three o'clock, Philippe was asleep in the lower bunk and Raoul and I were deep into the financial details of purchasing a canal-side building in a place called Aiguillon near Agen. I'd already told him on the phone that Joëlle would be getting to Agen by train if my present mess didn't resolve itself soon. We also discussed a corporate structure with shares to both of us, to Christine and to Joëlle, Philippe and Marie-Thérèse and we chatted about the various skills we could each bring to a joint enterprise.

After backtracking to Toulouse along the 'Autoroute des 2 Mers', we headed up the long climb into the Massif Central and into the heart of France. Raoul, then at the wheel, remarked that *Jester* was a remarkably lightweight tow from the feel of things, as we began taking the first of many uphill grades. I explained that this was because *Jester* was made mostly from aluminum above the hulls' gunwales.

The two principal hulls alone were of steel, and fairly thin plate at that. And I had taken a lot of care with the necessary steel framing – I'd cribbed from aircraft design – making it strong enough and then some, but as light in weight as possible. Pushing needless weight cost fuel. Raoul and Philippe were impressed. "At this rate," said Raoul, "we'll be in Nantes by this evening."

Dawn caught us high in the mountains on a twisting road that was only sometimes a four-lane autoroute. Mostly it was just two lanes, but there was not much traffic. By six in the morning, we arrived in Brive about a hundred and twenty gruelling uphill miles north of Toulouse. Two hours later we stopped at Limoges, about sixty uphill miles further on, to fuel the truck at an Elf-Antar autoroute stop… at $50 U.S. to the gallon. Raoul, Philippe and I also enjoyed some coffee and a *croque monsieur*, France's ancient precursor to an Egg McMuffin. Mariko slept in the locked cab.

On checking the rig at Limoges in the full light, I saw that my vegetables had not survived the wind of the truck's speed. I had not expected them to. Philippe helped me to lower the planter boxes enough to cover most of *"Folderol Jester – Toronto"* on the stern, and we tied the boxes down with a web of nylon to keep them from swinging.

Philippe drove on from Limoges and Raoul took the lower bunk. I learned that he would be doing with his rig what Raoul and Christine had done with theirs. Bringing Raoul's flour from Bordeaux to Aiguillon and then my urgent errand had been the first business that he had had in a while. He and Marie-Thérèse were on welfare. She was a part-time clerk. Things were very tough. Raoul's proposition seemed to be a way out but, unfortunately, they didn't have the money to buy into it. However, now, so he understood from Raoul, I would be buying in.

"You're included. You can repay us over time, was how we figured it. Talk with Raoul and Joëlle about the details. I can't remember them."

"Mais, in tout case, merci... Monsieur Rennsaler."

"Thank *you*, Philippe... and it's Marc," I told him. "Joëlle has to approve the place and the deal," I cautioned. "So, nothing's carved in stone yet. But any building that Raoul would want will probably be okay with Joëlle. By the way, Philippe, what's this Aiguillon place really like, in your opinion?" I asked as an after-thought. I already knew from Raoul that Aiguillon was thirty kilometres west of Agen on the Garonne just outside the town of Tonneins. Aiguillon, he explained, was at the junction of the Lot River. Raoul had been interested in the property for some time.

Philippe explained that the actual warehouse in Aiguillon was located beside another and smaller stream nearby, a sort of navigable private backwater. That's why I probably hadn't noticed it. As for the place itself, it was very large, a big low stone-built warehouse with a couple of concrete silos and its own wharf. Philippe had not seen too much of it because he was unloading flour from the truck to the barge until it got dark, then he'd gone with Raoul to meet me outside of Carcassonne.

Philippe concluded that the location was superb for canal commerce. The warehouse itself needed some interior work, but was fundamentally very strong and secure.

I mentally shrugged. The place sounded promising. I had some confidence in Raoul's careful and meticulous approach to things, and even more confidence in Joëlle's business acumen and planning knowledge. For some time in the truck cab's dim lighting I had also been noticing a distinctive tattoo on Philippe's right arm. Finally I asked and he told me what his tattoo proclaimed, that he'd served with the French paratroopers in Cote d'Ivoire. Short of the Spanish Foreign Legion, there is no tougher outfit.

Just before Poitiers, I called Joëlle to keep her abreast of what was happening. I suggested that, since her Moissac job was becoming iffy anyway, she might seriously think about a career change. Say, CEO of a canal barge company headquartered in… where was it?… Aiguillon.

"That's only eleven kilometres from where I was born," she said, surprised. "Tonneins is just down the river."

"Six miles? I had forgotten that, Joey."

Anyway, I told her that Raoul would be in touch with her by tomorrow and would probably see her the next day. I pleaded with her not to go back to the apartment, even if she went back to work, and she agreed. However, I suggested that it would be better for all concerned if she took the next train to Agen and put up at a hotel there. That would make it easier for Raoul to meet with her. Since my phone's batteries were low, I had to leave it at that.

By Poitiers and noon, Mariko had awakened. She squeezed down between us on the wide front seat with her wig and sunglasses in her lap. I noted that these were not the red-framed and heart-shaped ones of last night. So, thankfully among the things she had purchased at the grande surface were new sunglasses with slightly less dark, but adequate, lenses set in steel rims. Philippe noted the wig and glasses, but said nothing and tactfully pulled into the first autoroute station that appeared on our side of the road. Mariko donned the wig and glasses as the rig slowed on the way to the parking area.

While Mariko freshened up, we ordered Quarter Pounders, fries and coffee. Everything but the coffee tasted just the same as in North America. The coffee had just a suggestion of the French roast bitter taste, not Colombian smooth, but it all tasted surprisingly familiar. The only foreign touch was that sugar came in paper tubes and not in flat paper packets, and it was large grain brown and not small grain white. Just like at *Le Port Romain*. I decided firmly not to pursue that mental association.

There was a McDonald's in Narbonne, right beside the Canal de la Robine and, whatever the French say, it offered the best food value in the town. It was usually crammed with people, whereas the neighbouring local restaurants suffered. And deservedly. However, if there was a McDonald's in Bordeaux, well, I hadn't discovered it. And there wasn't one in Moissac. I realized outside of Poitiers that I had been suffering from acute hamburger deprivation.

"Real Yankee cuisine," I said, as Mariko came to the booth. "Don't look like that, Mariko".

"I've had a Wimpey Burger," she said.

"So have I," I assured her. "This is much better than a Wimpey Burger, Love." The British, for all their efforts at making hot dogs and hamburgers, just couldn't do it for some reason. I had had a hot dog once in London's Victoria Station that "was just like they serve at Yankee Stadium" the vendor had assured me. Right.

She took a tentative bite, chewed, and brightened. "This isn't at all bad," she conceded. "It's not rubbery." It turned out that she liked the fries, too, and finished off mine after she had eaten all her own.

Curiously enough, although Philippe would glance at Mariko, and chatted with me about innocuous matters like the quality of Narbonne's McDonald's, he never said a word directly to her. I attributed this to the fact he must be aware of Joëlle and her contacts between Raoul and me of the day before. Possibly confused about the relationships, he lay low.

We rumbled into Nantes on the Loire just as the sun set. We didn't unhitch at the Nantes Club Nautique because it was too dark to launch *Jester* and besides, I was too tired to do anything. We parked the rig under some spreading chestnut trees overlooking the boat ramp parking lot. Raoul and Philippe walked the two blocks to a disco bar. As for me, I climbed carefully onto *Jester* and helped Mariko first up and then down.

We had no electricity except dim little lights from the 12-volt battery. I had shut the boiler down in order to empty it. This had saved at least a little weight on the haul up into the mountains. I think that Mariko intended to read for a while by the low light. She was flipping through the *Almanach du Languedoc*, anyway.

"By the way, it's okay to use the toilet," I remembered to tell her. "It flushes into a chemical catch tank, not outside." This reminded me that I had to get it pumped out.

"Don't you worry about a thing, Marc Rennsalaer." She smiled and actually seemed fairly rested. "Do you want me to come over for a little cuddle?"

"Sure, that would be nice," I said. Mariko set the almanach aside and I shifted from a sitting position on the settee to stretch out on the bunk. But I went to sleep almost as soon as I was horizontal.

31

I didn't awaken from my preset mental alarm, but from a soft knocking on the hull. Rolling out of the bunk and glancing at my watch, I saw that it was just 5:30. Strangely enough, I felt more or less refreshed. But then, of course, I had had almost eight and a half hours of sleep, a decided improvement over what had become usual since falling in with Maruko, so to speak. I stood up in the corridor fully dressed in jeans and my usual flannel shirt because I had flaked out that way.

Mariko sprawled on the bunk, which she had not bothered to make up, in briefs with her jeans and jersey snuggled up to her chest. Her face looked less grim than yesterday in that the wrinkles around her eyes had smoothed out a little and the shadows beneath her eyes were not actually grey, but were only a deeper shade of apricot. That was all to the good.

The knocking came again and this time I reached up barely above head level and rapped definitively on the steel ceiling. I didn't want to call out through one of the cracked-open portholes for fear of awakening Mariko. But the knocking ceased and Mariko awakened at the same time. She hmmmed and rolled more onto her back, letting the crumpled jeans and jersey spill to her side and making one exposed full breast quiver like a generous bowl of Jello with an unlikely butterscotch topping. Not being able to think of anything better to do, I grasped her breast softly and very gently jiggled it again. And again. The dollop of butterscotch started to become piquant and her eyes fluttered open.

She gazed up at me. After a moment she said: "A perfectly delightful way to be awakened." She dimpled, yawned and stretched.

"We're launching the boat…you'll have to get up."

She nodded and swung her knees off the settee. "I'm up."

Raoul and Philippe had already undone the nylon tie-downs and had stowed theirs away in the truck cab. *Jester's* nylon tie-downs lay neatly rolled on the pavement and so I ignored them, leaving them for Mariko, as I jumped the last two steps down from the hull. It had been my idea to launch *Jester* so early and I wanted to show as much get-up-and-go as they had.

"Bonjour, Guys," I said. It was barely pearly under the trees and there was no one around the Club Nautique's ramp area. I could see a distant figure on some boat in the marina part of the Club. The problem with *Jester* was that she would attract too much attention if she were launched under curious, knowledgeable and nautical eyes.

We reversed the procedure we had performed on the canal. We launched the two hulls folded together. Raoul and I tied the large boxy thing to the launching dock while Philippe hauled the truck cab and Ivory back up to the parking area. We stepped the two slightly outboard main masts by a mixture of wading alongside and working from the launching dock. Then we all took a breather while we looked around for curious spectators and gauged the wind. The breeze had not yet picked up from the Atlantic, or else it had not yet come inland to Nantes. Broad chestnut leaves drooped ashore above the truck and trailer.

Now we hauled mightily to raise the front hull up, vertical between the masts and then let it slowly down onto the water. The loosened outriggers naturally canted outboard during this fall, but when they encountered the water their flotation pushed them outboard. So far as we could see, no one had noticed this most crucial part of *Jester's* transformation. Now she just looked like a boat, albeit an unusual one.

We were all waist deep astern of *Jester,* screwing the locking beams forward with turns of the big wrench – and this was much easier than before, though still difficult – when we heard Mariko call out "Boys…? Come and get it!"

Raoul was the freest of us because he was then just double-checking that the three other beams were in place, while Philippe and I were actually wrestling the last locking beam forward into its socket. So I gestured for Raoul to splash forward and around *Jester's* bow to assure Mariko that we were still around. I heard him lowering the front ramp now that the forward hull was virtually secured.

When I dripped up the ramp with Philippe about five minutes later, I was both gratified and a little amused at what the 'it' had also referred to in her 'Boys, come and get it'. Aside from coffee and croissants, Mariko certainly knew, or more likely had only learned quite recently, what tired young men enjoy for breakfast. And, whereas I was not quite young enough to be included among boys, except in a figurative way, I was still young enough to share some boyish appetites. Indeed, as I reflected upon them, I realized that I had not indulged them for far too long a time. So, as we wolfed down coffee and croissants – the microwave would work, for a brief time, on battery power alone – crowded on *Jester's* deck and slouched against the wheelhouse, we also visually ingested the fair amount of Mariko not covered by micro cut-offs and threatening to escape from the most inadequate of halters. Even as we ate, the Atlantic breeze began playing with the long strawberry tendrils of her wig and she'd begun to toss her head from time to time to keep hair out of her face.

I had been among tough men long enough by now to know... I hoped... that Mariko's offering was accepted and fully enjoyed as symbolic thanks, and not as any present or future invitation. From the open and easy way that Raoul and even now Philippe included her in our breakfast chatter, I felt certain that I had not under-rated Mariko... or them.

Philippe had seen her in her natural short-haired and semi-Oriental-eyed state before we had stopped for lunch in Poitiers. "What's with the wig and glasses," he asked her directly at one point.

Mariko explained in much better French than my own that it was a disguise. I added that it wasn't because of the law, but to hide from stalkers. Philippe waved a hand to encompass *Jester* and the truck, saying that he now understood the urgent night drive through the mountains. Raoul cautioned, however, that none of this had ever happened and that Mariko didn't exist. This last was manifestly absurd, but Philippe grinned broadly at us. "Mais certainment."

I could detect no hint of subdued calculation or assessment of future possibilities. In fact, as far as Philippe was concerned, Mariko's display had put an end to his wonder. The breakfast goodies were her way of thanking *them* for helping *me* to help *her*. Until and unless Mariko wasn't with me, that was all there was to it. Although, of course, if she ever happened to be without me... But this was only natural and proper.

Observing carefully because I myself had a future to calculate that might well be affected by the character of these two men, I was gratified to have my faith in truckers and bargees vindicated yet again.

That was why, when all was said and done, I had remained faithful to the Western World and to the Far Eastern one. I had rejected both the Jewish and Islamic intolerance of the Middle East as a psychosexual aberration that had always endangered humanism on all sides of its geographic domain. Adult males who could not accept natural female sexuality were simply psychological cowards, and those who sought to suppress it were socially dangerous. This took in Judaism, Islam and the Near Eastern foot-in-the-door called orthodox Christianity.

Also, I reflected wryly, many modern and more educated men, who prided themselves on their cultural superiority, could not have grasped such civilized sexuality, which came so naturally to Raoul and Philippe. I had mostly encountered such men in media interviews and also in the values of sophisticated and suborned women whom the society had poisoned. In my view, which was admittedly considered eccentric whenever I had discussed it with sophisticated people, this undercurrent of civilized sexuality was the cement and mortar that had always held worthwhile human culture together. Modern women, the Western "feminist" leaders – and, of course, they were almost all Jewish – were just deluded fellow travelers in their retreat from human psychological truth, distorting and burning healthy growth wherever they went.

This progressive destruction and distortion of natural human sexuality was, indeed, at the root of rampant progress and globalization, which had brought about the present energy crisis. Middle Eastern peoples and cultures were unable to make love, not war. I had begun to suspect that there was a genetic reason for this. In the Judeo-Christianized Western World, a true and mutual appreciation of men and women survived only among the lowest orders of people, remnants of the original megalithic population before the Middle Eastern, Indo-European-speaking invaders arrived. Thankfully, and due to the energy crisis, these orders were once more coming to the fore.

Mariko's breakfast fare proved so nourishing to male bodies and self-conceptions of chivalry that Philippe and Raoul did not leave, as previously arranged, to let me handle the considerable detail of returning *Jester* to a proper boat. Together, Raoul and I bent to these chores, which mostly concerned securing the outriggers, but which also included stepping the mizzen masts and then re-erecting the smokestack with its accessory whistle-tubes.

I noticed when we got around to them that Raoul regarded these whistle-tubes in a puzzled way while examining the breeches and the air fittings closely. Then he glanced up at me as he secured a brass flange on the wheelhouse. He smiled just slightly in query and I gave him an almost imperceptible nod.

"These days, Raoul," I said blandly, "every boat should have a proper whistle."

"Awesome," he replied. Then, after a pause. "Maybe I could rig something the same on our barge."

"I think we'd better," I said.

Since Mariko had gone below with cups and saucers, we discussed the matter of equipping *Mer-Cedez* similarly. He had not yet named the barge according to my earlier suggestion, but I did in our conversation. Meanwhile, ashore, Philippe had unhitched Ivory, had wheeled it clear of the truck and had almost completed the task of shortening her wheel-base from trailer to mini-vehicle proportions. This was done by telescoping the steel tube frame into itself, much like the four main locking beams that held *Jester* together underneath the hulls. Philippe was tightening the last of several through-bolts that secured the shortened frames in place when Raoul and I came up to him.

Philippe gave a final tug on the wrench and stood up, wiping his brow and glancing at his watch at the same time.

"Sept heures, Raoul. Nous y allons."

"Oui, bien sûr," Raoul replied. And we all walked over to the truck's cab.

I peeled off many, many francs from a very depleted sheaf of large denomination notes. I added most of the American dollars and all of the German marks and handed the wad up to Raoul behind the wheel. He tucked it all into a breast pocket and I heard Mariko squeaking across the pavement toward us in her Adidas. I knew that she'd come up near me when Raoul nodded his chin on his crossed arms on the truck's high window sill.

"Joëlle will handle everything," I assured him in French. "Explain to her what we talked about this morning about the share structure. She might have better ideas. She has full authority, Raoul, to act for me." And here I handed him a blank, signed cheque drawn on the Bank of Perseval's Well. "Don't lose it," I said. And grinned. "And don't you dare let Joey try to go back to our apartment by herself no matter what she says."

"No way," said Raoul. "I have an interest in her". He smiled back at me. "No worries, Might," he said, reminding me of Bouchard. *Crocodile Dundee* had mightily, no pun intended, influenced French truckers. He then coughed the engine to life and let it rumble for a few seconds. He and Philippe threw a glance and a wave to Mariko, and Raoul tipped me a quick and very casual salute with his hand. He glanced in the side mirrors and jerked the big cab ahead with a roar and a burst of diesel exhaust. I knew that they wanted to be back to Agen by dark. It was barely possible along the coast autoroute with no load to pull. I felt Mariko's hip brushing me and we waved together as they turned out of the launching ramp parking lot.

"Joëlle…," she said when the truck had gone. "Is that her name… your… friend?"

"I have many friends, Mariko O'Shaugnessey," I intoned expansively. "Raoul. Philippe. Marcel Bouchard… I think. Inspector Gabereau… I hope. Frogs… especially. Beasts of the field. Denizens of the air… like bats. Fishes of the sea… like sharks… which are not fishes, come to think of it, but boneless Selachians. Newspaper articles."

She sighed. "Your… special… friend…"

"Yes."

"From what I heard you tell Raoul, you're doing some long term planning."

"I am."

"Accordingly, you must intend to return."

"Not necessarily, Mariko. That depends on what happens with us," I said. "And to us," I added more quietly.

I turned and took her hand and we walked back toward *Jester*. Even though it was early on a weekday morning, I had to move *Jester* from the ramp dock as a courtesy to others who might want to launch their boats.

"It's like this," I mused. "Whatever happens... Joëlle will need some security, a way of making a living in a... a... rapidly evolving world." I smiled the euphemistic phrase down at her.

It was common knowledge that governments were under pressure to reduce their reliance on computers and to hire old-fashioned clerical workers instead. I had no doubt that computers would still be used, unless we fell so far back that the technology of them couldn't be sustained, but probably only in increasingly rarified areas of data processing and technical design. As more people became unemployed due to decreased production, there was already public pressure to hire people to replace machines. Joëlle's job in Narbonne had disappeared because of that, and Moissac's city government was rumoured to be thinking along the same lines. But private business might be less affected than government, especially small businesses. Proposed legislation was now ambiguous.

"It happens," I continued, "that there's an opportunity to build something for the future with Raoul and Philippe... for the future that seems to be coming, that is. Joey has a legitimate place in this business with her skills, and among people I trust." I didn't add that Raoul's warehouse was uncannily close to Joëlle's place of birth on the Haute Garonne. Not being at all superstitious, of course, this had carried no weight with me.

"Are you... pairing her off with Raoul? Is that his interest in her?"

"I doubt that Christine would like that very much," I said dryly, pulling her to me. "Besides, do you think I am in any position to 'pair Joëlle off', as you put it... or would be that ruthless to... to get rid of her... always assuming that I was in such a position?"

"Back at the little lake... with the helicopter. There was a certain ruthlessness."

"Hmmm. Who was shooting the cannons, I wonder...?"

"There is that."

I paused. "Raoul's interest is in my money, and Joëlle handles it. She will probably always handle at least a part of it."

"Oh." I felt her slow and stiffen slightly as she walked, but made no move to take my arm from around her waist.

"Oh, indeed." We arrived beside *Jester*. I tethered Mariko's unruly wig in cupped hands so that I could kiss her. "Why shouldn't I be concerned with my future... and Joëlle's? You're concerned with your future... and so am I. Right?"

"Therefore..." she said finally, "...I should mind my own business and otherwise do what I can to help... since, being so ruthless, I don't want to go to the National Trust," she added.

"That's about the way I see it."

"And what can I best do? Besides sex, that is?"

"Me? Mariko, I'm undecided on that," I said seriously. She waited, so I continued. "I know that you're a delight just to look at. And I know that you're sexy as hell... but..."

"Ye-es...?"

"But I suspect that you may even be just as good a linguist... If you ever had any time to be one, that is," I amended.

She laughed and turned back toward me. "You're a veddy odd man, Marc Rennsalaer."

Sorry that you... ah... fell in with me?" For an answer she cocked her hips and tossed her head slightly, fingering tendrils of her wig back. She said nothing and I regretted that I couldn't see her eyes behind the sunglasses because I suspected they would have been lowered in Oriental modesty... Right. Sure. They would have been flashing a menacing oceanic comber at me. When I started to embrace her again, she stepped nimbly aboard *Jester* on the landing craft ramp. I watched her saunter along the deck and swing up onto the poop deck using the big hinges as a purchase for her Adidas.

Just before she disappeared into the wheelhouse, she rested her chin on the threshold of the hatchway. "So it is written, so it shall be done," she intoned. She smiled. "Consider, Marc Rennsalaer, that the big problem is to find out what's been written." She disappeared below.

32

I was tired of rushing around, so I took a lazy hour to do all the things necessary in order to move *Jester* from the launching ramp wharf out to a visitor's berth on the floating marina docks. I also thought that the hour or so would give Mariko time to calm down from our little confrontation beside the ramp. *Joëlle will probably always look after at least part of my money?* Hmmm. A challenging assertion, that.

First, I drove Ivory down from the parking lot and backed the vehicle aboard *Jester*. This was a bit tricky because the old converted Norton motorcycle engine, used as a compressed-air motor now, had never been noted for its smoothness anyway. Even when new and powering a motorcycle. It had not been used for a while and very recently it had been completely submerged twice, once at Carcassonne and again at Nantes as a part of *Jester's* trailer. It squealed horribly for the first few revs because of last night's rust and then began whuffling with the screech gradually dying away. It clanked until some lubrication had built up and then it clanked less loudly, but then it also snorted fiercely. My Rube Goldberg belt and chain drive had always whirred and chattered, but it worked. However, with patience and care, plus a good deal of *sotto voce* profanity, Ivory jerked and shuddered to its appointed place straddling the hatches that covered the amidships well. I took some care backing and forwarding not to put a wheel on these hatches because I had never been certain that they would bear the weight of the vehicle even empty, never mind loaded. Calculations are all very well, but...

After that, I started up the electric pump in order to fill the boiler with filtered Loire water. Reminding myself of the hazy plan I had in mind, I valved the engine's steam outlet into the radiator, and the pump into the radiator's outlet and back to the engine. *Jester* would run on recycled water now, at least for a while. Because of various losses in the system, however, the fresh water would have to be topped up every two or three days.

All the while I was doing this, and later while I was backing *Jester* slowly out to the visitor's docks, I was casting glances toward the Clubhouse office to see if there were signs of life. Just as I was tying up to the visiting yachtsmen's' wharf, I noticed someone adjusting blinds in the restaurant. It was just eight.

Now, back in Carcassonne I had not had a great deal of time to think ahead. My first notion had been to ask Raoul to trailer *Jester* all the way to Cherbourg for a quick Channel crossing. But, by the time I had actually called him, I had rejected this idea. The extra distance, return, would keep him away from the Garonne too long. I had decided on Nantes, not that I knew exactly where it was, but I thought I knew it was somewhere near Brittany to the south. In the truck I'd found road maps and had been relieved to discover that this was, indeed, true.

There had also been a town plan insert map of Nantes, which had enabled me to direct the truck directly to the Club Nautique on the Loire River. I had studied the general geographic lay of the neighbourhood. It was clear that from Nantes I could carry out our original idea of going through the Brittany canals to Cherbourg. We'd saved about two and a half weeks of time, maybe more, at a high cost in money. However, the cost of staying at Carcassonne would have been a good deal greater.

I stood up from the bollard and called through an open porthole under a half-open steel cover: "Mariko, Love, what about a lazy sit-down breakfast? In the Club…" I added with a little emphasis. "While we wait for the laundry…" I hoped that she would perceive that the micro cut-offs and precarious halter of an earlier hour might not be entirely appropriate for guests in a marina restaurant.

"Why Marc, Darling, that's a simply marvellous idea. I'll be right up… Dear." So I lifted the garbage bag full of dirty clothes from the deck beside the wheelhouse down to the dock. This bag had held the clothing that Annette had loaned. I had no plastic bags so large aboard *Jester*, never before having been in the throes of so much and so lengthy nautical domesticity. Maybe I would have to get a package of larger garbage bags soon.

The Annette Collection had proved to be eclectic. In a minute or so Mariko climbed out of the wheelhouse wearing the Jordache jeans and a nearly-matching navy-style denim blouse. French navy, and this meant a little beret-style cap with a red pompom on top. Cute. She had blue sneakers, which, from the look of the soles, were brand new.

I handed her up my keys and she closed the hatch and locked it. "What's with the shoes?" I asked. "They can't be from Annette."

"I bought them in that mall in Carcassonne."

She hopped down on the dock with the help of my steadying hand. "So why all that squeaking around in oversized Adidas this morning? …not that you didn't look and sound beautiful."

"Like a sexy little Oriental mouse?" she asked, handing me back the keys.

"Knock it off, Mariko."

She squeezed my hand and gave me a genuine kiss. "Squeaking just made me think of mice, that's all. No sarcasm intended."

"Right. And the emphasis on the sexy part?

"Because I've discovered that it is true," she said simply. "No sarcasm intended. Truly."

"All right."

We turned to walk along the dock toward the Club Nautique de Nantes complex and there was no squeaking. "I would have worn them except that I couldn't find them."

"In *Jester*?"

"Well, you told me to stow things away for the trailer ride, and there's not a lot of stowage space... So I put them in the microwave along with some other things."

"Risking fillet of sole?"

"I found them only when I wanted to warm up the croissants this morning, but I was in a rush and didn't want to take the time to change shoes." Farah Fawcett's hair suddenly smothered my face as we walked out of the shelter of a large, high cruiser. Mariko had to clap a hand down on her cap to keep it from blowing off the wig as a gust of wind swept in off the river. Flags fluttered and wire halyards tinkled against aluminum masts. Atlantic breezes were coming alive.

Nantes is about sixty kilometres inland from the Atlantic and even here the Loire is a wide river. The famous resort of St. Nazaire is at the mouth of the Loire that by then has become an estuary about ten kilometres wide. Some thirty kilometres north along the coast from St. Nazaire is the mouth of the Vilaine River, the entrance to the canals of Brittany. So, Nantes turned out to be a fairly good destination, all things considered.

Although the energy crisis had reduced tourism significantly, there were still some British yachts that maintained the hallowed tradition of a summertime cruise to Brittany. There were not so many yachts as before and, of course, Nantes was a fair day's run from the Atlantic coastal resorts. The reason for going upriver from the coast was, of course, the famous fairytale fantasy of Late Medieval castles that were displayed bend after bend. The castles of the Loire valley.

This sightseeing traffic was also much reduced, whether by private yacht or by tour group river boats. Nonetheless, the Club Nautique's restaurant advertised "English Breakfast" on a sign intended to be read from out in the river. I had seen it from the visitor's dock. Also, of course, I needed detailed charts and Blondel's tide tables.

"You know," said Mariko, "even if it is windy, it's really getting warm now. It was such a cool and stormy spring. That's why I headed south, you know, not that the direction mattered at all at the time. But now it'll be officially summer in just a few days."

That stopped me. Mariko stopped too and looked back. I pulled her to me and gave her a big kiss. "Mariko O'Shaugnessey," I said, "you're beautiful."

"You've been telling me that, but why now particularly?"

"Because you just saved me from making a stupid mistake."

We were nearing the Clubhouse entrance. "The summer solstice will make for huge tides, Lovey, and we could have been caught in them." I opened the door for her. "And it's been so long since I've had to deal with tides that I just plain forgot."

I strongly suggested that she take care of the laundry since I was likely to shrink or fry delicate fabrics. I explained that usually marina laundry facilities were somewhere near the restaurant. Mariko fully concurred with this and, taking the garbage bag from me, said that she would be in the restaurant waiting for me and would order the advertised English Breakfast.

"How do you like your eggs?"

"Scrambled."

The marina's nautical shop was just being opened up. First of all, I paid for the use of the launching ramp, for the pump-out to come and for *Jester's* day berth. Then I bought charts covering the south coast of Brittany and tide tables by Blondel. Ambling slowly toward the restaurant, I consulted Blondel about solstitial and equinoctial tides and upcoming lunar phases. Later, between mouthfuls of eggs, bacon, sausage and toast, I pointed out my ideas on the folded charts on the table between us.

Mariko readily agreed that we badly needed a few ordinary unexciting days. I pointed out that we had been missing, as far as *they* were concerned, for about thirty-six hours. If all went well, they might think that I had locked *Jester* down through Carcassonne during the night. This was illegal, but not impossible. The locks were worked by hand on the Canal du Midi, so there was nothing to stop anyone from doing this except the lockmaster's vigilance. At, say, three o'clock in the morning, a lockmaster could reasonably be expected to be asleep. Locks could be worked very quietly, too, with care.

Therefore, we *could* be in the étangs around Narbonne and Béziers. Gabereau might not have any reason to look for us at all. *They* would need a helicopter to find us, and we had taken care of that. I refused to believe that they could afford two helicopters, although another one could always be chartered. Still, the Narbonnais was a big place. Not only that, but most of the étangs have channels to the sea. The Mediterranean was even bigger than the Narbonnais. Much bigger.

"Does Inspector Gabereau know *Jester's* capabilities?" Mariko asked sensibly.

I considered this and, in fact, had been considering it. "He knows that she's an odd-looking boat. It wouldn't surprise me, given my background, if he suspected that some firearms might be aboard. But he wouldn't do anything about that so long as I kept my nose clean..."

"What...?"

"...caused no trouble," I smiled. "But he doesn't suspect anything else...or he would have taken us into custody at Lac des Doigts. *Jester's* large enough that he wouldn't think of folding capabilities and a trailer. At a pinch, I'm sure he knows I'm capable of operating canal locks illegally by night." I chewed, and added after a moment. "Besides, Mariko, how could I tow something like *Jester* on such short notice? These days? The only vehicle that Gabereau would associate with me is little Ivory. Everyone knows about it because I used to use it for hauling lobster tanks on board back around Narbonne."

"By the way," Mariko said. "Why... Ivory... when the thing is dark blue?"

"Integrated Vehicle On Rennsalaer's Yacht."

I honestly thought that she would choke and I blamed myself for not noticing that she had just taken a sip of coffee. But she managed to swallow it with only a few coughs and a bit of dribble. "Jesus," she wheezed. When she was breathing normally again, she dabbed her mouth first and then under the glasses with her serviette. Trying not to laugh or cry, she said: "Marc, seriously. I can't take any more. I simply cannot."

"All right."

"Please...?"

"I promise, Mariko." Then, after a moment. "Can you think of a better designa – name?"

"Easily."

"Let's have it."

She gazed a moment, thinking. "What about Achilles?" she asked.

"The Greek warrior...?"

"He sulked because he didn't get a certain slave girl he wanted in the division of spoils from some raid, and he therefore refused to fight. That's *The Iliad*, basically."

"Oh. Well...?"

"From what I heard, your engine is reluctant to start. Also, Achilles always did everything 'with a fearful clashing of arms', his Homeric epithet. And judging from the terrible commotion I heard earlier, the name is entirely appropriate for that vehicle."

I laughed. "Done."

"Therefore," said Mariko, daring a sip of coffee again, and returning to the subject, "we're on the Atlantic coast of France miles from where they think we are…"

"Three hundred miles."

"That far?"

"Roughly. As the crow flies. Airline miles."

"What are we going to do now?"

"Disappear for two or three days more. Maybe then they will think that we've vanished into the Med somewhere."

"Do you think that will work?"

"Not really. They're too persistent. I think they will probably try to establish some surveillance on all French coasts, but with special attention to the Mediterannean shoreline. They will set up something here too, but it might take them a few days."

"And now they know you, me and *Jester*."

I nodded and changed the subject. "Mariko… what do you need in order to translate that page of parchment?"

"Mostly just some time to think." Then she said that she had brought a couple of dictionaries from Oxford in her suitcase. Hebrew-Arabic-Aramaic. Also, she had photocopied most of the known variants of the Tiffinagh alphabet. There were about twenty. They had been filed away in the briefcase, and were still badly wrinkled. But she had taken my advice and had scanned them to store the Tiffinagh alphabets on diskette.

"Would the Internet help?"

"Immensely. I could pull up similar parchments for comparison."

"Okay, Marko, this is what I have in mind." I turned a chart around so that she could see it. I pointed at a speck in the Atlantic about sixty kilometres from St. Nazaire off the mouth of the Loire. "That's the island of Hoedic," I explained. "There are no settlements on it, but it's inhabited anyway, by scattered families of fishermen, visiting yachtsmen and archaeologists."

She looked up a question.

"For the menhirs," I said. I looked down at the chart, pointing. "Anyway, in Narbonne a Dutch yachtsman said that there's a little cove on the north shore of Hoedic that's fully protected. It's a tidal pool, really, because when the tide goes out you can't get out over a ledge. Now he could get in because he had a Zuider Zee leg o' mutton barge… I don't want to go into nautical details, but they don't draw much water."

She nodded. "Like *Jester*."

"Precisely. And therefore no other yacht is likely to have appropriated the place, either."

She looked up, smiled, and rubbed her chin. "Since it is a pool... part of the time... then the water will be calm. For the Internet connection with the satellite dish, like back at the little lake."

"I'm impressed." I pointed again. "Now, just here northeast of Hoedic, is the mouth of the Vilaine River. That's how you get into the canals of Brittany."

"How far?"

"From Hoedic to the Vilaine? About thirty-five kilometres. Call it twenty miles, give or take."

"Your thinking is that after we've had some peace and quiet... and after I've cracked that page of manuscript... we make a run for the canals." Her fingers were tracing the route. "What if we can't find that cove? Or if someone's already there?"

"See this speck just north of Hoedic?"

"Houat," she read.

"It's also inhabited... sparsely... and by the same people for the same reasons. Between the miles of shoreline represented by Hoedic and Houat, we're bound to find a good little tidal pool or a sheltered cove. But if worse comes to worst, Mariko, I'll just beach *Jester* during the ebb. That'll give you almost twelve hours a day on the Internet. But that's a last resort. I don't like beaching boats, especially something like *Jester*. The stress can bind hinges and locking beams."

"Yes, Marc. I can understand that. Truly."

"I know."

"Not bad for having to improvise at Carcassonne. Thank you."

"You are most welcome. Of course... Miz O'Shaugnessey... there's a price for everything..." I said, folding the chart and putting Blondel on top of it.

"I do not intend to work on that parchment all the time," Mister Rennsalaer.

"Glad to hear it," I responded. "By the way, Mariko, the inspiration is free."

She cocked her head.

"Lady of the Lake," I smiled, "you will be in the middle of Lyonesse." I'd written a Brittany travel article about this a few years ago, but I had forgotten most of the details.

"That's off Cornwall, Marc."

"Quite so, depending on the pronunciation, that is." I removed Blondel and turned the chart around for her again. I pointed at the Brittany mainland just north of the offshore islands of Hoedic and Houat.

"Cornouaille..." she read.

"Precisely." I paused and sipped disgusting, cold coffee. "Mariko... my Sweet... would you mind filling this with something warm?"

"Not at all. Just as soon as I put the clothes in the dryer. I do coffee," she smiled.

"Good."

As she disappeared to the laundry room that was conveniently next door to the restaurant, I scanned the chart carefully myself. By the time she returned, I was more certain of my ground. I swivelled the chart at her on the table. The waitress began clearing our plates. When the clatter died away, I traced the hundred fathom line on the chart with my finger. "The British are so insular. Just because the Scilly Isles off Land's End were a part of Lyonesse, Mariko, that doesn't mean that they were all of it. See these banks here… the shallower bits dotted along the line?"

She nodded, and traced them out herself.

"They're fishing banks now. Shallow places. It's reasonable to think that these banks were once islands, like Hoedic, Houat and the Scilly group still are. If so, Mariko, Lyonesse was once a sizable place. A sort of mini-Indonesia between Britain and France." I pushed the chart all the way to her so that she could look at it.

I enjoyed warm coffee… English Coffee, they called it here. Smooth Colombian. The coffee is one of the most difficult little things about France for a North American – or a Briton. Not only is French coffee usually extremely expensive, but it is also both strong and bitter. It upsets all but French stomachs.

Unfortunately, I love coffee. That's why I had the luxury of a coffee maker aboard *Jester*. Of course, that was only half the battle, the strength. The other struggle was finding Colombian grounds or beans. But this could be done with dedicated searching. In the second-last grande surface I'd been in, I had bought ten 1-kilo plastic packages of vacuum-packed finely-ground Colombian beans. This, I figured, had helped me stay fairly sane and had kept my stomach lining intact.

"Have you read Caesar's *Gallic Wars*?" Mariko asked.

"No."

"It's curious that he doesn't mention anything about Lyonesse. Conquering it, I mean."

"It had probably sunk by then, except for a few bits."

"That's… ah… relative, as you like to say, Marc." She smiled over the rim of her cup. She sipped, and then again. "Good coffee… There was more of it… ah… unsunk back in King Arthur's time. Several Arthurian characters supposedly came from Lyonesse."

"I didn't think Arthurian stuff was your field."

"It's not," she admitted. "But we had to read some as an exercise in how to cope with degenerate Latin. Gildas. Nennius."

"I see."

"At any rate, according to some sources, Arthur's father... or grandfather? I can't recall... came from Lyonesse. Tristan was a prince of Lyonesse and King Mark 'of Cornwall' was Arthur's ally."

Now I remembered: "And Merlin's summer home was in the forest of Brocéliande."

"Wherever that is," Mariko commented dubiously.

"About sixty kilometers from here, as the crow flies. Merlin's Oak is still there, supposedly, and the Forest of Paimpont is certainly there. That's the remainder of Brocéliande."

"Supposedly."

"Supposedly."

"At any rate," Mariko continued, "if it was more... unsunk... less sunken... in Arthurian times, it must have been even..."

"Larger...?" I offered.

"... larger... five hundred-odd years earlier in Julius Caesar's time. Yet Caesar doesn't mention Lyonesse that I recall."

"By some other name, maybe...?"

"Nothing that fits. He writes about mainland Gaul." She sounded definitive on that subject. It was time to find a new one.

"Mariko..." I said pensively. "Assuming that we both live to translate that page, steal the rest of it and translate that... have you given any thought as to what you're going to do with the parchment?"

"No. Oh," she said, surprised. "I hadn't got that far in my thinking."

"I can understand that." I replaced my cup in its saucer slowly. "But it bears thinking about. Even if all goes well with us, Love, you can never come out and admit that once having taken a fragment of the parchment on impulse, you returned to Glastonbury on purpose to steal the whole thing. Bad for your career, and all that."

"Yes," she smiled wryly. "I can appreciate that."

"So, you had to have found it somewhere else. A plausible elsewhere, that is."

"Do you have a suggestion?"

"I certainly do."

"Let's hear it."

"Lyonesse." I tapped a finger on the chart. "If, as you say, Mariko, more of it must have been above water back in Julius Caesar's time, then it would have been a viable culture when Joseph of Arimathaea supposedly came to Glastonbury after the crucifixion."

"But that's just a silly legend."

"I thought the same thing when I wrote a story on the Glastonbury Thorn for the *Ottawa Citizen*. However, Mariko, it's a Palestinian variety of thorn tree; not the species typical of northern Europe."

"It is?"

"Absolutely. I quoted several botanists in my article. Anyway, silly legend or not, it is certainly a convenient one… for you."

"I begin to realize that," she said, studying the chart.

"Who's to say where we found that silver box? Some of these fishing banks, ex-islands of Lyonesse, are in international waters. Things get dredged up all the time. If the box had been sealed with lead, well, it could easily have come up intact."

"Therefore…it would be legally mine."

"Well, you'd need a boat… wouldn't you?"

"I could have chartered one."

"Except that that can be checked."

"In a way, Marc, I *have* chartered one…" I let her complete her own thought. "…except that I haven't paid for it."

"Hmmm."

She came to it herself, and she did it quickly. "All right, Marc Rennsalaer, we'll share… fifty-fifty. She stirred her coffee. "You know, Marc, I'm terribly slow at some things. Yes… assuming we live, I can translate the Gospel, if that's what it is. I can release a learned paper with all the pages illustrated with photographs so that other scholars can check my work. That's as far as I'd got." She finally sipped, and smiled. "But, of course, it would be priceless and would be worth a great deal of money in addition to making me world famous."

"Indeed." I said. "I think that Southeby's could probably handle its sale. But, if I were you," I added, "that's not the way I'd go."

"No?"

"No. I would make a deal with the British Museum or something. Oxford or Cambridge, maybe. Take less money, Mariko, but cement your reputation with an ultra-reputable academic institution."

"That sounds right to me. Otherwise private collectors might get it."

"Or worse. What if some organization acquired it by auction, then a couple years later, announced expert study had revealed it's a forgery? Not by you, of course, but some medieval forger. You're not a criminal, just incompetent. The manuscript itself can disappear so that the only evidence remaining of it would be the photos of the pages in your learned book… but these alone will not prove or disprove authenticity."

"Oh, my God."

"You see? But in the vaults of the British Museum or some other place like that, the original will be preserved… and so will your reputation, as long as your translation's good, that is."

"Thanks again, Marc, for pointing that out. Is fifty-fifty agreeable?"

I nodded.

"Where did we find it?" she said after a moment.

I turned the chart so I could see it. "My guess, Mariko, is that we found it southeast of the Great Sole Banks, south of the Brittany mainland... ah... not far from Hoedic, in fact. I'll work out plausible co-ordinates."

"How?"

"We dredged it up."

"On purpose?"

"Absolutely, Mariko. From historical and linguistic snippets, you suspected Lyonesse had been a going concern in Early Christian times. You wanted to dredge in places that might have been Lyonesse islands back then, but you lacked the reputation to finance a scientific expedition and you lacked the money to charter a research ship. But you could afford to go to southern France on more Lyonesse-related research jaunts and there you met this Marc Rennsalaer. He's an odd and eccentric fellow with a strange boat that has the minimum required capabilities. Marc's previous articles prove his prior interest in the subject of archaeology. You... ah... *fell* in with him ten days after leaving Britain for France. Sheer accident. They happen in Moissac as elsewhere. Rennsalaer, intrigued, went on this hunt with you. And you two dredged up the box. You'll have to write something like that, Mariko."

"It's almost the truth... almost."

"It's always better to stick as close to the truth as possible," I observed unctuously.

"Can *Jester* dredge something up, Marc?"

"From the Great Sole Banks? A piece of cake. The water's only six and a half fathoms deep there... thirty-nine feet. My winch and the diving well can handle that. We might need a grabbing bucket to make the story more plausible, but I can always say it snagged in rocks later and I had to cut the cable."

"Do you have a... a... grabbing bucket?"

"Now that's one thing I didn't think of, Mariko... until now, I mean... but I may get one."

Mariko shivered across the table and folded her arms on her chest.

"Cold?"

She shook her head. "No... It's just that..."

"What, Mariko?"

"It's just that this story could have been... could be true."

"You'll have to find out a little more about Lyonesse, Mariko." She nodded absently, so I went on. "Me, I can't wait to get to Hoedic. And,"...as I glanced at my watch... "the sooner the better."

33

I awakened at an early hour after only the second truly secure and restful night's sleep I had enjoyed in over a week. As soon as my eyes opened, the boat's motion again told me that all was calm. The blue-green liquid reflections from the open ports were soothing. And, for that matter, had it been only a bare week since Mariko O'Shaugnessey had dropped into my life? I pushed the light blanket aside and rolled out of the bunk to make coffee.

Mariko was wrapped like a mummy, not only in her light flannel sheet, but also in the heavier wool blanket that she had folded at her feet. I had warned her that even midsummer nights could be cool out in the Atlantic off Brittany.

We had cleared our berth at Nantes about 10:30 two mornings ago after I had heard the weather forecast and, dropping down the Loire at five knots, had been abeam of St. Nazaire a little before six in the evening. I had considered stopping there for the night, but I didn't want to risk being spotted by anyone at this obvious port-of-call. Someone might remember a boat like *Jester*. But also, the tide would be high around Hoedic by the time we could reach it… if we pressed on.

Jester was fit for coastal sailing in fine weather, but I didn't think that she could handle a serious storm. The forty miles of open Atlantic between St. Nazaire and Hoedic were, as far as I was concerned, stretching *Jester's* capabilities.

Our only chance was good weather and the forecasts had continued to be extremely reassuring. I had therefore wanted to reach Hoedic while the winds and tides were auspicious. We had drifted in the middle of the wide estuary only long enough to fold *Jester's* cut-water panels forward into the shape of a vee in front of the blunt bow. It had required only a few minutes to lock them in place with bolts inside the apex. After that, I had made sail while Mariko steered temporarily. Hoedic's high hills could be seen, just barely, near the limit of visibility and I had told Mariko to keep them poised over *Jester's* now pointed prow.

Presently, I had felt the lift and rhythmic surge of a vessel under sail and saw with satisfaction that we were making a bit over seven knots in a breeze that averaged about fifteen. This wasn't great performance considering *Jester's* potential, but then again I wasn't trimming and steering for maximum speed. I was just enjoying the feel of sailing, a rare experience during the past couple of years since I'd sailed from the Balearics into France. I'd done some sailing in the étangs around Narbonne and once or twice in the Gironde estuary out of Bordeaux, but not nearly enough, it seemed. I didn't realize how much I had missed broader waters until I had taken the wheel from Mariko. She had brought me a sandwich and some coffee about eight, but we hadn't talked much. We had watched the sun drop between Hoedic and the distant hazy tip of Brittany until finally it sizzled into the sea, leaving a mist on the horizon.

Out of the Garonne valley, the days seemed much longer because the sun did not drop prematurely behind constricting mountains. Of course, in an absolute sense, the sun was also moving toward the summer solstice, the longest day of the year.

Jester's white sails had become pink for a while in the sunset and then had remained mother-of-pearl in the long solstitial afterglow. The wind had backed into the northwest since noon, but *Jester's* Chinese-style full battens had kept the sails filled on a westerly course, almost due west, from St. Nazaire for Hoedic.

Hoedic trends southwest to northeast and a little after 10:30 in the evening we had come close inshore of the island's southeast coast. Now it was a curious thing, and it still puzzles me, but dead ahead had been a gap in some rocky outcrops that led into a fair sized lagoon or tidal pool. We could see it clearly from the wheelhouse in the milky light. It had been high tide, but it had nonetheless been a bit risky to put in because of the twilight. I had sent Mariko forward to look down over the ramp-door and warn of rocks. I had doused the sails and the engine had pushed *Jester* through the entrance. Both the chart and the Eagle sonar agreed that the entrance shelf had three feet of water. *Jester* drew two feet. Inside, the depth rapidly dropped off at between six to twelve feet to a sandy bottom with small rocks. Just like the Dutchman had said.

But the curious thing was that the Dutchman in Narbonne had emphasized that his tidal pool had been on the other side of Hoedic on the northwest coast. But, otherwise, this lagoon fitted his description perfectly. By eleven o'clock, I had settled *Jester* to my satisfaction. The cut-water panels had been folded back again, the broad bow had been run up on the beach half an hour after high water and I had put down the ramp door. I had taken two lines ashore, one from either side of *Jester's* stern and, with Mariko's help with the searchlight, had snubbed them around rocky outcroppings that might have been standing stones for all their convenient shape. The Dutchman's story still bothered me. Seamen seldom made mistakes in giving directions and I had always prided myself on careful listening. Still, for all that either I or the Dutchman might know, perhaps Hoedic was ringed with tidal pools like this.

We had turned in after having a cup of hot chocolate on deck and had watched pale stars in the glowing north and Aldeberan blazing in the black velvet south. What with the fresh air and the gentle rocking of water still flooding into the lagoon, we had begun to yawn and nod to sleep. But we had managed to get below and even to make up proper bunks. I think that we had fallen asleep in the comforting darkness before we remembered to say good night. And it had been a restful sleep, not simply a harried search for rest.

The next day, I had profitably occupied myself with domestic chores. Now, whatever mix-up had occurred between me and the Dutchman, I had immediately perceived that this lagoon was much better for our purposes than any tidal pool on the northwest coast would have been.

Here we were in the lee of Hoedic and under high ground at that. The clouds told me that the Atlantic westerly winds, which could be brisk, were deflected high above us.

Our pool was barely rippled in cats' paws and mill pond flat most of the time. But that also portended discomfort from midges.

My strategy for the day had been simply to stay on deck as much as possible and to keep out of Mariko's way. I had not thought much beyond that but, looking down into the dead calm water now isolated by the ledge from the mud flats and ebb tide outside, I had noticed much movement on the bottom. Scuttling. Crabs. And this had given me an idea. But first I had gone aft and had aligned the satellite dish until the red light showed me that we were receiving signals from space. I had checked that the gimbal mount was actually working because the water was so unruffled that I couldn't tell for sure. Standing there on the extreme stern, I had heard water starting to run beneath my feet and knew from the splashing that Mariko had just begun showering.

Taking this opportunity, I had gone went below for some Black Forest ham for the crabs, the only bait I had, and two nets. One of these nets was for the crabs, but the other was for the midges. I had rummaged briefly in my narrow closet and had finally found the bottle of insect repellent at the bottom.

I had also taken the Walther and its shoulder holster as a precaution against greater dangers than midges. I vowed to wear it faithfully from now on, in spite of the apparent security of our surroundings. As days passed, the more likely that *they* would have time to set up surveillance other than around Narbonne and along the Canal du Midi.

After having donned the Walther, I had felt more secure and had begun my domestic day. In North America I had equipped *Jester's* portholes with standard aluminum insect screen. A summer's experience with Narbonne and the étangs had proved definitively that French midges were smaller than the mesh. They reminded me of the *no-see-ums* of the tropics from Florida to Indonesia. Their bite or sting is like fire and they raise small watery blisters. I had changed the screen to smaller French-made stainless steel mesh. This was fine for the portholes, but I could think of only fibreglass gauze for the wheelhouse hatchway. So, I had contrived a net that could be draped over the aperture and snapped down.

These tiny midges seem to be a coastal phenomenon. Lac des Doits had been too high for them, perhaps. Anyway, they have no flying power and any respectable breeze will blow them away. The problem was that our lagoon had no breeze at all. This was great for the Internet, but even better for the midges. As soon as the sun got higher and the sand warmed up a bit, I had expected them to come out in force.

So, I had rigged the insect net and had doused myself with the citronella. One big breakfast per week was about all that I enjoyed and I had known from my sense of rested wellbeing that I wouldn't be hungry before noon. I therefore had got on with my plans. First, I had pushed Ivory… Achilles… forward and clear of the amidships well. Folding the two doors back flat on the deck to either side of it, I had looked down onto amber sand and had seen some nice large crabs crawling only three feet beneath *Jester's* hull. I had rigged my net.

Unfortunately, this was not a proper crab net, but just a large diameter aluminum framed Canadian landing net originally intended for pike or muskellunge. I had first twisted the plastic grip off the aluminum handle and had tied a cord to the frame. I'd baited the middle of the net with ham by tying the meat into the mesh and had dropped the baited net through the three-foot by four-foot aperture of the open well. I'd had to dunk it several times before its hollow aluminum tube frame finally filled with water and it had sunk flat to the bottom with the ham in the middle. My idea was that if I jerked it up quickly enough, then the crabs would fall into the deep net before they could scuttle to safety beyond its frame.

This proved to be true in practice when I had jerked the net up two hours later. I had kept one crab as bait for its colleagues and had planned my strategy with this success in mind. Then, I had got on with pounding out the dent made by the gunmen in Moissac. After that, I had sanded down the repaired area, had treated it with primer and late in the afternoon I had applied a coat of *Jester's* white hull paint.

Otherwise, I had kept us fed with a light lunch and dinner consisting of the dehydrated soup I had bought in Carcassonne's 'La Nouvelle Vague' grande surface, the little fresh fruit I had also bought there along with imported English cheddar and Boursin cheese. It was plain that Mariko had had a frustrating day, so I had turned in after reading for an hour or so. When I had lowered my privacy partition in the cabin, Mariko's face, just a few steps along the corridor past the galley, had been illuminated by the Toshiba laptop's screen. For reasons of saving space, I had no separate monitors.

But this morning, arriving on deck with my coffee, and feeling smug with virtue after my domesticity of the day before, I rejoiced because of the sun just topping the horizon directly astern over blinding, invisible St. Nazaire. I really noticed for the first time the smoky green little valley, covered in coarse marram grass not yet burned yellow, that swept down to our beach from the high hills at the northern end of Hoedic. Nearby, just ashore above the beach, were a few small dark oaks and beeches in their deep green brocade of summer foliage, while higher on the curves of the hills grew small clumps of white-trunk birches partly smothered with brighter green lace.

Far up to the north, I could see curious little bumps silhouetted against the sky and I took these for the tops of standing stones that were, I knew from the chart, arranged in a ruined circle.

I felt a little adventurous. Also, I had to be adventurous. The steam engine had been running slowly on recycled water in order to power the boat for the better part of two days since Nantes. It needed fresh water and the chart and pilot claimed that it was available across the island. A steam engine will run on sea water, for a very short time, but the salt rapidly clogs everything.

I'd planned a good shore dinner for tonight with the water problem in mind and with my crab-fishing experiment of the day before. So, I rigged the net just as before, but this time baiting it with my hapless captive instead of ham. That being taken care of, the next thing was to acquire some fresh vegetables and a big pot. This called for a journey across the island in search of the necessary water, a garden plot and a resident who might loan, rent or sell a steel bucket, a big pot or a wash tub. And, in the way of things, this, in turn, required some work with Achilles that I needed to carry the water anyway.

Not that I was averse to this, for I believe in keeping equipment ready for instant and reliable use. I also did not discount the possibility that the vehicle might be urgently necessary in the immediate future.

However, as grateful as I was for Mariko's new name, and I could see her point since the vehicle wasn't ivory but blue, I had been a bit stung by her description of its mechanical noises. I knew what was wrong, and it was irritating…

About the time when the Norton engine was almost re-assembled, my phone trilled. I leaned against the side of the boat and answered: Joëlle informed me that my account at the Bank of Perseval's Well was nearly dry. The balance she reported made my mouth dry. But, in compensation, I was part owner, major owner, in fact, of a very large stone-built warehouse in Aiguillon. And yes, the Moissac apartment had been both broken into and ransacked when she, Raoul and Philippe had got there in the truck to move our things. Joëlle had no idea yet what might be missing. She would have to go through the stuff carefully and she had had no time for that. She thanked me for all the warnings not to return there and now she knew that I had not been exaggerating.

Joëlle explained that, in gratitude, Raoul and Philippe had insisted that we have the office corner of the big old warehouse. The office had a silo adjacent to it because, apparently, there had been nowhere else to add it when the building had last been modified back in 1953. It was the only area having divided rooms, including semi-bathrooms circa 1954. She thought that she could get a shower, at least, installed fairly quickly and maybe a large bathtub.

"What about a Jacuzzi?" I suggested. "Or a sunken bath?"

When I was informed that one of the bathrooms already looked a little sunken, I wasn't thrilled, but Joëlle promised that she would do her best although cash was now in short supply. She also had to organize some sort of kitchen, but as Hervé had some old appliances, this might not be too difficult or expensive. All things considered, she thought that it had been an excellent decision the way things seemed to be going in the world. Her future with Moissac's municipal government had been getting more problematical by the day. And, of course, it felt very good to be back so close to where she had been born and had grown up.

Joëlle thought that there was great future potential in the barging business. And yes, Raoul and Philippe had moved all of hers and my home computer equipment, along with other possessions, from Moissac to Aiguillon. It was being unloaded now, as she spoke. I strongly suggested they use my old satellite dish instead of installing cable Internet. Unfortunately, the electricity wasn't yet hooked up. Maybe tomorrow or in a few days. I said I knew how things were these days.

Now, when was I coming back… or was I coming back? Of course, I was under no obligation to return and they would all get along somehow. She had some savings and some severance coming. Raoul and Philippe had very good prospects with canal haulage. She could certainly help them achieve greater efficiency, but she would also try to get a job in Agen. It wasn't too far to tricycle, especially with the moped. By the way, she had chosen the largest office for my bedroom because it overlooked the wharf. It would always be there – whenever I returned.

I told her that I wasn't sure of anything. But that since she'd trusted me up to now, and this trust had not proved misguided, she would have to trust a little longer. I would keep in touch and would let her know as soon as I could about my future plans.

When I looked up from ending the transmission, I saw Mariko gazing at me through that polycarbonate front window of the wheelhouse. She held a coffee cup in her hand and gestured, it was plain, if I wanted some. I nodded, perhaps a bit brusquely, because I really couldn't see her all that well. True, the polycarbonate wasn't so clear as glass, but the real problem was the tears in my eyes.

By the time I had got the Norton back together again, my eyes had dried. And only then did Mariko come out with a cup of coffee.

"If I can get Achilles to produce a slightly less 'terrible clatter of arms', I'll go across and try to get the makings of a shore dinner," I said.

"Clashing of arms."

"Oh."

She was wearing that Mongolian ponytail again because, of course, there was no need for disguise here. She looked exquisite in the micro cut-offs and a Tee shirt and she said not a word about my phone conversation. She slapped her arm and scratched her thigh, so I handed her the insect repellent. "If you're out in the open during the day, you'll need this." I glanced up at the wheelhouse hatch and saw the net in place.

But she handed the bottle back to me. "You'll need this more than I," she said. "I had best get back to work downstairs... below." She kissed me gaily, and went back up to the wheelhouse. She was careful with the midge netting.

I put my coffee cup on top of Achilles and carried on. The insides of the engine had been buffed free of rust and swiped with engine oil. I now tried to pay attention to the drive chains and belts, but my mind kept wandering to Aiguillon. I had to focus it firmly in the general area of engine parts at least.

On October 27, 2000 the Evolution automobile had been unveiled at the Auto Africa trade show in Johannesburg. This was the brainchild of Guy Negre, renowned for his design of Formula One racing cars. With this design, he had set out to make "the most cost effective and eco-friendly car on earth."

The Evolution was enthusiastically received because, hardly a month earlier, the oil crisis had begun. Negre's Zero Pollution Motors had caught the big car manufacturers flat-footed. It had accordingly never got much publicity in the United States.

The idea was devastatingly simple. Negre built a car that ran on compressed air. It had its own electric air compressor that could be plugged in. In Negre's sophisticated design, the air tanks were an integral part of the frame structure, the ordinary piston engine was lightweight and conceived from the ground up by a racing car genius and the car's performance was therefore extraordinary. Carrying one passenger, it would achieve 80 miles per hour and would run for 125 miles before it ran out of compressed air. It would carry six people at lesser velocities and for lesser distances. It was the perfect urban automobile.

After four hours with the compressor plugged into an ordinary electric outlet, the Evolution was ready to run again. There was no pollution at all, and lubrication used vegetable oil. Of course, the car used fuel – electrical energy. But some countries produced much electricity from hydroelectric dams while others had nuclear plants. Electricity could also be produced by burning coal, by solar cells and by windmills. The Evolution had solved the problem of carrying and burning fuel in the car itself.

Unfortunately, of course, although the orders for the new French-designed car far exceeded the production capabilities of five factories in Europe, South Africa and Mexico, not nearly enough could be manufactured to offset the petroleum shortfall for the millions of conventional vehicles. And the concept had not been applied to trucks, which might prove impractical to do anyway, so that Negre's design had not alleviated distribution problems that had escalated into the current shortages. In fact, even the Evolution factories themselves had now been slowed to a production trickle because of curtailed energy and materials availability. The Evolution had profoundly affected me and *Jester*. One could even argue that it had already saved my life and Mariko's.

Back in 1999, *Folderol Jester* had nearly been completed... except for the vexing problem of the on-board vehicle. Ideally I wanted the on-board vehicle to be amphibious.

But this was difficult to achieve on something intended also to be a trailer that could accept *Jester's* boxy keel. The only place for an engine was just in front of the box-trailer body almost on top of the hitch. As per Murphy's various laws, however, this would unfortunately be down near the water and where water would splash most continually on an amphibious contraption under way. When used as a trailer in the process of launching or recovering *Jester*, the engine would be submerged completely. Both steam engines and gasoline ones need air to breathe. Water drowns them. Nonetheless, I had been willing to go ahead using a cumbersome system of high and hopefully above-water intake and exhaust pipes.

My first idea had been to power the vehicle with a motorcycle engine for as long as gasoline was available. And then to make a small-size version of *Jester's* steam engine to replace the gas engine if and when petroleum became too expensive or even absolutely unavailable. I had already gone far along my garden path, although I had modified my thinking. I had acquired a third-or-fourth-hand 500cc Norton motorcycle engine and, just like Raoul, had had a cam ground to convert it into a two-stroke. The notion was to use it as a gasoline engine as long as feasible and then to install the new cam and use the same engine for steam with only the addition of a boiler. I had purposefully looked for an old Norton because it was both solid and antiquated. It had a single big piston and a long stroke that best suited the inherent properties of steam.

I had thought all this to be very clever, if cumbersome. However, the Evolution had been in development for some years before its official unveiling in late October 2000, and I had got wind of it in early 1999. My pride in my cleverness quickly evaporated when I had realized right away that the Evolution idea was even more applicable to my own *Folderol Jester* concept than to other and more conventional vehicles. Why hadn't I thought of this myself?

The major breakthrough for me was that a compressed air engine could run even if it might be completely submerged, and compressed air has exactly the same properties as steam. But the concept had other aspects that made the vehicle truly integrated with *Jester*. The on-board vehicle's air tanks could become the storage tanks for *Jester's* air compressor and, if I used standard scuba tanks, these could be removed from the vehicle for use also in diving and salvage. Installation of the compressed air tanks in the on-board vehicle meant that the tanks didn't have to take up *Jester's* already limited stowage space. Of course, the air tanks in the vehicle had to be connected with *Jester's* air compressor in order to fill them and with the pneumatic cannons that would deplete them. But this could be done with hoses and off-the-shelf fittings from the ever-handy Canadian Tire stores.

With such a large storage capacity of compressed air, the pneumatic cannons cried out to escape from the drawing board and onto the wheelhouse. As I have said, I couldn't think of a situation in which the vehicle would be used simultaneously in conjunction with either cannon-shooting or diving.

So, once hearing about Negre's Evolution, I had installed the two-stroke cam and had tried the Norton out on compressed air. It had wuffled and snorted and had worked beautifully. And so I had re-built the box trailer to have a false floor beneath which was a neat flat array of many scuba tanks. I went ahead with *Jester's* smokestack and whistle tubes. Our battle at Lac des Doigts alone had justified the integrated compressed air-carrying vehicle.

However, the Norton engine was so ancient that it had been made from cast iron parts. These tended to rust a little whenever the engine got completely submerged because, in the antiquated Norton design, water could seep into the valve train. This was all right as long as water kept leaking in. The problem began when the water drained out completely and it evaporated off the damp iron into rust. The splashing of normal amphibious operation wasn't too bad because the engine was up out of the water, and rust could be dealt with by an oily rubdown. But total submersion was something else. Achilles had been submerged as a boat trailer both at Carcassonne and at Nantes. At some point, I was going to have to replace the Norton with some sort of aluminum or stainless steel thing if I wanted to avoid tearing it down after each submersion, but I didn't know what.

At any rate, after my corrective surgery, the Norton now only wuffled and snorted. It didn't screech or squeal. Nor was it reluctant to join the fray of life. In short, I was well satisfied… and I needed a run… somewhere. Judging from the mud in front of *Jester's* ramp, and the soft sand higher up the beach – from which even now midges were probably emerging – and the steep marram-grassed valley rising up before me, it was obviously the better part of valour to convert Achilles into a half-track.

Achilles, as also a boat trailer for *Jester*, had two rear axles to carry the weight and a single fat front tire wheel like an all-terrain motorcycle – except, that like a boat trailer's accessory wheel, I could crank the front wheel up and down. This is necessary anyway on a heavy trailer for getting the hitch on and off a towing ball. On a paved road, I could crank the front wheel upwards, lowering the front end and this would raise the rearmost axle off the ground. That way, only two rear wheels were on the road. This reduced highway friction. Not having been designed by a genius like Guy Negre and having been cobbled together from existing pieces, Achilles was only about half as efficient as an Evolution. In this crouched-down highway mode, I could get about 55 mph on the road, but could only go about sixty miles before running out of compressed air.

However, Achilles, while not being as efficient as an Evolution, was a good deal more versatile. With the rearmost axle raised up and suspended by springs, it wasn't too difficult to work bands of conveyer belting around the two tires on each side. Cranking the front wheel down to make the front end higher also pressed the rearmost axle down against the ground and tightened the conveyor belting around both tires. The original conveyer belt had been used for carrying ore out of a Canadian mine and so my bands of it had a raised rubber herring-bone pattern. In this 'reared-up' mode, Achilles had great traction on land. The vehicle could only go about 25 mph as a half-track, but the huge piston of the Norton gave it immense power using compressed air.

In the water, the belting worked as elongated paddle wheels and the fat front tire gave clumsy steering as a thick rudder. Ivory, now Achilles, had made me a lot of money in the étangs of the Narbonnais. The lobster fishery on these 'ponds' was conducted by many individuals using big skiffs. These families lived around the lengthy shorelines and their catch had formerly been collected by 19th century buyers with horse carts and later by 20th century buyers with pick-up trucks or vans, who took the lobsters to markets and later to processing and refrigeration plants.

But the price of lobsters, and most other commodities, had skyrocketed when gasoline prices had soared back in September 2000. Operating a 20th century vehicle to collect lobsters was expensive. And there were not enough horses, at least not yet, to revert to 19th century carts in which to collect lobsters.

However, I could reach the wharves of even the most isolated lobster fishermen from out in the étangs and carry heavy plastic kegs of water and live lobsters back aboard *Jester* with comparative ease. Once aboard, compressed air could be carried in lengths of old hose pipes and aerated the water in the plastic kegs to keep the lobsters alive longer. There might have been some animosity among the former truck buyers, and I did experienced some, except that they knew that the fishermen themselves were generally poorer than most people anyway and couldn't make a living without selling their catches to *someone*.

Once the distribution system had become badly crippled, especially for refrigerated goods, live lobsters commanded exorbitantly high prices inland. Achilles could deliver hundreds of lobsters directly to scores of restaurants' doors. I had cut out several middle men with Achilles and the profits had been almost as good as with Raoul's more recent flour coup. But back in Narbonne, I had really just been playing around with *Jester* and Ivory while getting used to France and Joëlle. The really serious work had begun when we moved to Moissac.

Thereafter, I moved great quantities of wine and other merchandise on *Jester*, using Ivory – Achilles – for rapid loading and unloading and for efficient delivery to the customer's door. The quicker turn-around time with the ATV on-board truck was the reason I could make pretty good money in spite of *Jester's* limited carrying capacity.

Time is money, and the vehicle's half-track capability had already made substantial profit. When Ivory... er... Achilles... was used as a boat trailer; these flattened segments of conveyor belt folded inside the trailer box and acted like a shock-absorbing cushion for part of *Jester's* bottom. The rest of the hull was cushioned by the seat and back of a flat-folding bench as wide as the vehicle. One climbed into Achilles over the side because the vehicle had no doors. Doors made for leaks in an amphibious contraption.

34

Achilles, no longer sulking and whining, seemed more than eager to surge off *Jester* and into the struggles of life. The herring bone treads made a brief drumming on the plywood-covered front deck and they made a satisfying clatter down the steel ramp.

Running more smoothly now, the vehicle swished through the damp sand near the water and churned easily through the heaped little dunes higher up the beach. Heading for the easiest ascent up onto the grass, Achilles bucked and reared up the slight elevation from the beach, the treads crumbling clods from the lip of real soil.

The two plastic barrels in the bed, which otherwise took up space on the upper bunks, drummed hollowly as they bounced around.

Once up onto the marram grass meadow, I made boyish zigs and zags that were not due entirely to high spirits or hormones. The idea was to test the steering. The handle bars turning the front wheel seemed obvious enough, but a half-track cannot be steered that way. I had contrived a linkage so that when the handlebars were turned in one direction the belt-clutch on the inside of the turn loosened so that no power was transmitted to the rear driving wheel on that side, but the outside belt remained tight and driving. Pointed straight ahead, both belts remained tight. This system provided a differential of sorts and worked equally well with tires on the road.

To my mind, it was turning a little better to the left than to the right. Belts sometimes stretch unequally, especially after they have been soaked. After a few adjustments between zigzags, I was satisfied and wuffled up the valley in the direction of the stone circle.

Glancing back, I could see *Jester* growing ever smaller below, nestled snugly in her shrinking cove. Brittany has some of the highest tides in the world, after Canada's Bay of Fundy, but, and it was of great interest to me, absolutely nothing moved out on the exposed tidal flats or beyond on the distant sparkle of water.

I had not explained to Mariko, but these muddy tidal flats had contributed substantially to Hoedic's appeal for me. For about a third of the time, they made it impossible to approach the island closely... unless one had a contraption like Achilles, that is.

However, I couldn't fail to notice that the flats showed a distinctly greenish tinge and that the high tide line was delineated in some places by strings of green weed. So, this was the *marée verte* or 'green tide' that was even further ruining Brittany's coastal tourism, aside from mere oil economics. From what I had seen on television shows about it in both Narbonne and Moissac, Hoedic was considerably better off than other places along the coast. It really concerned Mère Lalie again. The five thousand pig factories of Brittany dumped their effluvia either directly or indirectly into the sea. This had stimulated an explosion of green algae growth all around Brittany.

It was killing fish and also making the shoreline even more unpleasant than most tidal areas always are because of an even stronger smell than usual. According to the experts on TV, even if all the dumping stopped immediately, it would take fifteen years for the environment to recover. Looking at these tidal flats from high up on Hoedic, I figured that in twenty years or so the mud would be black once more. Of course, there would be many fewer tourists by then to appreciate the rehabilitated ecosystem.

I don't know what I expected to find at the ruined stone circle, but it was certainly not a small group of puzzled people all staring downward into the ground. Then they suddenly all looked up because of the wuffling approaching them down the gentle knoll into the shallow dell where the standing stones were. I stopped beside the menhirs. After satisfying myself that *Jester* could not be seen from ground level at the broken ring of stone, I got out of the vehicle and was met by the French anthropological liaison officer, as I quickly learned. I explained that I had just come up from a Canadian vessel down on the south coast. I was scouting out locations and vistas to get good TV footage of the green tide damage for a freelance Canadian documentary. Later, the camera would venture onto the flats… and I gestured toward Achilles.

He seemed more than satisfied with this explanation of myself and my curious vehicle and so I asked what was up. *They*, in this case, proved to be a Danish archaeologist and three of her students along with the young and bearded representative of the French government. They had an exciting and unexpected problem, as I perceived when I stared down into the ground myself.

Beneath the butt end of a nearly toppled menhir, they had uncovered a burial. This was a curled-up child's skeleton that had been laid to rest in a hollowed-out segment of a split log. Oak, probably, I was told. The top of the rude coffin had already been removed and was lying on a white plastic tarp at the edge of the hole. Not having expected anything like this, they had hiked to the site on foot.

They had no ready way of moving the log segments since, as I could see for myself, they were about three and a half feet long and almost half as thick. Aside from the fact that they must have weighed at least two hundred pounds or so together, the archaeologists didn't want to disturb the skeleton and dirt inside the one half-log until both it and the skeleton could be meticulously examined *in situ*. Yet, the burial container just couldn't stay there because showers were being forecast for later in the afternoon or tonight.

I pointed at Achilles and explained in a mixture of French and English, because the Danes all spoke English – more or less – that the thing they were looking at could carry both log halves securely to anywhere on the island they wanted.

This offer provoked a flurry of conversation, and was at last accepted. I was relieved about this for both scientific and personal reasons. Naturally, I didn't want the discovery to be rained upon, nor did I relish so much activity within view of *Jester* if anyone should tear himself or herself away from the site long enough to climb the nearest knoll. Gilles, the liaison officer, seemed uncertain about removing a French artefact from French soil, but without any means of communication to some higher authority and with rain supposedly coming on, he rose to the occasion of a command decision.

During a half-hour in which many photographs, measurements and soil samples in plastic Zip-lock bags were taken, I altered the vehicle to rise to its new challenge. One glance had told me that with the empty barrels in the modest bed, we could never get the logs aboard as well. I therefore tossed the barrels out onto the springy grass and, with Gilles' help, lifted the insert out of the truck's bed. This could be flipped over and bolted down as a roof to shelter cargo, but it could also be used right side up as a trailer because of the down-pivoting axle with retractable wheels. Not that it would carry very much, a little less cargo than the bed itself, but it had expedited the job of carrying lobster tanks on the étangs.

When we had hitched it behind the truck, we lifted the log halves gingerly into it. The logs couldn't fit side by side, so the empty one was put lengthways and the burial one crosswise. This cargo was carefully cushioned by a collection of windbreakers, sweaters, backpacks and camera cases. The sweaters and windbreakers were quickly contributed because it was now getting uncomfortably warm in the sun. After the barrels were upended back into the truck, the archaeologists themselves clambered onto the seat and perched wherever they could. Then we all wuffled very gently the four kilometers up and down to their camp somewhere on the northwest coast.

Surrounded by the excited conversation of Jergen, Erica and Björn, Dr. Lis Hauglund sitting on the front seat beside me commented after a while: "Ve Danes say dat...*th* – at... our langvage iss not a langvage so much ass a disease of the throat."

I laughed politely and dutifully and said that I hoped it wasn't contagious. "But seriously, Dr. Hauglund, is the find extraordinary? Everyone seems so very excited."

"It iss almost unique. There are only a handsful of oak-coffin burials, und I haff never heard of a child haffing been interred zat vey before."

"Any idea of the date, Dr. Hauglund."

"Vell, it is megalithic for sure." Dr. Lis Hauglund, warming to her subject, explained that since the skeleton had been found beneath a partly fallen menhir, the burial had probably been made before or during the construction of the stone circle. Last year, her team had recovered a red deer antler pick from the same site. It had been carbon dated to about 3500 BC by labs in both Paris and Copenhagen.

"The flora?" I asked. "Pollen analysis?"

I figured that Hauglund needed little prompting, having found one attentive listener beside her own students and in unlikely circumstances. And so, over the next half hour of snail's pace driving, I learned that both Danish and French experts had been puzzled that the soil contained spores of plants not now native to isolated Hoedic, but more typical of the mainland's variety of species. These samples had come from various megalithic sites on Hoedic and Houat, including the burial hole at the stone circle.

For example, the oaks of Hoedic were puzzling, if I understood correctly. As seeds, new acorns cannot be carried very far by any wind. They are too heavy. For the same reason, they don't float. They sink. Acorns are not food for any birds that might have eaten them and then have flown to Hoedic to excrete them. Only wild swine, my wild sangria again, are known to eat acorns. And they can swim. But twenty miles in the sea? They *could*, maybe, have got to Hoedic and have excreted acorns, thus accounting for the oaks. But it seemed unlikely to Hauglund.

"So, do I understand, Dr. Hauglund? You're suggesting that once, within the time of cultured man... ah... humanity, that Hoedic wasn't so far from the mainland?"

"Ja... yess... dat's... *th* – at iss the qvestion. Vas Hoedic vonce part of ze mainland or vere dere many ozer islands around zo *th* – at the channels between zem vere narrow enough for schvine to schvim?" Or words to that effect. I admit that I rather enjoyed Hauglund's accent and enthusiasm. Her accent thickened as she became more excited.

And to think that the public believes scientists to be dispassionate. Perhaps that is true in the hard physical disciplines like mathematics and chemistry... but I doubted it. However, I had read Ceram's *Gods, Graves and Scholars* and so I *knew*, at least, that archaeology and associated humanistic disciplines were both passionate and romantic – just like linguistics, for example. I wasn't surprised at all, therefore, to see Hauglund's steel-rimmed glasses foggy on a hot day and to note her skinny jean-clad legs scissoring with the passion of paleobotanical ecstasy. She was the physical opposite of the woman on *Die Lorelei's* ruined Tee shirt.

Hauglund pulled herself together when we breasted the top of the last hill and we could see the camp's three tents down below. She became suddenly controlled and rather stern, as befitted the team's leader. Try as I might, I could see no sign of the Dutchman's tidal pool along this coast either which, it was apparent, was markedly less steep than the southeastern side of the island. There was enough level land, in places, for scattered small houses and garden plots. The plot closest to the tents, about a kilometre south, seemed to have several rows of half-grown corn, if the stalks weren't sunflowers. It was hard to tell at this distance. A few brightly coloured boats enlivened the drab tidal flats that, however, were visibly narrower now.

I was invited to stay for lunch, which was a catch-as-catch-can smorgasbord of canned herrings in tomato and mustard sauce, canned sprats, canned and devilled ham, cheese and thick slices of dark rye smeared with canned Danish butter. But, as far as I was concerned, the large screened tent offered better conversation than food.

It quickly became clear that there was a French and a Danish school of thought regarding Lyonesse. For the French, the pre-Celtic megalithic culture of Brittany was of little interest and of no historical importance. The Danes, by contrast, leaned toward the idea of a populous and agricultural megalithic society on the Atlantic coast from Denmark and Norway south to Spain and Portugal. Dr. Peter V. Glob's name came up fairly frequently among the Danes. He had studied the preserved bog people, I learned. Glob leaned toward the idea of a fairly large Neolithic and megalithic population that had worshipped pre-Celtic fertility goddesses.

It was Erica who broached the idea that there had once been many more islands like Hoedic and Houat around Brittany. I was interested to hear that there had been a major subsidence about AD 400 to 500 and that a lot of people had relocated to the mainland. Erica spoke of a King Gradlon and of a fairy called Mélusine as folk memories of this migration.

Gilles, the French government's representative, dismissed these stories as myths. He was particularly derisive of the idea that Paris had been named after the city of Ys. According to Erica, there had been a large offshore city called Ys on the island of Avvalon. When Ys went down, the next largest settlement in Gaul was called *Par Ys*… 'like Ys'…which became Paris.

"Erica," I ventured to ask in French, "why doesn't Caesar's *Gallic Wars* mention this offshore… ah… country?"

"Because it didn't exist," Gilles put in with a chuckle.

"He did mention it," Erica insisted. I learned that Caesar had mentioned the land of the Retz, not further referred to in his Gallic conquests, that lay between the mouth of the Loire and the sea. Erica explained that now there was nothing between the Loire and the sea, as I knew well along with everyone else there, but if there had once been a complex of numerous islands off the Loire, then the sea could be regarded as starting beyond them. Perhaps this group of islands had been the land of the Retz.

Taking my leave of the archaeologists, I asked Dr. Hauglund if they had a bucket or a large pot that I might borrow. The expedition's spaghetti cooker was produced, a fair-sized and upscale container made of thick stainless steel. I was also given a can of Danish butter and a loaf of rye when I explained my intention of cooking crabs. Danes, apparently, liked hot buttered crab meat on toasted rye. I promised to leave their pot up at the stone circle if I didn't return it personally.

The stalks I had seen proved to be corn. French people do not eat American corn themselves because they find it tasteless. However, they grow it as feed for cows and pigs. In this case, however, the three pigs had been sold on the mainland in May because of the pork shortage and correspondingly high prices. Therefore, the corn was for sale. The ears were small at this time of year, but well formed, and so I took a dozen of the ripest ones at a franc apiece. I pumped water from the well, insisting on payment at ten francs a barrel since I knew that later in the summer the well's water level might drop significantly.

By the time I could look down again on *Jester* from just above the megaliths, the tidal flats were gone and the sea had returned to the shore. Between Hoedic and the distant smudge of the mainland, I counted ten boats, about half-and-half yachts and fishing craft. None of them seemed to be heading for Hoedic.

35

I threw another piece of driftwood on the flickering bed of embers, and it licked to life with the spattering green sparkles which salt gives off. A slight onshore breeze from the southeast brought the fishy smell of tidal flats to us, kept the midges away and also bathed us in warmth. It was even strong enough, sometimes, to rustle the oak leaves.

This wind, which had been from the northwest and had now veered all the way around to come from the southeast, made me uneasy. This clash of weather fronts had probably caused the earlier prediction of rain that had concerned the archaeologists.

But it might also portend a storm, and I could not imagine what a south-easterly gale would do with the solstitial tides. Because of this change of wind, our little tidal pool had suddenly become a lee shore.

With the combination of an onshore storm and higher tides, we could be embayed for two or three days. I thought that we would be safe even if surf came into the lagoon, but I was uncertain.

There was a substantial lip from the sandy beach up onto the true turf. Perhaps that lip was the shoreline in unusual conditions of wind and tide. I didn't like the idea of *Jester* being cast up among the oaks ashore. However, there was nothing I could do about it until high tide because we could not get out of our pool until then anyway.

The northern sky was just light enough to distinguish the few small clouds and, of course, there was no sign of rain in the starry sky. I would hate to be a weatherman in Brittany because the climate is so variable. Rain is usually safe to forecast for Brittany, but the weather can occasionally be perverse as well as changeable.

The buttered crab on rye toast and corn-on-the-cob had gone some way toward soothing Mariko. But she was still fretting. "Perhaps it is simply a medieval monkish cipher, after all," she said for about the third time in as many hours. She had tried almost everything. Left to right. Right to left. Boustrophedon which, I learned, was back and forth like a ploughman makes furrows. But the inscription on the parchment still made no sense in any of twenty or so first century Middle Eastern languages that Mary Magdalene might reasonably have known or used.

Mariko had pulled up hundreds, it seemed, of inscriptions on the Internet. Many were in Tiffinagh and some of the variants were additional to her photocopied examples. But even using these other modifications of the alphabet, the inscription made no sense. She had then turned to the Ogham rebus that was the last inscription, or illustration, on the single page. I had seen this at Lac des Doigts, a rough circle somewhat resembling a facial portrait, composed of hash marks which, I knew vaguely, were Ogham letters. Mariko had also explained as much. Using something called O'Flattery's alphabet, today she had discovered that the Ogham spelled out 'Mary Magdalene' in a circle, a kind of mandala. But she had known that much already from the Tiffinagh phonems she had read before.

For my part, I had recounted my time spent with the archaeologists. Then, I had asked her once again, to go over her original story about finding the parchment in the little church in Glastonbury. Mariko may have been despondent about her day's success, and so her dispirited and nearly flat rendition of the familiar tale had been just a little different than before. Her preoccupation with the day's disappointments had freed up another memory from her subconscious as she idly ate buttered crab on rye. I didn't mention this new detail to her at the time, but it made me somewhat happier. All things are relative, of course.

I picked up the archaeologists' large stainless steel pot beside the fire and went down to the water's edge to scrub it out with sand. Mariko sat staring into the embers with her arms around knees that were powdered with sand. Sand, I noticed, also threatened to invade the crotch of her micro cut-offs. Our feet had gradually transferred small sand dunes up onto the blanket.

After letting the pot drip somewhat dry, I put it in the truck bed. Then I walked over to Mariko and held a hand down to her. She finally noticed, looked up and managed a small smile when she grasped it. "What are we going to do, Marc?"

"Go up to the menhirs," I said. "I promised to leave the pot there."

She nodded in a preoccupied way and I helped her to her feet. She brushed sand from her hands, knees and bottom. "Let's take the blanket," she said.

"Why not?" So I took one corner and she another and together we energetically flapped it downwind, turning our heads and closing our mouths and eyes to keep the grit out. I bundled it up and tossed it beside the pot in the back of Achilles. Mariko climbed over the side of the vehicle with fire glow shadows rippling inside her thighs.

I drove up the valley very slowly, taking a great deal of care, because the darkness doubtless hid bumps and rocks. The single motorcycle headlight seemed easily swallowed by the gently waving grass. When we got up on the knoll overlooking the circle, a few scattered and distant lights picked out the mainland curving from the north around to the east where St. Nazaire glittered like a single gem on a delicate bracelet.

Also, up here the breeze was just a little stronger. Coming from southern France and Spain, the wind was like being in front of a blow-drier on low speed. We walked down the knoll to the circle. The stars and the afterglow high in the northwest gave just enough light for us to walk with much care.

Only four of the stones were actually still standing straight. Two leaned precariously and three had toppled completely. I had already told Mariko about the burial and as I spread the blanket out on another fallen stone across the circle, because it was somewhat flatter, she went over to look down into the excavation. Not that there was anything to see, and certainly not in the dark.

Finally, the ghostly shape of her white Tee shirt grew larger and she swished through the coarse grass to come up beside me.

I glanced at the luminous dial of my watch. "The moon is supposed to rise in half an hour, Mariko," and I pointed to a slight yellow glow on the horizon, forgetting that she could barely see my hand. She sat down beside me on the blanket. The day's heat seeped up through the wool from the stone.

"Is Joëlle all right?" she asked after a time.

"Yes, Mariko. She is in a place called Aiguillon with Raoul, Philippe and their... wives. She will be okay now."

The glow on the horizon seemed a little more definite. I put my arm around her shoulders and urged her a bit closer. "You know, Mariko, Joëlle thinks that Mary may have been more like a title than a proper name." She said nothing, but I could feel her turn to look at me. "Think of all the Marys there are in the New Testament. Joey thinks that it was edited that way in order to disguise the fact that one Mary was very important."

"Yes. As I said in the beginning, Marc, I think that too."

"A wife."

"Probably."

"But Joey goes further, Mariko." I considered how to say it. "She thinks that the... ah... divinity... was actually Mary's. Jesus was her consort."

"That is also possible... many feminists tend toward that way of thinking."

"Joey would take it further yet..." I stood up to see the horizon better – the yellow glow was quite definitely stronger. I stretched, and then turned to sit cross-legged on the grass in front of Mariko. "If I understand correctly all that she has said, Joëlle thinks that the oldest Christian religion came from the west. Not from the Middle East. Christianity… ah… as we now know it… is only one more version of the same old story, but the original story came from out in the Atlantic somewhere."

"Atlantis." I could hear the smile in her voice.

"Why not?" I shrugged.

"I don't know about the coming from the west part, Marc," she said quietly and seriously, possibly to erase any idea that her previous humour could be construed as ridicule of Joëlle, "but otherwise that is well known. Many experts have seen Christianity as a variation on the 'earth mother and dying god' theme of ancient fertility religions."

"Right. Now, Mariko, given all this… doesn't it make a bit of sense to ask where Mary's own mother came from… that is, if there's a female lineage of supposed divinity? In writing a Gospel, well, maybe Mary used her mother tongue, as it were."

"Her allegorical mother, you mean. And – which Mary?"

I shrugged in the dark. "Any Mary, Mariko… if it's more of a title than a name. I just don't know the Bible well enough, and since this… all started… well, I haven't had a chance to look into it."

Mariko held out a hand to me. I felt her fingers on my shoulder, and gathered them in. "Let me see," she mused. "I know the Bible very well, really. I was raised a nominal Catholic. I just have to think about it."

"That's why I stopped to meet with Joey in Moissac, Mariko. Well, at least that was part of it. She was raised a Catholic too."

"Mary Magdalene's background isn't mentioned. Neither is that of Mary of Bethany, although she is presented as probably some relation of Joseph of Arimathaea."

"What about the Virgin Mary?"

"Jesus…" She said after a second or two.

Since it had not been said piously, I waited, then asked: "What…?"

"Sorry, Marc, I was off on a train of thought. Her mother…The Virgin Mary's that is… was supposed to have been St. Anne of Brittany…"

"It says so in the Bible?"

"No. Anne isn't mentioned in the Bible, it is just part of Christian lore… oral tradition."

"Brittany sticks out into the Atlantic, Mariko… And Joey said that 'Mary" means 'of the sea.'"

"It does. That's what I was thinking," she said quietly. "Atlantis… and all that."

"There is something else, Mariko, although I'm sorry even to bring it up. Joëlle mentioned that 'Magdalene' supposedly comes the word

'Magdala' which was a fortified town or something. In paintings and sculpture, she said, Mary Magdalene's crown looks like battlements. Is that true?"

"I never paid much attention to Roman Catholic iconography in art, Marc, but, yes, I vaguely remember something like that."

"I know it is dumb, because languages have changed and so on, but don't you find it odd that 'Magdalene' has nine letters and we are sitting here in Brittany in a circle of nine stones. The stone circles in Britain often have nine stones."

Mariko laughed. "Jesus. As you say, Marc, give me a break. Now we throw in numerology?"

"Maybe not." I grinned in the darkness because I knew exactly how she felt. "It's just that I've heard before of nine stones in a circle. Or multiples of nine. Maybe these standing stones became battlements in later art after humanity had cities, and 'Magdalene' was a way of saying an old name that also had nine letters and had been the name of the megalithic Mary."

"Letters… or syllables… Perhaps. But I would rather not speculate so far. Ugh!" She shuddered a sound of shivering and I imagined rather than saw her arms cross over her chest to hug herself.

Since I felt rather sheepish, I shut up for a while. Then I had a question. "What language did they speak?"

"Who's *they?*"

"Brittany people… Britons, I guess."

"Bretons, with an 'e'".

"Okay."

"Celtic. That's what 'Breton' or 'Briton' means. Brythonic. It was a later dialect of Celtic. Later than Goidelic, or Gaelic."

"Before that then, before Celts."

"No one knows."

"Make a guess."

"I cannot, Marc, because there are no written documents from that time."

"Then we're talking about the language of the megalithic folk?"

"Well… ye-ss… I suppose so."

"Have DNA studies begun to influence linguistics, Mariko?"

"Marginally."

"Well, I remember that back in 1999 or 2000, DNA samples from Celtic speaking students from somewhere in Wales that I can't pronounce caused a lot of surprise. They, the scientists, concluded that the students' supposedly Celtic ancestry was more or less local stretching back to the Neolithic and Palaeolithic 10,000 to 20,000 years ago with some evidence of DNA patterns also common to North America distanced at about 12,000 years ago… or so. More or less."

"Really?"

"Yes. That's why, when I met Joëlle and learned about this belief of Elysians as Atlantean refugees, well, I've always kept an open mind… I also remember a hot debate between some academics about what the word 'Celtic' really means now, if it can mean anything at all. The idea seems to be growing that they may have been some sort of Russian steppe aristocracy of a warrior class that came riding horses along the Danube into Western Europe. They may have brought some linguistic and artistic and maybe religious elements with them all right. But these eventually merged with local languages and cultures wherever they went because of gradual intermarriage and mixing with a much more populous conquered people. Submerged into the local is more like it."

"Yes, that's a very recent theory," Mariko confirmed. "Professor Colin Renfrew leads that school of thought, I believe. I never gave it much credence because I didn't know what evidence it was based on. But perhaps the DNA sampling was the evidence. Norman French would be a similar example of the same argument. The Normans invaded Britain in 1066…"

"..and all that." I saw the brief flash of a small smile.

"Yes… but modern English is mostly still Anglo-Saxon."

"And maybe it was also basically that before the Angles and Saxons invaded, and before even the Celts came. And, well, if that is the case, then maybe local common people spoke very basic Celtic and Teutonic before the Celtic and Teutonic overlords invaded."

"Now, Marc, how can that be?"

"What I mean is that thousands of years ago, people had to use river routes for travel. Perhaps basic megalithic and Neolithic speech migrated from the Atlantic inland. Later, when steppe Celts and Teutons migrated the other way, they were influenced by these languages en route along the same river valleys. Maybe scholars were confused and assumed that the languages came from the east toward the west without realizing that languages had already been established along river valleys."

"You've just undermined a century of classical linguistic teaching about the Indo-European language group," she responded somewhat dryly. Can you give me a specific example. A word."

"Axe," I said. "It is listed in the vocabulary of Teutonic and Old Anglo-Saxon, but it actually comes from the Ice Age twelve thousand years ago, not from Caucasus maybe five or six thousand years ago. It is the sound of a blade striking a tree."

"You are totally amazing, Marc Rennsalaer. Newspaper articles, I suppose?"

"Well, yes. I also read about some other basic words that still survive. Like *boy* and *girl*. They didn't originally come with the Teutons or Celtic invaders from Russia; they were already words of the old Ice Age language. The poorer classes, the conquered people, retained these words for thousands of years until they became acceptable even within the imposed Caucasus speech."

"And the genetic consistency of some of the British population has been confirmed by DNA studies?"

"As I understand it, Mariko. So, maybe there was some consistency in language among these people too over thousands of years. They were influenced by the Indo-European invaders, of course, both genetically and linguistically, but many of them are basically what they always were."

"Perhaps. Go on."

"Now, Early Christians generally preached to the masses, to the lower classes that have always existed since megalithic and Neolithic times, and so maybe your parchment is written in some form of fundamental and basic Celtic or Anglo-Saxon. Ever think of that?"

"No," she said quietly.

The horizon was lighted as if a candle burned just beneath it. I squeezed Mariko's hand. "Look, Mariko. Not long now."

We watched in silence for fifteen minutes while the moon peeked up, rose and lifted clear of the horizon. It was huge and buttery and it bathed a swath of milk across the marram grass. The stones suddenly cast moon shadows around us.

"Hell, Mariko, maybe I'm barking up the wrong tree... but I seem to get there by two different routes."

"What is the other one?"

"Forget ancient linguistics for a moment. Take simple religious expediency. Well. You found it, the parchment, at Glastonbury. Legends say that Early Christians supposedly came there. Who were the best candidates for conversion at that time?"

"The local Celts, of course."

"Maybe not, Mariko. I read that the Celtic aristocracy accepted Christianity fairly easily. Once the Romans allowed it, that is. The real hold-outs were the Druid leaders or priests of the pre-Celtic people, and the Romans officially stamped them out. But in the boondocks... in the... ah... countryside," I amended, "the common people still revered old religion and customs until the last century. There's a revival of these beliefs now."

"Ah, yes, the New Age and the Druidiots of Stonehenge," she had cynical humour in her voice. She paused. "But seriously... there actually were no martyrs in Ireland," she mused. "Not for the Celtic Church, anyway."

"Maybe that's because they already had something very similar. I once wrote an article about a character called Yesu who was revered by Druids, but this was maybe two or three hundred years before Christ."

I could see her brief nod in the moonlight. "William Blake... the poet... wrote something alluding to Christ in Britain... before it was called Britain. Back when it was called Albion. That would presumably be back in, as you say, megalithic times. Scotland is still sometimes called Albion or Albany because Celts retreated there with remnants of the old culture and the oldest dialect of Celtic language. Gaelic... from Goedelic. Go on."

"But even in early Roman times, there were Anglo-Saxon and Jute incursions. They got a lot worse, as we all know. But my point is that an early Gospel might have been written in some form of Anglo-Saxon or Teutonic, both for the local peasants and also for the Anglo-Saxon invaders from across the North Sea. On the top or literary level, the Celtic and Anglo-Saxon languages may have been fairly different, but who knows what your average Saxon oarsman or British farmer may have spoken? Their languages may have been very similar, for all we know. And they were the ones who had to be converted, after all."

She was silent after I finished. "Mariko...?"

"Yes, Marc..."

"Mariko, what does the word 'Gospel' mean?"

"Good news."

"In what language? Greek or something?"

She sighed audibly. "I hate to say it, but it is Anglo-Saxon," she said very quietly. "Gut spiel," she spoke up and pronounced it carefully. "The word was in use throughout the Mediterranean world by the second century AD."

"But there weren't many Anglo-Saxons around the Mediterranean. Isn't that a bit odd?" I asked.

"Yes," she said. "It certainly is." She paused. "I will go back and see if the inscription responds to an assault of basic Anglo-Saxon."

I considered this. "Can you stay here and respond to an assault of basic Anglo-Saxon?"

She was quiet for a moment. She removed her hand from mine and used it to peel the Tee shirt over her head. For an answer, she lay back on the blanket in the moonlight. I stood up and looked down at her stretched out on the fallen megalith. "Speaking of the moon, matriarchal megaliths, sacrifices and so on. Marc... If I were you I would take the offering fairly soon... unless you like your victims bloody as well as sandy. It is about that time."

I thought I caught a hint of that ancient sharp scent. "Right."

"I think I can very easily manage being a moonlit sacrifice to mysterious powers," she said softly. "They are certainly abroad in this place." She shivered again and hugged herself, not with cold because the warm wind sighed heavily like the breathing of something vast and near, but invisible. I first forcibly unfolded her arms so that she lay naked to the slow panting of the variable breeze. I wished that I had had something to tie her arms up with, but was uncertain how far Mariko had come down the road – or primrose path – of broadmindedness. However, she had come far enough to understand what I wanted and gripped the tapering top of the megalith above her head.

I unzipped and removed her micro-cutoffs so that I could enjoy the heartbeat palpitations and also the slower undulations of her torso. Since she obviously looked like an ancient sacrifice, as a high priest of the ancient urges, I slowly, intimately and lecherously examined and teased the wench with·feather-light caresses on her softer flesh and ribs and boustrophedon exploration of her furrow. I used judicious applications pallid but firm violence to keep her arms stretched up whenever the sensations became unbearable for her.

Finally, she was properly terrified of imminent intrusion and was desperately sensitive enough for really satisfactory gloating. When her breasts were surging back and forth in the moonlight with her helpless rocking, when the long moon shadows on her belly deepened with ragged gasps and when her thighs began alternately clamping one over the other in hopeless defence, I judged her ready for fully enjoyable impaling.

Her one high cry floated out over the silvered moonlit grass and crooked stone shadows, I then made certain that this time she whimpered and writhed solely for the lengthy gratification of the darkest and most timeless gods of men.

And these, possibly, were even older than the earth mother.

36

By the time we got back down to *Jester*, the moon was floating higher and a bit smaller although it still looked like a big pale yellow balloon. The tide was maybe half an hour from full flood and little rollers were creaming over the shelf into the lagoon. Our beach fire had already been inundated. Waves licked far up the sand to the very base of overhanging turf. *Jester* was prancing ponderously at her warps like a frisky plough horse. Her excited prow had gouged a deep fan-shaped excavation in the sand.

Our agreement was that Mariko would go below to try the parchment once more. As soon as she could, that is, for she wanted a long, warm bath almost as badly as she wanted to translate the parchment. She said the sit-in half tub would be sufficient if she directed the hot water strategically. She claimed she was sore. She said that she would not be able to sleep, anyway, unless she tried our new approach.

As for me, I brought Achilles aboard and rigged *Jester* for sea. Like most nautical decisions, I was taking a calculated risk and could only hope that I was figuring correctly. The waves were higher than when we had come across from the Loire. But they were nothing to worry about – yet. My concern, however, was to get off this lee shore while we could, and the nearest sheltered coast was now exactly where I wanted to go anyway. And that was twenty miles or so to the east, and a bit north, into the modest estuary of the Vilaine River.

We had six hours to make it before the tide returned to the ebb. But this would be no ordinary ebb because it was the day of the summer solstice and, in addition, the moon was full.

Therefore, before *Jester* ever surged over the ledge under steam, I had studied the chart very carefully. For most of the crossing I did not have to worry much about depth, but in a few hours I would have to be in the channel that the Vilaine had inexorably cut into the seabed over the past hundred and twenty-odd centuries since the end of the Ice Age. That channel would still have enough water to float *Jester* and so would the Loire's, but between them there would be only mudflats and a bewildering maze of tide-cut channels. Some of these were tentatively shown on the chart. All sailors know, however, that tidal channels can change season to season and storm to storm. I'd much prefer to find us at ebb in the ancient and thus reliable channel cut by the Vilaine.

The wind was southeast enough to call it a beam reach – if it didn't shift again, that is. Also, I felt, it could freshen just as suddenly as it might shift. In either case, I didn't want to scrabble with sails because Mariko could not be of help, and it was night, so I made sail only on the starboard mizzen and jib. This steadied *Jester* over the waves, four to six footers, and the cut-water prow sliced through these while throwing a fair bit of spray. There was enough moonlight to sparkle the cascades and droplets, and perhaps there was some phosphorescence too, making *Jester* into a fickle woman trying on necklaces and just as gaily tossing them aside again.

Not having what a blue water sailor would call sea legs, and because it was night, I had clipped my safety harness to the wheelhouse. Because of *Jester's* design, the spring-loaded reel gave me scope enough to handle the sails if necessary.

These Chinese sails were pushing us along a gilded swath of moonlight at about four knots. It reminded me of an *orembai* I had once been aboard, with Mei Ling, long ago on a milky tropical sea somewhere south of the sun and west of the moon. And then, also, the wind was coming from the direction of Aiguillon. So, the salty droplets on my cheeks were not wholly from the spray.

I heard the heavy cabin door suck open and chunk shut again with a click of the old cold-room lock. Presently, Mariko's head and shoulders appeared very unsteadily in the hatchway. She regarded the deck dubiously and finally turned around to sit down in the hatchway with her legs dangling down into the wheelhouse. Mongolian ponytail and jersey again.

"I feel a dunce" was her opening line.

"It broke? Or… it didn't break?"

"Oh, it broke – in all of twenty minutes."

"Then why 'dunce'?"

"I should long ago have thought of what you thought of."

"Maybe ignorance is bliss."

"But I'm supposed to be the linguist."

"You are."

"You could have broken it yourself, Marc. I heard you back at the little lake. You speak a bit of German."

"A very little bit."

"That's all it would have taken. In a few hours, you could have got the gist."

"Hopefully, you got more than the gist."

"Oh, yes. After it broke, I went back to fill in the blanks and get the nuances. I have a fairly clean translation now. Believe it or not, your CDs of the complete Oxford and American Heritage Dictionary of Indo-European Roots were of the greatest assistance. That's all it took. No need for more detailed Germanic etymologies, although they might help to polish the translation. However, polish is irrelevant. Would you like to see it?"

"Later, Mariko."

"Yes, of course." She steadied herself in the hatchway as *Jester* slid into a trough and the cut-water flung spray from the rising hump of the next roller. "Are these waves dangerous?"

"Hardly, Mariko." I paused to give her a reassuring smile. "Truly. Just normal. Now tell me the story."

"It is obviously the final page of the document, as I had suspected before. I always thought that I had taken the final leaf of an unbound roll. Also, it ends without using all the vellum. It is the conclusion of her life story. She was old and dying. But she was at peace. It was written in Avalon. Her daughter, by John... the text makes this clear by using the Scandinavian patronymic 'Ionesdottir'... had got married to someone on the mainland named Drustans and has two children. One of each. The boy will become the new Yesus."

"Now *that,* Mariko O'Shaugnessey, is about the biggest mouthful of words I've ever heard."

"Isn't it?"

"Can I start with geography? I'm better at that."

"Certainly."

"Since the writer is in Avalon at the end of her days, but her daughter has moved to the mainland, then this Avalon is manifestly not Glastonbury where you found the parchment. Glastonbury was almost surrounded by marshes and meres at one time, maybe, but it was an island only in a symbolic sense. One would not normally contrast it with a mainland."

"Yes. I agree."

"Therefore, this Avalon was a real island at some distance from the mainland. I suppose that it was Erica's 'Avvalon' that I told you about, one of the islands of Lyonesse."

"Perhaps... or rather, almost certainly."

"But where was two-vee Avvalon?" I mused. My archaeologist Erica thought that it had been somewhere near here, near Hoedic. When you suggested that we check out someone called Giraldus Cambrensis, we found that he gave a king list of Lyonesse, for what that may be worth, and a description from which one can make a crude map. One of the islands of Lyonesse was Avvalon with two vees. But it results in a bad and more than questionable map, even as medieval maps go. It is clear that by the time of Giraldus, the geography of Lyonesse had been forgotten and muddled."

Mariko sat head down in thought. The swath of moonlight and the glow coming up from the wheelhouse made her look, at that moment, because of the skin tones, cheeks bones and the curved shadows around her eyes, almost wholly Oriental. She looked like Mei Ling. I swallowed and more salty spray came aboard. I continued. "All that I believe we can say is that there was a true island called Avvalon at that time, Mary's time, but whether it was here south of Brittany near Hoedic or somewhere else, possibly nearer England, is anyone's guess."

"I agree with that," she said.

I continued: "And I think we can also say that this island sank at some point between Mary Magdalene's life and now. For surely, if the island were still above water, the name would have clung to it tenaciously, just like it has clung to Glastonbury as poetical Avalon. Its name would never have changed."

"Absolutely, Marc. Therefore, we can say that the area around Glastonbury was named Avalon after this lost island, the two-vee Avalon of Lyonesse. The parchment was written on this island and was later taken to Glastonbury to its still above-water symbolic home."

"Drustans…?"

"A variant of Tristan, Tristram, Tamtrist *ad nauseum*. Prince or warrior of Lyonesse."

"Tristan the Dislexic," I quipped.

"Just so. In fact, I rather enjoy that phrase. It should have been his epithet in the romances. However, the Drustans of the parchment must be an earlier man of the same name. The Drustans or Tristan of the Arthurian romances was a contemporary of King Mark of Cornwall who is said to have lived shortly after the time of Arthur, most probably between AD 550 and 600."

"The Drustans and daughter of the parchment were young and old enough to marry about AD 50, give or take."

"Right." She smiled.

"Is it a reasonable inference that Drustans became a popular or revered name because of our parchment Drustans? That later, men would have been named after him because of his Mary and Holy connections?"

"That is possible, of course, but not necessary. I have come across that name before, Marc. It was a Roman patrician name. For example, Emperor Claudius who invaded Britain… and I forget just when, sometime around AD 50… was the son of a Drusus. Drustans could have derived from that name."

"So, our parchment Drustans could have been a Roman, maybe an officer – or maybe even a relation of Emperor Claudius himself."

"Right," she said again.

"John's daughter...?

"Well, the obvious candidate is John the Baptist, isn't it? The preceding part of the document should clarify that."

"The *new* Yesus...?"

"Now we come to it," Mariko said. She smiled and shook her head slightly, her eyes sparkling in the moonlight. "It sounds like a title, Marc." She paused. "If, as your Joëlle would have it, 'Mary' was a title, then 'Yesus' appears to have been one too. If the Druids did indeed have a 'Yesu' before Christ, as you say..."

"I did research that article carefully, Mariko."

I could see her nod tentative acceptance. "...then Yesu was also revered in Western Europe before the Jesus we know in the New Testament. If it was a title, as appears from the phrase in the parchment, then there were successive Yesuses." She winced. "That sounds terrible."

Most of my mind was occupied with uppermost concerns, but a few thousand neurons meandered on biochemical byways. "Mariko, I have never really looked into it, but from what Joëlle has said over a couple of years, I suspect that the first name for the earth mother, the first recorded name, that is, may well have been Isis. She had a sacrificed husband and a son who was really the same person as the husband. What if Yesu or Yesus is just a way of saying Isis?"

"Isis was female, Marc. A goddess."

"Even I know that, Mariko. But I wonder if, over time and changes from a matriarchal culture to patriarchal ones, the gender got changed and scrambled? Mary 'of the sea' substituted for Isis and the name Isis was transferred to her husband-son."

"I suppose that anything is *possible*, Marc. And after your suggestion of trying Anglo-Saxon on the parchment proved correct, I am in no position to dismiss anything. However, it sounds highly speculative and unfounded to me."

"Just a thought," I replied. "I am afraid that my real concerns are more immediate, if you know what I mean." She looked up a question and grasped the sides of the hatch as *Jester* again dropped and tossed spray back toward us. *Were* the waves higher? Maybe a little. I looked up to study the sails. *Was* the wind getting stronger? I honestly couldn't tell. Maybe a little, but not much. Now that the Lucite sheet was gone, I had taped the folded chart onto the top of the wheelhouse. It told me that we had gone almost half way. I shrugged, and turned back to Mariko. "We have reason to think, from what we saw in Carcassonne, that at least one of the organizations... er... *displeased...* with you is the Roman Catholic Church, the Vatican."

"Now we know why," she said.

"True. But, Mariko, I have been wondering mightily why our North German Grail Crusaders are apparently working with the Church."

"It would be nothing new," Mariko answered in a wry tone. "After World War II, the Vatican helped many Nazis to escape to South America."

"Right," I replied. "And maybe it is just as simple as that. However, Mariko, I want to explore this because the Vatican has other and more obvious muscle. There is the Mafia and the Union Corse, for example, that were used so frequently when people were closing in on the Banco Ambrosiano."

"I remember that only vaguely, Marc. I was very young. Father told me about it. He was incensed."

I didn't ask her why. My, but time flies. I had been a truculent teenager then while Mariko, like Joëlle, had both been in little girl skirts. "I wonder if these Grail Crusaders, who have a lot of money and organization, have a more... ah... pressing reason for trying to prevent the parchment from coming to public notice rather than mere old times sake with the Vatican."

"I don't understand these things, Marc."

"Perhaps you do, Mariko, but just don't know it."

"I hardly ever read newspapers or even popular books."

"That is just what I mean." I paused, thinking about exactly what to ask since I was not at all certain what to ask. "Back in Moissac, Joëlle and I got into a conversation about the Holy Grail. As I understood it, the Grail is only a cup or a chalice in an... er... *obstetrical* sense."

"Pardon me...? She looked at me curiously.

"One theory has it that it was or is a bloodline from Jesus Christ and Mary Magdalene."

She smiled and shook her head. "You sometimes have the strangest way of putting things," she said. "But now I get it." She hesitated. "But if this parchment is true, we can forget about any offspring from Jesus and Mary Magdalene. Her children were by John the Baptist who held the title of the *Jesus*."

"But maybe she had children by two men. Jesus – or Ye'shua in Hebrew – was a common man's name in Palestine. We're not yet certain Jesus was only a title. We have to read the rest of the Gospel to find out. But the point is, let's say, the Grail derived from Mary one way or another – or through Mary Magdalene may be a better way of saying it."

"All right..." she conceded.

"Now, Mariko, since I don't know anything about this, I can rely only on what Joëlle and you have said."

"About the Grail…?"

"Yes."

"But since I have never mentioned it, what did Joëlle say?"

"She said," I began, "that even Perceval had to learn the right question to ask. She was impatient with my ignorance, you see." I thought that the sea might be running just a little higher, not much. I eased off to port by few degrees, but I didn't want to point too far north.

When I looked back at Mariko, she was again head down in thought. "Whom does the Grail serve?" she said suddenly in that eureka tone of voice. "Whom does the Grail serve," she said again.

"That was the question that Perceval had to ask…?"

She nodded. "It took me a while to remember," she said. "Arthurian romances are not properly my field."

"Are we ever given the answer in the romances? Are we told whom the Grail serves?"

She was doing the head down thinking bit again. She looked up and brushed her hair back and then shook her head. "Perhaps. In some romance or other. Because it is not my field, Marc, I haven't read all of them. But we don't get an answer in the ones that I have read."

"Maybe we already know the answer, Mariko. Part of it, anyway."

She said nothing, but nodded for me to go on.

"We didn't have much chance for sightseeing in Carcassonne, Mariko, but the tourist board puts out posters about Languedoc as the 'Pays des Cathares'. There's even a bank, head office in Carcassonne, called the Bank of Perceval's Well."

"You're joking."

"Not at all. I… we… have an account there. Scout's honour."

"All right, I believe you."

"So, we know whom the Grail does not serve. Cathars believed in the Holy Grail. Their poets invented the phrase. Provence and Languedoc were both invaded by the Church of Rome. So, the Grail does not serve the Vatican."

"We already suspected that," she pointed out.

"But also, it does not serve the Nazis." Dead ahead over the bow, an occulting light flickered on the horizon. The buoy marking the Vilaine River channel to the sea lock. I roughly figured my height of eye and made it six miles, more or less. "Did you know that when the Germans occupied the Midi, they searched for the Holy Grail?"

"Jesus," she said wryly.

I ignored Mariko's cynicism. "That's just the point. Not Jesus, Mariko. Not even John the Baptist, as the parchment indicates. Hitler had already obtained the Spear of Destiny from the Vienna museum when he invaded Austria in 1938…"

"The Spear of Destiny? Marc. Please."

"The supposed spear of the Centurion Longinius that pierced the side of Christ. You know, John Wayne in *King of Kings*. 'Yea verily, little sister, this man was truly the Son of God' and 'Romans… Yo.'" Naturally I did my John Wayne imitation. "You will be pleased to know, however, that the spear was recovered from the Reichstag by the U.S. Army and returned to the Hapsburg Museum in 1945."

"Is this all true…?"

"Absolutely. Trust me." A few lights of Pénesin peeped up over the horizon dead ahead, while down south off the starboard bow I could make out lights from le Croisic. With these headlands now somewhat to windward, the waves quickly became noticeably smaller.

"Right," She grinned and shook her head slowly. "Want some hot chocolate, Marc?"

"I don't think there is any. Anyway, he – Hitler – that is, wanted the Holy Grail from southern France after the French collapse of 1940. For him, Hitler, you see, it was a solid object sometimes also called Solomon's Jewel Case. This had been lost by the Moors when King Roderick defeated them at the Battle of Juan de la Frontera in AD 736. The House of ibn Da'ud, that is the House of David, had been in the vanquished Moorish entourage and had coughed up the relic. It was gradually taken into the Pyrenees as the Visigoths retreated from the Moors. It eventually wound up in southern France." I glanced toward Mariko to see if she was following all this.

"There's no hot chocolate?"

"I think we drank the last of it on the way from the Loire."

"All right," she sighed. "Go on. I am paying attention. Truly."

"The Nazis believed these objects had been given to the Aryan Race by the gods in the distant past as tokens of their special favour. Gott mit uns, and all that. They were stolen by the Jews and falsely claimed. Gott mit uns, and all that, and still is, for that matter. The Aryans wanted these tokens back because only with the spiritual strength of these artefacts could the Aryans win World War II. At base, obtaining both the Holy Grail and the Spear of Destiny was the rationale for the Nazi Party."

"What about the mass unemployment and incredible inflation in the Weimar Republic, not to mention probable insanity," Mariko asked in a decidedly dry and dubious tone. She had, after all, studied conventional history – 'the lie commonly agreed upon,' as Napoleon had called it. 'Bunk', Henry Ford, with typical American terseness, had called it.

"Pifflesnits," I said, tossing her comments off. "They were merely minor contributing factors to the rise of Nazism, Mariko. The reduction of the world to mundane materialism was one of the things that really rankled Hitler, by the way."

"I see," Mariko said. "Marc, does all this have a point?"

"Consider, Mariko," I said, as she sighed, "if this Grail is a human lineage from Mary Magdalene, and not another material token of esteem from Aryan gods, then it undermines the mystique of the Fürher, the special nature of the Aryan Race and the soul of Nazism. We're forced back into relying only on your unemployment, inflation and insanity again. Mariko, there's nothing very romantic or spiritual about unemployment, inflation and insanity. Almost everybody wants a piece of the Grail, and preferably a claim to the whole thing. Even the Vatican. Their Grail was the Cup of the Last Supper. Your parchment takes the Grail away from the Nazis as well as the Vatican. Naughty Mariko O'Shaugnessey. What's a nice girl like you doing in a spot like this?

"I admit that I have found myself in odd positions recently, Mister Rennsalaer, most of them since I met you."

I laughed. "Touché," I conceded.

Assuming," she began. "Assuming that I believe all this, is that enough for neo-Nazis to be involved in trying to hunt me down?"

"Ever heard of *Kreuzzug Gegen den Graal*, by Colonel Otto Rahn?"

"No."

"Well, it was prerequisite reading for admission into the SS."

"The helicopter! The Grail Crusaders..." she connected. "But can men be motivated by mysticism?"

"They always have been, Mariko. The soul, if you will, of all religious wars. And make no mistake about it, from the Nazi point of view; World War II was a religious war too." She said nothing, so I added a thought. "Of course, Mariko, it helps a lot if righteousness can be combined with a great deal of money. That, too, has never changed."

"I have not forgotten our talk about possible Israeli involvement in all this," she said softly.

"Yes, and that would contribute a great deal to the financial resources of our enemies. If it is true, that is. I cannot help but wonder."

Mariko, like Joëlle, was too young truly to appreciate the murderous capabilities afforded by righteousness allied with money – as in the case of the Vatican and Banco Ambrosiano. Neither young woman had even vaguely recognized the name of Roberto Calvi, for example. I tried to put it in a more modern context. "Think of it all as Al Gore and Joe Lieberman," I said, "defending American democracy on behalf of the Israeli lobby back in 2000." But I was not sure whether even this fairly un-hoary example of the process was relevant to younger lives.

37

...WISE [likewise? text "L-I-CH"] THAT IS BEAUTIFUL[,] COURAGEOUS AND FULL OF LOVE [? text "F-O-L-B-E-L-E-E-B-T][.] AND SO[,] I SAY [text "I-K-S-P-R-K"][,] SOON TO DIE AN OLD WOMAN[,] ONE WIDOWED YOUNG[,] I AM NONTHELESS CONTENT AT THE END OF MY DAYS IN AV[V]ALON[.] JOHN'S DAUGHTER [text 'I-O-N-S-DO-T-R] IS NOW [? text "YE-T-Z-T] MARRIED TO A GOOD MAN[,] DRUSTANS[,] ON[? IN?] THE MAINLAND [? text "GROS-R-LA-N-D"] AND HAS TWO [text "Z-F-I"] CHILDREN [text "K-N-D-R"] AND THE BOY [text "K-NA-BE"] WILL BE A NEW [? text "N-A-U-Y-S"] YESUS. MARY [text "MI-R-YA-M"] OF [text "FON") MAGDALA.

"Wow," I said, extending the hand-written sheet of paper back to Mariko. She accepted it with a modest smile marred only by her somewhat garish lipstick. The Bausch and Lomb 7 X 35 binoculars nestled on her French Navy blouse. The strap around her neck was lost in flowing Farah Fawcett tendrils because a fairly stiff breeze was blowing seaward.

Last night had played out in a minor navigational error. In brief, I had under-estimated the strength of the ebb current. True, I had seen the lights of what I had thought was Pénesin to the north and east, but now it was plain that I had really seen the lights of Piriac some fifteen crow-flying kilometers south. A current had set me southward during the crossing from Hoedic. Not wanting to head too far north, I had not headed far enough north. However, for all that, the Eagle sonar had proved faithful and had deposited us in a deep channel.

Being charitable about it, this channel could be called, well, an *extension* of the trough that the Vilaine River had scoured through the sand and mud bottom. The long and the short of it was that *Jester* lay to two anchors with a lot of scope in thirty feet of water about two kilometers northwest of Le Croisic. Most of that distance now consisted of mud flats. We had slept out in the channel with *Jester's* riding lights shining from the masthead.

I had explained to Mariko that although Blondel's was about the only source available for Brittany tides, many sailors had discovered that Blondel's tables were not infallible. The pilot book spoke darkly of the need for local knowledge, but after reading a great many books about navigating this coast, it had dawned on me that local knowledge was invariably contradictory. So, I had stuck to basics. I had kept enough water under the keel so that *Jester* was still floating; heartened by the knowledge that even if she was set on the bottom she would at least remain right side up when the tide came in.

"Thank you, Marc," she said, taking the page, folding it and stuffing it fairly carelessly into a hip pocket of the jeans. "I will do a more elegant translation when I have access to more books, but that is adequate for now."

"It certainly is, Mariko."

She raised the binoculars and looked toward Le Croisic. It was a fairly large town at the end of a major road. What remained of the legendary forest of Brocéliande crowded behind the stone buildings and down to the beach on either side of town, but we could see the waterfront. There were boats heeled over on the mudflats and there were shops ashore. Small vehicles and ant-like people scurried past on the coast promenade. I could see the occasional flash of sun off a windshield. "Marc," she said, torturing herself with the binoculars, "can we sail over there? I need some… things… and I would dearly love a chocolate bar."

I knew women enough to know those symptoms. Looking back, I recalled that our shopping in Carcassonne had been rushed and focussed on urgent necessities in the time available after our obligatory visit to Gabereau's office and before closing time at the grande surface. Mariko had not had much time to herself. Perhaps not time enough to buy what she might well consider necessities. On broad waters, like Lake Ontario and the St. Lawrence estuary in Canada and even around Narbonne, I had been careful to keep a small quantity of feminine supplies aboard.

You would be surprised how many women forget to carry extra tampons or panty liners when they come for a day's sail... because they don't realize that the wind doesn't operate like a bus schedule. Or, there could be a storm. You can be hours late getting back to the marina.

Also, I have noticed, there is a strange tendency for young girls to get their first period during a day of sun, water and fresh air. In Canada, some of my friends had children, and some of these kids were naturally young daughters. It is true, though, about first periods, and I discovered it the hard way with a few aborted day sails and much needless embarrassment. Thereafter, I took to ensuring that a package of pads was kept aboard. I also stocked Midol. After some time, this began to seem only reasonable and civilized. After all, there are two genders, and sometimes both are on boats.

However, I had fallen out of this habit on the Canal du Midi. First, I seldom had women aboard and also there was almost always a village within a couple of kilometres. There was not much difficulty, on a canal, about simply tying up to go into a store.

Nonetheless, I had remembered Mariko in Moissac's marketplace when I bought the package of briefs and when I had withheld one package of Prima pads from Joëlle. The briefs had been appreciated by Mariko because at the time she had been without her suitcase. The problem was that I had forgotten all about the package of Prima. It was still in the bottom of the backpack.

I told Mariko as much now. After a casual interval, she went below.

When she came back up, she looked much happier. "But I would still like to go ashore somehow, Marc. I am positively craving chocolate. It started last night."

"*Jester* is not going anywhere until early evening," I said.

"But we could go right over to that wharf there," she said, looking expertly through her Bausch and Lombs. It was said a bit archly, I thought, with a hint of edge to it.

"Keep watching," I replied. "Very soon there will be no water for miles and miles and miles."

"But there's water now," she wheedled, with the sweet reasonableness of the chemically challenged. "There is water right up to that wharf there. I can see it."

"But there won't be in an hour," I explained. "That isn't enough time to get to that mecca of chocolate over there and get back. I don't want us and *Jester* stuck on shore in Le Croisic." I could feel her stiffen beside me on the break of the poop. "You see," I said, "the flow of tide is controlled by the position of the moon. It was full last night. And today is the summer solstice. This will be an unusually low tide. Watch."

However, I am a compassionate soul. I left Mariko up on the poop and went down to open and fold back the cutwater doors. I lowered the landing-craft type of ramp-door in *Jester's* bow to an incline into the water supported by the cables, and I unshackled the vehicle from the cables and turnbuckles that clamped it down to the deck at sea.

When I returned to the poop, I had worked up a small sweat because the wind was partly blocked down there in the hull and the sun was hot.

"Marc! Look! The water is going," she said in subdued awe.

Within minutes, there was almost no water off Le Croisic, except in our narrowing channel. We stayed afloat in our little Ice Age river, and far out there was a distant sparkle of water that was the sea. Mud flats stretched all around us, glistening in the sun and extended all the way to the tiny thread of sand that was the beach separating the tidal flats from the Forest of Brocéliande.

"We will have a few hours of this," I said. In truth, I was not at all happy about going ashore, much less leaving *Jester* at anchor in a tidal channel. However, realistically there was not much current now and the anchors had worked themselves deeply into the mud. And naturally, I wanted to avoid a hormonal mutiny. Death by chocolate, or lack thereof.

So, I chivvied Mariko into the vehicle and we wuffled off the inclined bow ramp and splashed into the water. I was glad to see that Achilles leaked hardly at all. Only enough to keep Mariko busy baling with the cut-down plastic juice container. But, there was some current still running in the channel, and small waves, so I was careful to avoid spray by keeping the speed down. The half-track drive splashed us slowly through the moat of water separating *Jester* from what could barely be called land. Then we churned up onto the greenish mud flats.

We could only make about fifteen miles per hour over the mud, and sometimes not so much, but Achilles never bogged down completely although this mud was soft and sticky in many places.

We finally came to the end of the mud, which stank mightily of dead things of the sea, and churned through the strip of seaweed-adorned sand up to the coast road. I was somewhat nervous about this. The vehicle had an experimental international plate, and also French experimental plates I had acquired in Narbonne. Nonetheless, the thing attracted attention. I had been stopped once on the étang roads near Narbonne simply because the cop wanted to examine the vehicle. And once again in Toulouse while delivering lobsters, another gendarme had stopped me for the same reason. The ensuing conversations had been friendly and had consumed about twenty minutes before desultory checks of my plates had sent me freely on my way. But what if Gabereau had sent out an alert? Then if I was stopped I might find myself in jail.

However, for a couple of years the mere existence of the strange vehicle had resulted in my being stopped only twice. Therefore, I had decided to chance it. For some reason, there appeared to be rather heavy traffic on this coast road, once we churned up the sand onto it, and I figured I was safe enough in the stop-and-go. Stopping Achilles out of mere curiosity would cause inconvenience to other motorists.

All along the mud flats and sand near the shore were many stranded boats and some people walking. Some vessels, of course, were the local brightly painted inshore fishing and crabbing skiffs. They had been purposefully beached. But some had come to grief. Most of these recreational craft were small day-sailors, but some were larger yachts, motorboats and cabin cruisers. Their crews slipped around in the mud, little knots of colourful clothes becoming a rather sickening grey-green-brown, focussed around a particular hull, with many a Sunday Skipper, identifiable by a yachting cap, usually white, dangling from his hand, scratching his head. And just about here, but for the grace of Mariko's comment back on the Loire, *Jester* might have been too. No damage would have come to her, just as these stranded boats would come to no harm, but she would have waited an embarrassed five or six hours until the tide surged in again. But for Mariko, I, too, would probably have been surprised by the suddenness of the ebbing tide.

Once on the coast road near the town's waterfront, I drove slowly into Le Croisic with the herring-bone tread thrumming on the asphalt. Not only was the traffic considerable, but cars were parking carelessly along the side of the road, adding to the congestion. What was going on, anyway? Mariko pointed to the first pharmacy that came into view, but I explained that, in France, pharmacies *per se* sold only prescription drugs. Did she have a prescription that needed filling? When she shook her head in the negative, I suggested that we wanted a magazin général or an épicerie. We found one near the end of Le Croisic's waterfront promenade not far from the Club Sportif's entrance that blocked the street ahead.

I shoved some money into Mariko's hand, and said that I would wait. "And Mariko, don't forget the garbage bags," I called out as she was about to disappear through the door. She gave me a hip wiggle in acknowledgement.

While Achilles rested at the curb, I saw a small Fiat 128 sedan cruising up the street. Achilles naturally intrigued the driver. He slowed as he approached, and unabashedly looked out his window. When the time came for him to look at the driver of this Rube Goldberg vehicle, and make some suitable insult, his face at first registered only humour... then puzzlement... then surprise... and then alarm. Instead of throwing me a good-natured insult as he ought to have done, he abruptly squealed the Fiat past me down the street. He turned, but I thought he would probably go around the block and take another look.

At last, it seemed to me, Mariko emerged from the store. Smiling as she munched chocolate. I gestured urgently to her. As soon as she had climbed over the vehicle's gunwale, so to speak, I pushed her as far down as I could. Our treads drummed off along the pavement.

"They're here," I said. "At least I think so."

"Oh, my God."

I glanced in the side mirrors. A Fiat 128 leaned around a corner behind us, squealed onto the promenade's pavement and lurched in pursuit. "Keep down." There was only a driver in the car, and I doubted that he could shoot and drive at the same time. Only about thirty yards to go to the Club Sportif entrance. It was going to be close because our speed with half-tracks on was much less than a car's.

I clattered through the entrance and veered around a curve with boat cradles to either side. I saw the sign for the boat ramp just ahead and wasted no time turning onto it. Going down the Club Sportif's boat ramp at top speed, I saw in the mirror that the Fiat had also turned onto the ramp. But it braked hard to avoid rolling into the mud and slid sideways on the slippery green algae at the high tide line. Once out onto the muddy tidal flats, I turned parallel to the coast to head back toward *Jester* but I kept a hundred yards out from the high water shoreline.

As we rounded the gentle curve of Le Croisic's waterfront, we beheld a wondrous sight. Mariko beheld it from beneath a large straw hat that she unfolded from one of the plastic bags she had brought from the magazin général. This floppy wide-brimmed thing actually suited her. Gay and bright yellow, it effectively put most of her face in shadow in addition to her sunglasses and the wig. I should have thought of this, of course. Anyway, when we rounded the curve we saw hundreds... maybe thousands... of French dads, moms and children scurrying over the mud flats like so many ants. They were raking, shovelling and dumping mussels into pails. The sound of their activity was like muted surf.

They were after the crustaceans and shellfish that were being exposed to them on this extraordinarily low spring tide. Their determination to harvest these creatures was amazing and frantic, because of the few hours they had in which to do it. Now, I should mention that on this part of the Brittany coast, it is usual for a family to stake out a small section of the seabed as a private shellfish preserve. Stake out is literally accurate, for they mark their territories with slim branches which are stuck deep into the sand and mud every few inches to form a fence around a family's plot. These stakes, by virtue of their slimness, seem to stay in place in spite of the flow of tides and winds. I don't know what they are called in French, but visiting English-speaking sailors usually call these fences 'withies' and they constitute yet another navigational hazard not marked on any chart.

These withies are a veritable forest on the ancient land of Lyonesse. It is a much less enchanting forest than Brocéliande because, as slim as they are, these stakes can poke a hole in the bottom of a wooden cruiser or yacht if a wave sets the hull down on one in the wrong way.

It is the French family custom in these parts to go out on weekend low tides and delve in their staked-out plot of sand and mud for Demoiselles, Coques, Couteaux and Escargots de Mer – shellfish. Spring tides are always eagerly awaited because more of the seabed is exposed. But this spring tide, coinciding with the solstice and full moon, occurs only once every twenty years or so. Much more of the seabed was now exposed, and it was obvious from the crowds that this event had been anticipated in crustacean-collecting circles even if some weekend sailors had been taken by surprise. Or, no surprise. In France, la gastronomie is much more popular than sailing.

The mud flats were so packed with people that I had to be careful steering through the initial congregation near the beach. The hordes were much too demented in their collecting frenzy to take any notice of us and our vehicle... and their madness was demonstrated by the fact that I sometimes found the vehicle frightening myself. My half-track steering mechanism took all my strength to work in this sticky mud, and tended to slide anyway, so that several French family groups never knew how close they had come to being run down. The coast road was now clogged and scores of cars were parked all along it. All this had happened in perhaps half an hour.

But, as we headed across the mud flats, I saw from the corner of my eye that some men around a stranded boat seemed to be following us... or, more accurately, trying to follow us. A group of men was running away from a beached speedboat and slopping through the mud in our general direction. Even when we had tracked fairly far out on the mud, these men still tried to follow us.

When we were beyond the winkle-hunting French families on the mud flats, I saw the men firing pistols at us. But we heard no shots, so they may have had silencers. It was too far to tell in a jiggling rear view mirror. But it was longish range for handguns, which is all they seemed to have, and I wasn't much worried.

My biggest fear was that a stray bullet could explode a compressed air tank, which would result in an explosion just like the one that had finished *Jaws*. But at this range, I doubted that a pistol bullet could penetrate a steel tank. Nonetheless, I was nervous and told Mariko to stay down. But she peeked backwards from time to time while I tried to tell her, over the engine and drive train noise, at full speed and then some, about the encounter with the Fiat driver.

I counted five men in the group and, as we both looked back in snatched glances, a strange thing happened. According to Mariko, two of the five just jerked and fell. This mystified us for, of course, we weren't shooting back and could not hear any shots over the racket. Heart attacks? It is hard work trying to run through deep, clinging mud. Mariko reported that they turned to look back toward the beach and the fringe of forest, and fell to the mud as if to take cover from danger coming from that direction.

But, whatever had occurred, it helped us because it put us beyond even fluke rage of their guns. And flukes can happen. We could only suppose that we had friends in the enchanted forest. But who?

Achilles took us back across the wide expanse of mud and then across the narrow tide channel to *Jester*.

"Thank you, Marc, for that excursion," Mariko said later from under the hat while pouring water over the treads from a plastic barrel. "I truly was craving chocolate."

"No problem."

"Only being shot at."

"There was that."

"If it hadn't been for this crazy thing, we would have been killed."

"If it hadn't been for this crazy thing we would not have been targets in the first place and you wouldn't have any chocolate."

"Quite true," she conceded. She poured another dollop over the tread while I herded some smelly clots of persistent greenish mud toward the 'midships well. "I've been thinking," she said.

"Hmmm?"

"I should not have imposed my passion for Classics upon you."

"What do you mean?" I asked cautiously.

"Achilles. After today, I have a better name for this contraption."

"Hmmm?"

"Victory," she said.

"Don't you think that is a bit overblown, not to mention premature?"

"Vehicular Integrated Compression Tanks On Rennsalaer's Yacht."

I stopped dumping mud through the well, and returned her smile. "I like that, Mariko. I really do."

"I thought you might."

By late afternoon, we were ready to proceed as soon as the tide had flooded more fully into the channel. Mariko had her necessaries. Not only chocolate bars, but also powder for hot chocolate and the tampons she preferred. And we had decisions to make. These were not wholly nautical.

38

Later that evening, quite tranquil with resolve and acceptance, Mariko and I readied *Jester* for the next phase of our voyage. In spite of the earlier ambush off the mouths of the Loire and Vilaine Rivers, I had definitely decided not to risk sailing around Brittany, across the Channel at its widest, to the coast of England. No matter what, I was going to enter the canals of Brittany and go as far as I could in sheltered waters.

It may seem foolhardy that I decided to enter the Vilaine River and the canals, so obviously near to the scene of our near-disaster off Le Croisic, but I had no choice. *Jester* was never designed for ocean sailing and the corner of the North Atlantic between Brittany and Cornwall was one of the most treacherous expanses of water in the world.

Also, after the fracas at Lac des Doigts, I wasn't about to leave *Jester* in any French port, while we took a car or an air plane flight to England. I did not know the status of Gabereau's ongoing investigation and I did not want *Jester* impounded, while we were away in England, where she could be subjected to a very thorough search. This would mean a cutting torch and her virtual destruction. Since, in so many ways, *Folderol Jester* was my life, I would not risk this.

Strangely enough, with these decisions firmly made, Mariko and I slipped into a warm and confident kind of contentment. Since Lac de Doigts, we had accounted for our one victim each, and then some, in retribution for the crew of *Die Lorelei*. Anything else would be another helping of gravy. And we both agreed we'd rather die fighting our direct enemies on land than fighting an innocent and impartial storm at sea.

Besides, I took that gunfire, which had come to our aid from the enchanted Forest of Brocéliande, as a sign that we would have friends to assist us at need. Who they might be, and why they were also waiting for us at Brocéliande, remained mysteries.

During a long and languorous afternoon, we had folded the cut-water back and had secured it. We had hauled the outriggers inboard again, and had lowered the masts and sails. I had insisted on doing this work first. By dusk, we were ready to leave quickly, if necessary – I was remembering that the tide-stranded speedboat could possibly pursue us when the tide came in again. We were ready to travel the narrow canals of Brittany.

Accordingly, as soon as the tide flooded our channel somewhat more fully, I had steamed right up the estuary of the Vilaine, and then the five miles up from the mouth of the river to the sea lock at St. Bernard de la Roche. Although this had once been a busy summertime Breton boating crossroads, presently reduced tourist traffic since the energy crisis meant that I had been able to find a mooring at the Club Nautique.

Naturally, I wore the Walther while working at the mooring at St. Bernard de la Roche, and vowed to wear it constantly until this episode was over. And I half expected that shots might ring out while Mariko and I were fully exposed on deck for much of that first late evening after we arrived. St. Bernard de la Roche was, after all, the most logical place to mount a watch with a limited number of people at hand, not Le Croisic on the coast. But nothing happened then or later in Brittany. 'The fog of war' is not just a cliché and, as Groucho Marx once put it 'military intelligence is a contradiction in terms'.

I finally concluded that *they* must have calculated that *Jester* would sail around the Brittany coast toward England. This coast was too convoluted and indented to maintain a search, and to mount a concentrated attack, without literally hundreds of people at their disposal. Therefore, having been thwarted in France, they would pull back to Glastonbury and wait.

After *Jester* was rigged for the canals, we checked in, about eleven o'clock that night, at Les Deux Magots, an inn and restaurant well known to yachtsmen in 'Roche Bernard', as the visiting British called it.

I had never been in Brittany on a vessel, but I knew Les Deux Maggots very well from both reading and also conversations in Narbonne. Several sailing books had mentioned it, including Ken Duxbury's delightful *Lugworm Homeward Bound*. My Dutch acquaintance in Narbonne with the Zuider Zee leg o' mutton schooner had also talked of Les Deux Magots where he had stopped en route from Holland. And, in this instance, he proved to be accurate down to the name of a brilliant mechanic at the Club. Boat people are a closely-knit family, and important information is passed around like gossip.

I have stressed that *Jester* was adequate for one person almost indefinitely and fun for two for a few days. But we had been aboard for almost two weeks. Mariko was not a born boat person, and had few inclinations in that direction. Also, it had quickly become clear; she suffered not only from decided PMS but also from cramps. So, during the few days we stayed at Roche Bernard, I got a big room overlooking *Jester's* mooring. I gave the vessel a thorough cleaning-out and freshening, sometimes with Mariko's help, but mostly not. I got the boat up on the yard's dry dock and scrubbed the bottom. I watched her repainted with anti-fouling. The prices at the Club Nautique were surprisingly low as an incentive to yachtsmen to spend their money there rather than at St. Nazaire. Roche Bernard had suddenly become a yachting backwater, not a nautical crossroads.

Now, the early first morning at Roche Bernard, while looking around for thick aluminum plate suitable for a grab bucket, I happened to see the wreckage of a Kawasaki 750 motorcycle in the inevitable treasured junk pile in the marina's workshop. The engine and connected goodies had not suffered in the crash, which had mangled the frame and which, I heard, had claimed the lives of both riders. It had been kept at the shop at Roche Bernard under the French equivalent of a mechanic's lien. I dickered. Since I could not get aluminum plate thick enough for a grab bucket in Roche Bernard, much of my next four days was spent with the mechanic, Emile, and the yard's welder, Jocelin. We replaced the Norton with the Kawasaki. The engine was not only 50 years newer in design, and all-aluminum too which made it a few pounds lighter than the Norton, but its valve train was sealed. It was also 50 per cent larger.

'Victory' as we'd now renamed Achilles/Ivory, went much better, and much more quietly, with this engine transplant. As it so often happens, especially in small places where there is not much business, Jocelin and Emile became almost as committed to the project as me. They got the idea to change the front of the vehicle. Between them, some old pieces of thin aluminum plate were found stacked in the back of the shop. This was pounded and welded into new frontal bodywork for Victory, a pointed and flared front end that resembled a boat's prow over the recessed trailer hitch at the bottom. We even primed it and then painted it matching blue.

Out on the canal, Victory showed significantly more speed without deafening noise. Her new shapely prow and flare tossed spray aside. As far as I could tell, and I calculated with some care, the Kawasaki gave a little better mileage than the old Norton even though it was half again as large. I attributed this to the fact that the Kawasaki used compressed air much more efficiently. No calculations were needed to prove a lot more speed and power.

Now, this facelift and engine transplant for Victory was not strictly necessary, but it gave me something to do while Mariko had laundry done in the marina's machines, had numerous hot baths, had lots of sleep in the wide soft bed and read a paperback novel. She had delicious meals in Les Deux Magots, and sometimes I ate with her.

As Emile and I became chummier while working, I learned of a war surplus dealer in Rennes who did not ask many questions. And so, one evening I was driven into Rennes in Emile's fearsome Suzuki Swift

DOHC 16-valve and bought enough 5.56 ammunition to refill my two banana clips. I bought a Beretta .25 automatic pistol. I also bought a partial drum, about twenty-five metres, of ¼-inch 1 X 19 stainless steel cable. We were back at Roche Bernard in time for me to wash off most of the grease I had acquired from the cable, dress a la mode Vrai Grand Capitaine and have a very late candle-lit dinner with Mariko.

After she went up for yet another hot bath, I took the time to amble to *Jester,* now back at her berth beside the inn. I went aboard and loaded the two banana magazines from boxes of the cartridges I had bought in Rennes at a somewhat inflated price, but not actually outrageously exorbitant. As for the cable, I wrapped it in one of the new plastic garbage bags and wedged it in a corner of my upper bunk.

When we left Roche Bernard, I was considerably poorer in some ways; richer in others. Mariko's bright eyes and old smile were back, and she wore Annette's shorts and halter in the hot late June sunshine. She needed her floppy straw hat, and her sunglasses.

The canals of Brittany are much different in character from the Canal du Midi. For one thing, they are much narrower – almost like the English canals – and pasture often comes right down to the banks. Cows grazed, and looked solemnly at us, with their forefeet lapped by *Jester's* smooth little bow wake. Birds I've heard called 'dabchicks' in England, although they look like what Canadians call coots, peeked from canal-side sedge. When *Jester* surprised one, it would run over the water, hurdling from lily pad to lily pad with great dexterity, until it could squeeze back into the sedge.

The canals were alive with small birds of all sorts, but the only kind I recognised seemed to be kingfishers – smaller but also bluer than Canadian ones. One thing I did miss was red-winged blackbirds. In North America, they would have thronged canals such as these, flitting from stalk to stalk of the taller water grasses, with their vermilion wing patches flashing like rubies in an ancient green-gold setting.

Brittany gave me the impression, and Mariko said that she felt it too, of being in an 'elder land' with many now-hazy memories and not a few half-remembered secrets. The occasional menhir or Celtic Cross still standing out on the hills, but usually askew, emphasised this impression.

Although the weather held hot and clear, a proper summer, the canals were sometimes so narrow that trees almost arched over them completely. Great oaks, beeches and elms. Then, we had respite from the heat and a charmingly dappled reflection stretching before us. We mostly ate on deck during the day. Bread, cheese, olives, tomatoes and sometimes even paté. Mère Lalie was still ubiquitous in Brittany, the heartland of her distribution turf, even if her gruesomely smiling face had gradually become much more scarce further afield.

As for our intimacy, it had become quite gentle. Mariko had raped me at the Lac des Doigts because of days of fear, bravado and confidence after winning the battle with the helicopter and the fear of an impending sexual relationship. I had always considered it a kind of pre-emptive strike. I had raped her on the fallen Hoedic megalith out of sheer lust combined with an appreciation for shallow melodrama. We were therefore "even" when we set out from Roche Bernard and could emotionally afford to be the people we were, and had become.

I kept the AR-15 out of sight, but close at hand in the wheelhouse on its ceramic magnets. Despite the heat, I always wore a shirt to conceal the PPK under my left arm. Needless to say, perhaps, the air cannons were vertical as whistle-tubes, but with no whistle inserts, and ready for instant downward pivoting. I had serviced the plate pivots and hinges with WD-40 at Roche Bernard and the mechanism worked as smooth as butter. With the masts down, we could not have data input for computer-controlled gunnery, but on this Brittany stretch the vistas were usually modest. We felt that manual aim might be effective... or at least off-putting. And, in spite of our apparent relaxation, Mariko and I were always scanning. The two pairs of binoculars were not only, or perhaps even mostly, for bird-watching. We were especially alert whenever *Jester* negotiated a bend.

I had bought the Beretta for Mariko's personal use and 'last extremity' protection. The day we left Roche Bernard she contrived a 'disco-holster', she called it, from a small disco purse that Annette had contributed. She wore the Beretta and holster on deck, slung low on her hip and tied around her thigh with a length of leather thong, like Billy the Kid. Out in an open area of countryside, she fired off several magazines in order to get used to it. She was surprisingly good at putting holes in lily pads as we glided past, and she killed no dabchicks.

"Not bad, eh, GI Joe?" she grinned. "I'm a real... real..."

"Annie Oakley...?"

"That's me," she said. "Who is Annie Oakley?"

"Was. She was a Wild West lady sharpshooter of the 1880s. She married Buffalo Bill... I think," I amended "Or Wild Bill. One or the other. *Annie Get Your Gun* was a Broadway musical based on her career."

"Did she die with... with her boots on? That's right, isn't it?"

"That's the right expression. Boot hill, and all that. No. Annie gave up shooting and became a fashionable New York lady. Wild... er... *Bill* anyway wanted it that way."

"Chauvinist."

"Probably. But he may have had his reasons, as I might also. Mariko, would you mind terribly not waving that thing in my direction?"

"Oh. Sorry." She checked the magazine as I'd instructed, checked the safety, and nestled it back into her jaunty holster. Then she stood with her legs apart, pulled the brim of the yellow straw hat low over her eyes and posed with her hands on her hips. Her lips curled fiercely. A gay Matt Dillon in Dodge City at high noon. Or, since she was undeniably female in the cut-offs and halter, perhaps Sharon Stone in *The Quick and the Dead* was nearer the mark. "Do I look scary, Marc?"

"Absolutely." I decided firmly that it would be a good idea to hide the Beretta and holster before PMS came around again.

"Good." She relaxed and grinned, pushing the hat out of her eyes. "I am certainly learning different skills than I learned at Oxford," she said. "Academically, mechanically and… and… psychosexually."

"Speaking of your new skills, Annie, would you like to steer for a while?"

We had practised that, too, as soon as we got well clear of Roche Bernard's occasional maritime traffic. Steering was especially easy on the Brittany canals at this time of year. High summer had set in. Most days were balmy and windless and *Jester* just went where she was pointed with no side wind crabbing. Also, of course, there was a speed limit of 10 kph to prevent large wakes that would erode the canal banks.

Mariko steered for about half the time in Brittany. This gave me some hours to relax, read and decide on the best possible co-ordinates for having dredged up the parchment's reliquary box. I wrote an account of our dredging for Mariko. I also rigged the ¼-inch cable on the winch just beneath the wheelhouse front window and dragged the bitter end of the cable overboard in the water until the last few inches were properly rusty and frazzled.

Part of Mariko's off-watch was occupied with creating an account of her time since she had left Oxford almost a month earlier using my account of the dredging, the discovery of the parchment and the subsequent loss of the grappling bucket along with 30-odd feet of cable.

When we were on deck together, we would go over these accounts meticulously to search for flaws in the story. For example, could Joëlle, if questioned, swear that I had been en route to and from Bordeaux during the previous two weeks before meeting her at Moissac? No, because I had returned with gifts and a wad of francs. The gifts could have been bought in an hour, almost anywhere, even in Bordeaux, and the francs could have come from any source, including Mariko.

Could Bouchard or the wine dealer in Bordeaux contradict the story? Again no, because the actual drop off of one cargo and loading the wine casks had consumed only a day, thanks to Victory.

We decided in the end that Mariko had met me in Bordeaux. Her thinking had been, contrary to the usual opinion, that at least some of

Lyonesse had been in the south around Ile de Ré and Ile d'Oléron. Her research into legends of Lyonesse had uncovered the very common folk belief that, when the summer sun was just right, fishermen could sometimes see the shapes of sunken castle turrets and cities down in the water on the shallower fishing banks. This belief was current in the Bay of Biscay from Brittany in the north to Ile de Ré in the south. From our experience on Hoedic, we knew that stone circles and menhirs were usually located on or near the top of a hill. This was confirmed by Mariko's study of British and French large-scale topographical survey maps that she pulled up on the Internet. Therefore, it had stood to reason in Mariko's mind that the sunken castle turrets and cities of the fishermen were much more likely to be the remains of inundated megalithic stone circles and menhirs.

Carrying this reasoning one step further, Mariko had appreciated the well-known fact that early Christian churches had often been located on previously sacred megalithic sites. Here, a book called *Churches in the Landscape* proved particularly helpful by providing over twenty maps of Britain that demonstrated this phenomenon. Therefore, she had thought it entirely possible that Early Christian artefacts might be located by going to fishing banks in the Bay of Biscay where sunken castles and cities had been reported. At this stage, she had only been trying to prepare maps for some future expedition that she vaguely had in mind if she could ever raise enough money for it.

But then she had met this Marc Rennsaler in Bordeaux at a waterfront restaurant. She'd gone into *L'Ancre des Girondins*, in which I had actually eaten from time to time, for some dinner and also to ask around about the chances of hiring a boat that would take her out to Ile de Ré and Ile d'Oléron. She wanted to research legends and reports of sunken castles in the libraries of the island towns in an attempt to get closer to the original sources.

To her surprise – and their Englishified and American-accented French had quickly identified them to each other – this Marc Rennsaler had turned out to be interested in her ideas. He had an amateur's interest in archaeology because of his previous newspaper articles. Rennsalaer had also explained how his sonar could locate a sunken stone circle or a sunken ruined church fairly quickly on a fishing bank. His boat's grab bucket could delve down into such ruins. She had been excited at the prospect of actually finding a real artefact instead of just another literary reference. She had saved a little money to pay for Rennsalaer's time and boat. And one thing had led to another.

We had dredged around Ile d'Oléron for a week or so, but to no avail. Then, due to a prior commitment, I had had to load Marcel Bouchard's casks in Bordeaux and take them to Carcassonne, meeting

Joëlle at Moissac en route. Having little else to do, Mariko went along on this trip and had more or less enjoyed it. But there had been unexpected adventures. She had intended to keep a very low profile while in Moissac, at Rennsalaer's request for personal reasons, and had taken a room in an Old City pension.

Most unfortunately, while she was taking an early evening walk over the old medieval bridge, she was spooked by two men who had tried to abduct her. She had run across the bridge and had even scrabbled over the balustrade to *Jester's* storm mooring under the willows. Being much too frightened to return to the pension that night, and also because of the violent storm that night, she had stayed aboard in spite of the plan. But she had kept below and out of sight the next morning while Rennsalaer had met with his partner and girlfriend, Joëlle, at Moissac's old market. Only after they were again under way did she remember that she had left her suitcase and passport at the pension.

We had stopped at the Lac des Doigts so that Rennsalaer could see an antique *birol* and photograph lammergaiers for his book in progress, while she had taken advantage of the calm water to research more about Lyonesse on the Web. There had been the terrible nearby explosion – and then, because of the explosion of the barge out in the canal, Rennsalaer had become interested in the helicopter with the strange markings – and here we referred most carefully to the computer logs. He and Mariko had tried their best to identify it by using the Internet. And then there was all that shooting later when the helicopter itself had blown up. But that incident had duly been reported to Inspector Gabereau in Carcassonne, who had kindly retrieved her suitcase and passport from the pension in Moissac.

Not expecting to do anything except library research, Mariko had brought no rough working clothes with her from Oxford. But between Rennsalaer and Bouchard's girlfriend, Annette, she had borrowed some outfits to get by. They were not, it was true, her usual taste, but she had had fun at *Le Cheval de Septemanie* in Carcassonne anyway.

Re-thinking her slim data in Carcassonne, Mariko had then thought that maybe the major part of Lyonesse had been more to the north, after all. Perhaps it had been off Brittany, as everyone had always thought. And so, to save time, we had come across truckers willing to trailer *Jester* overland to Nantes.

From there we had dredged off Hoedic, finding the reliquary almost immediately, but losing our grab bucket a day later. She was certain that many other artefacts must be down there. She had come to England in order to translate the parchment and to do some additional Lyonesse research. I had come in order to replace the lost grab bucket, and we had always planned to return to the area of Hoedic in order to dredge for more artefacts. Mariko printed off a large-scale calendar on which we worked out a day-by-day and almost hour-by-hour account.

Not all of this material would be in the media account of the parchment's discovery, of course. But, if any reporter decided to check it out, the details had to agree with some actual events.

Die Lorelei, for example, was still a subject for decreasing press speculation and there was an ongoing official investigation. There were our signed statements in Gabereau's possession. I also wanted an account to send to Aiguillon so that everyone there would know what had happened and when. I did not think that any reporter would bother to research Mariko's story in such detail, but it was best to have it easily within reach in case someone did.

I worked out the nautical times and distances in my report to Mariko. After careful consideration, I even incorporated small mistakes into the co-ordinates for the dredging. When corrected by the media's inevitable navigational experts, these mistakes would place the location of the reliquary and parchment over even shallower water. It might seem improbable that we had found something so valuable after so short a time, but it was not impossible. We had, after all, spent a fruitless week dredging elsewhere. People have found treasures while gardening in their own back yards. Our story might be doubted, but it could not be disproved.

This story was adopted because it explained Mariko's whereabouts during most of the time since she had left Oxford and the only people who could contradict her were the men who had followed her and who had finally shot at her when she jumped off the bridge at Moissac. The small danger was that some train or bus ticket-clerk would remember her. That was possible because of her striking appearance, but she had, after all, really travelled to southern France as stated. Only some dates of travel had to be very slightly different. And since, in her fear and uncertainty, she had never reserved tickets, but had bought them for cash at the wicket, this was not a big problem. Perhaps a discrepancy of remembered approximate dates by busy clerks.

So, what with one thing and another, our days along Brittany's canals were filled.

In some places, the canals were bordered by roads – near towns and cities – but for the most part the canal meandered through open country. There was just one fly in the balmy ointment of this summertime paradise. Flies. This is not to say actual houseflies, though there were a few of them too, but night-time flies like mosquitoes and gnats. But I had contrived, as I've said, a solution for them once they had driven us below. And, in this northern latitude summer the days were long. By the time the biting flies came out, it was high time to go below anyway.

Even nights on the water could be balmy. If any breeze at all was blowing, we would leave the portholes open. On still nights, we buttoned up *Jester* as if for an Atlantic storm, I increased fuel to give 75 revs to the engine, and we turned on the 4000 BTU air conditioner in the cabin. Although we stopped at towns to buy our provisions, we berthed overnight out in the country where there were only meadows.

From Roche Bernard we wended our way upward to Rennes through toy wooden locks. At Rennes, by the way, the canal water was polluted with, among other things, the bodies of dead rats. From Rennes to St. Malo, we stayed in higher country and then came rather abruptly down again to the coast.

We arrived at St. Malo before the end of June, re-rigged *Jester* for sea, and made Cherbourg by the last day of the month. I remember this coastal trip mainly because we entered the kingdom of the tides again. Blondel was my constant companion. We also entered the kingdom of the midges again. They dominated the night all the way up the coast from St. Malo to Cap de la Hague. I think they were worst at Dinan. There, a warm drizzle and no wind brought them out in droves.

Blustery weather kept us pinned in Cherbourg for two days and, while berthed at the Club Sportif, we topped up *Jester's* fuel, last filled at Rennes. I was able to buy a barrel of coal oil at a lower price than in Bordeaux. It was evident to me that as we travelled northward into more densely populated areas of Western Europe, the distribution of necessities was, in some ways, better than in the Midi. Governments had made a concerted effort to supply regions of dense populations where social unrest would be manifested most quickly and most virulently. Except that almost everything was much more expensive than two years ago, it was almost as if there was no energy crisis.

Mariko, for example, had regarded the fuel crisis as more of a newspaper issue than something real. This was because she had never had a car and had mostly lived in university dormitories – and with her "mentor" at Oxford, of course. It was only when she had arrived in southern France that she had begun to see the effects of the fuel problem.

Inevitably, when the absolute shortages started to occur because of decreased production, the picture would change drastically. There would be seething unrest in the populous north while the Midi would be much less dependent on imported food.

Naturally, we sampled the two major gastronomic specialities of Brittany: crepes and mussels.

I had used up my French francs and was now into Swiss ones that I converted in Cherbourg. But since Carcassonne, Mariko had been helping somewhat with her traveller's cheques from her suitcase. I was almost down to British Sterling and my gold. Although I wasn't exactly staring poverty in the face, and had splurged on Mariko, *Jester* and Victory back in Roche Bernard, as possibly important future investments, I was now becoming concerned about money. We did not know what awaited us in Britain, and I could only hope that my Sterling would be enough to carry us through. In Cherbourg we discussed a price for the document if we could recover it.

It therefore came about, mostly over crepes and mussels, that we modified our plan once again. Originally, I had proposed that we take *Jester* by canal near to Glastonbury and use the vessel as a headquarters for a slow and careful assault on the problem of stealing the entire parchment. The incident at Lac des Doigts should have called this plan into question, as well as the confrontation with the men at Carcassonne. But we had stuck to it because it had been necessary to have some sort of general plan in order to guide those moves dictated by urgent necessity. After the incident at Le Croisic, however, and the pressing financial situation, I proposed a change in Cherbourg.

Although we had limited funds now, I would trade them for time. Time is money. I would berth *Jester* where we entered England. We would go to Glastonbury as quickly as possible and steal the box. Then, we would go back to *Jester*. While Mariko translated the document aboard *Jester*, I would work in Britain during the rest of the summer and into the autumn and winter if necessary. As a resident of the European Economic Community and pending French citizen, I *thought* that I could work in Britain. Especially if I was self-employed doing something useful, like carrying canal and coastal cargo. If this assumption proved to be incorrect due to British legislation, we would sail back across the Channel to Brittany, first, and then northern France. I could certainly work in France.

The idea was that, once having the manuscript in our possession as quickly as possible, we would keep moving and making a living until Mariko had a translation of it. Then we would publicize it and sell it. Then we would decide what to do from there.

Part Four

Even the renowned king Arthur himself was wounded deadly and was borne thence to the Island of Avalon for the healing of his wounds, where he gave up his crown to his kinsman, Constantine, son of Cador, in AD 542.

Geoffrey of Monmouth: *History of the Kings of Britain.*

39

I wanted to make the 74-mile crossing at night. This may seem strange, but if we left during the day, and were slowed by fickle winds, I might find myself approaching Portland Bill as night was falling. I did not like this idea even a little. Whereas, if I departed from Cherbourg about midnight, fickle winds or not, I would be able to deal with England's tricky tides and coastal currents during daylight. Also, I would be able to clear Customs, Health and Immigration in Weymouth, a Port of Entry, during business hours.

After two days in Cherbourg, the forecast for the third of July called for calm winds with a gentle breeze from the Southwest. More to the point, even in the dark I could see that the skies had cleared, the sea had smoothed and a warm zephyr had replaced the previous uneasy gusts. With my profound doubts about *Jester's* seaworthiness in the North Atlantic, I had been prepared to wait in Cherbourg almost indefinitely if need be.

We cast off at midnight and ghosted into Weymouth about ten in the morning after an uneventful crossing. Dousing the Chinese sails and being snubbed by a fairly professional, I thought, running Bermuda anchorage effected by me and Mariko, I came to a stop in the lee of the Bill in the quadrangle marked "quarantine" on the chart. I immediately ran up the yellow "Q" flag on the tallest mast – in *Jester's* case, the starboard mizzen. I waited.

The yellow "Q" flag flown in the proper quarantine allotment of harbour does *not* mean: "I am in the quarantine area because my crew is afflicted with scurvy, cholera, bubonic plague, blackwater fever, typhoid and/or yellow fever, etc." It meant: "I am in the prescribed quarantine area designated for vessels from foreign ports, as per Admiralty regulations, but my ship and crew are healthy. I therefore request Free Pratique."

I admit that Mariko *did* point out that these nautical protocols might not only be a bit out of date, though still official, but would possibly puzzle Weymouth harbour officials. Three other yachts, as we could see, were sailing into Weymouth on the tide, one from the direction of France and two others from the direction of Holland or Scandinavia. They were heading directly for the Customs and Immigration wharf. But I waited, and studied Mariko. She *looked* like Mariko the Linguist in her passport photograph. Well, more or less. Her skin had something of a tan instead of academic pallor, and her eyes were direct and challenging instead of furtive. Her body language was assured, not cringing.

After a while someone looked up the regulations, and the VHF crackled. A rather pommy voice intoned: "Registered yacht *Folderol Jester*, out of.... Cherbourg (a whisper)... Cherbourg ... you are hereby granted Free Pratique under law promulgated by King Henry VII pursuant to the charters of the Cinq Ports, effective in the year of our Lord 1507." Then, and with a much crisper voice... "Please proceed to the clearly marked Customs and Immigration berth."

I hauled up *Jester's* lunch hook from the patch of Weymouth's quarantine sand and Mariko fed steam for proceeding to the clearly marked berth. Since her helmsmanship was by now fairly proficient, I just ruminated on the degeneration of tradition while Mariko took *Jester* in. She came alongside the tire-padded wharf. Had we been carrying a cargo of eggs, she would not have broken one.

My ancient six-month British visitor's visa had long ago expired, but, as owner of a registered yacht from France, was renewed quickly once I lied that my visit was for pleasure along the British canals. "Yachtsman" means money, one way or another, for Inland Revenue. Mariko's student visa from the Republic of Eire had not expired. We had all the required inoculations. We had no pets aboard which required rabies isolation for six months. We were free to go.

I motored *Jester* up the small Wey estuary to the Weymouth Marine Sportman's Club. It was not nearly so posh as the Royal Weymouth Yacht Club, but it supposedly had a reciprocal agreement with my nominal Canadian yacht club, Queen City in Toronto. For the non-nautical, I will explain that yacht clubs all over the world have reciprocal arrangements whereby cruising members abroad may berth at each other's clubs. Under the arrangement, a certain number of berths are *supposedly* reserved just for cruising yachts that might happen to arrive from an associated foreign club. Now, these berths are theoretically reserved, even during the tourist season when, after all a cruising yachtsman might be expected to arrive, so that associated vessels can be more or less assured of a berth in a foreign port no matter how heavy the local tourist traffic might be.

Among the major cruising yacht clubs of the world, this reciprocal obligation is taken quite seriously. But smaller clubs, although they ape their betters in making these reciprocal arrangements, seldom or never have to make good on the obligations. For example, very few of the weekend day-sailing boaters at Toronto's Queen City Yacht Club are likely to sail their Tanzer 22 or Flying 14 to Weymouth and run up

Queen City's burgee on the starboard shrouds, as per yachting protocol, to request a berth.

So, when I did so, explaining to a sighing Mariko the finer points of yachting – she could have had a better teacher – I was somewhat surprised to see the *Lef*tenant Commodore *herself* pop smartly out of the clubhouse doors. She waved, and nodded, just as if she had seen a Queen City burgee before, which I strongly doubted. Mariko was amazed as the uniformed club officer walked down the pier, beckoning us to follow. We did, at minimum revs, and it was finally made clear that a huge berth, near the boundary of the club's domain, was intended for us. It was a berth which either (1) was under construction due to expansion of facilities but which had not yet been sub-divided into slots for the usual day sailors, or (2) had actually been intended for a largish ocean-cruising multihull.

Not having much choice with all this crisp hospitality, I turned *Jester* about in the middle of the greatly narrowed Wey River, so that her bow was pointing to seaward if I should require a rapid departure. And I used the impeller's side-thrust capability to shoehorn a fifty-eight foot hull – the cutwater had been extended at Cherbourg – into a sixty-foot length of quay. I took childish pleasure in this, and it was artfully done, if I say so myself. As soon as *Jester's* fenders were being securely squished by impeller thrust against the wooden chafing surface, and immediately after Mariko and I had leaped ashore to tie at least bow and stern lines to awaiting bollards, the Lieutenant Commodore threw me a smile and a careless salute."

"Welcome to Weymouth, Captain Rennsalaer... " She looked at Mariko and bobbed a greeting, "... and Miss..." which she let trail off into a "Misszzz..." and immediately turned back to me. "As soon as she's spronged..." and I could almost feel Mariko stiffen... "can you come into the clubhouse for drinks? Compliments of the Club." With that, she tossed another careless salute and a smile to both of us, and then returned to the clubhouse. I was interested to see that her spotless white uniform actually had a lower half that was a carefully tailored *skirt*. She wasn't in hastily-tailored and cut-down men's whites rapidly altered due to some unforeseen and lamentable club election.

While we rigged *Jester's* springs – criss-crossed lines running from aft of the boat to the forward bollard, and vice versa – I did my best to re-assure Mariko. To wit: that the word 'spronged', which Mariko swore was in no dictionary she had ever seen, had not referred to anything that should befall Mariko herself in the berthing process, but was an anachronistic nautical expression for "spring lines having been affixed". And that yacht club officers and members characteristically remained purposefully vague about the status, name or whatever of the skipper's guests until the situation had become relatively clear.

After pleasant informalities were done with, and we had been introduced to some of the members that happened to be there, I tuned in to the discreet smile of the charming Lieutenant Commodore and followed her into the business office. The office door was closed, ever so quietly, so that the serious business of piracy could be conducted with decorum.

To cut a long story short, this berth was not only the only one they had left reserved for associated members, but was actually one of the biggest berths in their marina. It was truly intended for a large ocean-faring multihull. I paid for it for a week, saying that I might call from somewhere to extend that for a week, so I paid a non-returnable deposit on that option. I left a Queen City burgee with the officer and she said that she would mount it among the visitors' burgees in a glass-fronted cabinet in their foyer. It was, she said, the first burgee from Queen City that they had acquired. I could well believe this. On impulse, I decided to lay on shore power, water and arrange to have the septic tanks pumped out. By this time, my sheaf of British currency was considerably thinner.

In return, though, I received some keys and a plastic card with a magnetic identification strip, and paid another small deposit on those.

Rejoining Mariko in the beamed-ceiling lounge, I found she was beguiling two old regulars who had long ago given up seawater for alcohol, although these liquids, as is well known, are closely related. She was explaining that although *Jester* was, of course, a registered yacht, "whatever that meant," she said with charming feminine ignorance, we had been out in the Bay of Biscay looking for evidence of Lyonesse. This was true... after a fashion, and delightfully did she embroider our adventures to include taking samples from the shallow banks offshore from Brittany.

She was vague about our actual geographic positions for some of this sampling, but one of her listeners expressed surprise that legendary Lyonesse had once extended into what were now international waters. Mariko was not very surprised, but she averred that she had little knowledge of such matters. Mariko was obviously doing the best she could to satisfy the avid curiosity and chronic loneliness of these old men, and she was thankful when I approached.

Declining the offer of further drinks from the two members for myself, I naturally bought them drinks while I proceeded with the plans we had made. Although Mariko had no car of her own, and had very seldom even driven one, the frightening reality was that she held a valid British driver's license so long as her student visa remained in force.

This bit of paper had been acquired at Oxford, through a student driving-instruction programme.

Accordingly, I sent her off in a taxi to the nearest car rental office. We had agreed that she must get either a mid-sized hatchback, or a mini-van. Since it was not yet approaching a weekend, I thought she might be able to manage this. Mariko went about that errand, and others if she could manage them, while I walked back to *Jester* and made ready for our imminent departure.

When Mariko swung into the club's parking lot two hours later, I saw her through the clubhouse's leaded windows as I sat in blazer and a doffed Greek fisherman's cap resting on the thick arm of an Edwardian sofa. Chart tubes and suitcases were piled around me, and I had added substantially to the blarney that O'Shaugnessey had spun about Lyonesse. Being a skipper, and a man, I had been able to show the original two codgers – and later one more – where our most promising grabs had been made – definitely in international waters.

I had also invited them to amble over to *Jester's* berth with me and look her over. I knew that no one would later actually go aboard without my permission... no club member, that is, and the marina had a tall chain-link fence, and electronic gates in it, to discourage the *sans culottes*.

I had told them to look between the rear wheels of the vehicle they saw on the foredeck, and they would discern a four-foot long by three-foot wide hatched-over diving well. The winch itself was mounted just above, a simple electric horizontal-drum affair which had once been on the front of a Land Rover. One could see instantly that this winch could do double duty. It could haul a loaded vehicle aboard if the load was too much for the modest engine on a slippery ramp. Or, the same winch could lift through the diving well, if the vehicle that straddled the well was pushed forward six feet or so, and bring up things from the bottom of the sea.

They had immediately perceived that the winch was operating at the centre of flotation and stability – *how clever* – and needed no boom to reach overboard. *Damned clever!* And yes, I said, and it was true, that the drum could hold 30 fathoms of 1 x 19 ¼-inch diameter stainless steel cable with a breaking strength of over 3,000 pounds. My mini grab bucket I said, had been of my own manufacture and design, but it had unfortunately got snagged on something during our investigations. The cable was taut just when a wave lifted *Jester* and it had parted.

Yes, the mini-bucket had had been the usual sort of clamshell affair. Capacity? Just three cubic feet. Yes, aside from the grab, of course I could shackle a hook to the cable to recover anything I could rig and that would pass up through the diving well. Like a nice bronze cannon, for instance... although I had never found one.

In truth, although I had not said this to my clubhouse companions, in designing this amidships well in *Jester*, I had always had Minoan amphorae and sunken sculpture in mind – for which there is a ready "no questions asked" market. And I saw no harm in this if the items were truly recovered in international Mediterranean waters. I would not pass up the occasional chest of Spanish (or Italian, French, etc.) jewellery or gold, either... and in such a case, my scruples about international provenance were much less.

But I had not confided all of these thoughts to my new fellow club-members because the British like to believe that they are law abiding. The most ruthless thief of Greek antiquities was, of course, Lord (Thomas Bruce) Elgin. But since he had Victoria's blessing and since he fenced his stuff to the British Museum, and since the Greeks couldn't do anything about it, well, this theft is remembered, by Brits, as the preservation of a great archaeological treasure. And this preservation had been due only to the well-known British respect for culture. If the marbles had been left in the care of Greeks, who had preserved them for the past 2,500 years, well, who knows what might have happened to the priceless sculptures?

However, I also know that Brits know the truth, even if they do not admit it. Nonetheless, it is considered bad form even to mention the truth. So, I had not referred to my hopes of artefact... er... *salvage* in national waters when conversing with my nautical cronies.

I knew that nothing of this Lyonesse treasure hunting *in international waters* would be lost in the re-telling to other club members. I also knew that they knew that 30 fathoms would reach to the mud of most banks off Brittany in the Bay of Biscay and most banks off Cornwall. I wanted this to be clearly understood and it was.

And the vehicle? Oh, it was an experiment. To see if a semi-commercial barge could load and unload cargo via a landing craft type of ramp-door for greater single-hander efficiency. And I explained all about Victory to an appreciative audience. *Capital! Damn clever, you Yanks!* No offence meant, of course. And none taken. Aside from anything else, I now knew that *Jester* would be watched over by some of the older regulars. Their visits to her, to show off the features to their friends would discourage anyone who might be tempted to risk the link fence. Not that any thief or vandal could do much to *Jester*.

I did stress to the club-men, however, that what we had found many fathoms down in ancient Lyonesse was easily small enough to fit in a suitcase. Don't know. Could be valuable, I suppose. We had to find out. They might just read about it in the papers within a week or two. And naturally, they were far too polite to ask what the nature of this discovery might be. I had planted some seeds, and invited some inspection, which would provide club gossip for some time. I thought this might be of help in the future, and would do no harm.

Indeed, *it could well be true*, I reflected. Just as Mariko had once realised. Part of my mind started to visualise a three cubic foot aluminum grab. Another complication, and a needless one perhaps, but an addition to *Jester's* capabilities. Also, it might bolster the Lyonesse story to have evidence of an attempt to replace the 'lost' grab bucket as quickly as possible.

About half an hour after we had returned to the lounge from visiting *Jester*, Mariko had appeared in the clubhouse. She helped me carry our luggage out to what proved to be a Plymouth minivan. I saw a well-used wheelchair in the back of the van.

"Did you find one of those carry-all wheelchair bags that hang from the push-handles?" I asked.

She nodded. "Thick vinyl, not too worn, a rain flap and a *tartan* pattern on the outside."

"Gee, Mariko... Do you have something against the ancient fabric motifs of your people? Well, half of your people."

She quite properly ignored this. "But I could not find any leg braces in any flea market in Weymouth."

"That's okay. There are flea markets all the way to Glastonbury. You done good, Mariko." She winced.

On the way out of Weymouth, with Mariko driving and me checking my seat belt, and gripping the seat while considering the merits of a contingency prescription of nitro, I asked her to keep on the lookout for a metal fabrication shop. She just nodded and slithered into another roundabout. Besides, she had given up wondering what I was up to.

40

Actually, we didn't find a metal shop until Frome, not so far from Glastonbury. Mariko waited while I went in. It was an hour before closing time and I had a chat with the owner-fabricator. Yes, Alcan 6061-T6 aluminum-magnesium alloy could be obtained from their London supplier within two days. I drew out my contraption, and we all agreed that it could be welded up in a day. They had MIG or TIG for aluminum. TIG costs more. I wanted TIG and counted out half the cost of the item. They gave me a card, and I said that I would phone within two days to see if the aluminum had got delivered. It was an urgently-needed contraption, I explained.

We arrived at The Friar & Firkin in Glastonbury just after six o'clock, but we didn't arrive as the passport Marc Rennsalaer and Mariko O'Shaugnessey. We arrived as one of those somewhat pathetic couples to whom most Britons extend an extra dollop of encouragement and sympathy. Mariko bore the fashion and hairstyle of a former skinhead girl trying to be at least acceptable and employable. Her husband, or 'partner', bore the marks of an ex-biker on him. Long, perhaps somewhat stringy, hair, yes, but jeans and a flannel shirt (doubtless covering arm tattoos) that were clean and pressed.

The poor chap was confined to a wheelchair, but perhaps he could walk for short distances because steel braces twinkled chrome from the jean cuffs and embraced polished boots. Somehow, the couple had made it out of the jungle, judging from their minivan, obviously an expensive necessity for the wheelchair. Their affectionate and good-humoured interaction between themselves, and their smiles and courtesy toward passers-by, demonstrated that they had somehow rejoined the British mainstream.

We clumsied our way into The Friar & Firkin, our suitcases riding on my lap and my chart tube balanced upright in my hand on the chair's foot support. Mariko pushed, smiled, and looked both affectionate and patient in spite of the inconveniences. We stolidly awaited out turn at the desk and cashier behind a couple who were paying for a lunch. The man gestured for us to go first, but we smilingly and definitely declined. Queing up was a British religious act, and not waiting for one's rightful turn was like unto grabbing the Host off someone's tongue at Roman

Catholic Communion. A Frenchman had once said of the British that "queing up was the only passion of an otherwise passionless race."

Mariko succeeded in registering us using her current and recent British driver's license as ID, along with current and recent Oxford student cards. None had photos of her. We were Mr. and Mrs. O'Shaugnessey for that time and place. But Mariko had been careful to scrawl her name in the best student tradition. *Perhaps* no one could read it. But we would be remembered. With our lack of plausible false identification, we could only hope that *they* didn't have the manpower to keep track of all the tourists passing through Glastonbury in early July. And, with luck, we wouldn't be here long.

We went immediately to our room once we were registered. Now that we were in Glastonbury, Mariko seemed a bit edgy. So was I. So, we went straight up to our room to talk some calmness into ourselves.

Mariko and I had now spent a lot of time together, and a frequent topic of conversation – one that drove her nearly to distraction on occasion – was *exactly* what she had done in the church after she had discovered the manuscript fragment. She had been giddy with both excitement and guilt, so her memory was genuinely impaired. But I doubted that she had just taken the parchment and had immediately stuck it in her briefcase. She was a linguist, after all, not to mention a woman, and surely she would have wanted to have an immediate look at it. I had taken her through it, over and over, and *finally* it had come out, words casually tumbling from her mouth while it was nearly full of buttered crab on Hoedic.

She had taken the parchment, and had held it up to her eyes. But the church was frightfully dim. So she had walked over to the open door, even stepped out a pace or two into the sunshine, and had had a look at the strange characters. *Then*, she ran back and did everything just as she had repeated *ad nauseum* to both of us.

This relieved me. Obviously, someone had the church under surveillance, likely with video cameras and telephoto lens. That's how *they* had got such a good fix on Mariko and how *they* had known she'd found something. With a good lens, and depending on the way Mariko had held the piece to the light, they might even have seen the characters.

Mariko looked puzzled. "Why have the church under surveillance?" "Okay," I said. "Now, Mariko, I admit this is a long shot, but here goes. In some way or other, *they* suspected that a document of importance was hidden in that church. Given what has happened to us so far, I'm inclined to think that *they* were planning to steal it themselves, sooner or later. But you came along first."

"Then the rest of the manuscript must now be gone," Mariko said.

"Not necessarily. You found it by accident. They may have suspected it was in the church, but where? In the altar? Below, in the foundation? Somewhere in the walls? *Their* assumption may well be that you *knew* where to look due to your somewhat specialized linguistic research. Now, that *must* be the case, Mariko, because they have been after *you*... Maybe, at first, they were willing to burgle the church, tear the place apart, and hope to find it on their first attempt. They certainly weren't going to get a second chance, once the National Heritage people were alerted and police deployed. But then you came along, found something, and so you must know where the rest of it is. You neatly repaired the altar, so they have no clue that's where it is. So..."

"So, if they can get me and learn exactly where it is, they can just walk in and get it. Nobody would even have to know if they put the altar back together as I did."

"Right. Now, Mariko... does that make any sense? Was there ever, to your knowledge, any sort of document – even a list – of books and relics held by the Celtic Church?" I paused. "It would have to be something that, say, the *Vatican* now has in its archives."

Mariko bit her lip, and I let her concentrate. Then, she nodded. "Perhaps... All right... after the Synod of Whitby in AD 663, the Celtic Church was supposed to make up a list of all non-canonical documents, relics and such in its possession. This list went to Rome, but not all of the things were recovered and destroyed. The Magdalene manuscript might have been mentioned on such a list. Only the Vatican would know."

"I see," I considered. "Now, for something as valuable as a *Gospel* by Mary Magdalene, why wouldn't the Celtic churchmen have conveniently forgotten it? Why wouldn't they just omit it from the list?"

"Because torture was involved, Marc. Also, your ideas about the word *gospel* might very well mean that some Roman investigators had known of a body of British writings. They might also have known – better than us two thousand years later – who most likely wrote the British gospels."

"So, knowing or suspecting that another Gospel might be in existence, Roman Church investigators used that knowledge, with torture, to make someone at least refer to it, to have it listed."

Mariko nodded slowly, realizing perhaps, how high the stakes were.

"But the Gospel itself was successfully hidden. The location was not betrayed," I pointed out.

"Yes... and I rather think that someone, perhaps several people, died hideously to keep that secret... " Then she shook off her mind's images, whatever they were, and tried to smile. "And how are we going to get it, Marc? If you are right, the church is still under surveillance."

"It has probably been watched for centuries, Mariko." I paused, the better to answer her question. "As for stealing it, Mariko, we are going to walk right in and get it. The simplest way."

41

The two of us left the Friar & Firkin about nine the next morning. We strolled, with Mariko showing off with her Farah Fawcett hair, floppy hat and sunglasses. And she needed the sunglasses that day. She pushed me in the wheelchair. We didn't hurry, and I helped her by pushing on the wheels. We came to the church, which was on the outskirts of Glastonbury to the southeast. One could see the Tower looming on the skyline to the Northwest and the huddle of the great ruined abbey below it. I was happy to see that there were a fair number of people about, strolling just as we were.

We wanted to walk all around the church insofar as we could, but here we were somewhat thwarted. There was a path of crushed or once-cobbled stones from Abbey Road and its sidewalk downward around a curve to the door of the tiny church. That path would be easy enough to take when the time came. But elsewhere, a little meadow ran down from the church to end in a marsh. So far as I could tell, this marsh extended from near Abbey Road all the way around the church. The wheelchair's tires were too narrow to cope with the spongy ground near the water. But we stopped on the meadow anyway, far from the edge of the meres, and Mariko rummaged in the tartan bag before handing me a sandwich and a bottle of fruit drink. She flopped to the ground to eat her own snack.

She skewed around so as to wave a bottle of orange juice in the direction of the water. While nibbling daintily at her ham and cheese sandwich, good English cheddar, not foreign Havarti, she explained: "In Roman times, Marc, there was an inlet of the sea so that ships could sail from the Channel all the way inland to Glastonbury. There are supposed to be the remains of old Roman wharves down in the lower town, but I have never seen them." She paused to swallow, and continued. "Four or five hundred years later, the land must have started to rise, and gradually access to the sea was cut off. By then, in King Arthur's time approximately, the sea inlet had gone to be replaced by a system of bogs, marshes, meres and streams. Glastonbury – or Caer Sidhi, as it must have been known then in Celtic – was almost cut off by water. It was almost an island, and may have even been one for a while... The Isle of Avalon."

I had nothing to say, so Mariko continued. "Now, at some point, but I don't know when, a causeway was built over the highest ground so that one could go dryshod to Frome. We drove in from Frome yesterday over this old causeway. But now, of course, the land has kept rising and you can get to Glastonbury from various directions between the bogs and meres."

"That *is* interesting," I mused. "Glastonbury went up as Lyonesse went down. A sort of compensating local tectonic shift."

"You're right. The same time, approximately. You know, I just never thought of that."

"Another thing occurs to me," I said, "just an errant thought."

"What...?"

"The Lady of the Lake," I said.

Mariko, looked up, startled and a bit questioning. I knew that she would remember our meeting, now seeming so long ago, aboard *Jester* at Moissac's old medieval bridge.

"If, as you say, in Arthur's time this water was more extensive... and since your small stone church is almost beside the water now, maybe, it is a slightly later and slightly grander version of Joseph of Arimathaea's first legendary mud-and-wattle church. And since it is dedicated to Mary Magdalene, well, perhaps this church was once called 'Our Lady of the Lake.'" I also took the opportunity to munch some ham and cheese, and sip some orange juice. "Maybe Arthur's sword was just kept in the church, the most sanctified place around, where no one would dare think of stealing it, and was supposed to be returned to the same sanctuary."

"Marc Rennsalaer, you're totally amazing... as I've had occasion to observe before," she smiled. But then a frown came over her face. "But I'm not sure... the Celtic Church wasn't really given to that 'Our Lady of such and such' stuff. That is more a Roman Church thing, and their lady is always the virgin."

"But both named Mary," I said. "Maybe the Celtic Church originally venerated Mary Magdalene and Mary the Virgin equally. When the Roman Church won at that Synod of... of... "

"Whitby. A.D. 663."

"Okay, when Rome won, then various things would have been renamed. This church, if it is on the same site as the first and special one, is still dedicated to Mary Magdalene. That stuck because folk memory was just too accurate and too stubborn to be undermined by Rome, but they could do the best they could by also, and probably officially, calling it 'Our Lady of the Lake.'"

"The Synod of Whitby was A.D. 663, Marc. Probably much too late for King Arthur."

"Maybe so," I replied, "but not too late for the various medieval chroniclers and troubadours who later wrote the Grail romances featuring King Arthur."

"And there's another little thought," and there was humour in Mariko's voice. "It is that the legend of Arthur's pulling Excalibur out of a stone may only refer to his going into the place of utmost sanctity and simply picking up the sword... say, from the altar..." and there she stopped.

I didn't want her to dwell on that altar, for obvious reasons, so I answered quickly "and it might repay some study... if all isn't lost by now... to find out why Arthur alone was qualified to enter this sanctuary. Was he the most direct descendant from Mary Magdalene?"

Before she could answer, and I wanted to keep her occupied, I handed her the binoculars with which I had been idly scanning the marshes, streams and the little stone church. And, after pointing at very real birds, and watching Mariko tracking them with genuine delight – a pair of swans winging very low over the mere, I asked her to have a look at the house, which was just opposite the church across the water. This was a narrow point in the water system, like a stream almost, because elsewhere to the southeast the marshes spread away from the church with a much greater expanse. Somewhere to the south, which we couldn't see, the mere system must turn and come back toward the church and Abbey Road where it narrowed to run between the church and the house on a point of meadow. The distance, as an oriole might swoop, from the church across the water to the house was perhaps two hundred yards.

A wooden Victorian monstrosity, a fairly posh summer home in times gone by, the house had one tall, round turret and was surrounded, from what we could see of its northern face, by a wide balcony. A square window in the turret faced us... and the church. From what I could see by following the restless pair of swans flying over the marsh, there were curtains on this window and they were moving ever so slightly. Now, there were other windows in this turret, but none of them faced the right way. It was obvious to both of us that there must also be some road access to this house which somehow connected with Glastonbury's back streets. But this was hidden from our perspective by the water-facing expanse of the house itself and by a heavy growth of willows and elders that formed thick greenery behind the house.

"Marc...?" Mariko had the Zeisses to her eyes. "I can't be certain, but I think there is another, duplicate turret on the far side of the house. It's not nearly as tall, though, and I think the windows aren't glass, but just open. No reflection. And this little turret is almost covered by tree branches..." Then, Mariko's sudden delight at positive identification "Yes! I'm seeing a carriage house behind there. The top of it. The windows are ventilators for the stables."

"Now garages for cars, no doubt." So, there must be a road from there leading into Glastonbury.

Mariko, in an unhurried way, cased the binoculars, and replaced the left-overs and trash in the tartan bag. As brassy as you please, we strolled to the church's entrance under the very eye of the turret, so to speak.

Mariko was right, this church was tiny, but its walls were thick. It once had windows, and perhaps still did, but they were boarded with neat plywood shutters courtesy of the National Heritage. The door was just as Mariko described it... not very tall at all, but the wood was solid. Now, Mariko had said that the door wouldn't turn all the way inwards, that one had to squeeze through because it got stuck. I prayed this was, indeed, still correct and that National Heritage had been lax in repairing it.

They had been lax. The door stuck. It was too narrow for the wheelchair to get through. With a very good piece of understated acting, Mariko simulated the latent anger of her sort. She pushed at the door in spite, seeming not to care whether she sprung or broke an ancient oaken door. She put her shoulder to it and, after scraping over a small, scuffing rock, the door suddenly slid back... and more than just open. We laughed, and she pushed my wheelchair into the church.

It was a terrible temptation, now that we were here, just to steal the box and document now. But I could see a skiff tied up across the inlet at a little dock. From what Mariko had said, few people visited this church. My assumption was someone from the turreted house checked it every time a visitor left the church. Since the skiff could cross the water in seconds, we wouldn't have enough time to get away – unless I wanted to introduce Glastonbury to mayhem not seen for many centuries. I didn't.

So, we stuck with our plan. This was, now that the door was more than open and part of it was hidden from view, for me to remove the screws of the modern hasp, snip them down with my small chain-cutter in the tartan bag, and replace them. The door would be closed by its own massive iron handle, but the ancient lock had long been inoperative. The custodian used a simple modern hasp with a padlock. When we left, after exactly twelve minutes, this hasp was not very strong.

Thereafter, we visited the famous abbey at the same slow pace, and I took a few faltering steps with the aid of my walking stick to get closer to the famous Thorn. We did some shopping, going into a big bookstore called The Glastonbury Experience where I bought an ordnance survey map of the area. Mariko found a quite thick Old Anglo-Saxon dictionary.

"Should I buy this, Marc? For good luck?"

"By all means."

So, we headed back to The Friar & Firkin in good time for a bath and tea. Mariko soaked for a long time in the big Edwardian tub. Meanwhile, I was able to see on the large-scale ordnance map that the Victorian house did, indeed, have an attached carriage house and that a road wended off the point to intersect in the lower town at Water Street.

42

Our plan worked fine – it was only our luck that went wrong. Just before midnight, we took the minivan and parked it about half a mile down Abbey Road from the church. On the way, we had noticed a few people abroad. The night was balmy, and could even be considered a bit too muggy for comfortable sleeping. A mist was seeping through Glastonbury and it got thicker closer to the water. We were already dressed as reformed skinhead and physically challenged partner. I hobbled to the back door of the minivan and did what I could to help Mariko swing down the wheelchair. I checked the tartan bag most carefully.

We rolled down the path to the church slowly, but in a relaxed way, and entered even thicker fog nearer the shore of the mere. But up above it was surprisingly light in these northern latitudes and a midnight stroll seemed fairly natural.

The weakened hasp gave way almost silently with the leveraging assistance of a big screwdriver. The door opened without a scrape this time, and it closed just as quietly with the addition of a black plastic light-duty tarp draped over its rounded top. Once inside, I padded this plastic all around the door. It was old, that door, and I suspected there were chinks through its planks and also around its stone jamb. So, I padded the tarp carefully around the door, and then rummaged in the tartan bag for the flashlight we had brought from *Jester*. This could be set up on a folding tubular holder to shine at almost any angle. I set it up, and it shined.

"Okay, Mariko. Go to it," I said, even as I looked around at the windows along the side of the church. Earlier in the day I had noticed that the National Heritage's plywood shutters had been in place so long that the edges, where the plywood met the ancient stone, had been filled in by several years' worth of dust, dead grass and small twigs carried by the wind. This debris had been packed by winter rain and wind so that I figured it was pretty well light-proof. This was probably true. I'll never know.

Above the altar, and at the back of the church, I have never known the nomenclature of church architecture, was a rose window. This had not been covered by National Heritage plywood. It wasn't original, either. Nor medieval. It was a rose window only by courtesy, because the glass was clear. Yet, in the dim light, this glass seemed thick and to have veins in it. Like a circular section from the wing of a dragonfly. Poor quality glass, this, and made before men had learned how to float molten glass on molten metal to give a smooth finish to both sides. I placed it at the mid-16th century, probably locally made.

This was of interest to me, even at the time. But of much greater interest was my estimate of whether the glow of Mariko's flashlight could be seen through this window from the turreted house. I thought that it could, barely, if anyone were watching. The glass was not only thick, it had not been cleaned for several decades at least. But this minor mental exercise was not much compared to the nagging sense of wonder about whether those in the turreted house had IFR sensing devices in addition to telephoto video. I assumed that they did because they had deployed a Sleipnir, and had blown up the *Lorelei* for no better purpose than to close a canal, etc., etc., etc. – as the King of Siam had been wont to put it.

I had been listening to rocky scrabbling for about three minutes.

"Got it!" Mariko whispered in exultation.

"Is the parchment in the box? Check carefully now."

"Yes. It's here, but it is drier. The same characters."

"Great," I said. "Now push it out of the way and reconstruct the altar just as it was. Take your time."

"Why aren't you helping?" She paused, and the scrabbling stopped. "I know why, Marc Rennsalaer. You don't want to be an accessory before the fact."

I sighed. "Mariko, keep scrabbling. Legally, I am an accessory before, during and after the fact. I am thinking."

"Is it really this easy?" Mariko giggled. Tension.

"Er... not necessarily," I said.

"Done," she said, after a couple of minutes.

"Be sure, Mariko. Be very sure." I was happy to hear some additional scrabbling, chinking and pats. "Okay? Now?"

"Yes. It is just as it was."

So, Mariko brought both the torch and the ruptured pewter box over to me near the door. I felt in the tartan hold-all for the roll of silver duct tape. She surrendered the Grail long enough for me to wrap the thing most thoroughly. I didn't want any scrap to fall out, and I wanted any fragile bit of pewter to adhere to the tape. Mostly, though, I just wanted the thing taped tightly shut.

"Can... can I hold it?" Mariko asked.

"Most assuredly," I answered. I paused, while dousing the flashlight and stowing it in the tartan bag. I opened the door ever so softly and slowly and I folded the plastic tarp into the tartan bag as I opened it. I made very certain that the AR-15's stock was just covered by the rain flap and that the banana clip was unhindered by tarps, flashlights or fruit juice bottles and sandwich remnants. While doing all this, I whispered: "You see, Your Honour, she insisted on carrying this thing herself. How was I to know what it was? True, Your Honour, I had carried a machine gun, a flashlight and a light-damping device into this church at midnight. But that was only to have an argument in case the confirmation celebrations got out of hand... oh, the midnight part, Your Worthiness? ... Well, I suppose we got the times mixed up."

Mariko giggled, but softly.

"Okay," I whispered, as I opened the door wide, "just wheel the chair out and wait for me." She did, and I closed the door by its still-solid wrought iron handle, and using the heel of my hand, gently knocked the modern hasp back into place. Not a difficult job with the truncated screws, and I thought they had enough bite left to fool the National Heritage for a week or so – until the hasp just fell to the ground when someone clinked the padlock into it just a tad too roughly.

Now, in view of this second theft, and remembering Mariko's natural reaction when she had pulled off her first solo one, I insisted on a stately walk up to the sidewalk flanking Abbey Road. Courageous person that I am, I hobbled along beside Mariko as we trundled the wheelchair up to the sidewalk. I was scanning, but the fog must have wafted up from the water surface. The infrequent streetlights on these outskirts of Glastonbury were befuzzed, not at all dazzling.

We were actually on the sidewalk when several things happened at once. First, we were *not* travelling immediately in the direction of the parked Plymouth minivan somewhat distant along Abbey Road. I wanted to maintain the guise of strolling a bit more, and to monitor events. I heard the unmistakable sounds of oars and then a boat shoving into soft turf, coming through the mist to me. And then feet running to the church came to me distantly. Then, the sound of shod feet running along the sidewalk behind us came almost simultaneously.

I shoved Mariko's shoulder forward. The taped box was clamped in both her hands against her chest. "Run, damn it! Run!" She ran, as I fumbled the AR-15 out of the tartan bag. I caught a glimpse of Mariko dematerialising into the mist, downhill, toward the water, and I turned to face the pursuers coming along the sidewalk.

But, as I was turning to bring the AR-15 up out of the tartan bag to level at the footsteps behind me, it came to me that I didn't want to spray Glastonbury with 5.56 slugs. Not with some strollers about and possibly within range, and, besides, my job was to buy time for Mariko. So, I held the AR-15 in my left hand – it was so light that this was easy to do, and checked that the Walther PPK was loose to hand under my flannel shirt. I stood there, with the wheelchair's push-bars in the small of my back, and waited. If they didn't shoot me outright, it would be my kind of fight. Depending, of course, on how many there were...

There must have been something odd about this mist, for it took them seconds to emerge out of it. I had thought that they were a lot closer. But I knew well enough that fog and water vapour in the air can play tricks with sound. All skippers with canister fog horns know this.

Five shadows loomed out of the mist and clattered to a stop in city shoes. But only for a second. One brawny giant, blond, I think, filled most of my left-side view and he hardly hesitated. He came on, after the barest hesitation, in a soccer-style kick aimed at my groin. I pivoted on my left leg, which was about all the knee was good for since some fragments from the Timor land mine had made it more steel-and-plastic than natural bone, and brought my own right leg around to meet his upcoming kick. The emphasis was on the "up," for him, since he clearly intended to send my balls zooming into some imagined soccer net.

So, as I swung my own right leg against his, and not having his momentum and speed, I just turned my leg ever so slightly with the idea of *ju jitsu* – literally the use of your opponent's own speed and anger to turn it back upon himself. In this case, the reflective medium was a heavy chrome-steel brace round my lower leg.

I *heard* the crack as his tibia, just below his knee, encountered this steel bar with all the force he was putting into the kick. That didn't stop his momentum, but it slowed it, and I'd been trained to be fast. The brace had a bar of the same square steel running beneath the instep. With the momentum of his charge I had only to change the angle of this a little, withdraw my flexed knee two or three inches, and then straighten it suddenly and viciously in order to feel the steel bar grip under the kneecap and rip it up and off. By this time, less than a second, I suppose, the nerves from the tib fracture had passed a message to the brain, the pain was processed, and the message was forwarded to the vocal cords.

The scream started when his face was about the level of my hip joint as he came over me. Since his mouth was open, wide, my back-flexed left arm just stuck the barrel of the AR-15 into that open mouth and the trigger got pulled by reflex.

I needed some room, and Stoner's baby gave it to me. Surprising what 3000 foot pounds of energy can do. The loud cough was muffled by deep immersion in the blond giant's open mouth. His scream was cut short, and, although his head exploded, the rest of him was snapped back to fall at the feet of his cronies. But I did not expect that the long front sighting blade of the AR-15 would get trapped behind his white and strong front teeth. And, even as these teeth spattered and cracked outwards in a pearlescent spray toward me, the rifle was jerked from my left hand and disappeared into the mist. Stoner's black plastic stock gave no hint has to where it might have landed.

This had all happened so quickly that the other four remained in hesitation mode, but then a lithe, black-haired giant, more stocky than tall, in a sheeny suit lunged forward. I saw the glint of his knife, held low, as he came for me. I knew I would have no time for the Walther, and so, as they taught me over and over at Fort Bragg, I knew that a good man with a knife *will* get you, and your only choice is *where*.

So, I took his low-held knife, meant for my gut, where I'd been taught to take it. By a quick twist, to take it in the muscles of the back over the kidneys. I shrieked as it stabbed home. And I came up in a rotating pivot with my locked arms to give more force to the left elbow I crashed into his oncoming chin. I had been careful to keep the actual angle of the radius bony nodule beneath the point of his jaw, and I heard a crack as his lower mandibles came apart, at one or both ascending ramuses of the coracoid processes. He arched back onto the sidewalk, but somewhat spilling over the curb into the street. I was later told that Rocco Bartolozzi had been dead before he hit the Abbey Road's pavement.

But the time taken with killing Bartolozzi had allowed the other three to move in. It was a scrabbling fight then, and I don't remember the way of it. I had taught them to be afraid of me and so they kicked and hit from a distance, taking their time. But it also took time because I was very good at this kind of fighting. Finally, of course, I went down. And then they booted me everywhere they could reach. I thought that I could hear my own bones fracture from time to time, but mostly it was the softer splat of internal organs. Finally, I couldn't take any more and began to sink down into black and pain. T.S. Eliot's lines came back to me: "This is the way the world ends, this is the way the world ends. Not with a bang, but a whimper."

43

I came to, if that's the right word, to some obscene gurgling noise. I tried to drown this out until, at one point, it reached a crescendo I couldn't ignore. I opened my eyes very reluctantly and gradually saw the source of the gurgling. But I could barely move my body from the shoulders down.

Mariko.

She was kneeling in an old Victorian armchair. Her back was arched over the top so that I couldn't see her face, just the heaving planes of her rib cage as she breathed and the soft sway of jelly breasts atop the ribs. Her legs had been splayed wide apart over the armrests. And, in that position, the deep cleft in the peach was stretched open. Vivid pink and red petals and girl parts glistened in the cleft. But just then they were working on her chest. One man, who was later had identified to me as von Theissen, was holding Mariko's arms above her head in his ham-like hands, while another man – taller but thinner than von Theissen – was manoeuvring to bring a rod down on a nipple dancing and swaying as if to escape. I could hear the capacitor whining and buzzing. At last he jabbed, and the capacitor buzzed as it discharged. The gurgle once more rose to a crescendo, and Mariko's chest heaved and flung from side to side, and sprayed droplets of blood all over the Victorian antimacassars. I tried and tried, and finally got my arms to work.

"Gut, Doktor. Now, the other one. But slowly, my friend." As von Theissen spoke, the other man – Doctor Franz Baumann, it turned out – lifted the rod from Mariko's right breast, and with this release of pressure, the breast quivered back into shape again. "No, wait Franz." Then the Germanic voice got softer, mandale he bent his head close to Mariko's. "Tell me, my little beauty, where the book is... We will find it anyway in the morning. It cannot be so far away. And all this agony for nothing... "But, I could see that the chest heaved because her head had shaken "no." Through an effort of sheer will, and through a blur of red pain, I could make my feet move.

I heard an angry, "Zap her Franz, deep and slow, but stay within the teat... . I'll hold her down... Ach, she's slippery." Out of the corner of my eye, I saw the rod lifted across her chest toward the other nipple. It was a cattle prod, but one modified for delicate work. The large metal contacts had been replaced with two sharp pins about half an inch long. The idea was to bury these pins in soft flesh, done slowly a nice bit of pain in itself, and then pass the electric current more deeply within the flesh between the two electrodes. The capicitor was whining again, and Mariko knew what that meant by now. She wriggled desperately. Slowly and carefully, Doktor Franz buried the pins in the aureole... and even this produced a frantic scissoring of the thighs. But when he pushed the button, I knew it because Mariko's body jerked and spasmed like a harpooned fish. And then the gurgling reached a new peak, the chest heaved and tossed, and the thighs would have clamped together over the cozy Victorian armrests had they not been restrained by grasping, brutal-fingered hands. I could shove myself off the floor, a little, but my head wasn't on right. Mariko's muffled screams were nonetheless deafening in my ears.

"We don't have much time here." It was von Theissen, and he sounded anxious.

"Then, with your permission, ve vill have to stimulate the clitoris."

I saw von Theissen nod, and grasp Mariko's upper thigh so that her leg was spread wide. Doktor Franz fingered into the cleft, found what he was looking for and sank the rod into the pink. He did it slowly, and I saw blood trickle down the rod and off along one labia as Mariko arched impossibly. But when the buzzer started, it was hideous. Mariko, held down by a strong man, jack-knifed off the back of the chair. She broke whatever grip von Theissen had and I saw a glimpse of her face as she surged up – eyes wide open and bulging and her mouth stretched open beneath the tape. The muted scream that came out of her must have rasped the skin off her throat, even as it deafened me. And yet her mouth was taped.

So that she wouldn't break away, von Theissen slammed his first into her belly and she doubled up. I hated myself, but I was glad his fist had knocked the wind out of her so that the scream was abruptly cut off. The agony, of course, seared between her legs as long as the buzzing lasted. This wasn't long. Maybe five eternal seconds until the capacitor had discharged and started whining up again. Doktor Franz had stayed faithfully with her though, and her clitoris had missed no 'stimulation' with her writhing.

"Where is the book, you little bitch?" ... von Theissen's voice.

Doubled over, with her head now hanging toward me, I saw the cropped black head shake no.

"Cervical stimulation will make her talk," Doktor Franz said calmly, but we have to secure her more firmly Herr Theissen."

Mariko, doubled over still and trying to breathe and scream at the same time, was lifted up and dumped upside down in the armchair. Von Theissen straddled her legs over the chair back, and then spread them to either side down the curved cushion. One aspect of torture is to strip the victim of all dignity and at the same time to emphasise the victim's total helplessness. Mariko, upside down with her legs open, certainly had no dignity. And she was totally vulnerable. I saw Doktor Franz walk around behind the chair, look down, and check the position of the vaginal opening. He didn't like what he examined, apparently, because he licked his hand with his tongue and applied the goo between Mariko's legs. "Must be moist for the best results," he said. "Now... "

Mariko, with bulging eyes and scrabbling hands could see what he was about to do, but with her hips held so high above her head by her knees bent over the back of the chair, she could do nothing. She was too weak to do much. Her hands scrabbled uselessly at her cleft, drawing runnels of blood, and her eyes fluttered and bulged. I heard a torrent of gurgling behind the tape and too easily imagined her "No! Please, God!". So must countless women in South America have screamed. In Argentina, Paraguay and such places, a cattle prod in the vagina was the usual mode of torturing females.

Unfortunately, in that upside down position, Mariko's head lolling off the seat of the armchair allowed her wide eyes to stare at me. Not that she could have recognised me any longer. She knew only agony by then. Nonetheless, I was impelled to move by those hopeless, beseeching eyes.

But just as Doktor Franz was about to insert the rod, with the capacitor now crooning at a high pitch for its prey, my ears were buffeted by loud 'phutts' and my limited field of vision was buffeted by vignettes of jerking bodies. Others had entered the room, but I saw only a man drag what was left of Mariko over the back of the armchair, which crashed to the floor, and using her has a shield with blood streaming from her chest and thighs, back away. I also heard brief, unsilenced gunfire in the room, but with dulled eyesight, and legs that wouldn't work properly, I stumbled after my hazy vision of Mariko.

44

I was told later that I dived into the boat just as it was putting out from the rickety wharf. We all went overboard. Von Theissen had a gun, but it was knocked into the mere when Mariko twisted away – and what agony that cost her, I don't like to think about. Now, he had only the boat hook, deadly enough, and he backed to higher ground up the shore of the water meadow of the turreted house. I was told that he jabbed me with it, and I must believe it because of the wound in my left shoulder. But I didn't care, and did not notice at the time.

While stumbling ashore, partly on all fours, my hand encountered some solid and thinnish object in the ooze. An old automobile spring? I jerked it out of the mud. As von Theissen jabbed the boat hook again, I flung this thin metal thing at him with eyes blurred by water and tears.

And even as I threw it, I felt bitter because I had just broken the rule. A particularly unforgiving instructor at Fort Bragg had always beaten it into us that if you have a blade, keep it. Throwing knives is for the movies. At best, you will miss and throw your weapon away. At worst, you'll have thrown your weapon to the enemy. I was falling, with excruciating pain in my neck, and with my body numbing, and knew that I had failed. But, to my amazement, though, the last image I had was of some dark blade-shape planting itself solidly in the middle of von Theissen's chest. A pause – and then blood spurted darkly all around it. I saw him dwindle, even as my own sight darkened. But, with my last measure of strength, because I'd made the unforgivable mistake of throwing that blade, I screamed and swung my right leg in the deadly circle of *harushi harai* with all that was in me. And I felt my ankle connect with his neck, as he fell back, and the steel of my false brace crunch into his neck. I didn't know until later that I had killed him twice.

I remember only Mariko bending over me as the darkness became total, her blood anointing me, crying and still gurgling with her taped mouth, and then nothing. Falling down a long tunnel, I knew that we had been ruined beyond any hope of healing in this world. And I screamed defiance of all gods all the way down into hell.

45

I had awakened several times and, as usual the first was the worst, with the thick, sick feeling of pain-killing medication in nose and mouth, and not knowing if one was still in hell.

Or, maybe it was only purgatory and things would get worse. The first time, you don't *want* to be awake. I remembered that too well from East Timor and even Germany. That first awakening had been brief. Thankfully…

Later, I came awake more often, and often to see Mariko, all in white, sitting in a chair beside me. But, fearing that she was an angel, I strove to go back under. At last there came a waking where the smell in nose and mouth wasn't unbearable, and where I knew that Mariko wasn't an angel. It was then that I learned that I would live, and not as a paraplegic. I'd feared this because I couldn't move much of anything during previous awakenings…

Still later; and I did not hurt much at all, it seemed that I awakened most suddenly and also wide awake to hear Dr. Geoffrey Whitticomb explaining everything and showing me nasty X-rays of my head and spine. I had gone through this before, too. Aside from the ribs that had been fractured by some frenzied kicking by scared men on the sidewalk, nothing internal had been irrevocably ruptured, except the spleen.

The worry had been, all along, the almost complete rotation of the atlas vertebra. I should not have even tried to move in that condition, much less jump into a skiff and indulge in a fight with Sigismund von Theissen. And only then I did I get the whole name of my nightmare opponent.

Although Geoffrey Whitticomb was much too scientific to ascribe my survival to a miracle, but rather chalked it up to an unusual degree of past physical conditioning which had still rendered the neck and shoulder muscles stronger than your average bear.

I had been lucky. Only the small atlas condyle had actually been fractured, and the spinal cord had stayed intact. But, the process of re-rotating the atlas vertebra to its erstwhile proper position had caused some anxious moments. I had been "out," more or less, for five days, and was now also out of the woods, so to speak. Complete recovery might be slower for a man of my age than for an Olympic athlete of, say, twenty-two. And that is when I really had a good sleep…

I awakened to Mariko again, and also to a tall and distinguished-looking man who could cross his long legs without making perceptible ruin of his creases. This interested me, if only because I've never been able to do it.

It was in this session of consciousness that I learned, and precisely in the order of immediate importance to me, that Mariko would recover, *had* recovered, fully – in a purely physical sense, that is. I had killed Rocco Bartolozzi and Kurt Gruenwald on the Glastonbury sidewalk, and I had killed Sigismund von Theissen by the boat dock.

Mariko and I had been in a private Somerset clinic for the past week. And, although bodies had once cluttered Glastonbury's sidewalks, evidence of Mariko and me had been removed along with the Plymouth van. Von Theissen's body had been recovered on the point of land beside the boat dock. The Frome metalworkers had not only been called, but the contraption was in safe keeping. The Weymouth yacht club had been called, and my mooring had been extended.

I did not quite grasp that the piece of metal I had thrown at von Theissen was now of considerable interest in certain quarters because analysis indicated that it might date from the mid-6th century. I did grasp, however, that the patina and mud on the thing had not been able to retain any fingerprints or DNA from any minute pieces of skin that might have adhered from the thrower thereof. So, I went to sleep…

I awoke to find the same creaseless gentleman, again with Mariko, explaining that it was the same day as all of the above had been imparted, and that Mariko wanted to talk to me as soon as I didn't fall asleep so often… and often in the middle of important sentences. I was to worry about *nothing* financially, which I already was, and he handed me a card which I read as "Malcolm Stuart" and nothing else. I gave it vaguely in the direction of Mariko who, I saw, stuck it into a small purse. This seemed very familiar. So I slept again.

Later, I felt fine. And, indeed, I wanted to go. But I found myself in a real wheelchair being pushed along a crushed-gravel path amongst manicured woods.

"Marc, you slayed the dragons… in spades, as you Americans say."

"Some Americans."

"But… but… perhaps… this princess can't be laid anymore."

"I wouldn't think so," I said, "after what they did to you."

"You know…?"

"I saw some of it. I hope to God I saw most of it. All of it. And I couldn't do a damn thing, for you, Sweetheart. I couldn't make anything move. I hate myself, Mariko."

"Oh."

"Yeah."

"You're an ass, Marc Rennsalaer... a hopeless, courageous, incredibly loveable *ass*."

"Give it time, Mariko," I said, with the steadiest voice I could muster. I knew that I was in the wheelchair, but that she had been hurt much more deeply.

"All right, Marc Rennsalaer, I will give it time. For you." But she said it without hope. "It isn't fair, I know..." she began. But then she continued more strongly. "I need you again... some more...."

"The manuscript?"

"Yes. While I was running... with the time you bought me, Marc... I hid it."

"I know that, Mariko. And I know that you never told them where. I *know* that."

"Mister Stuart... he has offered a... great deal of money... for the manuscript."

"I somehow suspected that, Mariko." And I detected a pause, an intake of breath, but she went on.

"And... of course, Marc... half of it is yours. More than half, if you want it."

"Half is fine, Mariko O'Shaugnessey." I paused when she couldn't answer right away. "And yes, Mariko, I will go with you to get it... wherever you were able to hide it." I knew she could not go by herself.

And I knew that she would never tell anyone else where it was. Skipping over a lot of things I could have said, but which I had already thought about, I asked: "Where does he want to meet?"

A pause. "The King's Arms, a place in Salisbury," she said.

I laughed. When I felt her stiffen behind me, I asked: "When?"

"In two days. At eight o'clock in the evening."

"Does that mean Whitticomb thinks I'll be... *ambient* by then?"

"Oh, yes," she said carelessly. "They want you out of here by tomorrow afternoon, or the next morning at the very latest."

"That is one way of putting good news, Mariko," I said.

"I thought it was the best way. For a man like you..." she answered.

46

Since I had a fair idea of who this creaseless "Malcolm Stuart" might be, and could assume the existence of very powerful, very efficient allies, I simply drove Mariko from the clinic to Glastonbury. But the Plymouth van wasn't parked at the Shepton Mallet clinic. Mariko explained that it had been returned to the Weymouth rental office, on time, after it had been thoroughly cleaned, vacuumed and washed. The wheelchair and braces had been suitably disposed of. So, what awaited us in front of the clinic was a dark green Range Rover. Mariko gave me the keys and helped me heave our suitcases from The Friar & Firkin through the back door. I noticed in the back seat a shrink-wrapped wicker and leather picnic basket with a discreet Harrod's tag. Hmmm.

We drove down a tree-lined lane, through an open wrought-iron gate. I glanced at Mariko. "Where's that tartan hold-all bag?"

"Mister Stuart said he'd have it at The King's Arms... and also that contraption of yours from Frome. He's been veddy helpful."

"Yes, I can see that."

It didn't take long to reach Glastonbury from Shepton Mallet, and we soon found a place that rented punts, although we did have to wait for the return of one, this being a Saturday at the height of the tourist season.

But within an hour and a half I was poling us toward where Mariko remembered hiding the book. The punt skimmed along with small ripples on the smooth mere, and Mariko reclined at the front in Jordache jeans and French Navy top. She had unwrapped the picnic basket and was sampling the goodies within. These were not totally English in nature, and I asked her to please save some of the paté and baguette for me, not to mention a slice of brie.

Now, Mariko had already told me about her adventures in the marsh before the people in the boat had caught up with her. Knowing that she was likely to be captured, she had hidden the taped reliquary in the split base of a huge willow tree that hung out over the water. She found a bit of rotten tree trunk and had shoved the box up into the soft core of the tree and had wedged it up there, out of sight, within the old tree body.

Mariko had experienced moments of panic in the clinic whenever she thought of some picnicking tourists discovering the thing by accident. But the panic was much worse out on the mere when she saw, by the light of day and without mist, that there were several willows matching her memory. Me, I was enjoying gentle and secure boating. I couldn't push myself to care greatly if we found the reliquary at all.

But we did find it. In the third willow we checked, a great giant whose trunk and branches resembled an ancient gnarled arm twisting upwards to a splay of branches knobbed and crooked like arthritic fingers. This old willow overlooked, and seemed to guard, a deep pool in the mere.

Mariko's relief was palpable. She chatted all the way back to the rental dock to relieve her tension. "Now, Marc, I can translate the entire thing," she enthused. "And it won't take long now, not with the dictionaries and everything at my disposal... "

"No, I suppose not," I said. But I was really looking at the swans. And also at the yellow webs of police tape I could still see strung around parts of the Victorian house on the point. From what I had heard, none of the opposition had come out of the fracas alive. None had been left alive, at any rate, which was possibly more to the point. Dead men tell no tales, to be corny about it, and the police would soon find that these particular dead men doubtless had long criminal records of some sort.

I thought, in the end, that the Somerset Constabulary and Scotland Yard might be inclined to be thankful that these types were dead and not be too interested in how they had got that way. At one point, the ever-helpful Mister Stuart had mentioned that the bodies had been searched most carefully and professionally. There was no scribbled note, for instance, that could lead to Mariko or myself.

Certain footprints and also Nike treads had been obscured in the soft mud. A 5.56 casing had even been recovered by Stuart's men from the grass beside the Glastonbury sidewalk. So, I enjoyed the swans.

As for the reliquary, we just popped it into the picnic basket, now that the basket's contents had been sufficiently depleted, and walked to the Range Rover after returning the punt.

We arrived at The King's Arms in Salisbury that same evening, a full day before our meeting with Mister Stuart. I was not surprised to find that we had a reservation, a double room. And this took some doing. The King's Arms is a popular inn in Salisbury, and more so since Peter Watson featured it in one of his art-intrigue novels, *Landscape of Lies*.

The name of the place derives from the fact that Charles I stayed there for some time when he was on the run from the Parliamentary Army. Indeed, it is said that in the hotel's burgundy carpeted and blackened oak beam-ceiling "Cavalier Room," Prince Rupert and Royalist officers plotted yet another military disaster for King Charles. I gave our Mister Malcolm Stuart the highest marks for a sense of humour. When I mentioned this to Mariko, she looked blank.

I slept in the same bed with Mariko, but not with her. Within arm's reach, yet far away, my heart despaired of ever finding her again.

Early Sunday morning, after a quite satisfying "Englishman's Breakfast," I left Mariko with her manuscript and Anglo-Saxon dictionary and I 'did' Salisbury. This means, mostly, the remarkable cathedral once built on a foundation of woven reed mats. I then looked in on Mariko who only looked at me in a puzzled way and said: "You know, Marc, if this is genuine, it changes the whole story of so-called Christianity... No wonder people died over this."

So, I went out again, took the car, and drove up to Old Sarum, and then the few miles over to Stonehenge.

At eight that evening precisely, we were informed Mister Stuart had arrived. We went down to meet him. He and Mariko shook hands like old friends and he gave her a fatherly embrace. Then he turned to me with an extended right hand.

"Captain Rennsalaer. I am happy to see that you appear to be almost fully recovered." Aside from being creaseless, he was a tall thin and rather scholarly man with dark-framed and fairly thick-lens glasses.

"Yes, thank you, Your Highness. I do feel a hell of a lot better."

"Oh…" I heard a little intake of breath from Mariko.

I turned to her with a smile. "Unless I am much mistaken, Miss O'Shaugnessey, this is Malcolm, Duke of Albion and H.R.H Prince of Albion … er… ah… Scotland."

"At your service," Mister Stuart smiled with a faint bow.

"Oh, Mister Stuart, I didn't know," Mariko almost stuttered, and bobbed a little curtsey. Then she turned to stare at me. "How did you?"

"Newspapers, Mariko." I paused. "With your linguistic background, you will doubtless know that the name Stuart derives originally from 'steward'. Although," I added, "some seventeenth members of the clan seemed inclined to forget that."

Mister Stuart laughed politely and herded us out of the plush lounge. "Yes, well, Captain Rennsaler, but now I did suggest the King's Arms didn't I?"

"So I observed to Miss O'Shaugnessey, Your Highness."

After a simple roast beef dinner in a private dining room reserved for Very Special Guests, and after conversation that rather put our whole adventure in a larger context, we concluded the deal.

In essence, Malcolm Stuart, a collector, bought the complete manuscript, including the reliquary, for $250,000. We were given to understand that the Celtic Church had put up some of this money and would, indeed, be responsible for the manuscript's safekeeping. It would be, however, on semi-permanent loan to the British Museum. I supplied a written 'provenance' for the artefact. It had been dredged up from international waters thirty-five miles northwest of Hoedic and in roughly 30 or 40 feet of water, give or take.

That, indeed, would be the gist of a press release that was necessary to get various organisations off the backs of Mariko and myself.

The entire manuscript would be photographed in London before anything else. Mariko O'Shaugnessey would make a first translation on behalf of Malcolm Stuart, his financial associates, the Celtic Church and the British Museum. After that, of course, other scholars could study the artefact and make their own translations. Stuart planned a facsimile photographic book with O'Shaugnessey's translation of the new Gospel in a page-by-page format. All this was most carefully written out as a contract, including, as addendums, the press release and the various already executed sub-agreements. About the time we were on our coffee, a rather stocky and elegantly dressed man entered the room along with a photographer draped with technical paraphernalia.

As HRH and I arose, Mister Stuart announced: "Allow me to present an associate Mister Kalil ibn Da'ud."

Mariko gave another intake of breath from her chair. Even she had heard of him, and even in the ivied halls of Oxford. She recovered, though, and gracefully extended a hand that was bent over and kissed. I shook a firm hand and looked into a pair of very determined black eyes. "Certain mysterious powers in the enchanted Forest of Brocéliand have suddenly become much more explicable to me," I said.

"Indeed," Kalil ibn Da'ud replied. The photographer was scuttling around recording all these introductions with whirring, clicking and flashing motor-drive Nikons. Mister Kalil ibn Da'ud's rather large worn leather briefcase never left his left hand until he set it reverently on the table. As Kalil ibn Da'ud sat down between Mariko and HRH, the photographer began to take pictures of all of us signing the various documents. Stuart planned to put out the release tomorrow morning.

We were each given our money from Kalil ibn Da'ud's briefcase in medium-sized bank notes, not new, and Mariko handed me $10,000 American right off the top for my expenses and assistance. We split the rest, in several currencies, evenly.

Outside in the King's Arms courtyard, while I helped transfer various items from a grey Bentley to the green Range Rover, I was both unsurprised and heartened to see a few discreetly suited men around the vehicles at the curb on the street beyond the inn's wrought iron gate. In parting, Mister Stuart told me quietly that there were Sentinels, as he called them, all over Europe – but mostly in Scotland and in southern France. Mister Stuart said that I owed a great deal to a certain Inspector of the French canal police. But, of course, I had already figured that out.

47

The next morning after reading what the larger newspapers had to say about us, Mister Stuart, Kalil ibn Da'ud and Mariko drove into London in a discrete small parade of expensive automobiles. I counted enough heavily-armed muscle in their escort to engage a small army. Their first concern was to get the individual pages of the document mounted between plastic plates and individually sealed by British Museum scientists and curators. During this process, small samples of the vellum would be taken for C-14 dating.

I drove the Range Rover to the Weymouth yacht club. I had help wrestling the aluminum grab-bucket out of the Rover and onto *Jester*. Lots of help. Gentlemen and ladies of the press had tracked me to Weymouth to expand on the story in the morning papers, and so were able to get photos of *Jester* and the replacement grab for the one lost on drowned Lyonesse.

Although I was interviewed, I admitted to very little knowledge of archaeology. I referred them to the person who had chartered my boat, Mariko O'Shaugnessey, the Oxford linguist, who knew all there was to know about the manuscript we'd recovered. I was patient with this because the cover story was vitally important to Mariko and me... mostly vital for Mariko's safety, but also for Joëlle's. At last, the reporters dispersed to file their stories and photos, and I returned the Range Rover to the address that Stuart had given me in Weymouth.

Then I walked to a branch of my British bank, made various deposits, transactions and transfers. I also bought some currency to replace my depleted secret sheaves. Feeling I'd benefit from the exercise, I walked back to the yacht club. There, I found my mooring fees had been paid. As Mariko had said, Mister Stuart was, indeed, very helpful.

Late in the afternoon, after I'd stowed my gear, I used the ebbing tide to take me out of Weymouth, bound for London.

I think I really knew even then that I should have set a course for France, but we had agreed to see how things would go in London. During what was left of July and most of August, I moored *Jester* in London in company with upscale houseboats and converted barges. Mariko had a suite at the Kensington Arms apartment hotel, close to the museums, where she worked on translating the new Gospel from excellent photographs.

We learned from the British Museum that the samples of vellum had consistently radiocarbon dated to between AD 900 and 950, so it was a copy or, as Mariko had said from the beginning, possibly even a copy of a copy. The reliquary was another matter, however. It was of pewter, that is to say a mixture of lead and tin. Because of impurities in the tin, scientists were able to say that the box itself had come from Cornwall.

For the same reason, the lead that had once been used to seal the box had first come from Rome, later from Cornwall. The style was similar to Cornish pewter work of the late First Century AD. Therefore, the box itself may well have contained the original manuscript and was thereafter reverently used for subsequent copies of the same work. There was no real decoration on the surfaces of the box, but an intertwined spiral motif beneath the rim of the bottom resembled Celtic work of the same era. Experts were still studying the box.

Me, I looked into the regulations for commercial barging on the British canal system. It was all definitely 'doable' and the money in it looked to be better than the Canal du Midi, but I gradually lost heart about it. I began to spend my days aboard *Jester*, doing very little, until it became evening when I could dare to interrupt Mariko's working day. Even I knew that this was no good at all.

It was not, of course, the lack of intimacy that caused me to give it up. I have more sensitivity than that... I hope. It was the fact that Mariko, in an attempt to insulate herself from the past hurtful cost of her notoriety, really didn't want me around as a remembrance of it.

Without me to recall both the joys and traumas behind her new success, she had a glittering new life and future. She was already something of a popular celebrity because of the discovery. When the translation was published, and the target date for the book was, of course, Christmas, she would be famous in the scholarly world as well. Since she naturally wanted the translation to be beyond any carping academic criticism, she wanted to do the absolute best that was in her as a linguist.

I suspected that she also wanted to use her translation in order to eclipse a certain former mentor... as well she might. So, I really did not see much of her during the short summer that we lived in London.

Finally, one late August evening I simply said that it was time for me to go. She nodded agreement. She had also become too honest, because of our mutual agonies, to delude herself or me. She said that she wanted to get on with the life for which she had studied.

Mariko came down to the Thames mooring with me. She brought a great bunch of roses with her.

"They are not as beautiful as O'Shaugnessey roses," she said, "but they are the best that I could find in London."

"I am certain they are not as beautiful as a genuine O'Shaugnessey rose," I replied. "But thank you, Mariko"

I climbed aboard and she handed the roses up. "And thank you, Marc Rennsalaer."

"Like the song says, if you ever need me, all you have to do is call."

"And I will send a copy of the book. Autographed, of course."

"And I will send you an address, somewhere, where to send it."

She tinkled a small laugh, smiled and said: "Now, that is nonsense, Marc Rennsalaer. You have a perfectly good permanent address in Aiguillon. I think you know that. Anyway, Aiguillon is where I'll send the book. You… we… have trusted Joëlle with so much, that I'm certain that I can trust her with a copy of a mere book. You know that too."

It was getting on for late in the afternoon when Mariko kissed me for the last time, and I kissed the tears on her face. She waved until *Jester* slid downstream out of sight...

Then, I turned to the mundane business of piloting. Passing through Gravesend on the last of the ebb, I thought that I would take the roses below. I had wedged them between the tubes of the air cannon and the smokestack so their paper wrapping would not blow away. But as the sea breeze picked up, I knelt from the wheel to retrieve them, thinking to put them in the wheelhouse for taking to the cabin later.

But they were much too beautiful, of course. And their scent was much too sweet for *Jester's* small cabin.

So, I tossed them slowly overboard, one by one. And as each rose went over the rail, I reflected that earthly loving, supposedly so robust, was pitifully fragile compared to loving within the long and ancient human continuity – eternity as we mortals can know it. Earthly loving was as vulnerable as the bodies and spirits of men and women who tried to sustain and preserve it for a brief lifetime. And both bodies and spirits can be so cruelly broken.

That may be the lesson of Sancta Sophia. Each of us stands alone at the point where earthly loving and eternal loving come together in vulnerable flesh. And right then, the loneliness of loving was difficult to bear.

Jester cleared Gravesend buoy with the sunset flaring behind us, lighting the rosebuds bobbing on the Thames.

Manor House Publishing Inc.
www.manor-house.biz
905-648-2193